The Purrfect Pack
The Pack Pets Omegaverse
Galadreal Simmons

Coffee After Dark

<u>*Dedication:*</u>

For My Tallest...thank you!

Music that Inspired this story and these characters:

Hello Anxiety – Bowling for Soup
You Shook Me All Night Long – AC/DC
Paint It, Black – The Rolling Stones
Closer – Nine Inch Nails
In the End – Linkin Park
The Anthem – Good Charlotte
I Love Rock and Roll – Joan Jett & the Blackhearts
Cherry Bomb – The Runaways
Buddy Holly – Weezer
Brain Stew – Green Day
Fake it – Seether
Dynamite – BTS
American Idiot – Green Day
All the Small Things – Blink 182
Self Esteem – The Offspring
Teenagers – My Chemical Romance
In Too Deep – Sum 41
How You Remind Me – Nickleback
The Middle – Jimmy Eat World

Contents

What do you mean by Omegaverse?

Omegaverse, often known as ABO, is an alternate reality where humans share some characteristics of wolves. In this one, we have fated mates and attraction based heavily on scent. Thus most people's scents will be compared to common items, our current female lead smells like thin mint cookies. You get the idea.

There are three known designations, Betas are like you and me, but with a better sense of smell, they make up 75% of the population.

Alphas make up 20%; they are predominantly male. Alphas often form familial packs of three to five other individuals, which may or may not include a beta or an omega. In addition to an average larger body size over betas or omegas, alphas are generally known to be stronger and more aggressive. Male alphas also come equipped with a knot for sexual purposes, specifically to tie the alpha and omega together and help increase the chances of procreation. Female betas can—with practice and patience—take a knot, but it's not something they're built to do.

Last are the omegas, approximately 5% of the population, which are predominantly female. Generally described as petite or waifish they lack the physical strength of alphas or even betas. Omegas are natural caregivers and peacekeepers, helping to balance their more aggressive counterparts, and are physically built to accommodate a knot during sex. They are incredibly tactile, craving touch and companionship. They go into heat approximately every six months which is their only fertile time. Heat requires medication, special toys, or the assistance of multiple alphas for each heat.

Due to their limited number and lack of physical strength, omegas are regulated in the sense that they are considered a protected group, a rarity that is often targeted for assault, kidnapping, human trafficking, etc. Thus laws that have been made to protect omegas often also restrict their freedoms and require that they live with a guardian or in an omega-specific complex for their safety. To make it harder for omegas to avoid these laws certain items, such as de-scenting products and heat suppressants, require the approval of a non-omega head of household to purchase. This does not always work out as intended, as it makes omegas without these products available easier to identify and therefore, take advantage of.

Simmons, or you can email me at galadreal.simmons.author @hotmail.com I implore you to NOT contact amazon, or use the "report to amazon" option on your kindle, I will be able to get it fixed much faster, and there will be less chance of it being removed completely if that happens.

Chapter 1

Candice

I stare at my monitor, squinting.

Eye strain...maybe? Do I need to update my prescription?

I take off my glasses and rub my eyes before trying again. *Nope; I read it right the first three times.*

Candyman: A hippo? I'm really gonna need you to provide references on that. I can't find anything.

Letting out an exhausted breath, I fully admit that I'm terrible at customer service. I hate telling people no. What if they don't want to hire me anymore? I can't lose customers, and there are a lot of NSFW artists out there trying to make a living.

Gotta make the money, gotta pay the bills, and gotta keep people from knowing who I am.

Getting doxxed is *not* an option, so I do as much as I can to keep my real and graphic design identities separate. No one knows the *real* me, just the online persona I made up for selling art.

Fox-Up: Yes, a hippopotamus. You're the artist, you should have lots of references to look at. I'm paying you for the art, so you can find the references.

I run my hands down my face, taking another deep breath and letting it out slowly. This is just one of the reasons I work online only. I've never been able to school my facial features well enough to talk to people in person.

Candyman: Yes, I can understand that, but none of my files or searches have come up with anything. Since it's your commission, I just need you to give me a better image to work with.

I can't afford to lose clients, even when they're incredibly picky and have rather...unique tastes. Don't get me wrong, most of my clients and commissioners are amazing people. They have things they like, or don't like. They work with me to get their art done, and they're chill. If I wasn't a complete shut-in, I would probably consider some of them friends.

But that involves leaving my house, which is just not going to happen.

In today's digital world, I can have my groceries delivered and do all my banking online. So other than a quick walk down to the mailbox, and sitting out on the back porch in the evenings, I rarely have to leave my cozy little house. Plus, I enjoy being inside. It has everything I need.

I shake my head to clear my mind and try to tune back into the long rant scrolling down my screen. I could do with one less client. It wouldn't be the end of the world, but if word gets out that I'm dropping clients, especially if it's assumed as a kink-shaming issue, who knows what could happen? But I'm tempted to risk it if this person doesn't stop soon.

I barely bother skimming through the tirade. It's all written down and if it's important, I can come back to it later. For now, I need to move or something before I let loose on someone who probably doesn't deserve it...probably...maybe?

> CandyMan: Ok. Yeah, no, I'll check again, and you can always make three changes to the final image if you don't like how it comes out. Now, do you want me to add a knot to that dick, or just the standard hippo?

I'm trying not to come off as sarcastic, mostly due to frustration—but clearly, I'm not keeping it as well hidden as I had hoped, judging by the angry reply.

> Fox-Up: Of course I don't want a knot. I told you, HIPPOPOTAMUS. Hippos don't have knots!

> CandyMan: Alright, well, if you can make sure you have all the other commission information in the message you send me, as well as a valid email address, I'll get a rough sketch drawn up and send that with an invoice. Once the invoice is taken care of and the sketch is approved, I can start working on a more solid pencil sketch.

How the hell does she know whether or not a hippo has a fucking knot? She can't even find me a reference to draw it, but fine, whatever. Ask and you shall receive, *I guess.*

I think I need a new motto.

She left the chat, so I just assume that Fox-up agrees. She's always been difficult to work with, but lately, she's gotten snarkier. Hell, I don't even really know if she *is* a she. I've never seen any of my clients in real life, and most of them are like me, trying to keep as much personal information offline as possible. That's ok, great even, but sometimes I feel like it would make it easier to talk to them if I knew them better. Oh well, my alarm to get up and move only had six minutes left, so I might as well get ready early. There isn't time to start any work just to stop again in a few minutes.

I set down my tablet pen and unfold my legs, stretching them out and wiggling my toes. I really need to put down a new rug in here or invest in more fuzzy socks. Sunny threw up on and clawed my last rug to death, and I haven't been able to find the time or budget to look for a new one. Speaking of that big asshole. I look over to see him just waking up from his nap on top of my printer.

He looks at me and blinks, stretching his long claws and yawning widely. Cat breath...lovely. But he hasn't been feeling well lately, hence the timer, so we're headed to the vet this afternoon. *Note to self; have them trim his claws before he gets stuck to the bed again.*

I pick up my favorite mug—white with rainbows and hearts and a black weeping skull that says, "I'm just a fucking ray of sunshine." I never thought of myself as particularly surly, but I guess compared to most of my designation, I'm a bit strange. Omegas are generally known to be perky extroverts. They want to snuggle with everyone in a big nest, have all their alphas service—

Nope, cut that train of thought off at the knees. I feel my skin crawl at the idea of being touched by anyone, so here we are.

After dragging myself into the kitchen, I swish my cup out to get rid of any leaf bits and put it under the hot water dispenser on my coffee maker. No, I don't really drink coffee (ok; I love a frappé decaf, but Omega and caffeine, not a great combo), but I love the hot water on tap aspect, so it was totally worth the splurge. I grab a new tea bag and figure I can let it steep while I get cleaned up real quick.

I make my way into the bathroom, peeling off my flannel top while turning on the shower to warm up. One of my favorite things about working for myself from home is that it's always pants-less O'clock. But, pants or no, it always feels strange walking around topless, so my wardrobe consists of a staggering amount of sweaters and warm fleece or flannel shirts, three pairs of stretchy yoga pants, and one pair of baggy blue jeans that have been worn a total of three times since I bought them. They're just so pinchy and rough.

The steam rising over the shower stall door says I've started zoning out and I need to get a move on. "Alexa, play my favorites!" I call out to my nest before I step under the hot water. I'm soon dancing to *Bad Moon Rising* while waiting for my conditioner to settle in and scrubbing down with de-scenting soap. I hate how paranoid I feel when I have to leave home, but it's better to be safe than sorry.

Chapter 2

Candice

Scrubbed and half-dressed, I hurry back to the living room. Iggy is sitting on the bookshelf beside the couch when I walk out of the bedroom, giving me the stink-eye for not immediately going to give her chin scratches.

After all of thirty seconds of hopping on one leg, trying to get these pants on over my *mostly dry* legs, I give up and lean down to rub my nose up her scaly snout in greeting. Taking my attention as an invitation, she leaps off the shelf, flying through the air, her tail whipping out and knocking over knickknacks.

Her scaly toes and long claws latch into my sweater and she scurries up my chest and around my neck, wrapping her tail over my shoulder. She burrows under my still-damp hair, and

I scramble to try to catch my grandpa's picture before it can hit the floor and shatter the glass.

She knows I love her too much to actually protest. Iggy has been my constant companion and cuddle buddy for the last three years, ever since Grandpa died. Most people don't think of iguanas as snuggly—it came as a surprise to me too—but when I went to the pet shop to get cat litter for Sunny one day, there she was, all alone. The runt of the litter apparently, the last baby iguana.

The pet shop owner said she'd been labeled "failure to thrive", and they didn't think she would survive. I looked into her tiny black and yellow eyes and had to bring her home—assholes still charged full price for her even though they were just going to let her die. So, then I had a pet iguana. Unlike me, she loves going on walks in her little harness, but today is all about Sunny and the vet. So I let her ride around on my shoulder while I finish doctoring my tea with copious amounts of sugar and try to lure my mean old grump into his cat carrier with treats. Which never works, but I continue to try, because what are my other options?

Keep going, keep trying...*things will get better*. They have to; I don't even know what I'm working towards at this point. Just put one foot in front of the other, one day at a time, surviving...Shit, I'm zoning again.

Fucking hell!

Thanks to that little brain detour; we're now running five minutes behind. I scoop Sunny under one arm, unceremoniously dump him into the carrier, and get it zipped up. He's totally going to throw up on me later for this, and I'll be lucky if I don't get retaliation poop as well, but my old man has been coughing a lot lately. I love the hairy old bastard, and we're going to the veterinarian's office whether he likes it or not. I'll deal with the retaliation when we're home safe and sound and he's feeling better.

Sunny's been with me for over half my life. We got him from the shelter after I left the hospital. I remember Grandpa leading me by the hand—he told me every little girl needs a kitten. And then there he was: a tiny ginger ball of fluff that was all needle claws and angry hissing. I loved him as soon as I saw him. He got along well with Grandpa and later helped me through when Grandpa got sick a few years ago. He's always been a grumpy puffball and is just as likely to curl up on my lap and purr, as he is to take a random swipe at me if I sit too close to him on the couch. Still, he's been the longest-running stable thing in my life, and I honestly don't know what I'm going to do when he passes.

Furry Friends Veterinary Clinic is in the same old brick building it's always been, and the familiarity is comforting in its own way. As much as I hate being out in public, they've been seeing Sunny since he was a kitten, so they know him pretty well. They've dealt with his annual shots and check-ups, his neutering, and six months of recurrent UTIs after Grandpa passed.

There was, of course, his obsession with fake Christmas trees—which meant a yearly visit for constipation and vomiting—until I finally just gave up on having a tree three years ago. Maybe one day I can have one again, but his discomfort isn't worth it, especially since it's just the three of us. Sure, we sometimes get a new veterinarian or a partner buys in or sells and moves off, but they're like a big family—and bonus—they recently got a new exotic vet that has experience with iguanas, so we'll get less strange questions when I have to bring Iggy in. I haven't met them yet, but Iggy's check-up is in another two months, so I will then.

I arrive only three minutes late, and unbuckle the cat carrier from the seatbelt; Sunny has, predictably, thrown up in the carrier and is yowling his deep old man meow to tell me how mad he is at me. So I trot inside to check in as fast as I can, before going back to my car and trying to get everything cleaned up without letting him escape. All is going remarkably well when I realize I was in such a mad scramble to get out of the house that I forgot to spray on the de-scenter before I left. I mean, really it's my own fault. With work, a sick kitty, and just life in general, I've been feeling overwhelmed and tired a lot. I'm almost out anyway, but I'm not going to be gone too long.

I mean, I used the shampoo and the soap, so I probably don't really need it, right? I just like the extra precaution. I rarely use it anyway because it's so expensive and a pain to get. It's not illegal to make or sell, but I can't buy it. My grandpa ordered as much as he was allowed to shortly after my designation came in. There are a few people I trust online to order it to ship to me, but honestly, it's a hassle, and one of the reasons I would rather just be home, cuddled in my nest reading, dancing, or even working. But nope. I wonder if I'm going to have to open for emergency art commissions to cover this vet trip.

I start to worry, because worrying is what I do, constantly, about everything.

Taking a few deep breaths I try to calm my mind. I can't do anything about forgetting the spray. Right now, I just need to focus on my cat and hope like hell no one notices. Shit, this extra stress is not helping.

Can I smell myself already?

Shit, no time.

For now—focus—take care of my old man kitty. Whatever's wrong, we'll get through this. Deep breaths. If I have to take on more work, I will. Yeah, my heat's coming up next month, and that's going to be miserable. Plus it'll put me out of commission for at least three to five days, but most of my regulars are awesome people. They know about Sunny, so hopefully they'll understand.

I feel like such a failure for forgetting things.

Why can't I do better?

What if something happens and I can't afford to get Sunny help?

They'll take a payment plan, right?

Why don't I have any friends other than my old cat and a lizard?

Am I that hard to like...

STOP...this is not fucking helping me. This isn't helping anyone.

Again, let's take some deep breaths...in....out...count of four. Come on, you can do this.

A throat clears beside me, and I see the vet technician, Maggie—according to her nametag—who came out into the parking lot to check on me. Apparently, I've been having my little freak-out for a while now, and they wanted to make sure everything is ok. i.e. get me into my appointment so I don't hold up the other appointments after mine or have to reschedule.

She comes over and extricates my poor cat—who apparently was getting squeezed hard enough in my panic that he had given up on escape and was just hanging in my hug, purring, and sounding like a motorboat engine. Almost as loud as one, too.

I mumble an apology, quickly wiping out the carrier with some paper towels now that I'm not juggling an angry cat and his carrier. I get Sunny put back in, and he just starts yowling again to be let out. With my head down, I shuffle after the nice, non-judgemental tech back through the office and into a room. There I promptly set the carrier on the exam table and unzip it to let him out—and he lies inside, looking smug, like he isn't the reason for this whole debacle.

Chapter 3

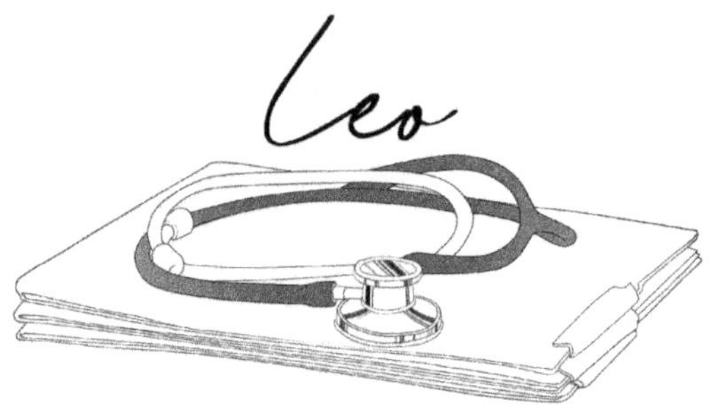

I'm counting down the time till lunch, and wondering what Jacks packed me today. I kind of love the surprise of it every day. I feel like a big nerd even admitting that, but it's always nice to know that someone's thinking about you—and cares enough to put thought into what you like. He always manages to do something special for each of us.

"Your next appointment is in room five," says Maggie, walking by and putting a thick folder in the file slot hanging by the door with the number five in bold black print.

Either this creature has had a lot of health issues, or it's geriatric. I guess we're going to find out. I finish drying my hands and pick up the overstuffed folder.

Name: <u>Sunny Manning</u>

Owner: Candice Manning

Feline – Male/Altered

Maine Coon Mix – Ginger

Age – 18 yrs, 6 months

Complaint: coughing, recurrent nausea and vomiting, lethargy; no change in diet or litter box.

Looking back at his history, this isn't the first time he's been seen for stomach issues, but it's not anywhere near the holidays. Still, we'd better get some imaging anyway, just to make sure there's not a blockage. Still scanning the file, I open the door and step inside. "Ms. Manning and Sunny?" I verify, without looking up.

"Um...yeah, that's us," is the mumbled reply.

"Good afternoon. I'm Dr. Leo Asher, but everybody just calls me Dr. Leo. How can I help you today?" I ask, still reading through the overstuffed file.

"Oh, uh, well, Sunny keeps getting sick; he can't seem to stop coughing. He'll cough so hard he just barfs...on everything. I'm really worried about him." The soft voice finally registers, and I raise my eyes to a tiny beta woman sitting on the exam room bench. She's wearing an oversized sweater and black leggings, her deep auburn hair is twisted up into some kind of knot at the back of her head, and I have the craziest urge to know what her downcast eyes look like. Her hand is stretched up, scratching the cat who looks perfectly content staying in his carrier on the table.

And suddenly, I can't breathe—*why can't I breathe*—why am I getting distracted right now?

Not the time, Leo, what is wrong with you, she is here for her cat, check out the cat!

It feels like all the oxygen has been sucked out of the room, but she isn't even looking at me, her attention is focused solely on the giant orange feline that she pulls out of the carrier and into her lap. Her eyes stay downcast, her lips curved down in worry. I fight the urge to reach out and smooth the wrinkle forming between her brows.

"If you could just put him up here on the exam table, I'll take a look." I finally get enough oxygen to speak and put as much encouragement as possible into it. She looks so lost, and for some reason I'm almost desperate to heal her cat so she'll stop being sad.

She manages to heft the increasingly angry animal onto the table, without getting more than a low growl from it. I reach out to rub his ears and try to help him relax so we can get a temperature and check for any noticeable physical issues.

"Now, it looks like Sunny has a history of eating things he shouldn't, so my first thought would be to ask if we can do some X-rays," I say, pressing along the underside of his stomach.

There are no noticeable blockages or hard areas, but there's no way to be sure without those scans.

I keep one hand on him, leaning back and calling Maggie to have her come take the cat for X-rays, while I look over at his owner again. I know I shouldn't, but I just can't seem to stop staring at her. She has big blue eyes, shiny with unshed tears, and she's staring up at me. I feel like a deer caught in the headlights.

Please don't let there be anything majorly wrong with this cat. I don't want to see this woman cry.

Honestly, I'm not sure how I would react right now.

Candice

This guy is huge.

He's tall, so much taller than me, but he doesn't feel intimidating. Honestly, his messy black hair and dark, almond shaped eyes help sooth my frazzled nerves.

Between his calm demeanour and his barely-there scent of oranges and chai, I'm less jittery than I was when I came in. I wish I could smell him better, but the purifiers and cleaning chemicals they use here block out almost everything. My instincts are screaming at me to climb him like a tree and not let go—which is a terrible idea really, but super hard to resist when he smiles like that, and when he looks at Sunny like he actually cares about helping him feel better.

I think my brain short circuited between worrying about Sunny and work. I know the name, Dr. Leo, but my brain feels scrambled right now, and I can't think. Was that the name of the new exotic animal vet that they brought in a few months ago?

I've been nearly frantic lately, how the hell am I going to afford any extra medication. I mean, I know I've read about pet insurance, and I kept meaning to look into it, but I haven't had the time, or money. Plus, I always thought Iggy would be the one to need it since she's considered fancy. Sunny is just a cat, an old cat...a cat I got when I was nine—*oh shit*—I didn't realize he was that old.

"Please old man, I know I told you to stop eating shit...er...stuff you find on the floor, but please tell me that's what happened this time." Sunny yowls loudly at me, indignant at the vet and his recent foray into taking my cat's temperature. I bring my forehead down to nuzzle against Sunny's fuzzy face. The thought just occurred to me that with his age, this might be something worse. I can feel a tear trying to escape, but I don't want to cry in front of this stranger.

What I want, really want, is for him to tell me my cat just ate something, suggest I give him some kitty laxatives, and take my old grumpus home. I'm suddenly terrified of what could happen, of what they could say about Sunny. I try to hold back the whine building in my chest, my nerves fraying. I can feel a tear slip free and run down my face into Sunny's fur.

I need to get a hold of myself. Nothing has been decided yet, they still don't know what's going on, and...the doctor's talking.

How long has he been talking?

I raise my head, trying to wipe off the tears before they start to itch, knowing my eyes and nose are probably already red and I look like I am about to have an ugly cry.

Tall, I just keep looking up from where I'm bent over my cat, up to broad shoulders, a thick neck, soft lips, kind eyes shadowed by black hair and...*WTF is wrong with me right now.*

Yeah, thanks, Dr. Hottie, now can we please focus on my cat.

Was he talking about Sunny...wait.

X-rays...shit, I can't afford—no, this is fine, I can deal with this. It's ok, I can figure this out.

I take a deep breath, let it out.

"Yes, X-rays, yes, let's do that."

Dammit, I sound like a babbling idiot.

Dr. Leo reaches back—*fuck this man is tall*—and opens the door; he calls for a vet tech. Maggie comes back in and they talk quietly while I go back to petting Sunny. His fur feels a bit oily and I think that when we get home I should give him a good brushing, even though I know he's going to complain the entire time. I alternate scratching under his chin and behind his ears until he's nothing but a big puddle of fluff by the time Maggie scoops him up and carries him away. Leaving me and Doctor Leo, aka: Dr. Hottie, alone in the room, waiting for the results.

Leo

Maggie has been here awhile, and she seems to know Ms. Manning and her pets fairly well. I normally only work with exotics. I would have met this tiny woman in a couple of months when she brought her iguana in for a check-up. But her normal doctor got called out on an emergency last night and needed to get some rest afterwards, so we offered to split up his patients for the day. While I am not sorry to have met this woman right now, I am very worried about giving her bad news about her cat. I am equally worried that she is going to hate me afterwards.

Sunny is old, and after just running the manual tests, I'm *very* worried about heart failure. He sounds like he has a lot of fluid build-up, and while I sent him back to imaging to verify my suspicions, I'm already fairly certain what they'll find.

"You also have an iguana, according to your charts. How is she doing? It looks like I'll be seeing her in just about two months?" I'm terrible at small talk, apparently, but Ms. Manning brightens considerably.

"Oh, Iggy's great, shedding a little bit right now, and I had to untangle her from my sweater before I left, but she's good. You know, kind of needy and demanding, but I love her." She sucks her bottom lip, biting with her front teeth enough to leave white marks. "Um, have you been in the area long? I was kind of relieved when I got the news that we'd be getting an exotic vet here. Dr. Harring is great, but even though we see him every time, he always refers to Iggy as a he, and asks the same questions. It'll be nice to have someone who knows more about iguanas." Her eyes suddenly widened. "Not that I don't appreciate Dr. Harring, I just mean...I'm gonna stop talking now...sorry." Her shoulders slump as she lowers her eyes, and I let out a little growl of frustration that I caused her distress.

Her head snaps back up, looking at me, pupils going wide. *Shit.* "Sorry about that," I grit out, "I'm terrible with small talk and I just...I feel like I should talk to you and try to get you to not hate me before they bring back Sunny." Clearly, pre-emptive apologizing is not my forte.

The edges of her mouth lift slightly, not a full smile yet, but it gives me some hope that I haven't completely made an ass of myself. "So, *have* you been in the area for long? I know you're new to Furry Friends, but are you just moving here or...?" She lets the question trail off, and I'm relieved that I'm not the only one here who's not great at small talk.

Honestly, I think I'd enjoy just sitting here and watching this woman, but that would just come off as creepy, so, I should attempt to have a conversation and not make a jackass out of myself. "No, my pack and I moved here a few years ago, but I only recently got my certification in exotic animals and..." She's backing away, spine pressed against the door to the lobby, eyes wide.

I almost don't hear her breath whisper out, "Alpha," as her eyes squeeze shut.

"Are you ok?" I don't want to try to touch her. Ok, I lie; I do want to touch her. I feel the overwhelming urge to pick her up and cuddle her until she isn't afraid of me anymore—but before I can move closer or pull myself away, the door opens, and Maggie comes back in carrying the giant orange tomcat—the reason I am in this room in the first place.

"Oh, look, Sunny's back. I'm just going to go look at those scans real quick, and then I'll be right back." Trying to sound upbeat, the cheer in my voice sounding fake even to my own ears.

Maggie eyes me suspiciously with one very raised eyebrow as I nearly run out of the room. "He was such a good boy, but I think he needs a cuddle. We'll be back in a few minutes. I'm just gonna talk to the doctor for a bit." I hear Maggie's voice drifting out of the room as I make my escape.

Dammit, I was a good boy, and I do need a cuddle—especially from Ms. Manning.

Then I realize she's talking about the cat. I can feel the heat in my ears as I scramble to the imaging room, breathing hard. This is more embarrassing than that time in high school, when I accidentally walked into the wrong locker room before the swim meet. Jacks's sister, Janey, was there and then I had to deal with an inappropriate erection—in a speedo—for the rest of the event.

Maggie follows not far behind me, chuckling and wiping her eyes. "I know I shouldn't be laughing doc, but if you had seen yourself just now. What happened?"

But heaven help me, I don't know how to answer.

I'm saved from my embarrassment when Josh, another vet tech, comes running into the room, panting. "Dr. Leo, we need you in the OR now...we just had a monitor lizard come in in critical condition." I feel torn—on one hand, I'm relieved I don't have to be the one to give Ms. Manning the news about Sunny, but I also want to be there to offer support.

It doesn't matter, the decision is out of my hands. So, I follow Josh to the operating room as he explains what happened. One of my regular patients, Freddy, had escaped. He tried to follow his owner to the school bus and—well, traffic doesn't always stop for big lizards.

One of his legs was broken pretty badly from when he was clipped by the car. They're getting X-rays to check for further damage while I scrub in.

Even though I've only been here a few months, I have more experience with monitors than anyone else—so I guess Freddy and I have a date.

Chapter 4

Candice

Sunny curls up in my lap, coughs a few times, and starts purring his loud old man purr. By the time he was six months old, he would barely fit in my lap. Now he only ever tries to snuggle this close when he's stressed, so I know he isn't feeling well. I stroke down his back, and talk quietly to him, assuring him he'll get a whole can of soft food when we get home, and some catnip for putting up with this ordeal so well, reminding him that he's a good kitty and I love him. Every word feels like not enough and the twisting in my stomach gets tighter until I feel like *I'm* the one who's going to be sick this time.

What's taking them so long? I mean, how hard can it be to look at an image of a cat's intestines and see that he ate something that got stuck—I know I'm oversimplifying things, but the longer it takes the more worried I get. I can feel myself starting to spiral again, my breath coming in short bursts, my eyes squeeze shut. Until a paw lands on my nose.

I open my eyes, tears finally slipping free down both cheeks. Sunny is sitting up, he's booped me on the nose, and is slowly dragging the pointy tips of his nails down my face—not enough to break the skin, but I know I'm going to have a few red stripes for a bit. I lift him under his front legs, bringing him up and draping his front half over my shoulder for a kitty hug. Turning my head to bury my face in his fluffy side, maybe I can pass off my crying as allergies when Dr. Hottie comes back, and it turns out to be nothing.

I don't know how much time passes, it feels like I'm almost asleep when I hear the door open. I raise my still red eyes to see Maggie and Dr. Marklon come in. Doctor Stephanie Marklon has been my friend since middle school. She wanted to be a vet for as long as I can remember, and I'm super happy for her that she was able to make it. I know she's worked hard to be able to buy into the practice so soon after graduating. I see her sometimes when I bring Sunny and Iggy in for check-ups, but we've been with Dr. Harring for so long, I didn't want to upset anyone by asking for a new doctor. Still, it's nice to see her, as she comes over and gives me a big hug, straining around the giant cat still draped over my shoulder.

"Hi, Candice, how are you doing? It's been a while, huh?" She pulls back, her brows furrowed, looking between my face and the orange fluff draped over my shoulder like a long, fluffy shawl. It *has* been a while. I haven't seen her since shortly after my designation came in. She was headed off to college, and I was just...stuck. Omegas can't go to public colleges.

My hand goes up automatically to keep stroking Sunny's back. "Yeah, no, I'm good." I try to force a smile. "Well, ya'know, I mean, I have my cat *here*, I'm worried about him. But if you can tell me what he ate, and how we can get him feeling better, I'll be glad to get out of your exam room. I know you guys stay pretty busy." I'm trying not to let my voice crack, but I can feel something wrong. Sunny chooses that moment to start coughing again, and I wrap my hand around him to keep him from sliding down into the floor.

"Oh, Candy." Stephanie looks like she is about to cry, too. "He didn't eat anything, sweety. We need to talk."

It feels like the world just cracked open. Has there ever been a conversation that ended well if it starts out with "we need to talk?" I can't remember one.

The knot in my stomach tightens further and I'm glad I haven't eaten recently. I'm also relieved that I'm already sitting down because suddenly I can't feel my legs. Stephanie comes and sits beside me on the bench, reaching out to run her hand down Sunny's back. "Sunny's pretty old now. I remember you told me you got him when you moved in with your grandpa. He's been a grump for as long as you've had him, right? Even as a kitten?"

Her hand strokes down Sunny's back, raising up enough not to brush against mine—she knows I don't handle touch well—before continuing along his spine. She gives him a few more pets before switching to his favorite chin scratches, and I'm surprised she still remembers how much he loves those.

"Candy, it seems Sunny has fluid build-up around his heart. While we can try to drain some of it, he *is* eighteen, and some times...well, the body just decides it's done."

I stare at my once close friend, not hating her so much, but wanting to deny the words coming out of her mouth. The pity in her eyes and the undeniable truth in her tone has me wanting to pack my cat back up in his carrier and take him home, where we can pretend this never happened. He'll be fine once I get him home.

I must look pretty blank, because Stephanie puts her hand on my wrist that's draped over Sunny, holding him in place. "I *am so sorry*, Candice. We can try to alleviate some of the pressure, but you'll probably be back here in a month or less. Your options now are to try to do that, or let him rest. We can give you a few minutes to think about it. Do you want me to stay while you make a decision? I'm here for whatever you need."

The words feel like useless platitudes. We were friends through high school, but we haven't really talked since graduation. I know it's as much my fault as hers that we grew apart, but with everything that's happening, I just can't think right now. My mind races, slamming into walls in a frantic scramble, trying to decide what's best. Of course I want to try to keep him as long as possible, of course just one more day would be good—anything. But, if he's uncomfortable—or worse, in actual pain—that's not fair to him. I rub the side of my face against him again, feeling the vibrations of his purr. Hell, I'm not even sure how I would afford to bring him back in a month. I don't want to make it about money. It *isn't* really, but my mind is a mess right now and the floodgates have opened on all my anxiety.

"I think..." I swallow thickly, my tongue feeling too big for my mouth. "How, um, how would that work? I mean, I want to be here for him. I want this to be as easy as possible for *him*."

Sunny lets out a loud yowl, and I loosen my grip on his fur, realizing I must have been holding him progressively tighter as we talked.

"Well, I would bring in a shot, and it would just make him sleep. Ideally, you would stay in here with him until it takes full effect. He won't know what's going on other than you being with him as he goes under. Then we'll take him to the back and give him another shot to stop his heart. It won't hurt him; he won't feel anything after that first shot, other than you
."

Stephanie's hand rubs up and down my arm. I know she's trying to offer comfort, but I just want to lash out at her for talking to me, for suggesting all of this, for touching me when I don't want anyone touching me except my cat, and now I'm about to lose that forever. I can feel more tears flowing down my face, a steady stream instead of a few solitary escapees. Knowing what you need to do never makes it any easier. "Yeah, ok, yeah..." I trail off; I can't even find the words right now.

Stephanie squeezes my arm and nods. "Ok, Candice, I'll be right back with the injection, ok? I am sorry, but I have to hear you say the words now. I can't do this without you."

She's really making me tell them to kill my cat? What the actual fuck. Misery flashes to rage and back again in quick succession. "Yes, please. I don't want him to hurt anymore." Stephanie leaves the room, leaving Maggie still standing by the door, looking near tears herself. She opens her mouth, then closes it again, probably wanting to say something, but knowing anything would be useless right now. I look at her, raising my lips and nodding, not really a smile, just trying to let her know that I know she hurts for me, but neither of us can talk right now.

It takes a few minutes for Stephanie to return with a capped syringe. The logical and still functioning part of my brain assumes they keep things like this under lock and key for safety. She's wearing purple nitrile gloves and carrying a blanket over one arm. Maggie takes the blanket and lays it out on the exam table. "Can you put him on the table, please? It'll be more comfortable for him." I manage to get my legs working. Then I reach up to detangle his claws from the back of my sweater and lift him up enough to be able to lay him down on the blanket. Maggie squeezes my fingers that are holding onto his fur before putting her own hand gently on his shoulder, holding him enough so he can't jerk when the needle goes in, but comforting us both.

Irrationally, I want to hate these people for taking my friend, but I know it is not their fault. The needle goes in and, while I feel Sunny's fur twitch beneath my fingers, Stephanie is good at her job and he barely seems to notice it. "We'll be back in a few minutes, but just open this door and call out if you need me." I barely acknowledge them, so intent on my friend, feeling his purr vibrating through my fingers for the last time as he closes his eyes.

Sometime later, Maggie comes back in and picks Sunny up, blanket and all, and leaves the room. I notice her eyes are red too, but I feel too detached to say anything. I hear the catch in her voice. "The doctor will be back in a few minutes to finalize everything, and then we'll get you out of here. *I am so sorry.*" The door closes and my legs unhinge, dumping me back onto the bench, as I try to hold back the sobs wracking my body.

Chapter 5

Candice

I'm in a daze as I check out. The receptionist is polite enough not to say anything about it though. She helps me set up a payment plan and gets me organized on how to deal with Sunny's remains; apparently, they work with a crematorium now. Which almost sends me into a fit of inappropriate and hysterical giggles, but I think I've hit the mental capacity that if I don't laugh, I'll cry. If I start that again, I don't know when I'll be able to stop.

I had a plan for today. Take Sunny to the vet, get him treated—since I was already out, take the car into the shop for an oil change, and while that was going on, go get a few groceries. I haven't actually been in the store, and upon further reflection, they probably wouldn't have been overly happy with my cart being full of cat carrier before I even started, but I guess that's a moot point now. My mind wanders, trying not to think too hard. Pretty sure I'm not going to make that appointment at the shop. I should probably call them to reschedule.

Before I realize what's going on, I'm standing beside my car. I guess it's kind of a miracle that I wasn't run over in the parking lot. No, wait, that's because Stephanie's still right behind me. She hasn't said anything, or if she did, I don't remember.

"Hey, I think you need to come inside so we can call you a tow truck and the police." Her voice snaps me out of my zombie state.

"Huh?"

"Looks like both your front tires are flat. Did you run over something on the way in?"

Fuck, I can't deal with any more shit right now.

I walk around to the front of my car, and sure enough, both front tires are flat. The driver's side at least has a large hole in the side of it—some asshole slashed my fucking tires. My mental state has gone from blank to rage like a switch was flipped. First, all this shit with my cat—cue the leaking eyes to start up again—now some asshole thinks it's funny to do this shit.

What the actual fuck.

I turn to Stephanie, and she's looking almost as upset as me. "Come inside, we can call that tow for you and see if the security cameras for the lot recorded anything." I follow her back inside seething, and the receptionist looks frustrated when I walk back in. Her pleasant mask slipping a little before it settles back into place. Yes, I know I'm a weepy mess, but now I'm a pissed off weepy mess. Thank you.

Stephanie leads me back to the main office and rolls a chair over for me to sit down beside a desk. "Be right back, I don't usually deal with the security stuff, so I'm not really sure where they keep the files. You can use this phone to call the tow truck while I go get someone who knows how to use this system." Well, I guess I'm going to the shop now regardless. Fuck, all I want at this point is to go home, hug Iggy, and burrow into my nest for the rest of the month.

I pull out my cell to look up the shop number, my mind going over all the other stuff I need to do when life gets derailed. I should probably post on my forum about Sunny. Let people know that things are going to be slow for a while. I'll need to open up for more commissions to cover the cost of tires and his medical bills, even with the payment plan. This is all overwhelming and I bury my face in my hands, taking a couple of deep breaths to fortify my resolve.

Gotta do shit or shit won't get done.

One of my grandpa's favorite sayings. I never realized how true it was until he passed. I pull up the search bar for the local garage I had an oil change scheduled with. Hitting the call button, I'm already late for my appointment there—but hopefully they'll understand.

The line finally connects, and I hear masculine voices in the background before, "Hello, Gabe's Garage, how can I help you?" The voice is rough and sounds a bit strained.

"I'm sorry," I reply, apologizing automatically. "I had a three-thirty appointment for an oil change and I've had a bit of an emergency." I pause to breathe and figure out how to word my question about a tow-truck, I don't speak to strangers often, and I get tongue tied easily.

"Yes, ma'am and it is now four-fifteen, we're gonna need to reschedule you." My brain short circuits at his words and I sit there gaping like a fish, hooked and dragged into the open air. "Ma'am...ma'am...are you still there?" But I can't seem to form a coherent thought, let alone a sentence.

Long fingers pluck my phone from my limp hand and hit the speaker button. "Hello, who is this?" says Dr. Leo.

"Leo? 'S Gabe down at the garage, what's going on, man?"

"Gabe? Ok, yes, I'm going to need you to send the tow truck down to the clinic. One of our clients had their front tires slashed in the parking lot and while we still need to call the police, I don't want this to wait until tomorrow."

A warm hand lands on my shoulder. I flinch, then look up to see Stephanie. She's always understood my need for personal space, but still needs to offer comfort. Her empathy is one of the things that makes her a great vet.

"Nah man, no problem. Go ahead and get the cops down there, we close up in forty-five minutes and I can come get it then if that works." I hear typing in the background. "This for Ms. Manning? She was supposed to be bringin' it in for an oil change this afternoon, so I should have all her information. But, if she needs to leave before I get there, just be sure to get her keys."

"Of course, thank you Gabe, I appreciate it."

A loud guffaw comes from the speaker. "Whatever, man, see you soon."

The call disconnects and Dr. Leo sets my phone down beside me on the desk before pulling over his own office chair in front of the keyboard. He pulls a pair of thick black glasses out of his pocket, settles them across the bridge of his nose then starts to type. His fingers fly over the keys opening files and suddenly a video pops up on the screen. It's the front parking lot, empty. He squints at the time stamp and drags the mouse across the desk. I watch cars arrive and leave in fast forward until I pull in.

He hits a button again and I watch the beginning of my panic attack from earlier. He glances over at me, and I think I see concern in his eyes before they flick back to the screen, back to fast forwarding but only at double normal speed. We watch people speed walk down the sidewalk, nothing really of note until an oversize pickup pulls in sideways behind me and blocks my car. The cameras are not angled to get a clear view of the driver, and when the truck moves later, my car is noticeably shorter.

"The hell?" a murmur from Stephanie. She's not touching my shoulder anymore, but still standing behind me watching the screen intently. "Can we see any information on that truck? Do any of the other exterior cameras pick anything up?"

Dr. Leo looks over again, "I'll check, if you can please go ahead and call the police. We don't want to keep Ms. Manning here any longer than we have to, yes?"

Stephanie raises one eyebrow at his stiff request. "Of course, doctor. We wouldn't want *Ms. Manning* to be here any longer than she needs to be."

I remember her using this same voice in high school for being sneaky snarky. Then she looks down at me. "Candice, do you want me to call them for you, and then I can give you a ride home after they take your statement?"

Dr. Leo jerks his head towards Stephanie, eyes wide at her familiar tone. "We went to high school together. Candice was one of the few friends I had. Everybody else thought I was weird for talking to animals."

The sad lilt to her voice makes my attention jump back to Stephanie; she's looking at the floor intently. Suddenly I feel very guilty about cutting almost everyone out of my life when my designation came in. I *have* missed her, but she was always smiling and cheerful. I never thought she would miss me too. Her hand lands on my shoulder again and squeezes so I reach up to squeeze it back, an apology and a promise to do better. The corners of her lips tilt up in a sad smile.

"Go ahead and make the call. Do you want to hit the diner down the street with me for dinner and catch up before I take you home? I know you've had a rough day, but I'd be happy to just listen if you need someone to talk to."

My own watery smile returns. "Sounds good. Let's get this over with."

While we're talking, Dr. Leo slides a card across the desk to me for the sheriff's office. "We sometimes have to call in cases of suspected animal abuse. We need to keep their number handy," he answers my unspoken question without looking back in my direction.

Chapter 6

Gabe

I was not expecting that. Honestly, when I got the call about the missed appointment, I was ready to be pissed. I hate dealing with the schedule but Kelly, our receptionist, is only part time in the mornings. She takes college classes in the afternoons. We could probably use someone full time, but her classes just don't leave room for that. Also, she's like a little sister, so I'm not going to fire her. Besides, she does a great job; I just *really* hate dealing with customers.

Picking up my grease rag on the counter, I make a failed attempt to wipe the handset off from where I rushed in to grab it earlier. The rag itself is already covered in grime, and just manages to smear an even bigger mess around thanks to my attempts. "Shit fire fuzzy and save the matches!"

We always keep a jar of Gloop under the counter, and I'm sure Kelly would rather the front desk smell like oranges than grease and alpha sweat. So, I proceed to smear the slimy shit all over the countertop and phone and wipe them down with a handful of blue shop towels. I just got the last of the gunk off the keyboard—I don't even know how it got there in the first place—when Trey comes in from the back.

"'Ey, boss, I'm 'eaded ou'. Ya need anythin' 'for I go?" Trey is good people, but super relaxed about everything, and I don't always understand what the hell he's saying. Pretty sure it goes both ways though.

"Yeah, man, you opening tomorrow?" I ask, and he turns back.

"Ya, boss, whatcha needin'?" I am honestly not sure if it is a regional dialect or just a Trey-ism...Hell, I'm not even sure where Trey is from, but he had good qualifications, all the right certifications I needed for the shop, shows up on time, and works hard. Can't fault a guy for how he sounds.

I reach up to rub the back of my head, realizing I've still got a handful of nasty shop towels just before I manage to slime myself, and explain, "I've gotta take the tow truck over to the vet clinic after we close up, somebody got their tires slashed. When you get in, can ya pull it into the bay and start gettin' it sorted out? Xan'll put the paperwork here on the desk. Looks like it's gonna need a couple'a front tires and an oil change." His only reply is a raised eyebrow. "It was already scheduled for the oil change before somebody got pissed off at it."

"Go'cha boss, no' a pro'lem." Now I'm not sure if he is just fucking with me, or if that's seriously how he talks, but fuck it, I need to get over to Leo's place and get that car. I should probably offer to stop and grab dinner at this rate. I better go ahead and call Jacks and let him know we're all going to be late so he doesn't worry.

About thirty minutes later, I pull up to the vet clinic. They're already closed too except for the emergency line. Sometimes it feels like the town rolls up the road at 6 P.M. Only things left open are the diner, gas station, and grocery store, and they close at eight most days. The car I'm here to pick up has seen better days. It looks pretty old, but well cared for. Not old enough to be considered a classic—just old enough to be considered almost worthless to anyone but the person who owns it. Why the hell would someone want to slash their tires anyway?

I park next to the police cruiser and look over the clusterfuck taking up the clinic's lot—we're gonna to need to get this thing backed up to get the bar under the front of it. I don't want to fuck up the suspension or rims by trying to tow it on the flats if I can help it, and I didn't think to bring a trailer to move it a couple of blocks. I step down out of the cab and head towards the group of people, easily picking Leo out as the tallest here. That man is tall even for an alpha, and he can look downright intimidating when he wants to—the closer I get, the more it seems he wants just that. But I can't understand his reaction to these cops until I'm standing right next to him.

"Ms. Manning, we can't take your statement here, you need to come down to the station to file the paperwork." The tiny woman standing next to Leo shudders, and I can barely make out her squeak of a reply."I...I need to get home, I can't...I...I can't..." She curls her body into Leo and starts crying. Poor bastard looks gob-smacked for a few seconds before he curls an arm around her back and holds her loosely against his chest. What the hell is going on here?

Another veterinarian is here too: *Sarah, Sasha...Stephanie! That's the one!*

Stephanie reaches over and puts her hand on the smaller woman's shoulder, rubbing up and down. "Officers, I've already told you, Candy...Ms. Manning has had a difficult day. I need to get her home. We can give you a copy of the surveillance files. If you can't take her statement here, I will personally bring her to the station tomorrow, but she *cannot* do it right now."

Stephanie puffs up looking like a protective mother hen, and I try to hide my chuckle with a cough.

Leo finally meets my eyes, his own pleading with me to step in. Leo looks big and dominant, but he doesn't handle confrontation well unless he has to—and then, well, let's just say I don't want to have to bail him out tonight. That man has the patience of a saint, but when it runs out...damn.

"Sorry, officers, I'm gonna need y'all to move outta the way here so I can get this car hooked up," I drawl, trying to play up my country more than usual. I never subscribed to the *Good 'ol Boy* way of thinking, but sometimes sounding like you do gets shit done—and right now, I just *need* to get shit done and go home.

I look down again and see the short woman under Leo's arm, her cheek pressed against his chest, eyes closed but facing me, and wow, ok yeah...I can see why Leo would let her cling.

She is so small next to him, but she looks soft and curvy pressed against his stomach, her dark reddish-brown hair is up in a bun, but falling out in wild curling flyaways. When she suddenly opens her eyes, I'm dumbstruck. Her pale blue eyes are flecked in green and gold, with a dark, almost black circle around the edge.

I've never seen eyes like that, and I stand there gaping like a slack jawed idjit for a moment—trying to shake myself out of whatever the fuck this is. I need to get this wrapped up and get gone, *now*.

I rub my hand up Leo's back, palming the back of his neck and skull. He glances at me and unwraps his arm from her—gently passing her off to Stephanie. "Come on, man, let's get this thing hooked up, I left Xan to fill out paperwork, and we need to grab him before we can head home for the day." I release his neck, sliding my palm down to his shoulder, giving him a final squeeze before pulling away.

I step over to Stephanie and Candy Manning—wow this girl's parents had a sense of humor, bet that name bit her in the ass in high school. "Ms. Manning." I can't bring myself to call her Candy. "Do you still have your keys, or didja give 'em to Leo, over there?" She looks up and up, meeting my eyes and sways slightly on her feet. I suddenly can't remember what the hell I was asking her for.

Her voice is small, and a bit hoarse, I would guess this isn't the first cry she's had today. "No, sir, I still have them."

Sir?

"Gabe, call me Gabe. Please." I try to swallow, my throat suddenly dry—*and what the hell is wrong with me.*

"Ms. Manning, if you could back your car up so I can hook the truck up to it, I sure would appreciate it."

There, a full sentence, great job Gabe.

"But, um, the front tires..." She trails off.

"Don't worry ma'am, we're gonna take care of that. Backin' up that far won't hurt 'em any more than just sittin' on the rims right now." She lets out a little squeak of surprise, and quickly scrambles into the car. It starts up quickly, and I realize that everyone else has moved out of the way and I have to jump to the side to keep from getting flattened when she puts it in reverse.

It stops and I knock on the hood. "Thank you, ma'am, that'll do it, you can shut 'er off." The two police officers are still standing there like useless statues when I hop back up into my truck, and holler, "Anybody who doesn't want to get run over better not be standing in front of that car when I get turned around."

Ms. Manning scrambles out of the car and trots back over to stand between Stephanie and Leo. The two officers wander over and I can hear the bigger one's obnoxious drawl. "You better come down to the station tomorrow, Ms. Manning. We can't do anything without a statement." It's a shitty power flex before they get back into their patrol car and leave. Finally moving enough that I can get my truck lined up right. Jackasses. What's their problem? I mean sure, she's kinda cute, but stop trying to strong-arm the woman into the station—that just sounds creepy. Hell, they caused so many delays I'm tempted to call the station myself and see if they were lying about not being able to take a statement on site.

My mind is wandering as I get parked and get all my cables hooked up. "Sir. Sorry, um, Gabe?" I try looking over my shoulder but end up having to turn around to actually see her face. "Yes'm what can I do for you?"

"Oh, no, please, call me Candice, if I call you Gabe it just feels weird to have you call me ma'am...I'm not that old." I can't help the smile that breaks free.

"A'ight, Candice, what can I do for you?" Better than Candy anyway. Then I realize, she's at the vet's office, she probably has to get her hamster or something out of the car before I hook it up. She kind of looks like a hamster actually, now that I think about it, short and cute, but cuddly. Something to put in your pocket and carry around so you can feed it snacks. "If you need to get your pet outta the car, can you please do it before I connect it to the lift, we don't want anybody gettin' hurt today." The second the words leave my mouth, the light in her eyes fades too.

I hear a sharp intake of breath from Stephanie and look up at Leo to see his face in his hands...Shit.

Foot, meet mouth.

Chapter 7

Candice

He didn't know and I *will not* cry. If I just keep telling myself that, maybe I can keep the tears in this time. "Oh, of course, no...no, we're good. I was just going to say thank you, give you my key, and ask if you needed more information before Stephanie takes me home." There we go, a successful effort. Lots of babbling and I feel the heat around my eyes and nose, but nothing feels drippy, so I'm going to call this a win.

The mechanic, Gabe, is big too—why are so many people around here so damned tall—but unlike Dr. Leo's sinewy grace, this man is built like a bear. A solid cylinder of muscle straight down. Topped with dark brown hair, shaved on the sides, and dark five o'clock shadow, he looks intimidating as hell, and the way he's staring at me with his whiskey-colored eyes full of impatience, it's taking everything in me not to scurry away and find a place to hide.

"Shit...I'm so sorry, ma'...Candice, yeah, if you wanna hand me your keys. I think we got all your information in our system already from your earlier appointment. If you could just write down your number, just to be sure...or...er...I can get it from Leo if that's easier."

I look back and forth between Dr. Leo and Gabe, oh...

Pack—alphas and pack—and no wonder they smell so good. Both spicy and sweet, but different flavors that I want to sample. Gabe reminds me of the cherry pipe tobacco Grandpa used to smoke, and Dr. Leo is both calm and refreshing with that chai and citrus. It takes everything in me to hold in the whine that tries to escape.

But of course—now I *am* shaking again. Thankfully, Stephanie knows my issues and is a lot more observant than I am right now. I don't even realize I'm backing up until she wraps her arm around my shoulders. "Let's go grab some dinner, then get you home. Ok, Hon?"

Leo starts to say something, but she cuts him off. "Later. I can text you over her number or you can get it from her file tomorrow. Now, she needs food and her nes—" I yank her arm and cut her off before she can finish that sentence. Keeping my omega status quiet has been difficult, and while I appreciate Stephanie's concern, she almost outed me.

Seeming to realize my abrupt change. "Tomorrow," she says again with finality to Dr. Leo and Gabe, before turning back to me. "Sorry, I know you're not a fan of sitting in the diner, but maybe we can get it to go. I can hang out for a bit when I drop you off?" She looks at me encouragingly. God, I've missed her.

"No, well, yes, but I mean..." I have to re-organize my thoughts. I'm more scattered today than usual after everything that's happened. "We can sit in the diner and talk for a while. I can't stay too late. Iggy's at home alone, and I don't want to leave her for too long—she gets destructive." One eyebrow goes up.

"Oh. Wait, yes, your iguana." She wraps one arm back around my shoulders—not completely touching, just offering comfort—and leads me to her car.

The ride to the diner doesn't take long, and there's no line. The Oak Flats Diner is one of only three places in town to get food, not counting the grocery store and the gas station. There's also the Jade Dragon Chinese Buffet over near the interstate. There's a generic burger franchise close to the interstate too, but the diner is the one closest to my house, so I've gotten takeout there a couple of times. They have good pi e.

Stephanie gets us settled in a booth near the back, and orders me a loaded chili and cheese baked potato and a milkshake. Not two flavors that really go together, but it seems she still knows my favorites. After everything else, I really appreciate her buying me dinner. I don't feel like eating, but I know I should, and the shake is cool and soothing on my sore throat after all the crying I did earlier.

She picks over her salad, and I finally manage a smile. "You still like that rabbit food?" I point at her plate.

"Well, no, not really, but old habits die hard, you know that." I manage a non-committal "hmm" around a sip of my shake. Not sure what to talk about. It feels like forever since we really talked last. We were so close until we graduated from high school. We used to have sleepovers at her house. Her dad made the *best* chocolate chip cookies.

She isn't really saying anything. She's trying to give me some space, and I appreciate it. But I have to say something. "So, other than saving fuzzy lives, what have you been up to?"

Her head pops up from watching the fork push a crouton around in a moat of ranch dressing. "Not much, honestly. Mom and Dad still live at the same place, but I have an apartment near here. You know I work at Fuzzy Friends. I did my internship there after college and was able to save up to buy in the partnership two years ago. No real romance prospects."

She waggles her eyebrows at me. "But Dr. Leo's hot." I blush, knowing she's teasing me. Stephanie likes men *and* women, but she actively avoids alphas, almost as much as me. Though her reasoning has more to do with not dealing with alpha-sized levels of bullshit than anything designation related. She likes to think of herself as a *drama free zone.*

"He is, and he's also an alpha. You know Grandpa taught me to stay away from alphas. And I'm not exactly standard omega material that most alphas are looking for anyway." I wave my fork vaguely towards my plate of melted cheese and chili goodness and my belly squish.

"Besides, I'm good."

Lie!

"I have my own house, steady work, and a few people I talk to online. And hopefully my friend back, if you're up for the random occasional hangout with a complete social introvert?" The offer seems to catch her by surprise, which I should have expected. We haven't really talked in so long. But her smile is encouraging. Deciding to take the plunge, I ask the burning question. "So, what do you know about hippo anatomy?"

By the time I finish explaining why I asked, she has given up on her salad and ordered her own salted caramel milkshake since I refused to share mine. We talk for a while about my work, some of my more interesting clients and the more risqué commission requests I get, until she's laughing so hard that the waitress comes over and pointedly leaves our bill, tapping on her watch and giving us annoyed looks.

"Shit, I didn't realize what time it was," Stephanie says, wiping a tear from her eyes. I had just been regaling her with a tale of another commission I had involving characters from a popular Saturday morning cartoon show, and anatomical additions that are not physically possible without dying of blood loss during arousal.

"Better get you home. Your lizard'll be worried." She leans into me, attempting a joke. But I feel bad for leaving Iggy home alone for so long, and I'm not sure how she's going to react to Sunny not coming home with me.

"You don't like iguanas?" I ask her, as she pays the cashier, and we walk out to her car.

"It's not that I don't like them…They're just so scaly. And they aren't affectionate." She looks at me, expecting me to agree, but I can't. "Ok, say, you have a dog, you get home, the dog is happy to see you, it runs up, wags its tail, and is overjoyed by your presence. You don't get that with lizards."

I smile slightly to myself, resolving to bring her inside to meet Iggy before she leaves me at the house.

Why are mornings so bright? I pull the covers over my head and try to burrow farther under the blankets, but no luck. I need to get up and check on Iggy. She was lying in her hammock last night when I got home, and nothing seemed destroyed. But we didn't leave the diner till late.

I didn't realize how much I had missed Stephanie, or human interaction in small doses. The diner kicked us out about two hours after closing time—which was still pretty early, really. So, when she brought me home, I invited her in. Iggy scaled her like a tree and Stephanie screamed and flailed a bit before finally admitting that yes, lizards can be affectionate.

Stephanie didn't stay long. After everything that happened with Sunny, I needed rest, and neither of us wanted to strain our newly restored friendship. Being at home, surrounded by memories of Sunny, I felt raw all over again. Stephanie gave me a brief one arm hug, more than I was really comfortable with, and excused herself since she still has to work today. While not in a hurry to do it again, having dinner with Stephanie was...nice. But I've reached my limit on human interaction for the year n ow.

No one else has been in my house since I moved here. After Grandpa died, I sold his place and used the money to buy this one. I didn't need anything that big, and other than the movers and the realtor, no one has been inside since I closed on it. So, even having someone here for such a brief visit was a bit of a mental strain, and I fell asleep shortly after she left.

Stretching over, I grab my phone from the charger to see four missed calls, from three different numbers.

Okay...

I pull up my voicemail, and the first one is from Gabe, telling me my car should be ready around one, and that he needs to talk to me before I go to the police station.

The second is from Stephanie, checking in.

The last voicemail is from the sheriff's department apologizing and saying they can take my statement over the phone, but please call them at my earliest possible convenience.

And the last missed call was ten minutes ago, from Gabe again, but he didn't leave a message this time.

Time...what time is it?

I shake my phone to take me back to the home screen, 12:11 P.M. Shit, how did I sleep so late?

Getting up, I try to wake up enough to call Gabe back. Dealing with finances on the car situation is gonna be a bitch, and I still haven't posted an update online. So much stuff needs done. I didn't even feel like showering last night, so I took a super quick one after Stephanie left. Not even bothering to dry my hair, I look like a dandelion after sleeping on it wet. That's ok. No one's gonna see it anyway. Twisting my hair up into a messy bun, I wash my face and grab a clean bra and a long flannel out of the closet—getting dressed on my way to the kitchen.

Iggy is sitting on top of the coffeemaker, looking imperious. While I don't like her up on the counters, I let her remain queen of all she surveys for a while longer so I can grab a bowl of cereal and pour milk on it before flopping back to the couch to try to wake up.

I curl my legs under me and hit the button to return Gabe's call while I wake up with my sugary overload drenched in moo juice. He picks up on the second ring, and instead of people in the background I hear a loud hum noise—*well, maybe they have a fan in the shop*—I'm sure it gets warm in there. "Hello, Ms. Candice, thank you for callin' me back," he starts before I can say anything.

"Oh, no problem, er, you said you needed to talk to me before I go into the police station, but now it doesn't seem like I need to do that."

I hear his low chuckle on the other end. "No, ma'am, you *do* not." The laugh is a bit heavier now, gruff and kind of growly, but not unpleasant.

"I also won't be able to pick up my car right now. I need to call Stephanie or figure out how to get to the shop. I only have the one means of transportation." I don't mention that maybe if I don't pick it up yet, I won't have to pay for it yet—I hope they won't press the matter.

"Yes'm, I'm sorry again about last night. Leo told me what happened. I'm sure I came off soundin' like an ass, but it wasn't my intent. As for a ride to the shop to get your car, well, I reckon I can help you out there. I just pulled into your driveway."

I let out a loud squawk, nearly dumping half my cereal on the couch trying to stand up. "I'm sorry, can you please repeat that?"

The phone hangs up, just as the doorbell rings.

Where the hell did I leave my pants last night?

Scrambling back towards my nest I yell, "Just a minute," at the top of my lungs. Iggy, seeing my struggle to get back into my pants as either time to play or time for a walk, decides to skitter down from her perch, across the floor, and claw her way up my still naked leg.

Fairly certain I am now bleeding down my thigh, I manage to get the waistband tucked over my stomach squish before opening the door. Gabe is standing there, eyes crinkled and trying not to laugh at either my appearance or the iguana hanging off my hair.

I realize a moment too late—when I open the storm door—that I haven't put on any de-scenter this morning. I look up into the scruffy face of Gabe. His pupils blow wide, the whiskey color of the iris almost completely eclipsed, all humor dropping from his features.

"Omega," he croaks out, right as I slam the door in his face and turn the deadbolt.

Jacks

Leo, Gabe, and Xan were late last night. At least they called to let me know, but damn, my lasagna was disgustingly dry by the time they got home. You can only keep pasta under the warmer for so long before you have a big noodle brick.

It's just as well they brought takeout instead of trying to eat it. Though, once again, if they had let me know in advance I wouldn't have bothered cooking.

Assholes.

Plus, they were eating cookies, fucking thin mints—love those things. Leo and Gabe both denied it, but I could smell it.

I wouldn't have been so upset if they had just brought me some, but no. Stuck at home with no chocolatey mint deliciousness.

I'm fine with getting takeout, but there's other shit that needs done too. If they aren't even going to appreciate the time and effort I put in—

Full stop—I'm staring down at the mess in front of me, banana bread batter slopped over the side of the bowl. Taking my aggression out on baking is clearly not working. I set the mess aside and go to wash the crushed banana mixture off my hands before taking off my apron and dropping it in the top of the washer.

Reaching up to fist my now clean hands in my hair, I tug hard. I need to get out for a while. They don't like me to leave the house, especially unsupervised. However, since I've taken over most of the household duties, I'm taking it upon myself to go to the grocery store. Maybe, if I'm feeling particularly benevolent, I'll take them all some lunch, after I buy myself a box of cookies—that I won't share.

While part of me wants to pry the hard lasagna out of the pan and box it up; I know they would eat it, just to make me happy. So instead, I go to the fridge and start getting out all the parts for an awesome loaded sub for myself...and the stuff to make Leo, Gabe, and Xander's favorites. Because their taste is shit...but I digress.

Twenty minutes later I have bag lunches all packed up, two turkey and Swiss overloaded with veggies and some freaky sort of mayo called aioli for Leo. Roast beef and cheddar, plain for Gabe. Ham and cheddar with mustard, mayo, pickles, and onions for Xan—thank goodness I don't have to breathe around him this afternoon. I toss in a few different flavors of chips and some bottles of water, and I am just a fucking happy homemaker.

God, I would make the perfect fucking housewife, not that these assholes appreciate it. Oh, I should probably toss in a few fruits too; none of them eat enough fruit.

I leave the house at exactly 11:45. That should be just enough time to drop Leo's lunch off at his office before his break and make it over to the garage for Gabe and Xan's before their 12:30 lunch break, then go by the store. We share the shopping app, but they never remember to update anything when they use it...we're almost out of tortillas, if I want to make tacos this week. Everybody agrees on tacos.

Humming, I get into the Jeep, it really is overkill to take it, but I don't want to walk six blocks back to the house carrying bags, or risk missing their lunchtimes. The whole needing a license thing is overrated anyway, I know *how* to drive, so everything else is legal shit.

Turning on the radio I crank the volume way up as *Paint it Black* comes on, before hitting the gas and bumping down the driveway. Ugh, I need to see about having a fresh load of gravel brought in. We live just outside the city limits—I use the term city loosely.

When we moved here, about four years ago, we were able to get a few acres out of town. It's not huge, but with Gabe's garage and Leo's veterinary work, we're doing well enough. Xander works at the garage for, or with, Gabe—not sure how that works exactly. I know I heard the word nepotism thrown out once but fuck it, they went to college together, and the place could easily be Gabe and Xan's Garage, but I don't think Xan likes to have his name on government paperwork for owning anything. He is a bit of a freak, but I love him.

Singing along as the song switches over to *Born on the Bayou*, I pull into Furry Friends. Hopping out of the Jeep, I grab the first bag of food and an apple from the pile of fruit I brought. They always argue over who gets stuck with the orange when I bring them lunch, so fuck it, they don't get a choice.

I swear sometimes it's like dealing with toddlers—not that I actually know what that's like—but I've heard it often enough to have an idea. I head inside and wave to Laura on my way through. She pales but doesn't dare say anything. Most people don't talk to me—I'm not sure why, but whatever, just making a delivery, then I can be on my way.

I push my head into the main office looking around; a pretty beta with short brown hair is sitting at the desk texting on her phone.

"Hey, you seen Leo?"

She lets out a little scream, before turning startled brown eyes my way. "Crud, you scared the heck outta me," she says, putting her hand on her chest as if to hold in her runaway heart. "Yeah, sorry...um, Dr. Leo is with a patient right now. Can I help you?" She has on her professional face, wondering why the receptionist didn't tell me, but since I haven't met this one before, I'm going to guess she doesn't know anything about Leo's packmates yet. I smile my thanks and she pales slightly but keeps her professional going, gotta give her props for that. I've been told I look a little crazy when I smile. I don't see it, but I rarely look at mirrors anymore, so maybe they're right. My smile always feels forced unless it's with my pack. Maybe I'm doing it w rong.

She starts to stand up. "Let me just go see if I can get him for you, ok?" She shuffles sideways past me to get out the door as fast as possible and almost runs down the hallway.

In less than a minute Leo is stalking up the hallway, glaring at me. "What are you doing here, you know better than to be out without me or Gabe? Wait, is Gabe with you, I don't..." He swivels his head around, doing a great impression of a black-headed heron...and I can't hold back the guffaw that bursts forth at that mental image or the look of confusion on his face at my outburst.

I clutch my stomach, trying to breathe through the laughter, and hold the bag out with the other hand. "Lunch," I manage to get out through my reaction at his perplexed expression.

Fuck, some people have no sense of humor.

I shake the bag at him a few times until he takes it, and I finally manage to collect myself. The laughter tapering off to giggles and then fading completely.

"You okay, Jacks?" He puts his hand on my bicep, squeezing gently, and trying to make eye contact.

Eye contact makes me twitch, I don't like it. Hell, people in general make me twitch. But with my pack, I don't expect them to do me dirty, so it's ok, I can handle this.

"Yeah, just, dinner was a bust last night, and I wanted to bring you lunch. You didn't tell me if you have any plans, I hope it's ok...I mean...you don't have to eat it if you already have something going on." I reach out to take the bag back, but he pulls it away.

"No, thank you. I...I appreciate it. I was just worried." His hand slides up to cup my cheek, tilting my head so I have to look at him.

"No." I know I sound like a surly kid. "My lasagna was ruined, you guys didn't bring me any cookies, and I'm going stir crazy sitting at home all the time. I feel like I'm losing what's left of my fuckin' mind, and I just...why am I so broken?" I have no idea what brought on this sudden bout of introspection, maybe I'm just as bat-shit crazy as everyone thinks, but I hate the desperate pleading in my voice when I feel like this. Something's missing, something's broken, and I can't fix it.

The last few weeks have felt like something's building up, and ever since last night it's felt like ants marching up and down along my skin—a deep inner itch—and I don't know what's wrong or how to fix it. I give up the fight, and lean into Leo, letting him wrap his arms around me, just breathing in his familiar scent for a few minutes and letting the comfort wash over me.

Finally, he pulls away, ducking his head to try to catch my eyes again.

"Ok, so, if you can give me fifteen minutes to finish up this paperwork, we can go over to the park and have lunch. Sound good?" Sometimes it feels like they're all just waiting for me to break again. They have to handle me with kid gloves so I don't fracture into a million pieces, and I understand, sort of. It already happened though, and while they helped me get my pieces all stuck back together, the cracks show if you look too close.

So, nobody looks close. They all just pretend it's normal and try to ignore when everything spills out again.

Shit…he's still looking at me…what was the question?

"Oh, I can't. I have food for Gabe and Xan in the Jeep, and I gotta get over there before they go on lunch. But tonight—text me what you want for dinner, ok? I'm going to the store after this, and can get it picked up, yeah?" I'm pulling away because his face is turning a rather unsettling shade of red, and I can feel the frustration spilling through our pack bonds. Normally they all stay closed off, but sometimes things slip through and this has to be pretty strong for me to even get a taste of it.

He looks like he's working himself up to a good rant, but I'm trying to make it out of the building as fast as possible. He has to work here and we don't need a scene. Making a break for it, I practically run out of the building—to the wide-eyed stares of the people in the waiting room, and the slack-jawed gape of Laura. I take a deep breath and let out what I'm sure sounds like a mad cackle. Gods, I needed this, just the fresh air and to get out for a while. Or maybe it was feeling connected to my packmates again. Things have been so busy lately, and affection has been strained. No one has time for snuggles on the couch or movie night anymore.

Taking a deep breath, I get into the car and buckle myself in. It's only a couple of blocks, but I don't want to add in any reasons to get pulled over. My foot on the brake, I reach up to put it in reverse and the pack bond blows wide open from Gabe's end with lust.

I freeze.

Then drop my hands, take my foot off the brake, and take a couple of deep breaths. What the actual fuck...This is the most awkward erection I've had in a few years, especially since I have no idea what's happening.

Suddenly Leo is climbing in the passenger side of the Jeep. "Go, we have to get to the garage, and Gabe."

Chapter 9

Gabe

My legs are about to give out, and I catch myself against the wall, dropping the coffee I brought along for Ms. Manning. I lean heavily against the brick beside her front door, my head swimming and my instincts going haywire. The hamster from last night, the one latched onto Leo, the one whose car is currently sitting in my parking lot—she's an omega. Fuck, but she smells good, like peppermint and chocolate.

Wait, was that why Jacks kept sniffing us last night and muttering about cookies?

I shake myself hard, looking down at my coffee splattered jeans. What the hell is going on? How did I not realize last night? And why the fuck does she smell so good? I've met omegas before, they all smell good, but I've never smelled one that makes me question my sanity.

One and all, great questions. But for now, I think I just scared Ms. Manning, Candice...Candy—well, she smells like a treat, that's for damned sure.

I wonder if she tastes as good as she smells.

What would it feel like to have her pressed against me, all soft and delicate?

My fist wrapped around that long dark hair, holding her head to the side so I can taste that fragile area right where her neck meets the shoulder.

Okay, full fucking stop. This is a customer who entrusted me with her car after someone vandalized it. For fuck's sake, her cat just died. I need to get my mind under control before I try this again.

Reaching out, but not really expecting an answer, I ring her bell again, then raise my hand and knock for good measure. "Candice, Honey, can you come out here please?"

Fucking hell, where did all these manners come from, and why the fuck did I just call a virtual stranger *Honey*. I need to get this shit under control *now*.

I try again. "Ms. Manning, I need to talk to you about your car, please answer the door." I hear the deadbolt click, and the main door slips open a few inches. Just enough that I can see her standing there, her fingers wrapped around the edge, knuckles white, and the fucking huge ass hairclip is still on her head. The scent isn't as strong through the glass of the storm door, but even if she sprayed herself with de-scenter, her house would still be saturated with that perfume. Just the thought makes me take a step back, needing to adjust my aching cock. These jeans were snug before but ever since she opened that door the first time, they could damn near be labeled as a torture device.

"Ms. Manning, can you please step outside for just a minute. I'm having a hard time concentrating over here, and maybe the clear air would help a bit." I feel my teeth grinding, trying to stay polite, when every instinct I have is demanding that I snatch up this hamster woman and drag her back to our pack house. Biology's a bitch, and I try to switch to mouth breathing. Which really does make me look like a bear, but at this point appearances are the least of my worries.

The glass door opens with a loud screech, and Candice steps out onto the concrete walkway. I know I'm staring; I can't seem to help it. Both her hands are full—at least she has good sense, since one of them appears to be a can of mace, and the other one is a bright pink cord—I mean, I'm not as kinky as Xan, and I don't think *I* will ever want to be tied up, but if she's offering.

No, wait, brain, stop.

Looks like it is a braided cord, a leash...once again, not *my* kink—I really need to get my mind out of the gutter here. But it is attached to that—that's not a hair clip. There's a big lizard sitting on top of her head, with a pink leash. And damned if that isn't strange enough to finally reset my fucking brain to at least some semblance of sense.

"Ms. Manning, I'm real sorry to show up unannounced this afternoon, but I need to talk to you about your car." She's standing in front of the closed door, and honestly, I'm not sure how she thinks that's going to work out.

If I was some kind of savage, she would have to step away to open it to escape. But I'm not trying to make her feel worse, so I just keep my mouth shut. I was trying to look over her head, see if anyone else is in the house with her; an omega living alone's in danger. But every time I try to raise my eyes over her head that damned lizard catches me by surprise. I don't know what the hell it is, Leo would. Hell, it's probably one of Leo's patients. But it *is* creepy as fuck just staring at me—shit, I made eye contact.

Wait, what is that little fucker trying to do now?

"Shit, Iggy, not now, what the hell!" is the only warning I get before the lizard is flying through the air, having leapt from her hair. I don't know what kind of crazy this thing is, but damn, there's no way in hell it can jump that far.

Before my mind can really process what my body's doing, I reach out my arm to catch it. Little bastard made it farther than I thought it would anyway. It lands with a squishy thud against my shoulder and scrambles around the back of my neck. Tiny claws digging into my skin and rubbing the top of its scaly head against the underside of my jaw on the other side.

So, I am tied to Candice by a lizard and its bright pink leash—my arm still hanging uselessly between us—covered in coffee, and *now* my phone decides to ring.

Xan

I just finished up with a spark plug job, pulled the car out into the lot, and am leaving paperwork on the desk for Kelly to take care of in the morning when the pack bond from Gabe opens up and I'm nearly knocked over with the shot of lust pouring through.

Did dude fall into a vat of pheromones or something, I mean, what the fuck even was that?

I lean against the desk, shifting uncomfortably, trying to figure out what the hell to do about the inappropriate work erection when Trey walks in. "'Ey, boss, I'mma head on out ta lunch..." He trails off, not finding Gabe in the office, but taking in my red face, fast breathing and hands holding a grease stained rag over the erection straining my coveralls.

He does a better about-face than I have seen in a long time and leaves without another word. I'm going to have words with Gabe after this, just as soon as I make sure that fucker is ok.

I pick up the office phone to check up on him, but my attention is diverted by tires screeching into our driveway. What the ever-loving hell is Jacks doing driving, and why does he have Leo with him? They both know better.

I hang up the phone. Clearly, having to deal with my wayward packmates takes precedence over whatever Gabe is getting himself into—or off with, if that surge earlier was any indication. Jacks slams on the brakes just outside the front door, and spills out of the driver's side door, dragging a handful of brown paper with him.

Thank fuck Leo is slightly more with it. Reaching over and turning off the engine, he brings the key with him as he takes a few shaky steps out of the car. I'm unsure if his wobbly legs are from Jacks's driving, or the same predicament my own boxers are losing the battle with, but Jacks scrambles through the front door making the bell jangle loudly and throwing what turns out to be a brown paper bag on the desk behind me before wrapping his arms around my shoulders and starting to suck on my neck.

Oh, he made us lunch. Well, that was sweet of him.

"Where is Gabe?" Leo grinds out as he shuffles in. Yup, definitely a shared predicament. Turns out scrubs hold in an erection even less than my work coveralls. Poor man looks like he's about to bust a fucking seam. Jacks is incredibly distracting, with his hand wrapped around my ponytail, gently biting up the column of my throat, and rubbing his hard cock against my hip. I grab his face and pull him away.

"Love, I know, believe me, I know. But this isn't the time or the place, ok?" I kiss him briefly on the mouth, nipping at his lower lip so he understands this isn't a rejection, just a delay. He pulls back and wanders over to the waiting area, rocking back and forth and muttering something about chocolate mint cookies again. I don't know where his brain goes sometimes, but he doesn't seem as agitated as Leo right now, so let's just deal with one emergency at a time.

"He took off for lunch early, said he needed to go talk to the owner of that little rust box out front. I don't know why he didn't just call." I shrug my shoulders. I don't know what our pack leader had planned. He didn't tell me in advance, but that's nothing new. I'll fully admit to some confusion and curiosity on my part, but I always assumed that if there was anything important, he would let me know.

Leo's looking out into the parking lot, scoping out the car that I mentioned before. "That car belongs to Ms. Manning; she was in the clinic yesterday. Someone slashed her tires while her cat was being put down." I flinch back—what in the actual fuck?

First of all, dick move at any time—but fuck me, no wonder Gabe wanted to be extra nice. I know for a fact that the car needed more work than it had done. Maybe he wanted to talk to her about it in person so she wouldn't feel as overwhelmed.

"Get her address, we're going over there," demands Leo, nearly in a panic—though I'm at a loss to see why.

"Now, just hold your horses," I tell him. "Let's try calling him first. If he answers, then we can just ask him what's going on." There, simple, practical, makes total sense—which is probably why Leo is gaping at me like a landed fish.

"Oh, yes, but I'm concerned. You see, the woman who this car belongs to...well, I wasn't reacting normally. I kept feeling the need to comfort her, and I fear what that may mean about her designation."

I blink slowly.

"Fuck man, just say omega like a normal guy—oh shit!" I snatch the phone from its cradle, hitting the speed dial for Gabe's phone, and barely registering Jacks's giggles getting louder from the other room.

The call goes to voicemail after four rings. So, I try again and it goes straight to voicemail this time. I quickly pull up the customer information in our files—her address is a few miles from here, not too far away.

Leo grabs Jacks and bundles him into the back of the Jeep while he throws me the keys and I get behind the wheel. I've already started backing up while Leo is still trying to get in. A hard turn out of the driveway has him cussing at me as he's slammed into the door hard enough for it to jar open again.

"Dammit, put on your seatbelt!" Jacks is still giggling from the backseat, and while that in itself is disconcerting, I can only handle one emergency at a time.

We barrel down the street breaking most of the speed limits in town, before sliding to a stop behind Gabe's truck in a little cul-de-sac. I've just managed to get the gear into park, when Jacks tumbles out the back door laughing hysterically. I can't even blame him when I see what has him gasping and sprawled in the street.

Gabe is lying on the ground tangled in a pink leash with an iguana perched on his shoulder, rubbing its face against his beard stubble. There's a short woman straddling his back, pulling on the leash. Leo lets out a loud snort as Gabe begins thrashing around, unseating both lizard and human passenger. The woman lets out a small, pained whine as she tips over and hits the ground. That sound brings everything else to an abrupt halt.

The iguana strains to get to its owner, slipping free from the harness, and darting over to her side. It turns towards us and starts hissing and clicking—clearly defensive of its person, despite using Gabe as a perch earlier.

Gabe is finally on his back, his wrist, still wrapped in a leash, is stuffed in his pocket. Apparently, he was trying to retrieve his phone when he went down. He's covered in bits of grass and yard debris and is using his non-leashed hand to brush it off his hair and face as he sits up, groaning.

Leo is focused on the iguana, or its owner, I'm not entirely sure. He's watching the situation unfold from beside me, and I can practically see the cogs in his mind turning.

Unfortunately, that means we've forgotten about Jacks. Panic floods me as I realize his laughter has stopped too, and I spin quickly, trying to locate him, but he's gone. Ice fills my veins at the thought of Jacks loose in suburbia. He's not a bad person, but he's not always safe for himself or those around him.

Before I can rally help, Leo lets out a strangled sound behind me. I turn again, feeling like I'm on a fucking carousel, and see Jacks. He must have circled the Jeep while we were focused on the spectacle in front of us. He's scooped up the girl and her lizard and is now striding purposefully towards her front door, bleeding slightly from the torn elbows of his shirt.

He's carrying her like a fucking princess, the iguana sitting on his shoulder, and a brown paper bag swinging from one hand. I have no fucking idea what's going on until I hear Gabe's voice, raised to carry across the yard. "Jacks, put the omega down. *Do not* go into that house."

Chapter 10

Jacks

ine. This one is mine. Her tiny green friend is protective, so she can belong to them as well, but she is *mine.*

I knew something was up, the twitchy feeling of ants crawling over me–that itchy tickle—should have known something was going to happen. But this has been a very pleasant surprise. Not gonna lie, I was upset when I saw Gabe tangled up in a pink leash, ropes have always been more my thing than his—and the absurdity of it all. My body wouldn't stop twitching, I could barely breathe through my fit of laughter, not even noticing the omega straddling his back until she fell, and then I couldn't breathe at all.

With my body on autopilot, I stand and grab the lunch I made for Gabe out of the Jeep, she needs it more than him anyway. She needs more, but that's all I have on hand, and I need to feed her. She's mine, and I need to take care of her, I just do. Marching around the front of the Jeep to avoid Xan and Leo, my body refuses to listen to reason as I bend to lift her off the ground. Her scent is intoxicating, and now I know why I've been craving those damned cookies.

I bet she tastes even sweeter, but before we can get to the tasting, I need to take care of her. Her small companion hisses at me again when I get close, so I pick it up first and hand it to her, that way it knows she's safe. My omega in hand, and her lizard clawing its way up my arm, I need to get her inside. Her scent is making my head spin, and I need to get her fed and into her nest for cuddles.

Mine.

Mine Mine MINE!

My mind screams out at me as I carry her towards the front door.

I just want to rub all over her bare skin. While I love her chocolate and peppermint scent—I want to lick her and see if she tastes like that too—I also need to make sure she smells like me. She's mine, and if my pack will kindly remove their heads from their collective asses, I'll be happy to share. But for now, they're all just standing around being useless—meanwhile our omega needs to be taken care of, so they're on their own.

I hear Gabe's voice calling out to me, demanding that I put down my omega and step away, but that's *not* going to happen. She lets out a dismayed whine at his voice and I am sorely tempted to turn around and beat the shit out of my pack leader for upsetting her. Doesn't she want me to take care of her, get her inside, away from other people?

There's a tear running down her pink cheek when I look at her. She's so cuddly, and I just want to bundle her up in soft blankets and purr for her until she only feels relaxed and content. Shifting her closer to me, my arm under her shoulders, I pull her tighter against my chest and bring my hand closer to her face. I rub my thumb down her cheek, wiping away the tear so she'll look at me.

"What's wrong, Omega? I've got you. Why the tears?" Her big blue eyes look up at me, wet, like she's going to continue to leak, and I have to strain to hear her whisper.

"Nobody knew...I've lived here for almost three years now, and none of my neighbors knew I was an omega. I can't...now everybody's gonna know, and I..." More tears start down her face. Her nose is turning red and I pull her closer still—rubbing my chin on the top of her head.

"It's ok, little omega, we'll take care of it, just rest."

I say we'll take care of it, but fuck me. I want to turn around and knock the living shit out of Gabe for not thinking earlier. Of course no one knew, it's not safe for omegas to live alone.

Stopping and repositioning her in my arms I get the storm door open, and her scent hits me hard.

She smelled delicious outside in the open air, but in *her* space, *her* home, it's pure concentrated ambrosia, and I stagger as it fills my lungs, making my mouth water and my cock go stiff as a fucking lead pipe behind my button fly. I push the front door closed with my foot. I'll lock it later, with my pack in the yard no one is coming in that way—and on the off chance they did make it in, I'm here, and I'm not going anywhere.

Looking around the entry, I take in her space. To one side there's a short hall with a bathroom and what looks like an office, then straight ahead is the living room with an open kitchen separated by a bar and a couple of stools. There's a closed door on the far side of the living room, and I'm guessing it leads to her nest, and another in the kitchen that probably goes to the laundry or a garage. These tiny cookie cutter style houses are easy to navigate, they have a few plans that they rotate through. But it's a cute little house, all her own, and I can see why she's upset at the thought of leaving it.

Setting her down on the couch, I pick up a blanket that's draped over the arm. It smells strongly of her, so she must use it often. I wrap it around her shoulders and stand back, appraising my omega burrito. Then I take the lizard off my shoulder and set it on a cat tree near the bookcases lining one wall.

I sit down next to her on the couch, but her arms start to flail, undoing my work. I try to purr, but she won't stop struggling, so I pull her into my lap, purring louder.

A muffled, "Stop!" comes from the tangled bundle just below my chin, and I freeze, feeling like my strings have all been cut. "Stop! You're bleeding. I need to get the first aid kit." My purr starts back up and I nuzzle against where I think her head is.

I'll take care of my bleeding arms soon. They don't hurt much, and I just want to enjoy a few more minutes of holding her before I have to get up and get her food. I look around for a clock, craning my neck. This has been a rollercoaster and surely hours have passed since I left the house. Nope, the microwave shows it has only been forty-five minutes. *Wow!*

But, bonus, that means the sandwich I brought in is still edible...maybe a little flat, but there's a banana in there too, she can have that while I cook something better.

I lift her off my lap, much to my body's frustration. My insistent erection is still trapped in my now too tight pants, and he is not a happy guy, but he's not in charge. My omega is, and until she says otherwise, he's going to stay right where he is.

"Here, I brought you a sandwich. Do you like roast beef?" I open the bag, and sure enough, flat sandwich. Maybe I can pass it off as a panini. Does she have a panini press? I can add some toppings, get it nice and melty for her. This is a good plan; I like this plan.

She's still trying to struggle free from the blanket, so I reach over and pull the top flap off from where I had her tucked in. Her messy bun is mostly out now, and the long auburn waves are frizzing all around her shoulders, making her look like a dandelion. I reach out to gently untangle her scrunchie and smooth down what I can while she tries to collect herself. I can't help touching her, my fingers itch with the need to run over her skin. But this is the best I can do right now not to freak her out, so I'll take it.

"No, well, yes. But you first, I need to clean up your arms. Infections are no laughing matter." She looks so serious, and so fucking adorable with her pout and her poofy hair.

"Ok, Little Lion, let me get your first aid kit. Where is it? Kitchen or bathroom?" I stand up—my knee popping—and put the flat sandwich back in the bag. We can do better than that.

She tries to stand up, still tangled, and face-plants against my chest. "No. Nope. Nope...it's in my bathroom, through my nest. I'll get it. You sit down and take off your shirt."

Her cheeks darken so quickly she looks like a cherry tomato. I'm not sure if the embarrassment is from the face-plant, giving me orders, or the thought of me without a shirt, but I kind of hope for the last one.

I peel my ruined shirt over my head and, admittedly, flex a bit for her while I do it. She goes even redder, and I can't help the grin that breaks out at her reaction, her jaw going slack when she sees my ink and pierced nipples—can't wait to show her my tongue ring—or let her feel it. Xan likes it, so hopefully she will too.

Her head snaps up to my face, eyes wide as if she was caught doing something embarrassing—like ogling my naked chest. She turns and tries to run, but her feet are still tangled in the blanket, and she starts to go down again. Wrapping my hands around her waist, I lift her out of the tangle of blanket and set her down on the other side, smiling unabashedly at how flushed she looks right now.

She draws back and I falter—I can look kind of manic when I smile, or at least, most people seem uncomfortable when I do. This smile feels more genuine, not like the fake face I have to put on for everyone else. I want to be around her, and it makes me happy.

She scampers off towards the door on the far side of the room.

Yup, nest, called it.

I head towards the kitchen to wash my hands and see if I can find a panini press, or just figure out what else I can cook for her.

Candice

I thought we were both doomed when Iggy wrapped her leash around the big growly one earlier, Gabe. He was spinning around, trying to get his phone out of his pants and unwrap from her long leash when he tripped. He landed half on me—holding Iggy in one hand since she decided she liked his stubbly beard—he seemed to be trying to protect her in the fall. I guess I'm lucky that I'm already padded, and he landed on his knees before he went over completely, face first onto my thigh. Being a bit squishy can be a good thing though, at least no one was seriously hurt.

By the time I wiggled out from under him, he had released Iggy, who was still leashed to him, and she had decided that his shoulder was her best option. I was sitting on his back, trying to untangle the cord, or at least get Iggy to move since one of his hands was still trapped under him. Then that Jeep showed up and things got even weirder.

Pressing my back against my bedroom door, I let out a deep breath. Ok, time to take stock. I have a giant alpha covered in tattoos, with his pierced eyebrow, septum, and nipples—I feel like I should look closer at those, just for artistic purposes, of course—standing shirtless in my living room, and don't think I missed the bulge in the front of his jeans. But those dimples when he smiled—fuck me, ok, yeah, so I'm a sucker for dimples. *Shit.*

But he's only shirtless because I told him to be—*I'm not sure if that is a positive or a negative.* I have three more large attractive alphas in my front yard doing who knows what, *negative column.* They just loudly shouted out my designation, so now my neighbors will all know that I'm an omega living alone——*definitely in the negative column.*

I guess it says something that Iggy tried to defend me from them, even if she is small enough to be stomped on. But she's still a traitor, climbing all over strange alphas, demanding attention, and letting them pet her.

A tiny voice in the back of my mind suggests that this isn't a bad thing, and they probably wouldn't mind if I did the same thing.

No, bad omega. There will be no rubbing on strange alphas, no demanding of attention, and definitely no letting them pet me. Completely, one hundred percent negative column.

But is it really? says the tiny omega voice again, and my alpha addled brain is having a hard time disagreeing with the little voice. But my logical mind is kicking me in the ass telling me to get a move on, get the first aid kit, and go patch up the stranger—who is doing god knows what in my living room right now.

The stranger with all the muscles...come on, one little lick won't hurt.

Clearly, my inner omega is a slut, and we are *not* going to listen to her.

I hurry to the closet and get out my first aid kit. I use it for first aid but it started out as a tackle box that I bought for crafts—but then I realized I don't craft often enough to need that much storage. But I *am* incredibly accident prone and it would work wonders for keeping bandages, tweezers, and other patching up stuff in one spot—and it glows in the dark because I am easily amused. It worked out well.

Scurrying back through my nest, I close the door behind me. I don't mind if Iggy goes in there for snuggles, but I don't want to risk hurting her if I go into there to flop and burrow when she's hiding. Glaring at her when I pass for her part in this. Her only reaction is to blink at me, and honestly, life is so crazy right now, I can't even stay mad at her. Frustrated, yes, definitely, mad, no—speaking of frustration where is he? I know I left a big guy with a *lot* of skin showing right here next to the couch.

A loud crash comes from the kitchen and a colorful arm pops over the bar. "Hey, do you have a panini press in here? I can't seem to find one." This is the strangest conversation I've had in a while, and since that includes talk of hippopotamus dick, I really feel that's saying something about where my life is right now.

Still carrying my tackle box/first aid kit, I walk around the bar to find the alpha sitting on my kitchen floor, going through cabinets.

When was the last time I dusted under there?

Shit.

God, but he looks good...like, all right there on display. Pale skin covered in a myriad of colors, but so well-defined, long and lean. My fingers are all itchy and tingly, and they really just want to reach out and touch—to bandage him up, of course. The tiny voice is trying to hijack my thoughts again, but since we already know she's a slut, we've got to ignore that for now. "Hi, sorry, I don't think I own a panini press. I'm not even sure what a panini is, or how to press it, sorry."

A shaggy strip of caramel colored hair emerges out of the cabinet and over the countertop, hazel eyes crinkled at the corners in what I think is a smile, but could be plotting my demise for my lack of panini knowledge. I'm terrible at reading people. "Sorry, but, I got the first aid kit, if you can stand up and come back over to the couch, I can get your elbows patched up, sorry. Is that ok?"

Wait, how many sorries was that? Do I apologize habitually, or am I just stressed out?

Ok, stupid question, of course I'm stressed. But, yeah, I should probably stop apologizing. I sound like a broken record.

He unfolds himself from my kitchen floor and I have to tilt my head back to watch his face. Okay, yes, that is definitely a smile, but he still might be plotting vengeance over the panini thing.

"Sorry, Little Lion." He walks towards me, all sinuous grace, brushing his hand down my back when he circles behind me before sitting down on the couch. That should not feel as good as it does, and I have to shake myself before sinking down beside him and focusing on his arms.

The blood's mostly stopped, but I still want to make sure there are no little chunks of road stuck in there, so I hold a clean towel up and upend the bottle of hydrogen peroxide over his elbow. I would be hissing and whining about it by now, but he's just staring at me with a goofy grin. It's starting to make me nervous. I wait for the bubbling to stop, smear him with ointment, and dig out one of my big bandages to put over the area.

Maybe he senses my confusion, maybe he just wants to talk...I like the sound of his voice regardless, it just makes me feel...right, somehow. He mentions something about last night, and a lasagna, and cookies. But I'm having a hard time focusing. The last twenty-four hours have been crazy and stressful, and I should be freaking out with him so close—and my mind is, sort of. But my body seems to think that all is right with the world, and that in itself is concerning.

Standing up, I cross to his other side to repeat the process. He leans towards me, still talking and nuzzling his face into my hair as soon as I sit down.

Kind of freaky, but I can't say I don't feel the same, he smells like cinnamon and coffee. I had a hell of a time earlier fighting myself to get out of his lap when he wrapped me up. Except even then, his scent was muffled by all the blankets.

Why does he smell so good?

This side isn't bleeding at all, but the skin is pretty scraped up. Once it's clean and bandaged he pulls me into his lap and starts purring again. I haven't heard an alpha purr since Grandpa died, he used to do it when I was little. When he would tell me about Grandma and stories of when Mom was little. As I got older, he would do it less often, usually only if I got hurt, and then just for a few minutes.

It's taking everything in me not to just close my eyes and fall asleep right now. Which is batshit crazy, because I still don't know anything about this guy, or why the hell he's in my house. I guess it's good timing that there's a loud knock, and then another strange alpha walks in, followed by Dr. Leo and Gabe.

Chapter 11

Gabe

I am so fuckin' sore right now. The first time I went down I landed on my phone, with my hand wrapped around it, so at least the phone was ok. But neither my thigh nor my hand are really happy with the situation. Then when I rolled over, I landed on her can of mace, that *is* definitely gonna leave a bruise—on my ass. Yeah, gonna have a fun time sitting at work the rest of this week.

Fucking hell.

I'm finally able to stand up, and work on brushing all the grass off. It's been a long fuckin' day already and now I gotta deal with this shitshow before I can finish work.

"Leo, Xan, gimme a hand here, I think I broke my ass." As expected, Xan lets out a loud bark of laughter, but then he comes ambling over to gimme a hand up off the ground. Leo starts brushing off my shoulders and back as I try to steady myself around my throbbing hand and aching ass. But I can't help the loud grunt when he smacks against my bruised butt trying to dust me off.

"What the actual fuck man, when were you gonna tell us you found our omega?" Xan whisper shouts at both Leo and me.

"To be fair, I don't think either of us was aware of Ms. Manning's designation until today, or even aware of Ms. Manning at all until yesterday," Leo replies.

"If you say so, but I don't know how you could have missed that. Hell, it took Jacks less than a minute to sniff her out, and he was farther away than either of us. Speaking of…" Xan trails off, as we all look towards the house. Worry pinching Leo's brows as we wonder what exactly our least stable packmate is doing in there.

Yeah, that is a concern. Normally Jacks wouldn't hurt a fly, but his reaction surprised me. He never likes strangers, and omegas tend to make him extra nervous. We better get in there and check on them both.

"I gotta warn y'all, I damned near lost it from her perfume when she just opened the door earlier. I don't know what it is about her, but fuck, we're probably gonna have a hell of a time gettin' Jacks out of there without scaring the bejesus outta her." Leo and Xan nod, looking thoughtful. I don't think they understand yet just how much her scent affected me.

Then again, judging by the front of Leo's scrubs, maybe he does.

Xan

I don't bother waiting after I knock, I don't want to give Jacks a chance to bolt or do anything too crazy—but I also don't like just walking into a stranger's house unannounced, it's...rude.

The first thing I take in is Jacks—shirtless—with neon green bandages on both arms, and the omega bundled up in his lap looking half asleep. I get closer before I hear him, and fuck me, but this is starting to freak me out. Jacks hasn't purred in years.

Not since Janey died.

I take in the room around me as I walk towards him, hands out to show I'm not gonna do anything. I trust Jacks with my life, but I'd rather be safe than sorry with how he is right now.

The house is small, made smaller by the four large bodies currently in it. One larger room that has a living room, kitchen, and breakfast nook. There's a tiny bistro set there, but it looks like it's covered in papers. I don't know how anyone could actually use it to eat. One long couch with Jacks in the middle and a roundish coffee table that looks a lot like a giant cable spool. I walk towards that and nudge it with my knee to make sure it is stable before I sit down, directly across from Jacks. He has a big stupid grin on his face, and while the whole situation is unnerving, it is a relief to see him happy.

Leo and Gabe sit, one on each side, and now the omega starts to struggle. Not that I blame her, but Jacks's expression falls, and he loosens his hold so she can slide free and bolt across the room. There's a huge terrarium over there, and the iguana has stretched out across the mesh top.

I don't blame you little buddy. This has been a long day already.

I stand up and turn towards her. "Ma'am, I really am sorry about all this. Just walkin' into your house and all, but I needed to get Jacks, and now we can get outta your hair." I keep my eyes lowered, and my hands up, trying to look as non-threatening as possible. I'm sure the tent in my coveralls isn't helping right now.

Gabe wasn't wrong. Her scent in here is making it hard to think and I'm already both embarrassed and in physical discomfort from my body's reaction to it. Hell, I was hard just from Gabe's reaction to it through our bond, and it hasn't exactly gone down since I smelled her myself. I'm torn, my mind knows the best thing to do right now would be to grab Jacks, and remove him from this situation, forcibly if necessary.

But my body wants to get as close to her as possible, my fingers itch to touch her skin, and smooth down her hair. To feel how soft she is, she's so tiny, I could probably pick her up without too much trouble. I'm not as big as the rest of my pack, but I do haul around tires and car parts all day, so I'm not a lightweight either. I bet I wouldn't have any trouble carrying her into her nest and peeling off those yoga pants.

I bet Jacks would even join me. Hey pack bonding exercise!

I shake my head—fuck—I haven't even introduced myself yet. She probably thinks I'm some sort of pervert like this.

I should probably do that

"Shit, I know it's a little late, but I'm Xander, or just Xan. That snuggly guy on your couch is my mate, Jackson, but we just call him Jacks. And it seems like you already know Gabe, our pack lead, and Leo." I raise my eyes, because eye contact is important, and she's wearing a very perplexed expression.

"Oh, yeah, sorry. This is really strange. I'm Candice. Some people call me Candy, but it always sounds like a stripper name, so I don't use it very often. Mostly people I went to high school with...and now I'm babbling and should probably shut up."

Her face is getting progressively redder, but she just can't seem to stop. I guess she's a nervous talker. I can't help the smile tugging at my lips. She *is* cute. Slowly I lean closer, holding out my hand to shake, but giving her plenty of time to stop me if she feels uncomfortable. She shakes my hand firmly, not what I'm used to with omegas, or even really betas. Shakes twice and then draws back.

"Thank you, Ms. Candice, it was nice to meet you, despite the awkward circumstances. Now we better get going."

Her skin really is like silk, and I want to linger on that handshake, but we need to leave. We retrieved our missing pack leader, now we have a hand on Jacks—I can hear Leo and Gabe behind me, whispering to Jacks, trying to get him to get up and go.

Gabe stands, hand around Jacks's upper arm, ready to pull him up and drag him from the room if he refuses. When I hear a loud grumble from Candice, my head snaps around and she's beet red with her hand on her stomach. "Um, sorry, I haven't eaten breakfast yet."

Jacks pops off the couch like he has a pogo-stick up his ass, almost knocking Gabe over in the process, and bolts around the couch and back to the kitchen—and it looks like we're going to be here for a while. Once he gets an idea to feed someone, we're better off just waiting it out.

Plus, I left the lunch he made me at work so I'm feeling hungry myself. He's a damned good cook. Leo drops his head into his hands and gives a defeated sigh. While Gabe turns to Candice and says, "Well, it looks like we might be here for a while, so let's talk about your car."

Chapter 12

Candice

By the time we got home yesterday it had been the worst day I've had since Grandpa died, well today is turning out to be the strangest. I haven't been up that long, but I need a shower, and there are four strange alphas in my house. Each one smells amazing. All together they smell like some kind of fevered sex dream. Nervous babbling aside, I think I am doing fairly well—all things considered.

And they're all hot, which is so unfair. I mean, Dr. Hottie, hello! Gabe who looks like some sort of professional strongman with short dark hair and stubble. *I just want to rub against*—I bet I'd get stubble burn if I tried. Jacks, who is standing, still shirtless, in my kitchen with a fucking mohawk...What is this, the 80s?

I wonder if I should get him an apron, it would be a shame to burn any of the colorful delicious skin.

No!

Stop it, slutty inner omega.

And now this new guy, Xan, he's kind of short for an alpha, and I can't see much of his body from the coveralls—*except the erection*, points out that tiny voice. Long dark blond hair.

I wonder how that would feel running over my legs...as he kissed his way up, nipping and licking—get thee behind me inner omega!

Well shit. Look, he has chin pubes, it isn't even a real beard, he isn't that hot, ok. Just...no.

But ugh, the tiny omega voice is right, they are hot, and they smell good, and I just want to go flop on the couch on top of Dr. Leo—who looks a bit shell shocked right now, actually.

Maybe I should check on him, he is gonna be Iggy's doctor after all, I don't want to make him uncomfortable.

He would be a lot more comfortable without pants.

Shut up, inner omega.

"Candice?" I was so focused on Dr. Leo that I missed Gabe coming to stand next to me. "Everything went haywire, but I *do* need to talk to ya about your car. I mean, that's why I came over. Things are...well, I'm not sure how safe it is to drive right now."

Shit

I take a deep breath—bad idea. "I'm sorry, I...what?"

Gosh, but he smells good.

No, wait, what?

I mean, yeah, he smells good, great, but what?

"I'm sorry, back up. My car, what do you mean it's not safe?"

His hand comes up like he is about to put it on my shoulder, but instead he pulls back and runs it through his own short hair. Whiskey colored eyes looking everywhere but at me. "Well, your front axle is loose. It's not broke yet, but I wouldn't feel right lettin' ya drive around with it like that, if it does break, ya could get seriously hurt. I'm not sure what ya hit, but it sure did a number on it."

He looks almost sheepish, like he's worried I am gonna go off on him for accusing me of running over something.

"But I don't drive it, I mean, I've taken less than four car trips this year, one of which was yesterday to the vet, the others have all been either to your shop for an oil change, or the one to the bank. I don't go anywhere if I can avoid it. Not saying I'm a shut-in, but people make me nervous." I raise my hand, indicating all the people in my house, currently making me less nervous than I would have anticipated.

"Shit...ok, well, um, I'm not sure what to tell ya, I can take another look at it, but I'm pretty sure it is gonna need replaced. Was it wobbly or anythin' yesterday when you took it to see Leo?"

I sigh, pulling at my own hair, I don't have the time or the money for this. But sometimes I need a car. "No, no, I believe you...I just...I can't afford to do it right now. I need to take care of Sunny's vet bill from yesterday, and I still have to pay for the tires and the oil change and I just..."

I trail off, my stomach bottoming out. Good thing I haven't had any food yet.

I'm suddenly exhausted—feeling overwhelmed by everything from the last two days, and unable to hold back a whine. I want a do-over. Let's just go back to last weekend, so we can redo this whole week. My hands come up cupping my elbows, and then a pair of big arms wrap around me, one hand still holding a spatula.

"What the fuck man—what did you do?" It's Jacks again, looking aggressive and staring daggers at Gabe. I reach up and pat his chest, not wanting a fight in my house.

"Shh, it's ok, he didn't do anything. Just some not great news, and I miss my cat. I'm sorry, I just...I'm sorry." I can't hold back the tears as the stress from the last couple of days comes crashing down on me.

"No. No. It's ok Little Lion, I got you." Then I'm being lifted off my feet and carried back to the kitchen. "Here, finish her pancakes." He thrusts the spatula into Xan's hand, before turning and marching me back towards my nest.

Once we're inside he closes the door and sets me down on the mattress. "Bunch of nosey old biddies, I swear. Don't worry about them. You stay here, rest, get a shower, just breathe if you need to. I'm going to finish making your breakfast, then we can talk once you feel better, ok?" He brushes my hair back and places a gentle kiss on my forehead, before leaving and closing the door behind him.

I can hear raised voices coming from the living room, but honestly, I don't care at this point. After going to lock my nest door I head towards my en suite bathroom. Once the shower's on, I turn up some classic rock to drown out the rest of the argument and just let the hot water and the music soothe my jangled nerves.

Leo

A scent match? How the hell did I miss that before?

Yesterday was busy all day with seeing all the new clients since Dr. Jerry had an emergency and called out.

And then surgery on Freddy—*I should probably call the office to check on him, I'm seriously over my lunch break. I should call to let them know how long I'll be gone.*

Then Candice's car.

Of course, I know I reacted to her yesterday, but how could I have not realized?

I run my hands through my hair again, yanking on it hard enough to make my eyes water. I feel like a fool.

"Hey, Leo, you tryin' ta pull start your brain or something? I may not be the one that went to the fancy medical school, but I don't think it works like a lawnmower." I smile up at Xan, he still has the spatula in his hand.

He has always been the jokester, the one who tries to make everyone feel better. And I appreciate him for that. He hides it well, but he's smart enough to have gone through medical school. He just said it would be too much paperwork, and he would rather play with cars all day. I don't begrudge him that, we're comfortable enough with the four of us, and honestly, I don't think he has the temperament for it. He can be soft-hearted, and losing a patient like I did yesterday, even though I saved another one...I think it would break him eventually.

"Do I smell smoke?" I pretend to sniff the air, in truth, I have been trying not to breathe through my nose since we came inside this house. Candice's perfume is everywhere, and it is making my mind fuzzy.

"Shit! Fuck! Jacks is gonna kill me!"

Xan scrambles back into the kitchen.

"Oh, you asshole, no, nothing's burning," he says with a smile, and I know he isn't really angry. Jacks chooses that moment to come back out of the nest.

"Man, you better not be messing up the pancakes. Those are the easiest thing to make. Can you keep on 'em while I start the eggs and bacon?"

What is this, a restaurant?

Gabe. He'll help!

He can help me sort out this whole thing—I'm not opposed to having an omega, but I don't think any of us really planned for it any time soon.

"Gabe, I need to talk to you. I fear I have something rather disconcerting to discuss with you."

He raises his head from where he's been staring at her iguana. "'Sup man?" Ahh yes, my best friend and beloved pack leader, eloquent as ever, while I feel like I'm about to have an aneurysm.

Walking closer, I take note of the iguana's large enclosure, heat rock, lamp, and ample water supply. I approve, she clearly takes good care of her pets. The aforementioned lizard is staring at me right now, and I wonder what it thinks of all these strange people in its house.

I wait until I'm shoulder to shoulder with Gabe, keeping my voice low. "How are you doing? You look a bit vacant right now? Did you hit your head when you fell earlier?"

He lets out a loud bark of laughter, causing the iguana to scuttle backwards and glare at him. "Nah, man, just...it's hard to think in here, you know, I don't know what it is...I feel like my brain is stuffed with cotton and I'm having a hell of a time not touching Candice. Just being close to her is driving me out of my mind." He lets out a deep sigh. "I'm jealous of Jacks right now because she was curled up in his lap earlier, and I want that. I want her to snuggle against me, I feel like I need to comfort her and hold her and I *need* to fix her car, to make sure she stays safe."

"Yes...and this is just a theory. I remember reading more about it in school, but I believe that Candice might be our scent match." The color drains from his face.

"But, no, those...those are like super rare, right? How? How would we even check that?" He looks almost desperate.

"Well, your initial reaction, for one. The bond blasted wide open and..." I gesture vaguely to my groin, which my scrubs are not hiding nearly enough. "Not to mention Jacks's reaction to her. I've never felt this drawn to anyone, even before I smelled her today. Yesterday when I met her in the office, even with the full scent dampeners on I was...compelled is the only accurate word. I felt like I had to comfort her and take care of her. It was the most puzzling thing. But this. I think this is why."

Gabe swallows a few times, licks his lips. He seems to be having trouble speaking. "Shit...yeah. Hey Xan, come here for a minute. Not you Jacks, you're good, just keep cookin'."

Xan ambles over, all loose limbs. I doubt he is feeling anything out of the ordinary. But if he does, he hides it well. "Yeah boss?"

"Gimme your thoughts on Candice." Gabe has all the subtlety of a brick to the face.

"Just...wow. I don't know what it is about her. I mean, Jacks is obviously already in love." We all send a surreptitious look toward the alpha currently dancing around in the kitchen to whatever song is playing in his head. "But yeah, she smells so good. I mean, my dick hurts 'cause...yeah. Hey doc, I know the commercials say if it lasts for more than four hours to see a doctor, but do you have any suggestions, 'cause it has been at least an hour now and don't wanna have to go back to work like this." He looks at me but keeps going.

"She seems sweet, but I haven't really gotten to talk to her much. Kind of anxious. I just want to hold her, and snuggle up, and see if she is really as soft as she looks...I also really want to lick her, but that seems totally inappropriate so not even going there." Gabe looks stupefied, opening and closing his mouth like a fish.

"So, I'm assuming that we all feel this way, and judging by how comfortable she looked against Jacks when we came in, we can guess that the feeling is mutual. I don't think there is any other test needed really." I turn to Gabe, and yes, he is still doing his best fish impression.

"But, but...I don' know nothin' about courtin' an omega. I mean, if she's ours, do we need to court her?"

Xan's brows draw low, and aggression blasts his scent into the room. "What the hell, if she *is* ours, of course we need to court her properly. I mean, not doing so wouldn't just be rude, it would be disrespectful. If your mom heard you say that, she would tan your hide."

Gabe ducks his head, appropriately cowed.

Jacks has stopped dancing and is watching us all, indicating that we did not keep this as quiet or secret as I had hoped.

"Wait, we're going to court her? So, we get to keep her?" He looks hopeful, his eyes brighter than I have seen in some years. We all turn to Gabe.

"Now, everybody just hold your horses there. We haven't even talked to her about this, and what the hell are we gonna do with an omega anyway?"

Too late though, Jacks is knocking on her door, after a few seconds of her not opening it, he reaches over the doorframe and pulls out a tiny key to unlock it—you know, that seems like a safety hazard. But in retrospect, I wonder if she even knew it was there, I doubt she could reach it without a stepladder.

Jacks's voice drifts out of the other room, "Great news, we get to keep you," followed by a high-pitched scream. "Oh, and how do you take your eggs?"

Xan

Candice comes out wrapped in a towel, dripping and mad as a wet hen, dragging Jacks behind her. Snatching the key out of his hand, she shoves him out of her room and relocks the door. Going back to finish getting cleaned up.

Jacks is out of her room and back in the kitchen finishing breakfast. Apparently, she likes her eggs unfertilized—her words, not mine—so she's getting them scrambled. Jacks is back to dancing around the room cooking. Gabe and Leo are bent together over the iguana's tank having what appears to be a serious discussion, and I have nothing else to do, so I might as well invade her privacy a little more.

I wander down the entryway and around the corner to what appears to be an office and a bathroom. The office has posters and drawings hanging all over it. Some of them I recognize as being famous, most I don't...quite a few are incredibly risqué, and I can't help my grin looking at some of the sketches.

Looks like we got a kinky one, awesome.

There are more bookshelves in here, loaded down with sketchbooks, so I guess she draws as well. Pulling one off the shelf, I open it and flip through it...and close it, quietly putting it back on the shelf. I can feel all the blood in my face as I leave the room and walk back to the living room to sit quietly on the couch and not bother anyone. That was... *jarring,* to say the least.

There were so many dicks, just on that one page...it was like a page of dicks. I don't mind dicks, I mean, I have one, and I certainly enjoy Jacks's. But I have to wonder why I just opened a book filled with them. I know omegas are supposed to have a high libido, but that seems excessive. Does she draw them? Are those from previous lovers? I feel like I should ask, but at the same time I am a little terrified to do so, as some of them didn't look human at all.

So here I sit, on the couch, trying not to think about those books and wonder exactly what we're getting into. Should I tell Gabe and Leo? I think they might want to know because some of those were really disturbing. I don't even hear her door open or realize everything has gone quiet until she sits on the couch beside me.

Should I ask? If we are planning on courting her, isn't this important information? I just can't wrap my head around how to ask and I must look like I have something going on in my mind, because Jacks comes over and pokes me in the back of the head with his spatula. He's finally finished cooking, and the counters are covered in food...I don't know who all he was planning to feed, but I'm fairly certain it is more than the five of us could eat in a day.

He piles two plates high, one with a stack of super fluffy pancakes, and the other with a generous helping of bacon and eggs. He brings them over and sets them on the coffee table in front of the omega, then goes back for a glass of water and one of orange juice, syrup, grape jelly, strawberry jam, and apple butter. The omega's fridge has got to be empty at this point. He sits down, pulls her into his lap and starts to offer her bites of bacon.

She squirms a little at first, but eventually gives in and eats what he's offering, and his purr starts back up, vibrating the whole couch. Getting up, I wander over to the kitchen.

There's a fancy coffee maker, but only a canister of decaf on the counter.

What the hell? It'll have to do. I grab a couple pieces of bacon, roll them in a pancake and start eating while my coffee brews.

Gabe's sitting at the far end of the couch, and he looks about ready to settle in for some sort of serious negotiations. "So, we noticed your office when we came in. What do you do for a living Candice?"

She doesn't get a chance to answer, because that is when I inhale the bacon roll-up I was chewing.

Thank fuck Leo knows the Heimlich.

Chapter 13

Candice

Jacks is an amazing cook. It felt a little weird having him feed me, but the little voice in my head enjoyed it, and kept talking about all the other things we would enjoy having him feed us. When I couldn't eat another bite, the guys descended on my kitchen and finished everything off. I guess it's been a stressful day for all of us, but I was kind of hoping for some leftovers to use for dinner tonight.

Now I need to order more groceries—one more hit to the budget.

Aside from some small talk, me avoiding questions about my work—and Xan almost dying on my kitchen floor—it was surprisingly relaxing. Xan and Leo clean the kitchen after they eat, while Jacks wraps me in his arms and goes back to purring.

He keeps running his fingers through my damp hair, detangling it gently, and it feels so good.

Why does everything with these alphas feel so good? Why am I so comfortable with them?

I admit, my experience with alphas is pretty limited. Grandpa was one, and I'm sure there were some in school, but my designation came in late, after I graduated. Which is how I managed to avoid going to an omega school, but after all the warnings he gave me, and my being alone for the last three years, I just don't interact with anyone really.

I catch my eyes drooping and it takes tremendous effort to not just let go and sleep, but as much as my body is telling me that everything's good, these are still strangers. Gabe is settled beside us, Leo is on the other end of the couch texting. Xan is leaning against my bookcases, his foot tapping up and down rapidly. When Gabe reaches over to touch my ankle, I jolt, and Jacks's arms tighten around me.

"Candice, I'm real sorry, but we need to go. I still need to talk to you about your car, but this's been…strange…Nice, but strange." Gabe's voice is soft, but I can feel Jacks's arms contracting more as he slowly shifts away from him. "We were talkin' earlier, and we wanted to ask if it would be alright…if you might be open to the possibility…"

"Oh, dear god, man," Leo interrupts. "Candice, I believe you may be our scent match, which I fully admit is incredibly rare, and we would like to know if you would be open to the possibility of exploring it with us. As such, we would like to ask your permission to formally court you. There, see how easy that was?" He looks pointedly at Gabe.

"Well, yeah, what he said, but we really do need to get back to work. Xan and I got a lot of work on the schedule, and while Trey can handle most of it, nobody can understand him when he answers the phones. And I'm gonna bet that Leo here has his own set of appointments he needs to get to, right?"

"Yes, well, I was just texting Stephanie to make sure everyone was covered for the moment. However, Freddy's owner is coming in about thirty minutes, and I *do* need to be there to discuss aftercare from his surgery yesterday." At my puzzled expression Leo continues, flustered. "After I looked at the scans on Sunny, I wanted to be there for you. Even though I was worried you would hate me for telling you what was going on. However, the problem was taken from my hands when an emergency came in, and since I am in charge of exotic pets, I had to take care of it. Now the patient, Freddy, the monitor lizard, is ready to go home, but his owner needs discharge instructions."

I read about monitors, much bigger and more aggressive than Iggy. But she was stunted anyway, so a lot of adult lizards were. Before I can voice any of this though, Jacks slides off the couch and is backing up towards the nest, still holding me tightly, one arm under my breasts while the other is pressed against my throat. My feet stumble slightly, not used to walking backwards, but he doesn't let me fall. Just keeps me pressed firmly against his hard chest.

The room explodes in a flurry of growls. Gabe launching himself off the couch and advancing towards us, Xan yelling for Gabe to stop, and Leo trying to offer me reassurance while not getting between Gabe and Jacks.

Xan

Fuck, this isn't good. I need to stop Gabe from cornering Jacks. I know neither of them is thinking straight right now, but Jacks's eyes are wild, and while I know he would never intentionally hurt Candice, I can't be sure if he's even seeing the same thing as the rest of us. My boy still blames himself for what happened to Janey, but I need him back in the now, not reliving that shit.

"You can't have her, you said she was ours...you can't take her away now!" Jacks is nearly yelling, and I can see Candice's chest rising and falling rapidly. It doesn't look like he's actually squeezing too hard, but if she starts to panic, she could still hyperventilate, and if she passes out, I know he is gonna completely lose his shit.

"Let her go, and step away. Now!" Gabe rarely uses his alpha bark, but clearly, he thinks this situation calls for it. It's not going to work on Jacks. I don't know if it's because he's broken, or his alpha is just that strong, but I haven't ever seen a bark work on him.

A loud whine stops everyone in their tracks, along with a powerful burst of perfume—ah, well it doesn't smell like she is afraid. No, Candice is wriggling against the hands that hold her, pressing back against Jacks's chest, her hands coming up to stroke his arms, until they loosen and droop on their own.

"Please, Alpha." It's a pleading breathy little whine.

Goddammit, I just got this fucking thing to go down.

She covers his hands with hers and moves them back up, one circling her throat and the other holding tight, pressed against the underside of her tits, and yeah, ok, now I'm just jealous.

"Alpha, nest. Please, I need my nest." Leo and Gabe both groan at the pleading in her voice, and Jacks is just staring down at the omega in his arms, eyes wide.

"Oh Shit...why didn't I think of that?" Jacks steps forward and hands the pleading omega to Gabe.

"We can't bring her home yet; we have to get her nest set up first." He starts picking up all the fabric around the room, rubbing each piece over his face and neck before putting it back exactly where he got it, as if he doesn't want to disturb her space. He marks the pillows, the blanket, and then leans down to rub along the back of the couch, before going into her nest and marking several of her pillows in there.

Candice looks dazed and glassy-eyed. I can see the muscles in Gabe's jaw flexing with how hard he is grinding his teeth.

When Jacks comes back, he looks around. Seemingly satisfied with a job well done, walks over to me and rubs his face over my hair as well as grabbing my ass. Lifting the Jeep keys out of my coveralls while I'm distracted, then he strides purposefully towards the front door. Meanwhile, Leo has taken a still-dazed Candice from Gabe's arms and set her gently on the couch, covering her in the scent marked blanket.

"Get some rest, little one. We'll talk soon, ok?"

Gabe stalks towards the door but is almost knocked aside by Jacks returning, picking up the iguana and rubbing it over his chin and neck then replacing it on its tank, before striding back out again

This, at least, finally snaps Candice out of her lust-filled state.

"Did you just scent mark my fucking iguana?"

I can hear Jacks's mad cackle, then, "Come on bitches, you got work, and I need to go shoppin'!"

Chapter 14

Leo

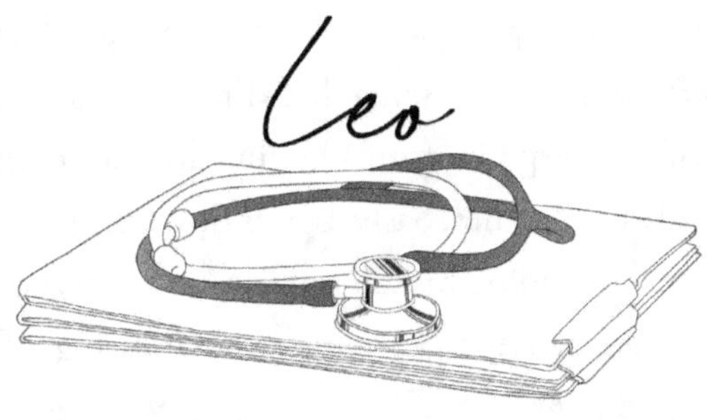

I arrive back at work in time for my 3 P.M. appointment, a pair of guinea pigs that need their yearly exam. All goes well, they seem happy and healthy. Their owners are attentive and while I question the choice of giving a child under ten the responsibility to care for a pet, these parents seem to be taking it seriously and have no problem stepping in or helping when necessary. Like today helping their son carry this precious cargo out to avoid jostling them.

Soon Sasha and her parents arrive to pick up Freddy, and we discuss how to care for his cast, if he needs a cone, and how to keep him hydrated while keeping his cast dry. I also discussed with Sasha the importance of always making sure the front door is closed when she leaves for school, so Freddy can't get into traffic again. She seems like a sweet child who cares deeply for her giant overprotective lizard, and I hope they have many years left together. She listens intently to my lecture, asking appropriate questions as Maggie brings out a still drooping Freddy.

However, as soon as he sees Sasha he starts to scramble on the concrete floor, his claws unable to find purchase and Maggie has to run to keep him from choking himself on the leash. When Freddy reaches her, Sasha bends down and scoops him into her arms, wrapping his tail around her waist, and gently holding his damaged leg to keep him from injuring it further.

What would it be like to have children of our own? We've never discussed it before. I've never really even thought about it before. Do any of the others even want kids? Does Candice?

I imagine her sitting in our living room, curled up between Jacks and Xan, rounded with child.

And I really need to stop this train of thought as it is going to become very awkward again since I am still wearing scrubs. I wipe all thought of family and Candice from my head, finalizing paperwork, confirming there are no more questions, and then watching this fourteen-year-old girl waddle out of the office with a fifteen-pound lizard wrapped around her like some sort of scaled sling bag.

I'll need to stay late to clean up paperwork from being out so long for lunch, and once I'm home, I want to do more research on scent matches. I pull out my cell phone to call Jacks and let him know I'll be late for dinner. I would say two nights in a row is inexcusable, but with the afternoon we all had, I believe he'll understand.

The house phone rings several times before I give up. I call again, and a third time, but there is no answer. I then call his cell, but it goes straight to voicemail. That isn't unusual, he often forgets to charge it as he rarely leaves the house. I then try the shop. Maybe he stopped back there after he let me off at the clinic. I'm still cross with him for driving earlier, but as he said, it was only for a few blocks, and he was being safe.

After three rings, Xan picks up at the garage. "Gabe's Garage, how may I be of service to you today sir or madam." Dear lord, Gabe would throttle him if he heard that.

"Yes, you ass, you can be of service. Tell Jacks I'll be home late today. I have a lot of paperwork I missed this afternoon. I don't want to leave it until tomorrow."

"Why do you want me to tell Jacks, just call the house and tell him yourself?" He sounds genuinely puzzled, and my stomach sinks.

"Oh, I don't know, why didn't *I* think of calling the house, *repeatedly,* and attempting to get in touch with the person I needed to speak to instead of calling you first and wasting both our time." I don't generally lower myself to sarcasm, but in this case, I think I can be forgiven. "Of course I tried calling the house, but he wasn't there. I assumed he was at the garage with you."

"Heh, you know what they say about assuming, old man? Makes an ass out of you and me." Xan chuckles. "Wait, did you say he isn't at the house?"

I hear the garage bell jingle over the phone line. "Xan, man, we are backed up out here, get off the phone and come get bay one cleared so I can bring in the next one."

There is a soft click as Xan sets the phone down, but I can hear Gabe's raised voice in the background. "What do you mean he isn't at home? Where the fuck is my cell? Yeah, pull up the PackTrack app...Fuck me...Where the hell is that?"

The phone clatters again as it's lifted off the counter.

"Hey old man, change of plans. Wrap it up now, looks like Jacks went into the city and is at the Plaza Mall. We'll swing by and grab you on the way over." The phone disconnects and I stare dumbly at it for a moment before pulling up a map. Yes, just what I wanted to do, drive an hour one way to go shopping.

Oh joy...and I'm *not* old.

Chapter 15

Jacks

My ass is vibrating, well, more specifically my phone in my back pocket is vibrating. With as many times as it's gone off in the last twenty minutes, I'm gonna take a stab and say they finally figured out I didn't go home—*took long enough*.

After all, I did take Xan's wallet, so at least I would have a license and his debit card. We don't look alike, but cops rarely bother to check everything if they pull you over, right?

Shit, maybe I should answer the phone.

But no, I'm almost done. I went by the mall because it has that candle store that'll make custom scents for you. It took longer than I wanted, but I finally got the right smell down for each of us. Xan's was the hardest to get right, that perfect smokey bourbon with petrichor. Too much one way or the other and you get either fishy swamp or s'mores, but I love his smell...so I got an extra one done for me. And, of course, some chocolate mint for the house. I need to be able to smell her, at least until she moves in.

Now I'm at Nest-N-Stuff, and honestly, the choices are a little overwhelming. I got a pretty good feel for what she likes when I was marking all of her stuff, but nothing here feels quite the same. Newer fabrics of course, none of them well-loved and broken in with repeat washing. But the colors.

Holy shit, so many colors.

It's like a rainbow threw up in here.

Her nest has several variations of blue, gray, and purple, so I'm going to get some of those...then maybe add in a dark green.

Personally, I would do orange and tangerine everything—maybe I can find some highlights in that, a splash of sunshine for my little lion. They have a whole area dedicated to framed prints, so once I get this pillow section figured out, I'll go over there.

I wonder if they deliver.

I wonder how soon they can deliver.

I should have brought the truck.

Ugh...FINE!

I pull my phone out, and yeah, twenty-five missed calls and eighteen text messages. But fuck it. I ring Xan back, not bothering to read the messages. I hear the rumble of the truck in the background, and Gabe yelling at me over Xan's relieved sigh.

"Man, I was really worried there. What the fuck are you doing? And why the fuck have you not been answering your phone?"

Ignoring his question, I have my own reasons for calling. "Hey, where are you guys? I'm gonna need a little help here." Silence meets the other end of the line. I only know they haven't hung up because I can still hear the rumble of the truck as it moves down the road.

"Motherfuck, if you *think* for one fucking sec—" Gabe cuts off as Leo takes the phone, and the background noise fades. Leo is often the level-headed voice of reason, mostly.

"Alright, let's start over. Jacks, where are you, and what do you need help with? We just passed Mile marker 105 heading south, just past that big glass factory, so we should arrive soon...unless someone kills us all in a fiery crash, or we get arrested for speeding. I'm not discounting either of those possibilities at the moment."

Wait, how did they know?

Tracking app.

Fuck.

It's ok, play it cool.

"Well, I'm at the big nesting store in Springfield. You know the one, or you can look it up. I may be buying more pillows than I can squeeze into the Jeep, and I still need to look at blankets. Do you think we should paint the walls in the nest, like, before she moves in, or wait and let her pick it out? I want it to be a surprise, but I also don't want her to feel like she doesn't have a choice. Her nest walls were a medium gray, but so was the rest of her house, so I don't know if it was an aesthetic choice, or if she just never got around to doing it?"

There's silence on the other end, and for a few moments I start to worry that the mute got hit on my end. Pausing in my perusal of fabrics and stuffing, I check my phone to make sure it didn't.

But I'm distracted again. I found their "build your own pillow" section, *and it is glorious*! There is a deep purple chenille fabric that I think she would love.

I assume they hung up, and I am about to press the end call button when Xan comes back on. "Ok, love, now, say that again. Where the fuck are you?"

Gabe is cursing loudly in the background, and even our good doctor sounds put out. "Well, what did you expect would happen? No, I have a box of suture supplies in the first aid kit. Yes, I know it's not normal, but just who do you think you're speaking to? Oh, really, well, I can let you bleed all over the cab if you prefer. No? Good, now shut up."

There are several pauses, and Gabe's yelling has stopped, so I am only getting one side of the conversation at this point. Fair enough. I need a store clerk anyway to help me with stuffing pillows. I'm only half paying attention to Xan.

Letting Xan know I'm at Nest-N-Stuff in Springfield, I continue, "According to maps it looks like mile marker 105 is about twenty minutes out from me...so you should get here just in time to help me load everything up...if I can ever find someone to help me work this damned pillow stuffer!" I say the last part less for his benefit and more for any customer service people who might be in earshot. This fucking purple pillow has now become an obsession and I am not leaving until it's stuffed and in my cart.

"Ok, well, we're gonna be a bit more than twenty minutes, man...Gabe was taking a drink of coffee when you called earlier and well...those plastic travel mugs aren't as sturdy as one would think. Leo is stitching up his hand now, but I'll take over driving afterwards. And we may need to make a stop to clean up some, I don't want to walk into a well-lit department store with a couple of guys covered in blood."

"Ew, no. Yes, take them, get cleaned up...I don't want anyone bleeding on my omega's pillows. Fine, I'll load them all when you get here, but then you have to take me out for dinner. Oh, I hear they opened a new Red Rogers in town here. I could go for a good burger."

"Yeah, ok love, just..." A loud sigh from Xan. "Just stay safe, ok. Don't talk to people you don't need to, pick out what you think she might like, load up what you can in the Jeep, and Leo can drive it home after dinner, ok? Just be safe, please?" I hear the worry in his voice. I might feel bad about it, if I hadn't finally managed to find a young beta woman to help me work the pillow stuffing machine. I would normally just fuck around until I figure it out on my own, but these need to be perfect, so better to bring in the professionals.

"I'll be safe. You be safe too, ok? I love you, and many snuggles soon, alright?"

"Love you too, Jacks. Just stay there, and I'll see you soon." The phone disconnects, for real this time. I owe Xan more than I can ever repay. We've been best friends since kindergarten, he was always smaller, and everyone just assumed he would be my beta as we got older. But, surprise-surprise, his designation came in when we were fourteen, before mine, actually. While he never got as tall as me, he is alpha in all the good ways.

"I'm sorry, sir. I'm not exactly sure how this machine works. I am pretty new. But let me call a manager for you."

Professional my ass.

Ugh.

I smile as politely as I can at the unhelpful clerk. "Thank you miss, I appreciate your time." I'm not sure what she sees in my face, but she nearly runs towards the front, and then I hear a call for a manager and security to the pillow stuffing area.

Well, fuck.

Chapter 16

Xan

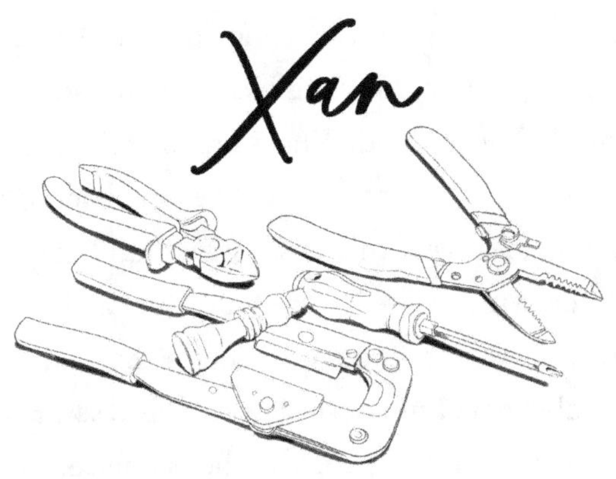

When we finally get to Nest-N-Stuff, Jacks is sitting outside on the folded down back of the Jeep. Bags with colorful fabrics spilling out the top are stuffed in the trunk behind him, and it looks like the back and passenger seats are full as well. Plus, he has three carts full of pillows in varying shapes and sizes parked beside him.

My love has been a busy boy, apparently.

He has his arms wrapped around a dark purple pillow and is rubbing his chin and cheek along the top seam, back and forth, over and over. He looks a little lost, and I wonder how long he's been sitting out here waiting. We got here as fast as we could, but I still worry about him.

Leo finally managed to talk Gabe down before we got here, but neither of them are happy, and they both stay in the truck while I park beside the Jeep and get out. I put down the truck gate when I walk by, but then go straight to Jacks and wrap my arms around his neck. He's still sitting down, and it sandwiches the pillow between us as I pull his face into my chest.

"Are you ok? You look sad. What were you thinking? You had me worried sick." I try not to sound like I'm blaming him, but even I have no idea what this was. "Why didn't you just shop online and have it delivered?" He pulls back and the look he gives me tells me what a stupid question he thinks that is.

"Ok, number one, I'm fine, just...they called security on me. Two, they had six different people in there, none of them knew how to use the pillow stuffing machine." At this point he's waving the purple pillow he's been scent marking around in the air. "They all kept taking it and trying different ways to get the machine to work, now it smells like them, and I need it to smell like us." He starts rubbing it up and down my chest and neck, and yeah, it *is* super soft.

"And to answer the rest of your questions, I was thinking that if I shopped online, I had no idea what colors I would really get. You know how nuanced colors get and while my setup is good, monitors never show exact colors. This, for example"—he waves the pillow in the air again—"could have looked like anything from black to lavender, depending on the monitor...and don't even get me started on texture. Do you have any idea how many different things are labeled as cotton...how many different types and thread counts of cotton there even are. I'm not even going to go into microfiber." He brings his legs up, wrapping his whole body around the small pillow, and rocking back and forth.

Clearly, my mate is feeling a bit overwhelmed. "Ok, well, let me get this loaded up in the truck, and move the things out of the passenger side, so Gabe can ride with Leo on the way back. Did you still want a burger?" He looks up at me and his eyes are bright with unshed tears.

"I just need a few minutes, ok. I got over excited and did something stupid, and it was all going fine, until it wasn' t...and they fucking called security on me. I didn't even do anything. I was being polite." His voice cracks at the end, and I just want to wrap him up and take him to bed for snuggles, but first I need to deal with this shit, feed him, and then we can get home, get a hot shower, and sleep.

I turn back towards the truck—I must have missed the sound of the doors, because Gabe and Leo are leaning against the side of the bed. Gabe's expression is thunderous and even our pacifist has a hard look in his eyes.

"Guys, come on. Let's just get this loaded up, we'll grab some food and head home, ok?"

Gabe marches over and I panic for a moment, until he reaches down and rubs his hand over Jacks's mohawk, before pulling him in for a quick hug. When he pulls back he looks into Jacks's sad eyes. "Help him get loaded up, a'ight. We'll be back in a few minutes." Then he pats him on the shoulder a few times before he and Leo stride towards the doors of Nest-N-Stuff.

Jacks slides off the back of the Jeep, his legs wobbly, and I help him load all his bags of pillows and blankets into the truck, as well as move a few things around in the Jeep so that Gabe can sit in the front seat when he returns. We're just pulling the bed cover closed on the truck when they get back. Leo still looks angry, and Gabe looks like he's ready to break someone in half, but he comes back over and gives Jacks a hug before leading him to the front door of the truck and getting him settled and buckled in.

"Fucking bigoted profiling assholes." Wow, it's rare to hear Doc cuss. He leans against the back of the Jeep, pinching the bridge of his nose, before running both hands down his face.

"Hey, Old Man, we were gonna grab some burgers over at Red Rogers before we head back towards the house. Y'all comin with?" I know I'm tired and my accent is coming out more. Most of the time I make a concerted effort not to talk like Gabe. People see someone who works in a garage and they automatically think uneducated or roughneck. We grew up in the south, and unless I try not to, my speech pattern reflects that.

But I'm too tired right now to put forth the effort, so I sound like I'm from the ass end of nowhere Alabama. And yeah, that's not too far from the truth, but I still hate sounding like it.

Food, apparently is the magic word here. "Oh, let me pull up my map, a burger sounds heavenly right now." We're still looking up directions when Gabe gets back from settling Jacks in the truck—he's listening to the radio, his head leaning against the window of the cab.

The restaurant is only a couple of miles down the road, back towards Oak Flats. "We'll meet you there, yes? Should only be a few minutes' drive." Leo lowers his phone and turns to Gabe. "Hamburgers, yes?" We defer to him as pack leader, but he rarely disagrees with us about anything.

"And thirty-two is not old, you ass." Leo pokes me in the chest, startling a burst of laughter from me.

"Yeah, yeah, just keep telling yourself that, *Old Man.*" This is a conversation we've had many times. Gabe is smiling again, barely, but I'll take it.

"If you want to play it that way, fine, *Short Stack*, I'll be happy to pick you up and paddle your ass like the young upstart you are."

Our relationship isn't like that. It's true that I see him naked all the time, we live together. And sometimes we sleep in the same bed because you just need a warm puppy pile to sleep. But they're closer to me than my own brothers ever were. Jacks is the only one I have a sexual relationship with, and with luck, soon Candice. Hopefully that won't make things weird, since she'll be with all of us.

Fuck, is it weird that the thought of her with my packmates, even the ones I'm not with is making me really hard?

But first, I need to take care of our caretaker. Get him fed, home, and into bed.

We load up into separate vehicles—Jacks has fallen asleep, drool running down the window. I wave at Leo in the Jeep as I pull back onto the road and start towards home. When we get to Red Roger, Jacks grumbles and sinks further into the seat, he doesn't want to wake up. We order his to go, and the rest of us bolt our burgers and fries in the parking lot—all of us ready to just get home and get in bed.

Leo gets a coffee shake—apparently *that's* a thing—to go so he can have caffeine and sugar to help him stay awake on the drive. It *is* late, and after the last thirty-six hours we're all exhausted. When I get back into the truck, I put Jacks's food in the back of the cab and pull him away from the window to keep from banging his head on the glass if I hit any bumps.

He flops the rest of the way over against me, pushing against his seatbelt until his head is laying on my thigh. He twists a few times, getting comfortable, then he starts to snore loudly, and I can already feel the drool seeping through my pants. I turn the radio over to an alternative rock station—something with a beat that will keep me focused. *Numb* by Linkin Park is just starting, and I sing along under my breath as I pull out of the parking lot and head towards home.

Chapter 17

Candice

It's only Tuesday, and this week has already been nuts.

Thank fuck my regular clients have been with me so long and they get the ups and downs of my life. The day after I met my pack—*when did I start calling them mine*—I went online and made the announcement about Sunny, having to take on a couple of extra auction streams to cover vet expenses, and now my car trouble. A few of them, who know more about cars than me, wondered what could have happened to my axle. Apparently, they don't just break on their own, and you need pretty specific long-term conditions, or a really hard hit. I don't know, and I've been putting off talking to Gabe about it since I already have too many irons in the fire.

Settling in at my desk, I check my DMs before starting work again. I need to see if Fox-up has replied about the sketch I sent for approval. Nothing yet.

Gaia sent me condolences for Sunny, they are sweet. They once told me that they have two iguanas of their own. Now I even get pictures occasionally, and we swap silly lizard stories.

Wishbone asked if I needed any help. He or she seems to have a well-paying job and often buys into the auction streams. But I don't want to take charity, so I say thank you but no, and tell them I will be doing another auction soon if they want to bid.

Bubbles sent me cat pictures, not in relation to Sunny, we just enjoy sharing cat memes back and forth. They also sent me a coupon for a free coffee in response to my announcement.

I skim through another seven messages, making note of whose art I need to check on, thank a few people for paying their invoices, and ask a few questions here and there about new art I need to start on.

Once those are all cleaned out I get started trying to sketch out a pose for a new piece I was commissioned to do, and what they want is very Esher girl. Spines just don't bend that way. My cell lets out a loud chirp, and I ignore it, because nothing pops up on my screen as an online message, and no one else ever texts me.

A few minutes later when it chirps again, I pick it up.

Unknown:

What's your favorite color?

Unknown:

This is Jacks!

Another two messages pop up in quick succession.

Unknown:

I stole your number from Xan at the shop

Unknown:

I want to get your room painted so you can come see it.

I'm super confused by what's going on at this point. Trying to figure out how to reply. I've been meaning to paint my nest, but that involves multiple trips to the paint store to pick out swatches, and see how they look in the room—and money. I just haven't gotten around to it yet.

Another chirp draws my attention back to the phone.

Unknown:

Did that little asshole give me the wrong number?

I can't help the laugh that bubbles free, and I pick up my phone and touch the screen to call back the number that's texting me. A puzzled, "Hello?" answers on the first ring.

"Hey Jacks, it's the right number." I can hear the smile in my voice.

"Pretty Little Lion. I wanted to surprise you, but I don't know what you like. Can you come over for dinner...it won't be as much of a surprise, but I need to get your thoughts on some stuff before I go any further."

Well, that is...vague and slightly ominous. "Sorry Jacks, my car is still at the shop, I'm pretty home-bound for the time being, but thank you."

"Oh...yeah...Oh, that's no problem, Gabe can pick you up on the way home. Do you like pasta, or...? Oh, I know, I still need to make you a panini. What kind of sandwiches do you like?"

What is with this man and paninis? "Oh, I don't know...I'll eat just about anything. Fix me whatever you like and I'll try it, ok? I don't want you to go out of your way for me. And maybe you should check with the others before you just invite me over on a spur of the moment thing. I'm not sure where you guys are, but I thought my house was in the opposite direction they needed to go to get home."

"Nah, they don't mind. I feed them and they do whatever I ask them to. It's all good. Plus, I know Gabe says he needs to talk to you, and Leo is super mopey, so this'll cheer him up. Come on, say yes. Please?" I can practically hear him bouncing around on the other end of the line.

"Ok. Ok, call them and make sure. I don't want to be sitting here waiting for a ride that never shows up. Let me know what they say as soon as you can so I can get cleaned up from work and find some clothes."

A low purring growl. "Little Omega, are you saying you aren't wearing clothes right now?" Several loud thumps sound from the other end of the phone, as if he's running up the stairs.

"Well, no pants. I don't usually wear pants when I work, it's comfy." I hear a lot of clicking coming over the line, like someone frantically typing.

"Stand up for me...do a little spin." Not knowing what the hell he's talking about, I stand up and spin around quickly before I flop back down in my desk chair.

"Those are some cute panties; I love the little pink polka-dots." What the actual fuck?

"Jacks, what the fuck...how...?" I trail off, because this is suddenly creepy as fuck.

"Sorry, Little Lion, I like watching you work. I hacked your computer camera a few days ago, so I can keep an eye on you. Come on, wave, say hi!"

I drop my phone on the desk and go out to the garage. It looks so empty without my little car, but at least it's easy enough to find what I need. I come back inside with duct tape and a pair of scissors and I hear Jacks calling to me from my phone. "Oh, come on, I just wanted to make sure you're ok. I worry about you, omega. What if someone else was to—no, wait. Fuck!"

"Can you see me now? Good." I know I sound a little snarky, but it's a defense mechanism. Having someone watching me work for a few days is freaky. I mean, what if I wasn't just working here? I do sometimes look for porn, though that's usually in my nest...*wait!* "Jacks, you didn't do anything to my phone camera, did you?"

"No, but now that you mention it, that's a great idea." I can hear him smiling again, and more key clacks.

"No! Jacks, no...I won't come to dinner if you don't agree to that. Leave my phone camera alone, ok? I need privacy."

There's a long silence, followed by a sullen, "Fine, but would you consider putting an app on there, just so I can make sure you're ok? It's just a tracker, they use it on my phone. It's super helpful if something happens and your car breaks down somewhere...or, you know...you run off without telling anyone to buy a lot of pillows and then need them to come help you bring everything home."

"Wait...what?"

"What, what? Nothing, dinner, paninis, yes? I'm gonna hang up, so I can call Gabe. I'll send you a link to that tracker app, and message you what time they'll be off work to pick you up. Ok, Bye!"

The phone hangs up, and I have no idea what's going on. I look over at the swatch of tape now covering my computer's camera.

What have I gotten myself into?

I get a new chirp on my phone—the pack, minus Jacks, will be here a little after 5:30 to pick me up.

That gives me a few hours to work before I need to get ready. I pick up my pen and start laying down lines.

I'm ready at 5:20, freshly showered and shaved. I didn't bother with my de-scenter. The guys already know what I am, and there's no point hiding it now, or wasting my expensive and hard to come by shampoo or spray. I put on a dark purple sweater, that could be long enough to be a dress, but since I feel like I need to put up as many barriers as possible, I still include the black yoga pants under it.

My long hair is brushed out and pulled back into a braid to keep from frizzing out, and while I don't expect the neatness to last long before I start getting flyaways, I *am* pleased with my current appearance. Some ballet flats complete the outfit and now I just have to wait.

And wait.

5:30 comes and goes—then 6. By 6:30 I've taken off my shoes, grabbed a bag of Doritos out of the pantry and flopped myself on the couch in front of the TV to find some kind of horrible monster movie—where the whole pack of obnoxious alpha jocks die, leaving the beta to escape with the frightened omega and blow up the monster. Seriously, it's pretty fucking formulaic, but that's why it works. The only difference is what kind of monster they have each time. Personally, I enjoy zombie movies, but aliens are awesome too. You just need to work in large quantities of monsters for the most blood splatter possible. The first movie ends, and the sequel starts automatically, higher body count, more blood. I really should be working tonight, but I feel like shit now, so fuck it.

My phone chirps once, and I don't bother picking it up. If it's a client, it can wait until tomorrow. If it's one of the guys…fuck it, they can wait too. Once the second movie is over I stand up, my hair is a mess now, and I really do look like a dandelion. I peel off these pants and my pretty sweater, now covered in chip crumbs, and ok, yeah, little wet spots from tears. But fuck it. I put Iggy back in her terrarium and pull the lid closed, latching it in place, and effectively tucking her in for the night.

My phone chirps again, but when I pick it up and see it is almost eleven, I just plug it into the charger. I didn't realize how excited I was to see them until they stood me up. Hopefully, I get an apology and a good reason, but I can't deal with it tonight. I crawl into my nest, burrowing under the blankets and finding a little patch of scent that hasn't faded away yet from Jacks's marking spree last week. I wrap myself around it as much as I can and just let go. Hopefully tomorrow will be better.

My dreams were really freaky last night, so I know I slept at least a bit, but I'm super groggy and it doesn't feel like I rested at all. My eyes feel puffy and hot, and the rest of me just feels sticky. My phone chirps again—is that what woke me up?

Reaching over and grabbing my phone—looks like there are twenty-three missed messages. The first two I didn't open last night are from Jacks, apologizing that work came up and they were all busy and couldn't get time to message me until later. Then asking if I was ok. Becoming progressively more frantic as the night went on. Finally, around 2 A.M., there is a text from Xan, also apologizing and saying Jacks won't let him rest until he makes sure I'm ok. Another one at 2:10 from Jacks, one at 3:18 from Gabe, threatening Jacks with bodily harm. Another four from Jacks, one from Leo at 5:30 asking if I'm alright, he can stop by on the way home and check on me if he needs to. Two more from Jacks, and finally one from Xan at 6:15 telling me that they're at my front door and won't leave until they know I'm ok.

Fuck, it's 6:20 now.

A tapping noise on my nest window startles a scream out of me. There's a privacy fence around the backyard, and I keep the gates locked, so this is freaking me out. The tapping is now a loud knocking, and I hear muffled voices, as well as someone rapping loudly on the door to my back patio. Wrapping myself up in a blanket—because it's too early to figure out clothes and this will cover the most area—I grab a small club that I keep by the bedside table.

I quietly make my way to the back door. The knob rattles and then the door swings wide. My blanket held tight to me in one hand, I have my club raised to bash whoever comes in over the—well, probably shoulder, depending on how tall they are. There's a tug on my blanket and I let out another scream—looking down. Jacks is squatting just outside the door with a credit card in his hand, grinning at me.

"Hey, we really need to get you a deadbolt on the back here, anybody could just walk in." He's pulling on my blanket and grinning up at my naked thigh when Xan ambles over from where he was tapping on my window.

"Hey, Pretty Lady, are you gonna bash him over the head or can we come in? It was a long night and I really need coffee."

Jacks unfolds himself, releasing the edge of my blanket to fall closed, and kissing Xan on the nose on the way up to his full height. "Sorry, love, I think she only has decaf." Then he walks into my house like he owns the place.

Chapter 18

Jacks

It's a delightful surprise to find that our omega had restocked the fridge since I was last here, and bought coffee...like real coffee, not decaf. Which shows she wanted and expected us to come back and drink it. I start a fresh pot and then begin sorting through the fridge to figure out what to make for breakfast. Technically Xan and I already ate, but food's food, so he will always eat again.

Oh, there's stuff in here for a frittata.

I wonder if she likes frittatas?

Does anybody not like a frittata, really?

That's a funny word, frittata...fritos...tatas...

I look over our omega, wrapped up in a blanket. From what I saw earlier, it's *just* the blanket, but her knuckles are white trying to hold on to it.

What could I ask her to help me with that would be difficult with just one hand?

"Don't fucking do it, Jacks, I know that look." Xan is glaring at me—and fair, he knows me better than anyone else.

I try to affect an air of innocence, but it never works with him. "As much as I love seeing so much of you, can you go put more than a blanket on, before Jacks gets us kicked out?"

My little lion blushes furiously and bolts towards her nest. The blanket flares from the wind and I still get a tantalizing view of her backside before she slams the door.

"Come on man, I'm trying to apologize here, don't embarrass her. She looks like she cried half the night already. Her eyes are redder than Gabes right now, and he caught a big lungful of smoke."

It was a long night, and once Leo gets him discharged from the hospital, they are gonna go get some rest before they have to start work. We need to rest too.

Xan looks at me, and sometimes it feels like he can read my mind. "We need to get home too as soon as I finish explaining things. I know you want to feed her now that we know she's ok."

I glower at my best friend and lover. I have a lot more energy now that I've seen my little lion. Of course, I don't have to go into a job that deals with heavy machinery or vehicle safety, or try to save any lives—pet lives, but still lives.

Fine.

Whatever.

"Fine...but drink your coffee first, she obviously got some for the next time we came over." I know I'm acting like a brat, but I still enjoy his look of surprise.

"Ok, guys, what was so important that you couldn't wait to tell me? In case it isn't painfully obvious, I didn't sleep last night, and I really want to try to get some rest before I start working." Candice comes back, wearing a set of blue flannel pajamas, and I just want to scoop her up and take her home—

There's an idea.

"Little Omega, we wanted to come get you, so I could cook for you, but alas, some foul fiend started a fire and we were forced to assist." I'm putting all the frittata ingredients back in the fridge and Xan is looking at me like I lost my fucking mind.

"Oh, my god, is everyone ok? Where are Leo and Gabe? Were any of you hurt?" She's wringing her hands now. Xan turns to put her out of her misery, but I beat him to it.

"Fair maiden, our pack lead hath suffered from smoke inhalation and is being cared for at yon hospital, but fear not, the all-knowing doctor is with him and shall text us when they depart forsooth unto our home. Shall you join with us, and meet them thus upon their return?"

Xan strides over and smacks me in the back of the head, with a snort of laughter.

"Sorry, love, he gets goofy on no sleep. We work with the volunteer fire department. They had an emergency. Probably arson, over at the old gym. We got the call just before five yesterday evening, and by the time we got there it had started to spread. No one was seriously hurt. The building was empty, but idiot teenagers sometimes hang out there, so we still had to check it out. Gabe got caught in a downdraft. He wasn't even in the building at the time, but he got a pretty big hit of smoke. Doc took him to the hospital to get him checked out. But we didn't get the all clear to leave until almost six this morning and we're all dead on our feet."

Candice visibly deflates as Xan explains. I don't know what's going through her head, but I know that we missed what was supposed to be our first courting date, and we needed to explain.

"Come on, Little Lion, the offer still stands." I take her hand and start to purr. "You wanna come over for breakfast and a nap? I think we could all use some snuggles right now, and I know it would help Gabe feel better." I waggle my eyebrows at her. Xan's right, I *am* feeling pretty damned loopy.

She chews on her lip for a minute. "Ok, but on two conditions. You have to bring me back this afternoon, I can't leave Iggy alone all day, and I really do need to get work done since I didn't work last night. And can you remind me later to call the locksmith to come out and put in a deadbolt on the back door?"

"Already taken care of, Pretty Lady." Xan leans against the counter beside me. "I texted Joseph, he's one of the volunteer firefighters we work with, and I doubt any of us have had a chance to crash yet. He runs a handyman business and will come out this afternoon at three after he gets some rest himself."

"Oh, ok...well...Um...let me get my shoes, I guess. And thank you." She reaches out to quickly touch Xan's arm before pulling back.

"Anytime, Pretty Lady." He wraps his arms around her and kisses the top of her head—smooth bastard.

Xan

Candice relocks the back door, grabs a tiny backpack for *personal care items*, whatever that means, and gives Iggy a kiss, telling her that she'll be back soon. Then Jacks is bundling her into the back of the Jeep before climbing in the back with her. We both smell like smoke, but she was kind enough not to mention it.

"Why is no one sitting in the front seat with me? I'm not a chauffeur."

"Oh...Shotgun!" Candice shouts before trying to squeeze through the bucket seats. It is a valiant effort, but she almost loses her pajama bottoms in the process. Not that Jacks seems to mind. I'm actually surprised he isn't trying to shimmy them down her hips. Then I see him out of the corner of my eye, pinching the fleecy fabric between two fingers, rubbing it back and forth, so I think he's just trying to get a feel for the texture at this point. He's been very interested in setting up her nest, and once he focuses on something he'll keep at it until he wears himself out, or it gets done. Often to his own detriment.

"My Lady! You left me...I mean, I can sit up front with you in my lap if you really want to be in the front." He starts to try to climb through the seats after her, but I punch the gas and pull away from the curb, and he has to sit down. "Now, put on your seatbelt, the sooner we get home the sooner we can have breakfast and sleep."

Leo messaged while we were waiting on Candice, and Gabe had been discharged. He said that they would meet us at home, and we're pulling into the driveway about ten minutes later. Parking beside the truck, I go around to open Candice's door.

"Wow, so I guess owning a garage pays pretty well, huh?" She laughs nervously.

Jacks wraps his arm around her shoulder. "Well, if you have four incomes and are willing to swing a hammer, you can work some stuff out."

Our house is old, not exactly historic district old, or fancy, but Jacks isn't wrong. We pooled our resources and bought a big fixer upper outside of town. It had a solid brick foundation on a good slab, and after the last few years of work, it looks pretty good. There are always small things we could fix up, but it's ours and it's home.

"Hey, come on, I need to show you your surprise!" Jacks pulls her towards the front door, staring at her to watch her reaction as they walk inside.

"Shit man, goddamit!" Gabe croaks, then bolts up the stairs in just a towel—we probably should have told them we were bringing Candice home, but oh well. It's too late now.

"What's wrong, do we need to go back to the hospital?" Leo comes rushing down the hall in nothing but boxer briefs with a towel around his neck, slides to a stop, sees us standing in the doorway and trips over his long legs trying to escape upstairs to his room.

Jacks is leaning against the wall laughing, tears running down his face, and Candice has turned the color of a tomato while staring at the floor.

"Great man...real mature. Now, do you want to show her what you've been working so hard on, or do you want to start breakfast?"

"You in the mood for sweet or savory, Little Lion?" Jacks asks when he can finally catch his breath.

"Well, I always like sweet. But it's your house, so whatever you feel like doing." I don't think she quite understands how much we want this to be her house too, but we need to ease her into it. Jacks taps his chin a few times looking thoughtful.

"Have you ever had a German Pancake?" She shakes her head. "It has a kind of a custard thing going on, so it's sweet, but eggy. Wanna try it? I can put on some sausages for anybody who wants meat."

He pulls her into the kitchen and sets her up on a barstool, and I leave them there to go find Gabe and Leo and make sure they're alright.

"So, I take it she was alive then, unharmed?" Leo is coming back down the hallway, wearing pajama pants and a tank top this time. It looks like he got a shower and is just about ready to crash.

"Yeah, she was still asleep. Jacks broke in through the back door." His eyes widen.

"He wanted to stay and make breakfast for her, so our compromise was that she would come over now, have breakfast, and then we could take her back home in a few hours on the way to work? That cool with you two?" I know Gabe can hear me, because I get a grunt in response.

"She's fine sleeping here, then? None of us are exactly great for entertaining at the moment you know?" Leo is drying his hair as we talk, waiting at the bottom of the stairs for Gabe.

"Yeah, apparently she didn't sleep well either. She almost fell asleep in the car just on the ride over here." Gabe joins us and we head towards the kitchen, where Jacks has just put a large pan in the oven to cook.

"I set the timer on that for about thirty minutes, don't open the oven, yeah? We'll be back." He grabs Candice's hand and practically drags her from the room.

Candice

"Ok, I got a surprise...and you don't have to use it...but if you want to you can...but no pressure." Jacks babbles along while pulling me up the stairs and down a long hallway. We reach a closed door at the end of the hall, and he tells me to close my eyes while he takes both hands, and I am totally having a Beauty and the Beast moment.

Somehow, I doubt I'm getting a library.

Still, the room is dark enough, even with the full sun outside, that everything is still black behind my closed lids. We stop, and he lets me go and I just stand there while I hear him circling behind me, the door shuts, and a switch flips.

"Ok, open up!"

I let out a scream; his face is directly in mine when I open my eyes.

"Oh, shit, my bad...ok...sorry," he mumbles, but steps to the side and I see the most amazing nest. It is bigger than mine back home, with plush rugs all around the room, and a low pack size platform bed, piled high with blue and gray blankets, and stacks of more in green and purple sitting in the corner. There are dozens of pillows—I'm not actually sure how anyone could sleep here with so many pillows—but I just want to burrow into them and hide.

Jacks shuffles sideways and grabs a dark purple pillow from the bed to give me. The fabric is incredibly soft, it has the perfect amount of stuffing, and it smells like him. No one has ever done anything like this, and I can't help the tears that start running down my face at what this sweet alpha has made for me.

He wraps one arm around me and tries to take the pillow out of my shaking hands. "Oh, no...what is it? Whatever's wrong I can fix it. I mean...I can get rid of anything you don't want...is it the pillow? I tried getting their smells off." He's speaking faster and faster with each word, trying to pry my fingers off the pillow without hurting me, until I let it drop to the floor and wrap my arms around his neck instead. His breath is coming out in harsh pants and his heart beats frantically against my own.

"The pillow is wonderful, it smells just like you," I say into his neck. "No one has ever done anything this nice for me, sorry. I didn't mean to make you worry." I tighten my arms around him, so he has to either stay bent over or stand up with me dangling off him. He wraps his other arm around me and lifts me up to walk towards the bed. When I'm standing on the edge of the mattress, we're just about the same height.

I slide my hand up to cup his face and kiss him, a soft peck on the lips, but his tongue comes out and licks across my bottom lip before nibbling it gently. I open my mouth in a shocked gasp and his tongue is suddenly in my mouth, sliding against my own.

Pleasure blooms down my body. It feels like an electric current is running from my lips straight to my core. He lets out a low moan and tips me back until I start to lose my footing. Then he lowers me down till I'm sitting on the mattress and he's kneeling in front of me. His hands unwind from my waist, pushing under my pajama top and across the skin of my stomach. I can already feel how wet I'm getting just from his kisses and his scent.

He lets loose another ragged moan and pulls back. "Please, Little Lion, I need..."

I don't know what he needs, but sign me the fuck up.

I feel like I'm about to combust as he leans in farther, lightly biting at my lips. One hand running up to cup my breast while the other slides down, gripping my ass and pulling me against him so I'm straddling his hips. Then he's grinding his hard length against my needy center.

I hear little whimpering and whining noises and realize they're coming from me as he plunders my mouth, and all I want is to tear him out of his clothes so I can feel more of his skin against mine. His hips rock out a stuttering rhythm against my core, and I am about to come just from that amount of friction, and the sounds of his moans muffled against my mouth.

He pulls back to look at me, his eyes bouncing between mine, but I don't know what he's looking for. I feel barely coherent at this point, as I wrap my legs around his lean hips and try to pull him back against me. Reassured by whatever he sees, he closes the distance between us again, one hand sliding up my back and wrapping in my hair. I feel his fingers from the other hand brush over my center as he tries to undo his own pants with one hand—while not looking.

A quiet knock draws our attention to the door, where Xan stands smirking. "Wow, smells like someone is enjoying her new nest...now I have a craving for a peppermint mocha. Also, your timer went off on the oven." He looks pointedly at Jacks.

"Shit!" Jacks stumbles back, tripping over his own feet when he tries to stand. His erection is painfully outlined against his jeans as he stumbles from the room, and I hear the loud thump of him running down the stairs towards the kitchen.

"Sorry to interrupt, Pretty Lady, but he gets kind of upset if his cooking doesn't come out right. Also, as much as I would love to watch the two of you break in your new nest, I really think we all need to get some food and rest." I know I'm still practically dripping from my kiss with Jacks, but I can feel my face getting red as my mind clears from the fog of lust.

And again, I want to just burrow into this wonderful nest he made me, but this time to hide until they all go to work so I can sneak out.

Xan stands there with a grin. "Don't be embarrassed. He *is* sexy as fuck. Hell, I have a hard time resisting him, even when we're this exhausted. But don't worry, there's plenty of time. We've barely started courting, and this is technically our first date." Great, now I feel even more like a slut. I bring my hands up to cover my face and groan when Jacks pops back through the door.

"Breakfast is ready, well, the sweet part is, so we can get you started. Oh, and I got you candles." The abrupt change in topic snaps my head up, and he is pointing at four covered jars on the table in the corner. I didn't notice that, or the other two doors in the room before, as I was so mesmerized by this beautiful nest. But now is not the time to explore, so I stand up, straighten my clothes, and follow Xan and Jacks out of the room.

There is German Pancake to eat, and from the smells wafting up the stairs, it's going to be delicious.

Chapter 19

Gabe

Coming down the stairs, they look like they've been up to something. I can smell the lust coming off Jacks and Candice, and Xan looks like the cat that ate the canary. Both of my packmates are sporting obvious wood, so I doubt they went too far. We're all exhausted, but her perfume is making it hard to remember why we don't all just go up, break in the new nest properly, and then pass out for the next twelve hours or so.

The thinking part of my brain knows why. We're waiting for her to be good with it. We want her to want the whole pack, and we need her to understand what that means and be ok with us taking care of her. From what I hear, she's been alone for a while now, and even before then it was just her and her gramps.

Lust is there, totally. I've been horny nearly all the time since I first smelled her. But Jacks isn't the only one whose alpha caregiving is riding him hard.

Trouble is, I don't know what to do. Most of my care taking of people has been more about responding to a need than trying to look for one, and it means I have to think more than I normally do. Because Candice has done a great job of taking care of herself for a long time, and she has a damned good handle on it.

The obvious thing is her car. I could get under there and replace the axle now that the tires and oil are sorted. Xan was the one who saw the axle was nearly busted so I need to talk to him about it. Something just isn't sitting right about it. Maybe after some food and rest my head will be a little less fuzzy.

Jacks has always been a great cook, but he really seems to be pulling out all the stops with her around. Sliced fruit, fresh squeezed orange juice, and I don't know what the fuck a German pancake is—doesn't look much like a pancake but damn it's good. Apparently, she thinks so too, judging by the noises she is making.

Fuck, I'm hard again.

Didn't I just take care of this in the shower?

Dammit.

The whole table has gone quiet except for Candice who doesn't seem to realize the effect she's having on the rest of us. I put my head in my hands and try to focus on something else.

Think about baseball, taxes...getting a colonoscopy?

Nope, no good, now I'm just picturing her in a little nurse outfit.

Fuck.

"Thanks for the food, Jacks, it was great. Just leave the dishes in the sink, I'll take care of 'em later. I gotta crash." I gotta take care of this hard on and sleep. I feel nearly fucking insane at this point and if I don't get away from her scent, I am gonna crawl into that nest with her, and then I don't know if we'll get *any* rest.

Everybody's looking at me...*what did I miss?*

"Sorry, I tend to ramble...I just wanted to thank you. Um, Jacks said you helped with the nest shopping, and I just wanted to say thank you...so...yeah...thank you...sorry."

I blink through my sleep deprived and hormonal haze. "Oh, yeah, nah, that was almost all him, I just helped with the pickup, he did all the real work. Sorry I'm not more chatty. I really am dead on my feet. Get some rest, Omega."

"Oh, ok. Sleep well," she mumbles, and I hear a loud sniff—and now everyone is glaring at me.

"Little Omega, the only thing I want right now is to carry you up to your nest and lick and nibble on every inch of your body, knot you hard, and then fall asleep wrapped around you. But I'm gonna be completely honest, I can't. I can barely keep my eyes open right now. I am tired, I am sore, and if I crawl in that nest with you I'll just fumble around. I want our first time together to be special."

I reach over the table and wipe her tears away with my thumb. "Because you're special, and I need to be coherent for that, to make sure you feel good. But I'll tell you what. If I don't manage to fall asleep within ten minutes I *will* come to your nest, at least to try to snuggle. Deal?"

"Yes Alpha." And I have to clench my teeth against the groan just from hearing that.

"See you in a few hours, Omega. Be a good girl and get some rest."

I make my way back upstairs to my room and tuck myself into my big empty bed, barely closing my eyes before I'm out.

I look down and nearly come just from the sight of her kneeling between my splayed thighs. Her hair hanging over one shoulder tickles my hip as she leans down to lick the tip of my cock. I'm so fucking hard it hurts, and the sight of her little pink tongue flicking up the underside has me leaking like a fucking faucet. She's holding herself up with one hand, while the other wraps around my knot and squeezes far too gently.

I groan when she takes the head in her mouth, tongue flicking over my slit, gathering what's already there, and swallowing around my length. I reach down to run my fingers over her jaw and then into her hair, not forcing her down on my cock, but just for the added sensation of her hair wrapped around me.

"Oh fuck, Baby, you feel so good."

Her mouth is so hot and wet, and I know I can't last like this. She's making little whimpering moans in her throat and it vibrates my entire shaft as she bobs up and down, rolling her tongue like a wave against the underside of my head.

"Just like that, fuck. Please, Baby. I'm gonna come. God, I'm so close. Fuck!"

I feel my balls tighten up, the vibration at the base of my spine, and I try to move her head, try to pull her back so I don't come in her mouth. But she won't stop and lets out a tiny omega growl that undoes me completely, and I can't hold back. I moan as my release hits, hot jets filling—

Nothing—I just made a huge mess in the bed.

Well, fuck.

Every night this week has been torture. Jacks put that fucking candle in my room, so everything smells like her. But this is the first fucking wet dream I've had since I was twenty-two. Goddamn, what a mess. I get up and look around. The clock says it is almost eleven, and the house is silent. I look at the bed, and I'm gonna need to change the sheets completely. Which will take time, and I'm still exhausted.

I pull on underwear and drag the sheets off the bed. Stumbling into the hall to throw them down the laundry chute—I can deal with them later. The bedroom doors are all open, except the one on the end, the nest, so I open it as quietly as

I can. Candice is asleep in the middle of the nest—still fully covered in her blue flannel pajamas—her head burrowed against Leo's chest, while his arm wraps around her shoulders. Jacks is pressed up against her back, arm around her waist. Xan mimics his pose, pressed against Jacks, arm stretched over his mate so that his fingers are brushing against Candice's waist too.

"Well, fuck it," I grumble to myself, crawling across the foot of the mattress so I won't wake anyone up. I snuggle against her legs, wrapping my hand around her ankle, and I'm out before I can even worry if this is a bad idea.

Leo

The alarm we set up goes off entirely too early. I rub my hand up and down the soft hair of the omega clutched to my chest. After Gabe left, she was upset and felt rejected. She said she understood, and that it's just hormones. I crawled into the nest while she was brushing her teeth, and Jacks and Xan came in after their own showers. She was already snuggled into my chest by then, and asleep, snoring softly.

I detangle myself from her to shut off the alarm, and stretch. My foot catching Gabe in the chest where he's curled around her legs in her sleep. I figured he would make his way in here at some point, but I didn't want to argue with him about it.

I try to extricate myself from the group without waking anyone else up. With luck I can get dressed and take care of this damnable erection before anyone else wakes. Just being near this woman puts me in a constant state of arousal, and since we are not that far along in our relationship yet, it's nothing but a useless distraction.

Sliding off the bed as quietly as possible, I pad down the stairs to the kitchen. I don't want to risk running the coffee grinder, so we'll just have to settle with the bagged for now. Once the machine is prepped and brewing, I start back upstairs to my room, peeling off my shirt on the way. There isn't much time, and I'll need to hurry to take care of my own body before I get everyone else up. When I reach the landing and start down the hallway towards my room Candice is there, standing just outside the nest.

With her hair disheveled and her pajamas askew, she looks like she's already been fucked and ready to fall asleep, and my erection gives another painful throb. It wants me to carry her back to the nest and give her a reason to look so rumpled. Her eyes drop to the tent in my sleep pants and I can see her pupils dilate. Her eyes flick back up to meet mine, just as I'm hit with the scent of her arousal, darker chocolate and sharper mint than her normal perfume, and my mouth waters. She takes a tentative step towards me, her head tilting back so she can watch my face, she is so tiny.

"Oh, I was just...Sorry, I woke up and you were gone." She's still moving towards me slowly, and I need to move. My mind isn't in charge right now, and anything she asks from me, I will gladly give. But we don't know each other well yet, and I don't want to rush into anything she might regret later.

I know the scent match means that we're genetically the most compatible, but she doesn't know much about our pack yet, and I don't want her to feel like we weren't honest up front.

She's very nearly to me now, her hand reaches out and lands on my bare chest and I try to stifle my involuntary groan at the connection. She slides her hands up to my shoulders, which presses her chest to my abdomen. She's only nipple high to me at the top of her head, and it means that her soft breasts are currently hugging the erection straining against my waistband. She tries to pull me down to her height, but my body acts on its own, leaning down long enough to wrap one arm around her back while I scoop the other under her ass and lift her up to me.

She lets out a shocked gasp, but then wraps her arms fully around my neck, kissing me softly—I can't stop the growl that erupts from my chest. She lets out a small gasp at the sound and I take the opportunity to flick my tongue past her lips and taste her more deeply. She still tastes faintly of mint from brushing before, but her scent of peppermint and chocolate is so pervasive I can hardly taste anything but that. She wiggles in my arms. Her hot core rubs across my stomach and I can feel the dampness through her pajama bottoms. I turn, carrying her, and walk into my bedroom.

I nip her lip before pulling back and looking into her eyes. "Please, Dr. Leo…" And I let out a quick burst of laughter.

"Really, just Leo is fine, unless I'm at work." She giggles and leans back in for another kiss, but I have to stop her.

"Candice, I want you, I do…but are you sure? You haven't known us for long, and in case it wasn't obvious, we have some issues. I don't want you to feel forced into anything. If we are together, I need it to be because you want us, not because you feel obligated since Jacks made you a nest, or Gabe has your car—I need you to be sure, ok?"

It's rare for anyone to be on eye level with me, even Gabe has to look up unless we're sitting on the couch. But she looks at me thoughtfully for a few moments, searching my face, before dropping her gaze. The most alluring blush suffuses her cheeks.

"Can I be honest, Leo, and you won't hate me?"

"Of course, I could never hate you, Kitten." I sit down on the edge of my bed, letting her slide down enough to balance on my thighs so I can tuck her head under my chin.

"I wanted you when we first met. I know it was horrible timing with Sunny and everything, but you being there helped. I mean, it was still horrible, and God knows I miss him so much. But you being near made it easier. I wish you had been with me when they took him away. I could have used a hug."

And now I can feel her tears striking my neck and running down my chest.

Well, goodbye erection, at least.

She makes a wet sniffling sound against my throat. "Still, I do want you, all of you. It feels weird to say that, like someone's going to accuse me of being a slut or something, but I do. You and Gabe. Jacks and Xan. The four of you together, you make me feel whole. Like something's been missing for as long as I can remember, but it's there now. Does that make sense?"

"Well, from what little I've been able to dig up on scent matches, yes. There's not much research on them, and they're rarely talked about, but I know what you mean. It feels like there was a little piece of us that we never knew we didn't have, until you came along, and now everything just feels...right." I hug her to my chest again. "And I don't hate you, pets are family and losing any family is an emotional experience. I wanted to be there for you as well, but I had to do my job...to keep someone else from losing their family. I was so worried you would be mad at me because I wasn't there."

She hugs me tighter, and the tiniest omega purr vibrates against my chest when I kiss the top of her head.

"I could stay like this for hours, but unfortunately we do need to get everyone else up and go to work." I smooth both hands up her back, trying to tame her wild hair on the way back down. She sighs against me and gives me one more squeeze before she slides off my lap.

"Oh, is this your room?" She looks around my personal space, light gray walls, my desk with the laptop on it. My degree hanging on the wall above it, and the few houseplants that I managed not to kill languishing in the corner.

"I'm not kicking you out, Little Omega, but I do need to get ready for work." I stand and put my thumbs into the waistband of my pants to let her know what's coming. "Or you can go try to wake up Jacks and see if he has an idea on lunch before we all have to go."

She stares at my hands, cheeks pink with an adorable blush, flicking her eyes up to mine before going back to my hands.

"Ok...I did warn you." I turn and push the fabric from my hips, walking to my closet to get into a clean pair of scrubs, but when I turn back around, she's already gone. I wonder if she liked what she saw.

Chapter 20

Candice

I scurry from the room as soon as Leo's back is turned. I can't remember if he was wearing underwear or not, but I knew I would be a drooling mess if I saw him naked, and he was right. We all need to get to work. The guys have places to go, I need to get home for Iggy and get work done myself.

I hurry back to the amazing nest that they built for me—Jacks, that Jacks built for me. And crawl across the mattress to them. Gabe was still asleep when I had to untangle my legs from him this morning, and he lacks the signature scowl I've seen on his face so far. I would almost say he looks peaceful, but I'm not sure if anything about this man could be described as peaceful.

I brush the fringe of hair from his forehead—if I am going to wake him up, I want to be as gentle as possible. But his face tilts up to my touch, and he rubs his mouth against my wrist, rekindling the fire I managed to escape with Leo.

He lets out a low groan. "Omega," and nips lightly at my flesh, and yup, there goes my perfume again along with my whine. His hand snaps around mine, holding me in place as his tongue laves across the area his teeth were just on. He lets out a purring growl, his eyes opening slowly—the way he looks at me makes me feel exposed, naked and waiting for him to sink his teeth into me.

Or another body part! Just a suggestion.

Ugh, I thought that little omega voice was done for a while.

I try to pull out of Gabe's grip, but it tightens to the point of almost pain. I have his full attention now, as he surges up and over me, bringing my wrist over my head, and pinning my hips with his. I can feel the hot bar of his erection pressing against my core, and I want to wiggle against it so badly. Chase some of that delicious friction that his body is promising me. He curves his torso over mine, bringing his face to my neck, and I can hear his low growl as he traces his tongue over the pulse in my neck.

With Gabe looming over me, I feel so small, surrounded by so much power. But I want him, I want to feel him, and I let my legs fall wider so he can settle deeper against me.

"Little Omega, I had a dream about you this morning." My nipples tighten with his growly words and his hot breath on my skin.

He rolls his hips against me, letting me feel the full length of his cock through both our pajamas. I can't help the involuntary shiver that runs through me, or the whining gasp at how good he feels—how right it feels to have him there. He rolls his hips again, and I can feel the hard swell of his knot rub against my clit, making my hips twitch and curl to try to maintain contact.

"You came into my bedroom and used that wicked little tongue of yours until I made a huge mess all over my sheets." He nibbles on my earlobe and his soft words are at odds with the low growl coming from his chest, and his hard body pressing me flat into the mattress.

He releases my wrist and traces his fingers down my arm, circling the edge of my breast, and the dip at my waist until he wraps his fingers around my hip tightly, rolling against me again. And I swear to fuck if he keeps doing this, I am just going to orgasm right here under him, with Jacks and Xan still asleep above me.

He lets go of my hip to slide under the waistband of my pajama pants, following the line down to my core, "Fuck omega, you're soaked...is this all for me?" When I can't do more than whimper and nod he slides one thick finger inside me, pumping a few times before adding a second finger and rubbing the palm of his hand against my clit with each thrust.

I feel like I am about to melt as he brings his mouth down to mine. I open for him, and then he's thrusting into me on both ends, his tongue in my mouth, his thick fingers into my pussy.

I moan loudly, all worry of waking up the pack gone as I writhe under him, panting.

His mouth, his hand, his hot length pumping against my thigh, suddenly there's another hand, I open my eyes and Gabe pulls back, allowing me to see Jacks kneeling on the mattress beside him. Gabe leans up, hand never losing its rhythm, and Jacks comes down, kissing me fervently. His teeth nipping and biting at my lips. His tongue flicking over the tiny abrasions he just made. He kisses down to my jaw, then my throat, and I can see Xan behind him, hands running down Jacks's back, staring at us, pupils blown.

Jacks makes it all the way to my chest, undoing the buttons on my top before he pulls it open, and rolls my nipple with his tongue gently biting.

I let out a squeak as he bites too hard and then Xan is pulling him back, hand fisted in the back of Jacks's mohawk. Xan is directly behind him now, pulling the taller man back against his chest, biting the side of his neck, eyes never leaving mine as Jacks shudders and moans, his own eyes slipping closed. I trace my eyes down the two of them. Jacks has lost his pajamas at some point and his cock is fully erect and bobbing against his stomach with every thrust Xan makes against his ass. Not penetrating, not yet. My eyes snag on something shiny, a glint of metal against the slightly darker skin of his shaft, but I can't focus.

"Eyes on me, Omega," growls Gabe, catching my chin in his big hand and turning it back to face him. Gabe withdraws his fingers from my core, and they're coated in my slick. He brings them up to his lips and runs his tongue over them. "Fuck, you taste good, Little Omega."

Then Jacks is grabbing his hand and sucking on Gabe's fingers frantically as Xan thrusts harder against him before pulling away and leaning towards the nightstand closest to him.

Jacks's moan is louder than my whimper as he tastes me on Gabe's fingers, and I try to pull Gabe back down to me. I roll my hips under him, I'm so close, and I need more friction.

"Words, Baby, use your words. I can't go any farther unless you tell me what you want."

Gabe's hips push against me, but we're both still fully clothed below the waist, I feel like I might go mad, or melt. Spontaneously combust if there isn't a release of pressure soon. I can barely form coherent thoughts, let alone sentences.

"Please, Gabe, please, I need you."

"Please what? What d'you need, Baby?" His hips continue to rock against my core, and the friction is so good, but not enough, not nearly enough to push me over the edge.

"Please, Alpha. Please fuck me, knot me. Please." It's barely a whisper, but still he hears.

A loud ripping sound is the only warning I have as Gabe's briefs are shredded, then he lifts my hips, and removes my pajama pants and underwear much more gently. Jacks moans loudly behind me, and I tilt my head to see him staring at me, eyes devouring my body as Xan squeezes a bottle of lube over his ass-crack. Gabe tilts my chin gently back to face him. "Do I need to make 'em leave, or are you gonna be a good girl for me?" Jacks lets out a loud snarl.

"No, Alpha. Please. Now, please."

He reaches down and rubs the blunt head of his cock through my slit up to my clit and back, and I whimper with impatience. "Almost there, Baby, but I don't wanna hurt you." Then I feel him pushing in, just the tip, and he is so thick. I knew he would be, but this feels nothing like my toys I've used in the past. He's so hot and hard and he rocks into me a few inches then withdraws, before surging forward again. I can see the strain in his shoulders, his eyebrows lowered in concentration as he rocks back and forth a few more times, penetrating me a little deeper with each thrust.

He releases a loud moan at the last thrust, bringing me right up to his knot, that throbs against my clit. The stretch inside is intense. I put my hands on his chest, holding him still. "Just...just give me a second, ok? It's...it's a lot compared to what I'm used to." He stills, but glares down at me, and I rush to explain, "Toys...I've never...um...With another person, but I use toys for my heats...This is the first time I've..." I shrink down with embarrassment, still impaled on his length, but he lets out another growl, leaning down to nip at my lips and chin.

"Oh fuck, Baby. Gonna knot you, bite you. Make you ours."

His hips are twitching, and his knot is bobbing against my clit better than any vibe I've ever tried before.

His voice is a barely restrained growl, and it vibrates through my whole body. "Fuck, I need to move. You ok?"

And he does feel so good, I reach both hands up to bring his face down to me to kiss him slow and deep, and whether he takes that as a sign, or he just can't help it, he starts curling his hips into me again.

Each time he pushes forward his knot hits my clit, and I am already so close. I can feel him getting bigger, stretching me, and it feels so good.

Coming undone, my head thrown back, I cry out his name. My hands scrambling for purchase on his shoulders, I feel my inner walls clamp down on him. My body spasms and all my muscles unravel. But Gabe is still going, moving inside me. The sound of our bodies coming together is echoed by Xan and Jacks higher up on the bed. I can scent all of my alphas, hear the grunts and moans of those around me, my body starts spiraling towards another climax as Gabe's swollen knot slams into my clit over and over again.

"Fuck, you feel so good Baby. Are you ready for my knot?" A whisper near my ear, it doesn't sound like a question the way he says it, and I can barely think so I just nod. His hips are grinding against me, and his arms are shaking. His teeth on my neck, biting, but not hard enough to break skin, just the slightest pressure, a promise of more to come.

"Words, Omega." He leans back and brings my thighs up over his forearms dragging me closer to him. I finally manage to get enough breath to form words.

"Yes...please, Alpha."

He snarls and his hips snap forward once, twice, and then I feel the stretch of his knot forcing its way in. It burns just this side of pain, a sharp ache before it slips inside and locks behind my pelvic bone, and the pressure is like nothing I've felt before. "Come for me, Omega, now!"

His knot is hitting nerves I didn't even know existed, and I come again. Fireworks exploding behind my eyes, my body locking up. Gabe is still going, rutting into me in short jabs, his cock growing impossibly bigger before he lets out a strangled cry and I feel him coming, twitching inside me as he releases load after load. There is so much that I can feel it leaking out around his knot.

He's still kneeling between my legs, locked inside me, breathing heavily. "Fuck, Baby, you milked my knot so well, you're such a good girl for me."

He leans down, kissing me on the forehead before folding his legs and pulling me upright into his lap so he can rub my back, and I melt against him, everything warm and relaxed against his purring chest, my inner omega smug at the praise.

Gabe takes a deep breath, pulling back to look into my eyes, "Unfortunately..."

I panic in that split second looking up at him with worry.

"I think we're gonna be late for work...sorry Baby." He kisses my forehead again and pulls me tight against him.

A hand runs down my spine, and Jacks nuzzles into my neck, before he touches my jaw, pulling my face towards him for a gentle kiss. He looks mussed and satiated, his eyes half lidded, and his cheeks still flushed. Xan is lying on the mattress behind him, spread eagled and still panting.

"Well fine, I guess I'll just be the one to call the offices then?" I look over to see Leo standing in the doorway. He sounds irritated, but going by the fact he is still holding his softening cock—and he has come on the front of his scrubs—I don't think he's really that upset.

Chapter 21

Jacks

Standing in the kitchen, I'm trying to decide what to make for dinner. After making everyone lunch and rushing them out the door, I started laundry. Between the nest and Gabe's sheets there'll be a couple of loads, no pun intended.

I should call Candice and invite her over for dinner.

Yes, she was just here, and I know she can't be here all the time. She works, but with us she won't need to...but maybe she likes it? She also has her iguana at home, and she can't leave it there alone all the time. Oh, I bet I could set up a habitat here for it, and maybe her computer in the office. I don't do coding often, just when we need some extra money, but it could be a nice, shared space for us.

I pull out my cell and text Leo to ask what we need to set up for her pet so she can bring it here and stay all the time. She won't want to give up her house, it's her safe space, and in spite of what happened this afternoon, she needs more time.

Fuck, this afternoon. Leo was flustered when he came in, but even he couldn't keep it in his pants at seeing Gabe fuck our sweet little omega. I wanted to join, but we need to ease into things, and I've never really thought of Gabe and sex at the same time. I love Gabe, but he and Leo are more like brothers to me than anything else.

Xan on the other hand...

I would love to make an omega sandwich with him.

Fuck, being in the middle of the two of them or having her in between us...Fucking hell.

I should probably stop this train of thought before—

Too late

My boner is now officially the thing that wouldn't die. Between the sights and sounds I woke up to and her scent all over the laundry I'm inundated with it.

Fuck me.

That's ok. I can deal with this. Call and invite her over, ask what she might like to eat. Polite shit. None of that needs to involve me driving over to her house and just hanging out for the afternoon and keeping her from work.

Nope, none at all.

And yet, I find myself in the Jeep, with the keys, backing out of the driveway.

Gabe is gonna be super pissed...but fuck him, he actually got to knot our omega this morning, so he can suck it.

Hmmm...suck it.

Goddamn it!

And we're driving, yes, good, focus on the road.

I should have left a note.

Oh well, they track me anyway...Wait, did I pocket my phone? I could just stop in and tell them I was going to her house.

But then they'll want me to go home to "give her space."

I'll just text Xan when I get there, and *then* we can go grocery shopping to get what she might like for dinner so I can cook for her and have snuggles.

I got a goddamned plan!

Kevin Bacon in Tremors is a classic.

Pulling the Jeep into her driveway, I give a side eye to the truck parked there when I know that *her* car is in the shop. I quickly hop out and ring the doorbell. She's smiling when she answers and I'm on high alert. I smell another alpha, and she seems happy to see him.

Curiouser and curiouser.

"Hi Jacks, come in, I was about to call and thank Xan again for calling Joseph to help with my locks. I didn't know you knew him too." She's still smiling and seems relaxed, despite having a strange alpha in her house.

I know for a fact that Joseph is already packed up with his own omega. He's a few years older than Gabe, but he's lived in the area forever. He did our training when we signed up for the volunteer firefighting bit.

"Hey, man, how's it going?" I say cheerfully, curling my arm around Candice and pulling her tight against me, just so he doesn't get any ideas.

Joseph turns towards us and his face falls when he sees me. "Jacks? Sorry, I expected Xan would show up...um, you feeling ok after last night?" He knows I have some...well, let's just say I have issues and leave it at that.

"I'm fine, Gabe's fine too, since he's the one that had to go to the hospital, thanks for asking...all fine here. How goes the deadbolt install?" Not that I want to rush him out of my omega's house, but I totally want him to get the fuck out before the whole house smells like him.

I walk over and pick up a throw pillow to scent mark it again. *Fucking hell.*

"So, you two know each other? How long's that been going on? Does Brice know?"

Way to play it cool, jackass.

Candice comes up behind me and wraps her arms around my waist...rubbing her face on my back, and holding me close, both reassuring and marking me.

"Joseph lives next to my grandpa's old place. He's ten years older than me, but I grew up next to him. I was even the flower girl for his pack mating with Brice." She pushes her face around my waist. "How's his jewelry making going? I still have those earrings he made me when I turned sixteen."

Joseph's smile is more genuine now. "He's good, actually. The business never took off as much as he wanted. But he loves shiny things and just being able to create something, so he still does it as a hobby."

Candice smiles back at him, and Joseph turns back to his work. She pulls on my shoulder to bring me down to her level. "Hey, sorry, I need to go save my work. I was right in the middle when he showed up. I'll just need to go to the office for a minute, ok?" Taking her hand off my shoulder, I kiss the knuckles before gently pushing her towards her work room.

"Whatever you need is ok, Little Lion. I just came over to see what you wanted for dinner."

She blushes and fuck she's adorable. But she doesn't answer and just bolts from the room back down the hallway. I slowly walk after her, intent on seeing more of that blush, or causing it to get deeper. Yet when I walk into the office she's sitting at her desk with a pen and it looks like drawing on her computer screen...weird screen though.

Oh, hey tentacles...and...well.

That is certainly, um...detailed.

I turn away from the screen as her keyboard clicks and pull a sketchbook off the shelf. It isn't flush with the others and that draws my attention. I open it expecting flowers, or still life fruits, maybe rough figure drawings.

Nope...Dicks. So many dicks.

And putting that back.

I turn to see her staring at me, her mouth a little 'o' of surprise and her face bright red.

"A lot of people commission not-safe-for-work art. I practice...er. I need reference material and practice drawing specific anatomy. If you had just picked a different book...I have hands, feet, poses..."

Her voice tapers off and she is staring at her feet. Her next words are so soft I have to lean down to hear them.

"I'm not a freak, I just need a job. This pays my bills and lets me work from home. It's a way to support myself. I don't...I'm not a pervert I just...."

The first tear hits her bare foot, and then my arms are wrapped around her.

"No. No, no one said you're a freak. Well, ok I am sure people online do because people online are anonymous assholes. But we do what we have to do to survive, yeah?" I put my fingers under her chin and gently lift her face to mine.

"I'm so proud of how you take care of yourself, Candice. You've been through so much, and you just keep going." I wrap my arms around her, trying to offer comfort that I don't know if she wants, but I need to give. She remains stiff in my arms, and I'm about to let go when she finally relaxes against me.

"I just...nobody knows what I do. None of my clients know me. I have acquaintances online who know a little more about me, but mostly I have to hide everything, and I was worried that if you found out, you all would think I was some kind of pervert or a freak." I can feel her tears soaking into my shirt as I hold her and sway back and forth.

"And then this morning, with Gabe, I felt like I was being dishonest. I like you all, a lot...like more than it makes sense to. But I also felt like I was lying to you, like, technically yes, my degree is in graphic design. But mostly I do commissions. They pay better, and I don't have to meet clients in person."

Her voice is muffled against my chest, so I lift her up to put her face in my neck and fold myself into her office chair. It's a pretty tight fit and the canister lets out a hiss before sinking to the floor. I rub her back and purr for her.

I suck at words, never knowing what to say, but this...this I can do. Swaying back and forth, purring, and rubbing her back, I lose track of time—until Joseph knocks on the doorframe to her office.

"Hey, Candice. I got your new back door deadbolt installed and re-keyed, so it should work with the key you already have for the rest of the doors. I left my card on the counter, so just let me know if you need anything." Candice mumbles something into my chest and I nod to Joseph, who lets himself out. I swivel around and see we only have an hour until the guys'll be getting off work, so I pull out my phone and send them a text to let them know where we are. Leo has already sent me back a long list of items I'll need to order for Candice's pet to stay at our house, and I continue to rock with her while I do some shopping on my phone. Once I have it all ordered, I brush her hair back from her face.

"Little Lion, Little Lion, what should we hunt for dinner?" I sing-song in hopes of getting a smile out of her.

The eyes that meet mine are red and puffy, but no longer leaking. "You mentioned lasagna the other day?" it isn't exactly a statement.

"I did love, and I will make that for you soon, but there's no time today. What's your favorite food?"

She looks thoughtful. It *is* an important question. "Pizza?" Another not statement.

"Ok, then how about we go to the store and get stuff to make a pizza bar? I don't know what you like, but Xan is one of those pineapple on pizza weirdos, so we'll need to do multiples regardless. But I *do* love him, so if you could not judge him too harshly, I'd appreciate it." This, at least, gets a smile.

"Is it safe? I mean, I don't go into the store unless I have to...and I haven't used de-scenter today." Is it safe? Nobody is gonna fuck with my little lion while I am around.

I kiss her on the nose. "You smell enough like Gabe, and now me, nobody'll mess with you." I leave out the part about how good I am with a filet knife, and she climbs out of my lap to go get her shoes. I stand and stretch, pulling my phone out, again, to message the dinner plans to my pack. There is a surly response about my driving from Gabe, a message to be careful from Xan, and some more iguana information from Leo. At least he's taking this seriously. I stuff my phone back into my pocket before peeling the tape off my omega's computer camera, or at least off the lens area, and then watch her scurry around the house looking for a lost shoe while wearing her iguana.

Chapter 22

Candice

The trip to the store is uneventful. It's kind of strange—once we get all the stuff we need for pizza, Jacks suggests hitting the ice cream aisle to make a sundae bar to go with the pizza bar. But every time we go to a different area, it clears out. Nobody gets close enough to be able to catch my omega scent, and with Jacks behind me, I always feel safe.

Shit, Jacks is like walking Prozac.

Hell, they all are. Every time I'm around one of the pack, I just feel my whole body unwind. All the tension, the anxiety, the panic, all slowly draining away like someone pulled a plug. I still worry a lot, about pretty much everything, but I haven't had an actual panic attack since the vet's office. And even though it was only for a few hours earlier today, I can't remember ever sleeping that well.

"So, are we going back to the pack house, or my place?" I look at Jacks. "I worry about leaving Iggy alone too long; she's used to having someone around the house, and with Sunny gone…"

I trail off, words unsaid. Thankfully he knows about Sunny.

"What would make you most comfortable? I know we have more space at our place, but we already had breakfast there." He brushes my hair back to rub his face against my forehead. I lean into him while trying to do a pros and cons list in my head, but honestly, I'm stumped. I want to go back to the pack house and sleep in the big cozy bed again with all of them. It felt so good to wake up surrounded by my alphas.

They can't be my alphas, not yet. We still need to talk.

"I want to come back to the pack house, but I feel really bad leaving Iggy alone anymore. I feel like a bad pet parent right now."

He wraps me in his arms, pulling me close and resting his cheek on my head. "Don't worry, Little Lion, we can start bringing Iggy to the house soon. We want you to come stay with us permanently. But we need to talk before then. You need to understand what you're getting into with us…*me*…before you agree to anything. I wish we had talked before you and Gabe…this morning." He lets out a long sigh, still holding me close, and while his words do worry me, I have a hard time panicking with his arms around me, and my face pressed against his warm chest.

He pulls away and bundles me into the Jeep, and one coin toss later we're headed to the pack house. Jacks asks me if I want to set Iggy's home away from home up in my nest away from nest or somewhere else, but then we both agree that having an iguana watch us all having sex might be awkward.

We go back to the house and put up the ice-cream. We're chopping veggies for pizza toppings when the truck pulls up with the rest of the pack—home from work. They all give me sidelong looks during dinner, but the pizza bar goes over really well, as does the ice-cream, and soon I'm cuddled on the couch in Jacks's lap, facing a frazzled-looking Gabe across the coffee table. "Candice, we need to talk."

Who in their right mind starts a conversation that way, seriously?

There's no way I can handle two bad-news discussions in as many weeks.

I tense up and Jacks's arms tighten around me. I don't know if he knows what the hell is going on with his packmates either, but the worried looks they keep exchanging have me on edge even before those cursed words leave his mouth.

"What the fuck man, why would you even say it that way?" Xan is glaring at his pack lead.

Gabe looks confused for a moment. Before his eyes widen. "No, shit...about your car. We need to talk about your car. Fuck. Sorry, Candice. We pulled it into the garage today, it looks like somebody was actually trying to damage the axle. This wasn't a hit-a-big-rock or an armadillo sort of situation."

"No, you asked me if I hit something, I told you I hadn't...you didn't believe me?"

Gabe stutters, clearly not ready to make it worse, but thankfully Xan's there. "Normally, if someone has a damaged axle, they run over something. They don't always remember, but the car starts to wobble the worse the damage gets. Candice, I don't know how you could not have noticed, just between your house and the clinic. It's really bad. It looks like someone took a hammer to it. I mean, it's seriously beat to shit. I'm...well...*we're* worried. Someone slashed your tires, and now this. It seems like somebody might be trying to hurt you."

The air leaks out of my lungs as Jacks's grip grows tighter. Gabe leans forward, arms over his thighs.

"We really do need to talk. We're worried about you staying at home alone, but we also can't force you to stay here. We want to get to know you better, and to go at your pace, but we also want to go with you to the police department and file a report on this. It goes beyond just vandalism...and someone would have had to have a lot more time and access to your car—more than it took to slash your tires."

The sundae I had earlier curdles in my stomach. Why would someone do this to me? Nobody knows me. I've worked hard to make sure nobody knows me online. Plus I've only met my grouchy old neighbor, Mr. Sheldon, a couple times while I was out walking Iggy as he watered his flowers. I don't talk to people, so who could be upset enough with me to do something like this?

I don't realize I'm shaking until Jacks's purr starts up. He's rocking back and forth, holding me in his lap, and whispering quiet nonsense against the top of my head.

Chapter 23

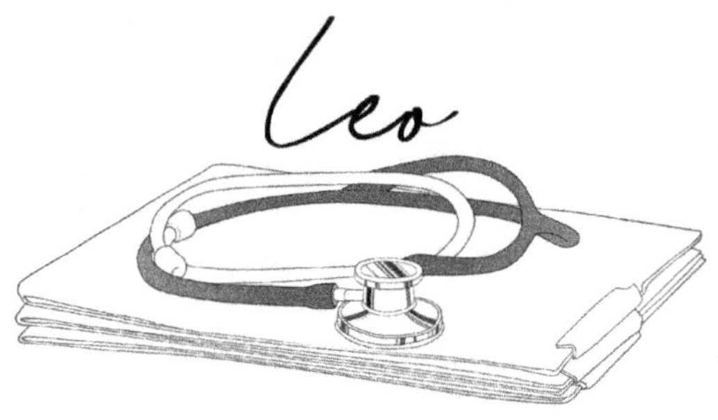

I don't want to take her home, but she insists, and we can't very well keep her against her will.

I go inside with her to check the house, and then make sure the back door and deadbolt are locked. Then I wait until the front lock clicks into place before I'm comfortable getting back in the driver's seat of the truck.

None of us want her to go home, but she needs to feel in control of her life, and Jacks is acting erratic and needs us. I wasn't sure if it was better or worse for her to be around him when he was like this. She'll need to know eventually, but until we talk about his past, his sister, and everything—she doesn't need to deal with that right now, she has enough going on.

I circle her block a few times, making sure nothing looks out of place each time I pass by, before driving home to talk more to Gabe and Xan. We'll pick Candice up tomorrow at lunch, and take her to the police station. But they need to get photos of the damage, and we're all feeling a bit strung out by the situation. It brings back too many memories.

We moved to Shreveport when I was thirteen, and Gabe was in my class. None of us had presented yet, but judging by Gabe's size and my own, we were both going to be alphas. He was popular—and it's no wonder, as he was a genuinely friendly person who just liked to talk to everyone. Even the new guy. We bonded over how hard it was to find size fourteen sneakers, and he invited me over to his house a few times to hang out. In truth, size was about the only thing we had in common. Being an only child, and moving around a lot, I didn't have any friends. But he didn't seem to mind my lack of social grace, and allowed me to tag along often.

One day at his house, I met his neighbor, Jackson. He was three years younger, and a complete goofball. He and his older sister, Janey lived next door with their three dads. Their omega mom had passed away when Jacks was two and he didn't remember much about her.

Janey was in the year ahead of us, and it was crush at first sight. She had already presented as an omega herself, and I admit I followed her around like a lost puppy. Turns out Gabe had been doing the same for a few years now. Jackson, of course, thought it was gross since she was his sister. While he was a tiny daredevil and a hellion, he was also incredibly protective of Janey. She was his whole world, and he threatened me more than once to stay away from her.

We would often see him and Xander outside, trying and failing to play basketball in the driveway. Xan was smaller but insanely smart, everyone thought he would be Jacks's beta. Gabe often called him over for help with homework, despite the age and grade difference, and I liked him right off the bat. He never bothered Janey, so he was safe as far as Jacks was concerned. He had surmised that at almost five years his senior, she would have no interest in him anyway.

We tried to play two on two a few times with them at basketball...but neither of us really liked playing. Xan could barely make a basket, and Jacks was so busy running himself in circles that eventually we gave up. Still, just being near the three of them made me feel lighter and it seemed the feeling was mutual. By the time we were in high school, we had already agreed that we would be a pack afterwards.

We were Juniors when everything went to hell. Gabe and I were finalizing our college plans, me to veterinary school, him to technical college. Jacks and Xan were both freshmen, and we were all inseparable. We had finally stopped following Janey around. She was still beautiful, but if Jacks was part of our pack, that wouldn't work. Besides, while she was sweet, she was now more like a sister to all of us.

We had been hanging out playing video games when she called. Summer was about to start and she had been invited to a graduation party. She shouldn't have been drinking, but at least she was responsible enough to call Jacks for a ride. She told him she didn't want to call the dads because they would be mad at her since she was still underage. So the four of us piled into Jacks's beater and away we went. It took us about half an hour to get there—the party was out by the lake, a bunch of drunk idiot kids doing drunk idiot kid stuff.

The police and ambulance were already there when we arrived.

Janey had been waiting for us outside. In theory, it was safer than risking passing out around a bunch of drunk idiots, but apparently someone found her half nodding off, waiting by the road—a small defenseless omega. Not as defenseless as she seemed, they were able to retrieve blood and skin samples from her nails where she had scratched and bitten hard enough to draw blood. Some of the blood was hers. Apparently alphas don't like being denied, and they hit her, hard and repeatedly.

Not that they needed samples, really. The guy was still there, bleeding from several deep scratches on the face and chest where she tried to escape as he....

He was her ex—a college guy she had dated briefly, but broke up with a couple months ago. Apparently, he had been stalking her, found out where she was going to be. He came out himself to "talk." Try to get her to take him back. She wasn't taking anybody back now. He hit her too hard.

No summer vacation, no college, no future pack or family.

No Janey.

When Jacks saw the blood and semen he lost it—completely off the deep end. It took three officers to pull him off. I'm not ashamed to admit we were no help. Xan was the only one of us who was able to maintain any composure and he was wrapped around Jacks in the back of the cruiser, rocking them both and purring as hard as he could for his best friend.

We tried, at first, but...the longer we were there the harder it was to hold back. There was a mess to clean up, police all over, the ambulance's lights continued to strobe as they cleaned the guy up. Stitching his chest and face up from Janey, and suturing his eyebrow from where Jacks attacked him. They said they needed to stop the bleeding before he could be taken to jail.

Why the fuck should he get patched up and sent on his way when he had snuffed out the bright light that was our sister? I saw Gabe move first, he was built like a big, lumbering bear. He pushed aside the barricade and started towards the ambulance, but the police from earlier were watching, and after Jacks they were better prepared.

They bundled Gabe into another patrol car, but they were so busy with him that they didn't notice me. I circled around, behind the car—through the crowd of drunken gawkers, staring at the white sheet that covered our sister. Around the front of the ambulance. They didn't see me lift the scalpel from the EMT cart. They finally saw when I jammed it into the guy's eye socket, and he started screaming.

But by then the damage was done...just like Janey. I couldn't kill him. There would be no coming back from that, but I could deal with an assault charge. Temporary insanity at seeing my pack sister's corpse, at hearing the devastated screams of my brother—yeah, I was pretty sure I could swing the insanity plea.

I got slammed to the ground, but I wasn't fighting. I'd done what I needed to do. I'm not sure where the extra police came from, but they were on me then. Looking up I could see the EMT was staring down at me, horrified. Fair enough, I'm not proud of my actions, but this fuck shouldn't get to walk away with nothing but a few scratches.

Jacks was screaming again in the back of the cruiser with Xan still clinging to him like a koala, Gabe was throwing himself against the inside door. I couldn't see them well from where I lay pinned to the ground. But I could hear it all. Two people were sitting on my back to keep me from moving, cold metal around my wrist. I didn't struggle. I knew I would get caught, but I couldn't just sit there. There's movement to the side and something slammed into the back of my head.

When I came to in the hospital, my pack brothers were in the room with me. One of the beta officers got a little too overzealous with a baton and nearly cracked my skull. I was being held for observation due to the possibility of a concussion.

My family came the next morning to bring me home. Mom was crying—I don't know if it was because of me or Janey.

Her funeral was the following week, the last week of our Junior year in high school. None of us bothered to finish the semester. It all seemed so unimportant by then, and Jacks couldn't be around people. He blamed himself too much. If he had just gotten there sooner. If we hadn't finished the kart race before leaving.

There were less than five minutes between her phone call and his car pulling out of the driveway. We went straight to pick her up. We all know that there is no real way we could have gotten there in time.

But Jacks still blamed himself. He retreated, just disappeared into his own mind. His dads were no better, so they couldn't really be there for Jacks either—but we were. Xan stayed at his house most days, sleeping over. If his parents had a problem with it, I never heard. He made sure that Jacks ate, slept, and showered. Gabe and I were there when we could be, but I had to deal with police and court stuff, and Gabe was my support. Thankfully, I was still underage enough to be treated as a juvenile, so I didn't go to jail.

By the end of summer, most things had returned to normal. Everyone else seems to have moved on, forgotten about her. But Jacks had lost a lot of weight, despite all of Xan's efforts. We went back to school, but he kept getting into fights. Finally, he broke a classmate's arm, and was expelled. The guy deserved it. He had decided to be a dumbass and talk shit about Janey.

Jacks didn't bother with any sort of school after that. His dads were essentially gone, they didn't talk to him—or anybody else for that matter. So we took him to stay at Gabe's house. Gabe's parents were cool, and it was right next door anyway. But Jacks was broken.

The guy who killed Janey, that fucking murdering rapist. He was nineteen and he only served a few years in prison.

"Shouldn't have his life ruined over one mistake" was the defense.

Life went on for everyone else. Not for Jacks, he was just stuck. And not for the rest of us, who were still with Jacks. He was, for all intents and purposes, our baby brother, we wouldn't leave him behind.

Chapter 24

Gabe

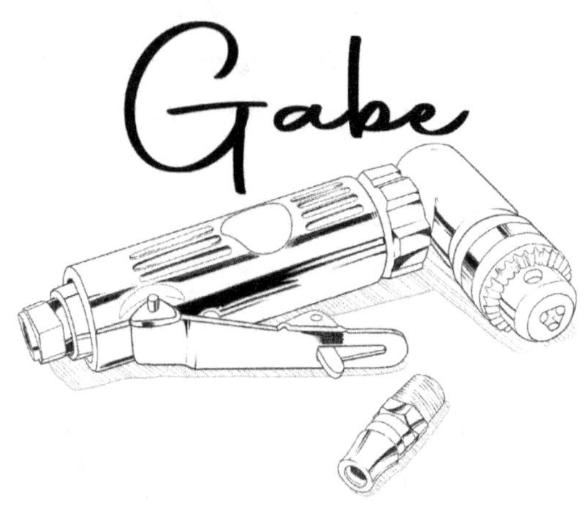

Xan and I take Candice in to file the police report. She's nervous and twitchy, and I can't really blame her. This is all sorts of fucked up. She says she made some announcements online on the forum for her job about her car and apologized again for delays. None of them know about her being an omega either, so she's trying to balance how much information she gives out.

A few of the people she works with step forward, offering words of encouragement, or money to help pay for car repairs. She says she isn't comfortable taking charity. One person blows up her chat with messages while we're waiting at the police department, insisting that they can help, and wanting to send money for support after everything she's been through.

I'm tempted to take the phone away and tell them off. *We* are here to support *our* omega, she doesn't need some random person online doing it.

Taking some deep breaths, I need to calm down. They don't know she's an omega. They don't know she's a female. They don't know she has a pack now. I try to take all this in stride while still paying attention to Candice and the officers she's talking to. It's taking all my control not to growl at some of these assholes who are getting too close to her.

The officers who saw her when her tires got slashed are there too, more alphas. I didn't pay attention before, but they're too close right now, giving our girl shit for not coming in sooner.

Hell, I can fix her car, that's not a big deal, but if somebody has it out for her, then we need to get the cops involved. But I hate how anxious she gets. I just want to bundle her up and take her home, stick her in the nest with Jacks, and let them keep each other occupied.

You know how Jacks would keep her occupied.

You just want her naked in bed again.

Ok, yeah, so not gonna lie, really lookin' forward to that.

But, no, for now take care of the stuff outside the house. Jacks is getting her iguana's new place set up in the living room for now. They can reorganize later if they want to. But he's a sneaky one, finding ways for her to stay at our place more often. He says his next thing will be setting her up a desk and drawing station in the office he shares with Leo. Not sure how in the hell they're gonna fit three desks in there, but between his brain and Xan's

I'm sure they'll figure it out. Those two are crazy as fuck when they get their brains working together.

Fuck, how much longer are these assholes gonna need us here?

Candice made her statement; we provided all the photos we took of the damage.

I guess she needs a police statement for her insurance.

Fuck my life.

I run my hands back through my hair. Maybe I should send Xan back to the garage to help Trey out. Poor bastard's been working mostly by himself lately with us jumpin' around like a frog on a hotplate.

"Um, I'm sorry, sir?" Candice raises her hand trying to get the attention of the officer that took her statement and then just left us here. When that doesn't work, she gets louder. "I'm sorry, but excuse me." Waving her arms at a different passing officer.

"Oh, for fucks sake, s'what I get for trying to be nice," she mumbles before slipping out of the chair and walking back towards the front desk, Xan trailing after her.

"Hey, I'm *really* sorry, but we've been sitting here for an hour, and I really need to get some work done. So can we please leave, or at least get an idea of how much longer this is going to be?" She stares up at the beta behind the counter and adds on a quiet, "Please?"

He looks dumbstruck for a bit, and I don't blame him. Candice has that effect on people. She just doesn't realize it.

"Sorry, Miss...?" He leans forward, prompting a low growl from Xan.

"Manning." She perks up, and he taps away on his keyboard.

"Oh, looks like you're done. Can you check this contact information here? We'll let you know if we find anything out." Now I'm the one growling. How the fuck long have we been waiting for someone to say we could leave? The guard unclips his taser and steps away from the partition, eyes never leaving me. A small hand rubs up and down my back, soothing me and changing my growl to a purr.

"So'kay, let's just go, ok?" She wraps her arms around me from the back, snuggling her face into my shirt. "You're like a big teddy bear, you know that?"

Xan snorts a laugh. "Yeah, boss, a big teddy bear. Totally what I think of when I think about you." He's chuckling now. We both know I can be a surly asshole.

I smile and pull our omega in closer, trying to shorten my steps so we can walk side by side, at least to the truck. She hadn't ridden in the truck before, and she is so tiny, Xan had to give her a boost to get in earlier. From the way her perfume went off, I'm guessing he had grabby hands.

Not that I am gonna complain, as long as she's good with it, I'll try not to be jealous, especially after yesterday.

Fuck me, yesterday.

I can't even blame Jacks, because if I had the ability to do what he did—getting her nest and everything set up, and trying to move her in with us—I would. But I carry the responsibility of the garage. Xan made the commitment to work with me, and he enjoys it. Leo has patients that count on him. But Jacks, he takes care of all of us. He's basically a house husband, and the guy is seriously a miracle worker. He cooks, he cleans, he does all the shopping and tracks finances. Which is why no one batted an eye at how much he spent on that nest.

That being said, I think he should have walked the fuck out and just not bought anything after they called security on him. Jacks isn't harmless, but mostly he just doesn't interact well with people. I can guaran-fucking-tee that they saw his tattoos, piercings, and hair and freaked the fuck out that there was a big scary alpha in their store without an omega leading him around. Hell, maybe they thought he was going to run off with his five carts of pillows.

Not sure how they expected him to manage that.

The important part is that Candice is happy with it, Jacks is happy to do it for her, and we are one step closer to having our omega move in with us. No pressure, but the easier we can make it, the better.

With all the damage to her car, and whoever fucked with it, it's gonna be at the shop for a while. So she asks if we can stop and let her get some sketchbooks out of the backseat. I can drop Xan off at the garage when we do that to give Trey some help. The man has put up with a lot of shit from us lately, staying late a few nights to help finish jobs, opening up when we were out all night for that fire. I don't wanna give him a reason to leave.

We pull into the parking lot and Xan helps Candice out of the truck and they hurry inside to grab her keys from the office.

I don't want to leave this all on Jacks. So we need to have a pack meeting, and see what he needs our help with in getting the house ready for her. I know he mentioned painting, and I can do that, but unless it involves putting shit together or fixing something, I don't know what other use I can be.

I open the door and stop dead...Candice is standing behind Xan as he digs through the cabinet for her keys. Trey is just standing there in the door that goes to the shop. He isn't saying anything, and they don't seem to even realize he's there—but he looks pissed about something, his hand squeezing around the wrench he's holding.

"Hey, Trey, sorry again about needin' you to open up this mornin'. I appreciate it, man."

His eyes flick to me, then back to Xan and Candice, his grip loosening. "'Ey, boss, yah'. Jus' gon' need ta make sure ay get off nes' Friday an de' lon' weeken?"

The last word lilts up, and I can't tell if he is asking for the weekend off, or...Fuck.

"Sure, Trey, whatever you need. You been coverin' for us enough lately. Take a couple extra days. Cool?"

"Ya boss, t'anks." He finally looks back at me and his smile gives me the creeps, but hell, he's been pulling an assload of extra hours. Maybe he's just tired.

Thankfully he takes his wrench and goes back into the shop, right as Xan pulls Candice's keys out of the drawer and she gives him a quick hug before heading back out the front to get her stuff.

"Xan, can you check in with Trey while I am takin' Candice home? He was looking freaked as fuck when I came in a couple'a minutes ago."

"Sure man, I can ask. Maybe he doesn't like omegas, or maybe we just startled him banging around in the desk, if he wasn't expecting anyone in here."

I chew on my lip. "Yeah, that could be it."

But why does that answer feel so wrong?

Chapter 25

Jacks

It's been a few days, but the new terrarium is set up, we got the heat rock and the lamps, food and water bowls ready, and a little mesh hammock.

I rearranged the office, but I need to snoop and find out what kind of work stuff Candice needs. I don't think I can fit another bookcase in here with the desks and terrarium. I wonder if we should swap a room out, or just add on to make this one bigger. I can talk to Xan when he gets home tonight, just to get his thoughts, my love kicks ass at Tetris.

Most of the daily stuff is done. I watered Xan's garden, he'll take care of the weeding this weekend. I'm caught up on laundry and cleaning.

Maybe I should start dinner, or plan out meals for the next week. I wonder what kinds of foods Candice likes? Maybe I should call her and ask, but I know she needs to get work done. I could go over to her place, get her, and take her to get groceries and help me with our meal plan. Or pick her brain about what she needs for the office. I can be sneaky about it.

Oh, so chocolate eclairs and turtle ice cream...and what kind of PC do you use, along with a detailed list of programs you need for art?

I don't think that's gonna work.

I just want to wrap her up so no one can hurt her. All this shit with her car.

Fuck. Our poor girl.

Maybe I should check in on her—see if she is sitting at her computer working.

Just a quick peek, don't want to bother her. But if she *is* working, maybe I can get her to bring Iggy over and they can stay for dinner, check out the new habitat. Then she won't have a reason to go home tonight.

Fuck, it felt so good to hold her a few days ago. I know it wasn't a proper overnight sleep, just a nap, but it felt so good to have her on one side and Xan on the other. I don't think I've rested that well since high school, before—

Yeah. So, gotta check in on her, then figure out dinner.

I fire up my desktop, and just a hop, skip, and a jump before I'm looking into her office—she isn't there.

Huh?

Oh, lemme check the security cameras.

There she is on the couch...

Oh.

Ooooohhh...

I probably shouldn't watch her without her permission...but fuck.

My omega is on the couch, her long flannel pulled up over her hips, nothing else on but a pair of black panties with her hand down the front, her other hand is tracing small circles on her neck, right where I need to bite.

My teeth ache. Just wanna keep her here in her nest and have snuggles.

Do I want to knot her? *Fuck yes!* I'd be lying if I said otherwise, but I *need* to take care of her, keep her safe and cozy, feed her, and protect her from all the hurt and crazy shit that she's been dealing with.

I should probably close this stream...but fuck. Should I call her, tell her to move to her nest? Would she get mad at me? Her breathy moans come through the speakers, the sound tinny and fractured from the cheap camera. Heavy panting and—*fuck,* maybe I should just go over to her place and check on her in person. I could say I just wanted to ask her what she wants for dinner. It was so hard to sleep for the last few nights, even with Xan in our bed, we both wanted her there.

I groan, hand lowering to my jeans, now strained over my erection, pressing against the denim, as if that'll do anything. Should I stay here and just take care of it, or should I drive over and offer to help?

"Jacks...Please!" Her cry comes through my speakers and I'm up and grabbing keys without even bothering to shut down the feed. I can be there in less than fifteen minutes.

Racing down the stairs, I almost knock Xan over as he's coming in the front door.

"Everything ok?" He takes in my flushed appearance and obvious arousal.

Shit. There goes my fifteen-minute time frame.

"Yeah, no, I'm fine. What's up?" My words are rushed as I am trying to escape.

"Oh, yeah, Trey flushed a radiator all over me, and I'm soaked through to the skin with coolant. So I needed to come home and grab a shower and get changed."

"Cool, cool, cool, very cool. Well, I'm headed out to the store to get dinner stuff, see you later." I try to weave around him to escape, but he knows I don't really drive, and grabs the collar of my shirt as I pass him.

"Dude, what the hell? Is everything ok?"

Fuck, now he looks worried. I hang my head, giving up on this grand escape.

"Yeah. Just...I went to check on Candice, and ok, so I got super horny"—my hand gestures vaguely to my groin—"so I was just gonna go see her, and talk to her about possible dinner options. See if she wants to come over, maybe take her to the store. Or at least see if she needs a hand—or a tongue—today." By this point he's grinning at me, but still smelling sickly sweet from the coolant coating his skin.

He steps into my space reaching up to cup my jaw. "Alternatively, you can stay here, and help me shower off, and then once we're both clean"—he leans into me, pressing his wet shirt against my chest, soaking it through—"and in fresh clothes, you can drop me off at work on your way over? Then bring Candice with you to pick us all up from work. It'll be a nice surprise for Gabe and Leo."

His hand slides from my jaw, cupping the back of my neck and pulling me down for a hard kiss. Xan is the shortest in our pack, but built wider than me. With his broad shoulders and tapered waist, he looks like he should be modeling men's underwear instead of wearing coveralls and those god-awful baggy boxers he loves so much.

I cup his face, kissing him back, biting at his lips, as he reaches down and starts popping the buttons loose on my fly with the hand that isn't pinning me to him. He pushes them down, and chuckles against my lips when he finds me bare underneath.

"Have you not found any underwear you like, or do you just go free-ballin' to tease me, love?" He nips lightly at my chin as he pulls back enough for us each to strip off our soaked shirts, and I shuffle towards the stairs, peeling my pants down. Throwing everything vaguely towards the laundry room on the way to the stairs.

Xan is sticky when he presses against my back, and as much as I want him inside me right now, we really do need to clean off first. This is itchy as fuck. He laughs and slaps my ass as I hop on one foot, trying to get my sock off, then he races up the stairs to get the shower started.

Our bedroom door is open, and I can hear the shower running in the en-suite bathroom, steam billowing out the door. I grab the lube off the nightstand on my way past the bed—just in case—and head into the bathroom. He's already in the shower, head tilted back, water running over his face and down his chest, and I want to follow those rivulets with my tongue.

Pulling open the door lets in a draft of cold air that swirls the steam around him and he leans forward, moving his head out of the spray.

"Don't mind me, I just need to wash all this sticky shit off." I grab the bar of soap and work up a lather in my hands before scrubbing my chest, and down my own stomach, using the slippery soap, I fist my shaft and pump it twice before stepping into his space and running my hands over his shoulders.

Seduction, yes please. But he still needs to get that shit off of him before I can lick all that delicious skin.

I run my soapy hands down his chest and stomach before circling to his back, pulling us flush from hip to neck so I can run one hand up his spine, while the other slides lower, squeezing one cheek and sliding my fingers along his ass-crack, pressing lightly against the tight ring of muscle. His head is tilted back again, rinsing the shampoo out of his hair, and I have to lean down to nibble on his neck and gently bite his collarbone.

He groans loudly, hips flexing against me, shaft sliding against my pelvis in an uncoordinated jab.

"Fuck, Jacks, are we clean enough yet?" It's almost a gasp as I start a rhythmic pressure against his back door with one hand, the other sliding between us to squeeze both our shafts together. He thrusts into my fist, adding pressure and pleasure to my cock as well.

I release the hand holding us together, and drop to my knees, finally giving in to the temptation. I stick my tongue out and catch some of the water dripping into the cut of his Adonis Belt. Letting his shaft rub against my jaw as I nip at the muscles there, and trace the groove with my tongue.

His hand fists in my hair, and he tilts my head back so I'm looking into his eyes. My hand that's been teasing his ass slides around, and I cup his balls. He releases my hair and leans back against the side of the shower, no longer directly under the spray.

With freedom to move my head, I follow close behind, running my tongue up his shaft, around the slight flare of his knot, and to flick the slit. Before wrapping my lips around him completely and sucking him to the back of my throat.

Confusion floods my mind when he pulls out of my mouth, turning his hips away so I can't reach him.

"I can't last when you do that." He smiles down at my puzzled expression, slipping his hand around my jaw and pulling me back up against him. He steps into me, pushing me out from under the water, until the cold tile hits my back, the shock drawing a gasp from my lips, and a shiver down my spine.

"I need you to feel good too, my love." Then he's kissing me again, holding my face, pulling my mouth to his, and I open because it's Xan. He's been my everything for so long, my best friend, my lover.

His tongue slides into my mouth, tangling lazily with mine before flicking up to lick my palate. His body leaning in. Pinning me to the tile with his chest, his hips against mine, rolling against me now, undulating like a wave. I run my hands over his shoulders, down his chest. Fisting us together again. I can't move my hips back, so I surge forward against him, finding our rhythm, like we always do.

He's moaning into my mouth, and breathing in my own gasps in return. His hand twists into my mohawk in the back, tilting my head so he can hold me in place while he bites and sucks on my lips, moving down to nip under my jaw and lick down to my shoulder, mouthing his bonding mark in that sensitive spot where the neck meets the shoulder, still rolling his hips, holding me prisoner with his hands and mouth and cock.

I can feel my balls tightening, and that warning tingle at the base of my spine. His face is still buried against my neck, his breathing coming in ragged gasps against my skin. He still holds my hair with one hand, but the other slides down to wrap above mine, making a double fist to stroke against. "Fuck, Jacks. I'm almost there."

I bring my free hand up to squeeze his knot, feeling his pulse as it throbs against the palm of my hand.

"I love you," I rasp out, my own orgasm hitting me and I have to lock my knees to stay upright as I paint his stomach in the hot jets of my release.

"Fuck, yes! Love you too, oh fuck!" Xan spasms against me, and I brace my legs apart in case I have to grab him to keep him up too. His knot swells, and I can feel his release twitching against my palm and my cock, almost scalding against my skin as it coats my hand, and splatters on the floor between us.

He wobbles slightly, and I release his knot to touch his shoulder, just in case. In case he needs me to hold him up, like he always holds me up.

"I think I am gonna need another shower before we go, or at least a rinse," he chuckles against my neck, before pulling back to kiss my chin. His hand finally releases my hair and caresses down my chest before flicking my nipple ring and making me squirm and laugh. He knows all my ticklish spots.

"Come on, we need to finish up and dry off so I can get back to work, and so you can go collect our omega for dinner, yeah?" I am satiated and relaxed, but yeah, that sounds like a good idea. I let him pull me back under the water to rinse away our combined release before we towel off.

I wander back to the laundry to get a new shirt and jeans, fuck socks. I'll just slide some sandals on before I leave. When I come back out, he's dressed, his wet hair pulled back into one of his douchey man buns to keep it clean at the garage—his name for it, not mine. I think it's cute and makes a nice handle.

He's standing in the doorway to the office—and I forgot to turn off the link I had to her security camera.

But she isn't laid out on the couch anymore, spread out like the most delicious buffet I ever wanted to taste. She's curled up in a tight ball, her favorite throw wrapped around her. Her phone is laying on the far end of the couch and she looks terrified of it, like it suddenly grew claws and tried to attack her.

Fuck.

"What the fuck were you doing, man?" All of our earlier affection has gone from Xan's tone.

"Ok, well, I know this looks bad, but I wanted to check on her, so I tapped into her security feed and was watching her on the couch, moaning...calling my name. And, to be fair, that is where I was headed when you came home."

Xan is still scowling. "Are you recording this?"

"I think that the security program records every time the camera's on, so let me check." All lightness gone from the room, I slide into my office chair and pull up the recording for the last half an hour. I have to bite back a groan as I start the video over with Candice on the couch, moaning, her hand moving frantically. Xan is gripping the back of my chair so hard his knuckles are white.

We double speed it, watching her come apart alone, stretching, relaxed and languid. Then her phone rings, and I switch back to normal speed. After the initial "Hello" all the blood drains from her face, and she pulls the phone away and ends that call. She looks shaken but takes some deep breaths, letting out a small scream of surprise when the phone rings again. I see her slide to the ignore call button on the screen. By the third time, she's cocooned herself in her blanket and is huddled into it on the couch, swaying from side to side as the phone continues to ring. The time stamp shows five minutes ago.

I hear the front door slam and I turn, but Xan isn't behind me anymore, and by the time I scramble outside myself, he already has the truck turned around, waiting for me.

Chapter 26

Work was going well this morning, I had already sent off two finalized images for approval so I could mark them off my to-be-finished art list. Two more were inked and awaiting color, and I had actually managed to go through all my messages and was caught up on things that needed replies. That part was easier than I thought it would be, a few people asking how things were going after Sunny, and how my car was doing. Three people asking about their owed images, and Wishbone, again, offering me money. It feels really awkward—and I don't want to be rude, because I really do appreciate it—but I just can't take it.

I was feeling pretty fucking good about myself.

Standing up to stretch, I head to the kitchen to get some water. Otherwise Jacks will nag me for not staying hydrated. Refilling my tumbler, I stretch out on the couch, just to rest my eyes for a few minutes since I've been staring at the screen for the last few hours.

Is it dumb to miss Jacks?

We see each other at least every few days, or at least talk, but I miss the snuggles, and how good it felt last week waking up surrounded by the whole pack. It never occurred to me that I could want that, but it just felt so right.

Of course, what happened with Gabe afterwards was also amazing. I'm not sure if he understood that I hadn't been with anyone else. I have toys, and I can't exactly say I was a virgin, not in the traditional sense since I've had to use toys when I get my heats, even on the suppressants. But he felt better than any toy I have ever had.

He wasn't really any bigger than my toys, but it was definitely a full body-experience, having him wrapped around me while he was inside me. And, yeah, I'll admit, I can totally see what the big deal is about knotting now. My legs were like jelly afterwards, and I had to fight myself to get out of bed and leave. Which isn't fair to Iggy or my customers, but it was just so good.

And I'm not going to lie to myself and say that I'm not looking forward to the next sleepover. For sex as much as the cuddles I never knew I wanted, that I never knew could be that good.

It's the strangest thing. I feel bad that I don't feel bad about wanting Jacks and Xan, too, and of course Leo. I mean, I had sex with Gabe, and while it's common knowledge that omegas have more than one mate, I still feel awkward about wanting them all, worried that I won't be enough to satisfy them all, or make them as happy as they make me. Of course it's less of a worry with Jacks and Xan, they have each other already, and fuck me but I want to be a part of that.

I mean, I've drawn plenty of guys together for commissions, but there's just something about those two that makes me shiver—makes me wonder what it would be like to have both their hands on me at the same time.

The way Jacks kisses me, it's more intense and feral than Gabe. It lights every nerve on fire with how much he wants me. Then Xan...the two of them are beautiful together. I rarely use that term when describing men. They're attractive, or sexy, or handsome—but even when they were fucking—almost primal—you could feel their connection, and I wanted to be part of it.

I'm starting to realize that while I've been thinking about them, my hands are wandering. My breathing is erratic and a slick warmth's growing between my thighs. I rub them together and sure enough, I'm wet just thinking about how they looked. I might as well release some pressure, since I'm taking a break. I let my hands roam as I play out the fantasy that's in my head already.

We're in the nest that Jacks made me, he's in front of me, with Xan pressed to his back, nipping at his neck and shoulder, his tongue tracing along the lean cords of muscle that stand out as Jacks's head tilts back. I lean forward, biting his collarbone, and then letting my lips follow the path of Xan's hand down over Jacks's chest and stomach. Stopping briefly to lave my tongue over his pierced nipple before I kiss a line down to his hips. Gently biting his hip bone and then sucking on the skin there before Xan cups my jaw, gently guiding my lips to Jacks's shaft. I trace my tongue from root to tip, lapping over the slit, then going lower to suck gently on the thicker swell near the base, trailing kisses and licks up and down until Jacks is moaning and rolling his hips against me.

His hands are twisted in my hair, gripping tight, but not trying to force me to move in any way. I look up to see him staring down at me, Xan's hands gripping his hips firmly while he thrusts against Jacks's ass.

"Little Lion," he calls me, though I don't know why. I never imagined myself particularly fierce.

"Come here. I want to taste you." His hands gripping my arms pull me up the bed, stopping when we're eye level, so I can kiss him again. Jacks kisses in a frenzy, all nipping teeth, and tongue, and passion. He rolls me onto my back to cage my head with his arms as he devours every gasp and moan that's drawn from my lips.

I hear Xan grumbling at the change in position before he's there too, pushing Jacks down to my neck so he can take my mouth. He's less fervent with long slow sweeps of his tongue, but there's no less passion in it.

Jacks is biting my neck, not hard enough to break skin, but there'll definitely be marks. One hand wanders down my body, tracking the line of my breast, plucking at my nipple, and cupping my waist before he drops his chest between my thighs. It's not the pressure I want, not the rolling rhythm I crave, but his warm body still feels delicious, and the kisses trailing down my chest and stomach have me squirming.

Xan pulls back so I can look down as Jacks slowly peels off my panties, raising his torso and my hips to slide them down my legs. All the nerve endings in my body are on fire, as Xan takes one nipple into his hot mouth, sucking and biting gently, while rolling the other in his fingers. I can't see Jacks anymore, but I can feel him, his fingers tracing up my thighs, and his warm breath against my core.

"Jacks...Please!" I cry out, feeling like I'm going to combust if he doesn't use his fingers or tongue on me soon.

He chuckles, "Needy Little Lion, don't worry, I'll take care of you." Then his mouth is on me, his tongue taking one long stroke from core to clit, before his lips wrap around it and suck.

My hips jerk and buck on their own, and my hand scrambles to find purchase in his hair. Jacks brings his fingers up, thrusting two of them into my hot center, and I'm so wet it makes an obscene squelching noise.

I look for Xan and he's kneeling above my head, watching as his mate makes me shake in pleasure. I reach out my other hand, finding his hot, hard length. I begin to stroke him in time with the thrust of Jacks's fingers until his head falls back and he moans.

"Oh, fuck, Little Lion, you taste so good. But I need to feel you come." Jacks's breath is a harsh pant against my core as his fingers continue to stroke in and out of me. He punctuates each word with a tongue flick against my sensitive nub until I'm squirming on the edge of release. I can't make out what he's saying, just words mumbled against my core, between his wicked tongue stroking and teasing me.

Then I'm falling, blowing apart only to be put back together again, my hips jerking spasmodically against his fingers and mouth.

When I recover Jacks is looking up at me, wiping my juices from lips and chin, and his eyes flick up to meet Xan's in silent communication before both their hands are on me, lifting and turning me till I'm on my hands and knees between them, Xan in front of me, his straining erection inches from my face, and Jacks at my back, his hard length pressed against my core.

Xan strokes my cheek, looking down at me. "Open wide, Pretty Lady." And I do, letting him slide into my mouth, his salty flavor bursting across my tongue. I feel Jacks lining himself up against my still weeping core, sliding up and down, gathering moisture. He grabs my hips with both hands and slams into me hard, pulling me back and away from Xan. Then they move my body. I'm still loose and pliant from my own orgasm as Jacks's hands on my hips shift me back and forth almost off of his cock until I am nearly choking on Xan's.

Forward and back, Xan's hand is still holding my jaw lightly, but I can feel the tremble in it as he wraps it behind my head, and twisting my hair around his fist, now helping Jacks shuttle my body between them. Jacks's fingers digging into my flesh as his hips thrust against mine every time he pulls me back. My eyes water with every push forward onto Xan's length as it slides to the back of my throat. Their combined moans filling the nest along with the sound of slapping flesh.

"Fuck, Omega, I'm—fuck!" Xan shouts, his hot seed coating my tongue in spurts. I try to swallow it, but there is so much, combined with his still-thrusting cock, that some dribbles around his length and drips off my chin.

My second orgasm blindsides me, barreling up my spine with no warning until I'm clenching down hard on Jacks, and crying out my release around Xan's still-hard length. Jacks's hands tighten to the point of leaving bruises and I feel his knot slam against my entrance, once, twice, and then he comes too. Pressed as tightly as he can be, without knotting me, hot jets of seed splash my inner walls before I collapse in a boneless heap between my alphas.

The phone ringing jars me out of my fantasy, and I pick it up with my not sticky hand. I don't bother checking the caller ID. Almost no one has my number, and I haven't gotten around to putting the garage or vet clinic numbers in my phone. "Hello?"

"You fucking slut! What're you doing with them? You're mine!"

I slam the end call button, finally looking at the number—Private Call.

The phone rings again, and I hit ignore.

What the fucking hell.

I need to call Jacks or Gabe, one of my alphas.

The phone rings again, and I can't even look at it. I just…I need…

I wrap myself in my blanket.

If I just don't answer…if I wait until they stop, I can call Jacks to come over, and he'll stay with me until I feel better.

My toes curl under as I pull the blanket farther over my head, rocking back and forth. The phone rings again, and a high whine starts in my chest.

I slide off the couch, away from my phone, and run to my nest. I know no one is coming out of the phone to get me—but the sound of it is sending me into a spiral, and I feel safer there, even though my logical brain knows that's all crazy.

My logical brain also knows I keep a baseball bat, a small club, and a few stabby knives under my nest, so it probably is at least a little safer.

I'm not sure how long I'm huddled there, long enough for my breath to slow down and my pulse to stop racing as much. The phone rings twice more. I can hear it from here, but I didn't bring it with me. I should probably go call Jacks now that I have myself under control. I pull out my club and shuffle my way back to the living room, picking up my phone. It rings again and

I scream, dropping it back on the couch, until I realize that the number on the screen is Jacks.

I scramble to answer. "Thank goodness. Where are you? I need you."

I can hear a car horn honking in the background, and someone yelling, Xan if I had to take a guess. "Are you ok, Candice? What happened?"

"I just...I need you, please. Can you come get me? I don't...I don't want to be a bother." Now that I hear his voice, my tight control is fading and I can feel myself cracking again—my eyes burning with the need to cry.

"Little Lion, you're never a bother. Xan and I are already on our way over. We'll be there as soon as we can, ok. Just...stay inside, keep the doors locked. It should only be a few more minutes. Can you stay on the phone with me, talk to me until we get there? So I know you're safe?"

Warmth swells in my chest. I do feel safer just talking to them. My breathing is easier hearing any of their voices. Jacks keeps talking, and while I'm focused on his voice, he's mostly talking about meal planning and going to the grocery store, and mundane things that help me stabilize and calm down.

A thought occurs to me. "So, wait, why were you on your way over before I called?"

The line goes quiet, and I hear Xan in the background. "Yeah man, wanna tell her why you were going to her house earlier?" He sounds like he is trying to make a joke, but the tension's still heavy in his voice.

"Ok, honey, we're pulling up in your driveway now. Can you come let us in?" Jacks's voice is softer now, and I don't hear as much background noise. I open my doorbell camera and wait until I see them, before rushing to unlock everything and throwing myself at Jacks. He pulls me close as he and Xan rush inside. Picking me up, he carries me to the couch and snuggles me into his lap. Purring loudly, his hands run over me, looking for any damage or injury.

Once he's satisfied himself that I'm safe, he just holds me, swaying and purring. Xan walks around the house, looking in my office and the bathroom, sticking his head in my nest, and sniffing, before coming back to the couch and sitting beside Jacks, his hand finally coming to rest on my knee as Jacks continues to rock me back and forth.

Xan rubs his hand in circles on my leg. "Ok, brief explanation. I came home from work to clean up. Jacks was perving on you, and then we saw you looking upset and rushed over." I'm still a little stuck on the part of Jacks perving on me, and turn my questioning eyes to him. He looks at me, then flicks his gaze up to my bookcase, where I have a security camera aimed at the living room in case anyone breaks in through the back door.

"How...um...how did you get access to that camera, and how long were you watching?" I can feel the heat in my cheeks and ears now, as embarrassment floods me.

Taking pity on me, or trying to save Jacks from my wrath, Xan abruptly stands up. "Ok, grab a bag with a couple changes of clothes, and your lizard...you can tell us what happened on the way back to the house, then I really need to get back to work."

Chapter 27

Xan

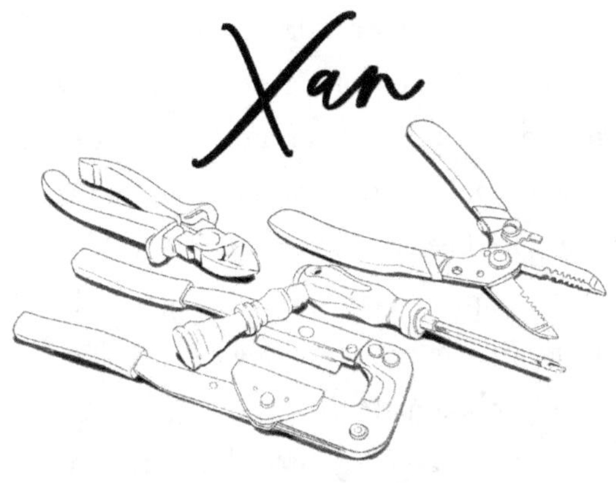

Fuck fuck fuck!!

What the actual fuck! Now we have to get the cops involved. Again!

I dropped Jacks and Candice off at the house and head back to the garage to confer with Gabe. He is, understandably, pissed. He texts Leo so we're all in the loop, and then we get back to work. There's still a lot of catching up to do, but I can tell he's pretty deep in thought. I know he wants to insist that Candice stay with us. We all want that, but we don't want to push her into something that makes her uncomfortable. Now, of course, it's a matter of safety, but I don't know if she'll see it that way or not.

All three bays are open today, and all three are full. Gabe is working on a bigger project—replacing a head gasket, and sometimes I have to step over to lend him a hand. Trey is mostly doing the basic stuff like oil changes and tire rotations, but he seems to be having a pretty off day himself. We end up having to delay pickup on a couple of bigger jobs so that we can get all the oil changes done by the end of the day. Trey can't even meet Gabe's eyes as he apologizes, before clocking out and leaving at five. That's fine, it's been a fucked-up day all around, but I have hopes that tomorrow will be better. I'll try to talk to him if he still seems out of it. We've been piling too much on him lately, and we need to get better about that.

I hate that Candice is going through all this, but at the same time, I'm super excited that she'll be staying with us for a couple of days. Gabe and I stop at the clinic to pick up Leo, and I take a few minutes on the way home to fill them in on the full situation of what happened today. I gave Gabe a brief version earlier, but with being so backed up, and Trey around, I just wasn't comfortable going into too much detail.

We get home and Jacks has all the doors locked, which is a first since we moved here. But I don't blame him for not wanting to take chances with Candice being at the house.

Jacks is in the kitchen putting the finishing touches on dinner, and it looks like a comfort food night of pot roast and mashed potatoes. He went all out and made bread too.

Damn, I'm gonna have to actually start working out if he keeps cooking like this.

Candice comes down the stairs, her iguana wrapped around her shoulder. Her eyes are red and puffy. She goes straight to Leo and snuggles against his chest. I'd be lying if I said I wasn't a little jealous. Leo folds her into his arms, and strokes her back, while Iggy scrambles up his shoulder.

"Hello, little friend. How are you doing?" He reaches up and scratches the iguana under the chin and its tail flicks back and forth, slapping Jacks in the face when he tries to hug Candice from behind. Jacks glares up at it, but then gives up and just drops to his knees, wrapping himself completely around Candice, burying his face against her back. Gabe is watching everything, a look of concentration on his grumpy mug—then he starts barking orders.

"Alright, here's what's gonna happen. Candice, you're gonna stay here for a few days, just to make sure you're safe. Leo, can you call in late tomorrow?" Gabe looks at Leo who just nods, then he continues.

"Yes, good. Tomorrow Leo and Jacks'll take you to the police department first thing to talk about the phone call you got today. I doubt they can or will do anything over one phone call, but better to get the ball rolling on it in case that fucker calls back."

Candice is still sandwiched between Leo and Jacks, but she looks furious. "You can't just tell me what to do Gabe, I have a life, I have work commitments I have to get done. I can't uproot everything just because of some asshole."

Gabe walks over to where her face is poking out from under Leo's arm and squats down so he's closer to eye level. "Little Omega, I know you don't like this, and I know you think I'm bein' an asshole, but I'm not gonna take a chance with your safety here. Jacks is a computer geek. He'll take you home after you talk to the cops, and help you gather all the stuff you need to keep working. Xan can help him organize the office, or if we need to set up a different space for you to work in the spare room...or if you need to swap spaces with one of us, we'll do that. Just, whatever you need to be comfortable, alright?"

He reaches out to cup her face. "The point is, we want you here, we wanted you here before all this shit, and now I won't be able to sleep unless I know you're safe here, got it? We'll get you whatever you need to work to make sure you can, but I need you safe, more than anything."

She blinks up at him, eyes glassy with unshed tears. "But, I don't want..." Her voice trails off in a whisper.

"You don't wanna be here?" he asks, swallowing hard. He turns an interesting shade of green, like he might throw up.

She rushes on, "No, no, I want to be here, but it just feels like you all are disrupting your whole lives to do this...I mean, I don't want to fuck everything up. Ok? I know you all have lives that don't revolve around me. You have the garage, Leo has patients. I'm messing everything up and other people are counting on you. I don't want to make things harder on everybody."

Gabe drags her out from between Leo and Jacks, picking her up and carrying her over to the couch, cuddling her into his lap.

Jacks gives him an irritated look, but goes back to the kitchen to finish getting dinner ready.

"Ok, first off, this isn't your fault. You didn't ask for this asshole to slash your tires, or break your car, or start callin' you with his shit. So any issues that come up are on him—not you. Second, like I said before, we want you here, we want you in that nest, we want to come home to you every day. Hell, in case you haven't noticed, Jacks is over the damned moon 'cause he gets to feed you an' take care of you right now."

"I can try to hire more help at the garage if things don't get better soon—if it comes to that. We own the fuckin' thing. If we want to hire people to run it instead of working there, we will. Yes, Leo has patients, but they did just fine without him—and before we moved here—so if he can only go in to see the exotic pets, we'll work around that until this is sorted out. You are our priority, Little Omega. I don't rightly care about what happens to anybody outside of this room right now."

She's leaning into his chest now while he strokes her hair, her eyes sliding closed. I think that saying she's emotionally exhausted would be an understatement at this point. I sit down next to Gabe, pulling her feet into my lap, and rubbing them through the fluffy purple socks.

"Yeah, we're gonna need to hire some extra help anyway. Trey is looking worn out himself. Pretty sure the man needs a vacation. Hell, we could all use a little R&R." Gabe nods to me, and I realize I just volunteered myself to be in charge of finding a couple of new mechanics...fuck.

Whatever. If it means I can spend more time here with Candice, I can do the extra work. I didn't know how relaxing it would be just to hold her, touch her, but I know I've zoned out when Jacks comes over and bites me lightly on the neck.

"Dinner time, love. You ok?" I realize Gabe and Candice are no longer beside me on the couch.

Fuck...maybe I'm exhausted too.

I'll deal with it tomorrow...tonight, food, snuggles, and sleep. In that order. I take Jacks's hand to let him help pull me off the couch, and into a quick kiss before whispering into my ear. "Dibs on being the big spoon for my little lion, you can fight with Leo and Gabe for who gets her other side." He grins like a shark and bolts from the room, cackling like a madman.

I mean, I knew he was a cuddle whore, but come on. That's just not fair.

Leo

Dinner was good, Jacks is an excellent cook, so I am not entirely surprised. It's just that I don't recall him bothering with making comfort food before. Still, I'm not complaining.

Candice insists on helping him load the dishwasher while he hovers around, trying to figure out how to get her out of his kitchen without upsetting her. She looked like she was going to throttle Gabe earlier when he told her she would be staying with us for a few days. She's just like a kitten, cute and cuddly but with sharp points on five ends.

Gabe asks Xan and me to join him in the living room. He wants us to help reconfigure the office to make space for her desk. Or we need to find an alternative area for her to work in if she doesn't want to squeeze in with the rest of us. Xan suggests we build on another room, but that will take more time than we have at the moment. I suggest that we move the bed around in the spare room and put her desk and iguana there, so she can have her own private space. The truth is that Jacks set up her nest, but she doesn't have a private room, and everyone needs their own space.

We agree to discuss it with her later—probably tomorrow, as we're all worn down after the events of today. Unless my kitten is amiable to any sort of bedtime activities, then I am sure we'll all find the energy. Right now, however, she just looks shaky and tired.

Xan puts forward that we all relax on the couch with a movie and popcorn.

Movie night has always been an affair, as none of us enjoy the same thing. Gabe always wants something with a lot of action and explosions. Xan enjoys mysteries, Jacks likes science fiction, and I prefer romantic comedy. There are a few that fit into multiple categories, but it's always a challenge finding something we can all agree on.

Apparently, Candice enjoys British comedies and anime. So, it comes as a surprise when she suggests a movie none of us have seen before with space traveling cowboys that use a lot of Chinese insults in place of profanity. Jacks makes popcorn, and Candice falls asleep in Gabe's lap within fifteen minutes of the movie starting. Which was *not* really a surprise.

He attempts to carry her upstairs to her nest when the movie ends, but she wakes up and insists that she can do it herself. He still insists on walking behind her up the stairs in case she falls over in her half-asleep state. Once in her nest, she seems to forget we're there, starting up a shower and peeling off her clothing while we're still in the room. Jacks has already called "dibs" on snuggling next to her, and Xan can't sleep unless he is touching Jacks, which leaves Gabe and me to throw rock-paper-scissors for who gets to sleep on her other side this evening.

While I appreciate and respect my pack leader, he always starts with rock, so it is hardly a competition before we're all relaxing comfortably in her nest, waiting for her to emerge from the shower.

Jacks is already asleep with Xan tucked around his back when she joins us in an oversized t-shirt. "Sorry, I usually sleep in nothing, but I don't want to make anyone uncomfortable."

Xan's head pops over Jacks's shoulder. "Sleep in whatever you want, Pretty Lady, as long as you get some rest."

He flops back, tugging Jacks tighter against his chest, and is snoring lightly before my little kitten is able to settle between us, snuggling into my chest with an adorable omega purr. Gabe, mumbling about getting kicked in the face, settles at the top of the mattress, hand stretched down so he can run his fingers through her hair.

I kiss the top of her head, breathing in the combined scents of my pack, her chocolate peppermint adding an extra comfort I hadn't realized was missing. Within moments, I fall into a peaceful sleep.

My first appointment isn't until 10:30, but I always wake up at 6:30. It drives Jacks crazy because he thinks he *has* to get up and make breakfast before work. I appreciate the effort, but I rarely feel like eating when I get up. Still, my internal alarm wakes me up, and for the first time in forever, I don't feel like I need to get up and start the day. There is a tiny, soft omega snuggled up to my chest. Jacks is plastered to her back like a koala, and Xan is laying half on top of him with his arms wrapped around them both.

One of her hands is tucked to her chin, and her forehead is pressed against my chest. Both Jacks and Xan have a hand wrapped around her hips, their fingers entwined. Her other hand is over her head, using her bicep for a pillow, and Gabe is holding her wrist. They all still seem to be sound asleep, and while I rarely sleep in a puppy pile with my packmates, I can see that being in the nest together will be a regular occurrence for all of us. She already feels like our center, and she isn't even officially a part of the pack. But I want her to be. Fuck, falling asleep near her, her scent mixing with ours, it gives me a sense of peace I didn't even know I was missing. Like all is suddenly right with the world.

Of course, that won't happen until we get rid of the asshole that's terrorizing her. She whines in her sleep and I look down to see my arms have tightened around her. I try to loosen them enough to keep her from being uncomfortable, but it's difficult. I know she wants to take care of herself, but she doesn't have to now. We want to take care of her. I'm unsure if it's the scent match, some sort of alpha imperative, or just her, but *I* want to take care of her, feed her, give her everything she could want or need. And fall asleep like this, every night, wrapped around her.

Which is the only real problem I see. We might have to make a snuggle schedule to keep Jacks from "calling dibs" every night. Regardless, I would put up with that happily just to be close to her every day.

Bending my neck to kiss her hair, I rub my jaw against it. I love how she feels against me. When next I look down, her face tips back and she's looking up at me.

"Sorry I woke you up, Kitten. I can't seem to hit snooze on my internal alarm," I whisper as quietly as I can, reluctant to have her move, or wake up the rest of my pack. She blinks at me a few times, and presses her face back into my chest, tilting her hips back against Jacks and stretching between us.

"So'kay, what time is it?" she mumbles sleepily against my skin.

"Probably shortly before seven," I say, stroking her hair. Her head snaps back, eyes narrowed on me.

"Hold up, are you saying I've gotten myself involved with a pack of morning people?" she huffs against my chin.

I try to bite back my laughter at how serious she suddenly is, but a muted chuckle escapes anyway.

"Nope, just me. Years of getting up too early for school, internships, and work have kind of conditioned me to be an early riser, whether I like it or not. The rest of the pack can sleep till at least ten if nobody wakes them." Running my hands up her shoulders, I gently squeeze the tight muscles in the back of her neck and her eyes lose focus.

That's a handy trick

Her eyes close and she nuzzles against my chest. "Ok, but...can you just stay here and let me use you for a teddy bear, for a bit longer, please? You feel so good."

The last few words are said as a mumble, and her lips moving against my skin send a shiver down my spine. I have to tilt my own hips back down to keep from grinding against her stomach, and soon she is drifting back to sleep.

Chapter 28

Candice

It's after eight when I wake up again, and I only know this because Gabe is grousing to Leo that he didn't wake him up, and now they're going to be late to the shop. Xan and Jacks are missing behind me, but the bed is still warm when I reach back, so they can't have been up for long. Leo still has his arms wrapped around me, rolling his eyes at his pack leader. "Well, you could have set an alarm, brought in your clock, or your phone. I didn't want to make Candice get up."

"Sorry," I mumble against his chest. "My bad, I don't normally sleep in, sorry." I rub my face over the warm, enticing skin in front of me. Hit with a wave of spiced chai and oranges, I'm torn between licking a long stripe between his pecs, and just closing my eyes and going back to sleep.

Then I remember why I'm here instead of at home in my own nest, and it feels like a bucket of cold water was dumped over me. We have to go to the police this morning, and then go get some of my work stuff, so I can work from here, at least for a few days.

Reluctantly, I roll away from Leo's warm chest and scoot off the edge of the nest. I have too much shit to do to stay in bed all day, even if it is surrounded by my delicious smelling alphas.

My alphas?

I'm not sure how safe of a thought that is, but my chest feels warm and fuzzy with it. And I want them to be mine, I just...I'm not sure how. It feels too easy.

It feels like I'm being a slut with four guys at once.

But they don't see it that way. Hell, judging by the way we all cuddled up last night, they seem fine sharing. I mean, Jacks is...intense, but Leo and Gabe were ok too, and they don't seem to be in the same sort of relationship as Xan and Jacks. I don't remember much about my parents other than I kind of remember my mom and dads all being affectionate towards each other...I had to move in with Grandpa when I was nine, and it was just the two of us at that point.

There's too much to think about this morning, and I can't deal with this on top of the police station and moving my stuff. I can't go down that rabbit hole this morning. I must have zoned out again. Gabe's hand is on my shoulder.

"You ok, Little Omega?" He looks concerned.

Shit, I'm staring, I should reply.

His eyebrows drop lower and his voice is louder. "Candice, are you okay? What's wrong?" He pulls me closer and I take a deep, shuddering breath.

"Yeah, sorry...sorry, just lost in thought. Sorry."

Shit, too many sorries again.

His big hand smooths my hair back. "No worries, Baby, you just looked a million miles away. I know you've got a lot goin' on right now. I'm just worried 'bout you. Sorry."

His arms wrap around me, and I just want to sink into his chest and not deal with life right now. But nothing is gonna get done if I don't do it. He lets me go when I step back, but he doesn't look happy about it.

"Sorry, Gabe, I just...my mind wanders sometimes, and I was thinking about family stuff." He looks like he wants to ask for more, but I can't think about that right now.

"I'll tell you all later. I don't want to think about it too much right now. Lots to do, ya'know?" I shuffle in place before turning and sliding towards the bathroom to get cleaned up and changed for the day.

So much stuff to do.

The police don't look surprised to see me again, maybe they expect repeat visitors when someone gets vandalized. I don't know, so I'm just rolling with it. Jacks and Leo seem to read my mood better than Gabe and flank me for support instead of trying to alpha me and be in charge. I appreciate everything Gabe is doing for me, but I've been taking care of myself for years, and while it can be hard—so fucking hard sometimes—I think I'm doing a fair job of it.

The police take my name and contact information, they record my statement, they ask for any information I remember about the caller, male or female voice, anything that stood out. They have me fill out a form so that they can get a copy of my phone records, if it comes to that. Which I do. I mostly use it for checking work messages, and now for the guys to contact me. Nobody has my number, which is part of what makes this all the worse.

I'm finally free to go get my stuff, and since Leo says he doesn't have to be at the office for another hour, he comes with us to keep Jacks from driving. I did offer to drive, but will readily admit that if I pull the seat far enough forward on the Jeep to reach the pedals, my boobs are squished against the steering wheel, so yeah, letting them drive makes more sense. Still, I don't want them to treat me like an invalid.

I'm short, not broken.

Fuckin' tall people.

I'm not mad at them, not really. I'm frustrated with the situation, and I'm mentally taking it out on them. I miss my cat, I miss my car, and I miss my nest. The one Jacks made me is nice, but it doesn't feel like mine, exactly. Maybe we can take some of my nest to the new nest, at least while I am staying there.

We finally pull up in front of my little house and I use my key fob to turn off the alarm. Nothing looks out of place, but there is a weird twisty feeling in my back, like almost a shiver...something's wrong, but I don't know what.

Jacks seems to feel it too and asks for my keys so he can check on everything. I grumble, but hand them over. I know he's trying to help. Instead of going through the front door, he puts both hands on top of the fence, one leg up and braces against it...then tosses himself over.

Can all alphas do that? Should I put in a garden behind the fence, with plant stakes...or a moat? What *is* the proper response when you find out that the fence you put up for privacy and protection won't actually do more than the bare minimum to keep people out?

Maybe barbed wire? my annoyed inner voice mumbles. I swear, these alphas are just throwing all my preconceptions about safety right out the fuckin' window. I know I'm grumpy from stress...but come on.

A few minutes later Jacks opens the front door from the inside, marches over to the Jeep and pulls me into a tight hug.

"I'm so sorry, Little Lion, we need to call the cops...again." He sounds both pissed and resigned.

Fuck.

Jacks

As soon as we pull up, I know something's off. Candice's scent had taken on a burnt sugar edge the whole morning with how stressed she's been, but this is different, more sour and worried. It feels like there's a low hum in the back of my skull. Something is definitely wrong, and I don't want my omega walking into it.

Once she hands over the keys, I hop the fence and make my way around to the back door. I don't need to pick the lock this time at least. But as I round the house, it looks like I wouldn't need to do that anyway, the glass on the back door is smashed in, and the door's hanging open, there are a few drops of blood on the concrete outside. I crouch low, opening the door as quietly as possible. But I don't smell anyone else in the house. Candice's scent is still everywhere, but there's something else, almost too faint for me to catch. Darker and heavier than her, angry. Stretching my elbow out, I try to flip the light switch without leaving any prints. Nothing happens, just a clicking sound when it goes up and down. Did this fucker cut the power? *Shit.*

I open the door to her nest and look in. The room is shredded, with blankets and pillows thrown everywhere. I don't go in, because the police will need to do an investigation, and I don't want to mess anything up. I walk quickly through the rest of the house...Iggy's terrarium is knocked to the floor, but it doesn't look shattered, at least. Several of her books are off the shelves and it looks like someone swept her photos and frames down. Glass litters the floor.

I walk to her office, dread filling me with each step. This was her sanctuary, and I'll find out who defiled it. I open the office door and swear loudly. The shelf with her sketchbooks is tipped over, ripping the anchor out of the wall. Papers are scattered over the floor where it looks like someone yanked pages out of them, the covers torn off. Her computer monitor is just a starburst pattern of broken glass across the screen, and her drawing tablet is laying on the floor, broken, and covered in plaster dust where someone slammed it repeatedly into the wall.

Her tower is on its side, dented, a boot-print well defined on the metal case, so I take out my phone and grab a photo, just in case. Her office chair has been cut up, stuffing and chunks of leather mixed in with the papers and other debris on the floor.

Fuck, I wonder if I can just take her home and forget about it. So she doesn't have to go through this today, after everything else.

I know I can't, but I also know she'll be devastated. My gut churns with anger and nausea as I imagine her reaction.

Fuck.

Better get this over with.

I head out of the front door. She's standing beside the Jeep, chewing on her thumbnail. Her eyes look up at me, and I see both hope and dread.

I'm gonna kill this motherfucker.

"I'm so sorry, Little Lion, we need to call the cops...again."

Leo is staring at me, and I shake my head. He pulls out his phone and dials the police while walking into Candice's house, and I hear when he starts cursing. Leo is the most laid-back guy I've ever met. Hearing him this upset is kind of disturbing. When he comes back outside, he's practically yelling into the phone.

"I was just at the station. I know there are no emergencies. Get some people down here now because we need to get this sorted out and get our girl home. I will not have her standing around all day upset because your department can't pull your heads out of your collective asses." Even Candice looks taken aback by the fierce snarl on Leo's face, as she reaches for him, rubbing her hand down his arm.

She shouldn't have to comfort him. It's her house that's trashed, but I think it must be an omega thing, as she pulls out of my arms to wrap hers around his waist.

Leo takes a deep breath and settles. "Yes, fine. I'm just...upset. Yes, someone will be here. But we can't go in or do anything to clean up until you arrive. Yes, I or one of my packmates will be here with her. No...just...please, hurry." By the time he hangs up, he's curled his big body around Candice, breathing in her scent, and offering her comfort as much as taking his own.

Once he's calmed down, he asks me to call the garage and leave a message for Gabe. He doesn't want to go into work, but Candice insists that people are counting on him, and only her demanding that he leave gets him to move. He can come back after his appointments and pick us up, or we'll have one of the guys come by and get us.

After he pulls away, Candice shakes herself and starts marching toward the door. I step in front of her, not wanting to grab her when she already looks like she is about to break.

"Little Lion, Candice, you can't...I mean...I don't want you to go in there, ok? The cops will be here soon, but they'll need to look around and do cop stuff before we can do anything. Alright? I know you want to see, but just...trust me, ok, I'll take care of it."

"Now, on that note, how much stuff was stored on your computer? How much might be lost if it got damaged?"

She looks up at me, tears in her eyes. "My computer? Mostly just recent stuff, unfinished sketches. I store everything online, so only a couple of days' worth of work. But my photos, stuff from my grandpa...all of that...I...how bad is it?"

Closing my eyes, I pull her into my arms as she starts crying. "It'll be ok, I'll take care of it."

I know I'm repeating myself at this point, but I'm not sure what else to do as I rock her back and forth against me with her tears soaking into my shirt.

Then we wait. I lean against her house, holding her against me while I text Gabe. After that, I leave a message with Kelly at the front. Candice doesn't want them to come rushing over and have even more to deal with at work. I want whatever helps her to be happy.

I ask her questions to take her mind off of what's happening, while my own mind spins and makes plans. We wait, because I can't do any of those plans until after the police leave. We talk about what color she might want to paint the nest, and about what she might like to do with her room at the house. We don't really need a spare room anyway, no one visits...and if they do, fuck 'em, they can get a hotel.

Finally the police arrive, they go through, take a lot of photos, but there isn't much they can do, take some samples, a few pieces of broken glass from the busted door that have blood on them, photos of the boot print. But there isn't a lot of evidence, no fingerprints or anything glaringly obvious. They'll send over a copy of the report for insurance purposes, and I seethe as Candice cries. Then we go inside and start sorting through her life again. She looks into the office, closes the door, and goes to her nest. More loud sobbing comes from there.

Gabe comes over for his lunch break, and helps us collect some of what isn't destroyed of her nest and clothes, and her broken computer tower. He takes us back to the house. After locking up, I pocket her keys. I'll need those later.

I bundle her into the nest at home, holding her until she falls asleep, then I go start cleaning up, washing all the nesting stuff she brought over to go into her room. Taking the side off of her computer tower, the asshole snapped the motherboard in half when he stomped on it, but the hard drive looks intact, so I'll salvage what I can. After dinner I'll take Xan over. We can board up the back door, and then clean up some. Even safe in our home, I won't leave her by herself.

I told her I would take care of this, and I will. Checking in on Iggy, I find that she's just chilling on top of her terrarium, so I pick her up and put her on my shoulder to have some company while I work on laundry and getting dinner ready.

So much to do.

Chapter 29

Xan

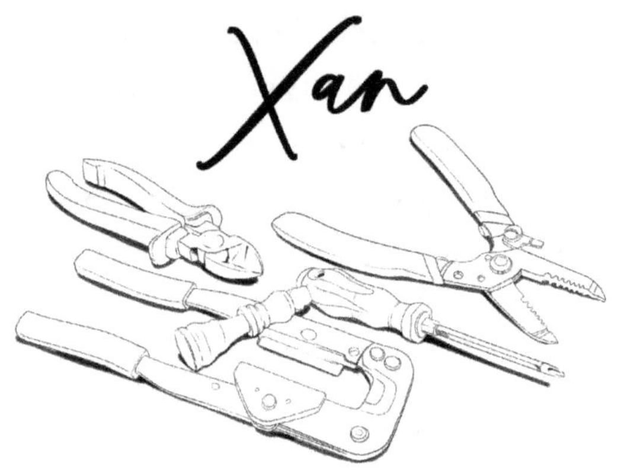

Work sucks. Trey called in, so we're already short staffed, and I asked Kelly to help me write up a job posting for a couple of mechanic positions. Even if we hadn't found Candice, Gabe still needs to take some time off. He runs himself ragged between work and the pack.

We're mostly done with renovating the house, or we were. I might set up some plans to build an addition. Maybe a large office space downstairs so we can all have one together. I'm not against Candice having her own room and office. I just think she might not want to work out of her bedroom. But that's more of a long-term plan.

I work together with Gabe to finish a couple of bigger jobs. If we can just get through those, everything else will be small stuff—oil changes and tires. Those are easy enough that we can do multiples at once and hopefully get caught up. Kelly comes out and tells us that Jacks called and left a message to call him or Leo. When Gabe finally finishes up and pulls out his phone, there's a lot of cussing before he manages to type something back. I don't know what to expect when he finally puts his phone away and comes to fill me in.

Apparently, someone broke into Candice's house and trashed it. Jacks is with her, but they have to wait for the police before they can do anything else. Gabe, of course, wants to leave now to go wait with them, but he doesn't want to leave me to work alone. He has some choice words about Trey calling in, but I don't blame the guy. We've been running him ragged, especially these last few weeks.

Kelly offers to stay late to help Gabe with the backlog of paperwork, which he isn't real happy about, insisting on paying her overtime, even though she doesn't work full time to start. She's practically family, so I go ahead and fill her in on the basics of how we met an omega, but then someone trashed her car. I point out the little beater in the parking lot as Kelly fumes about it.

We met Kelly, shortly after we moved to the area. Her mom brought her in with her to get her car worked on. Fifteen-year-old Kelly was fascinated with the shop, and she's hung around in one form or another ever since.

After all that, I tell her about the recent issues with someone stalking Candice, calling and screaming at her and now breaking into her house. Kelly is, understandably, upset on all of our behalf, but she's also super excited for us, and is practically wiggling as I finish giving her all the details. Except Candice's name, which, yeah, she could easily look up in our files, but she won't since I asked her to respect our omega's boundaries. Also, if things go the way we hope, she'll meet her soon enough anyway.

Gabe goes on lunch and goes to pick up Candice and Jacks, along with some of her stuff they manage to gather up to take to the pack house. When he gets back, I go by her house to have a look around.

Fucking fuck, this place is trashed.

Picking up the iguana's terrarium I put it back, but I can't get much done on my lunch break. I know that Gabe and Jacks already got all the clothes and nesting material they could. So I spend my time gathering up the photos that are broken and torn up on the floor. I see several of them are cut with broken glass, but hopefully we can salvage some of them.

I walk into her office and all her books are torn up. There are a lot of sketched images, not just dicks this time. But everything is ripped up and scattered on the floor. Sorting through the papers, I collect a few books that still seem to be intact and add them to my small pile of torn memories. Unfortunately, there's no time to take care of anything else right now. I need to get back to work.

At least I have enough time to stop and grab some deli sandwiches and trash bags on the way back to the garage. Gabe and I managed to each wolf down a sandwich between oil changes. Thankfully, Kelly's finished the job posting and asks me to look over it before she sends it out. After that, it's just playing catch-up with work until five.

Kelly left a couple of hours ago, but we're mostly caught up, finally. We *can* get the job done with two people, it just requires hauling a lot of ass. I don't often work full time, but I've had to for the last few months. Hopefully, this job posting will get me back to part time soon.

We don't have to stop and get Leo, since he still has the Jeep, so we make it home before he does. Jacks is just finishing up dinner, and Gabe and I each retire to our own rooms to wash off the garage grime. It feels like weeks since I was in here with Jacks, but it was just yesterday. I really need to schedule a date night soon. Maybe we can bring Candice along, see if she's up for dinner and a movie.

I'll talk to Jacks about it later tonight.

I shut off the water, my mind still going over what sort of date we can take her on. She isn't super social, so maybe a picnic and projector type movie. The truth is, we don't know that much about her. I mean, Jacks is already in love. He was gone as soon as he saw her. Gabe and Leo too.

Fuck, ok, fine I'll be honest, so am I.

Which freaks me out a bit, because I've always been the logical one, but Candice doesn't make any sense. The pack was already perfect...now it just feels...more perfect? Like, something was missing and I didn't even know about it until she was suddenly here. Maybe Leo's right, and she is our scent match, because every time I'm close to her I just wanna pull her into my lap and purr until she's nothing but a puddle of omega mush. I want her in the shower between Jacks and me, at least sometimes. I just feel like I need to be whatever she needs, and that freaks me out because I feel the same way for Jacks.

The introspective part of my brain wonders for a few minutes if my reaction to her is Jacks. He reacts to her; I react to him, so therefore I react to her...but I don't think so. I knew she was something special before he picked her up and carried her into the house that first day.

Clean and dry and redressed, I head back down the stairs to see Jacks standing by the table, hugging a sleepy-looking Candice. I wrap my arms around both of them and have to stand on my toes to bite the back of his neck. I'm not expecting him to go down and take her with him, but he nearly does, and I have to catch them both before they hit the floor.

"You ready for tonight?" I growl against his ear. He turns his head enough to look at me. We've always understood each other.

"Yeah, I got the truck all packed up. Thanks for grabbing that stuff. I already put it in the office to work on later."

Candice's eyes ping-pong back and forth between us. "What's tonight?"

I lean over Jacks to kiss her on the nose. "Nothin' to worry about, Pretty Lady. You are gonna stay here after dinner with our pack lead and veterinarian, and Jacks and I just have a few errands to run. Lots of time for snuggles when we get back, ok?"

She nuzzles her face against mine, kissing my chin, and then pretending she got a hair in her mouth, gasping and flailing...murmuring something about chin pubes...ew. Maybe I do need to shave, or commit fully to a beard. I'll worry about it later.

Jacks makes an excellent burger, and I love it when he goes all out with a burger bar, so we can each do something custom. Gabe almost always goes basic toppings with no veggies, but will always add bacon if it's an option. Leo enjoys a gardenburger, but decks all his options out with excessive lettuce, tomato, onion, and pretty much any other vegetables that are out. Candice asks for feta cheese and diced black olives to put together a Greek burger, and Jacks makes one for each of them. Sounds tasty, especially the garlic butter, so I slather that on and then put a little of everything else on mine...I can barely open my mouth wide enough to fit it in by the time I'm done, but I've never met a challenge I didn't meet head on.

After dinner we get Candice settled on the couch with Gabe and Leo. She and Jacks are both super clingy and he only lets her go after several hugs and scent marks. With what went down today, I don't blame him for not wanting to be apart, but we have work to do.

He already loaded up the truck, and I grab a spare sheet of plywood and some 2x4s out of the shop to toss in the back before we head over to Candace's house.

Time to do some cleanup.

We talk a bit about date ideas. I wanna make sure he's good with taking her on a date. I understand he wants to take her out, but I also know our time together is special, so we decided to roughly alternate. We can plan a date with her this week, and for just the two of us next time. We don't want to monopolize her time, especially since I'm sure Gabe and Leo also wanna get to know her better.

When we get to her house, Jacks helps me unload the wood, tools, trash bags, and gloves. He goes inside to start picking up glass and cleaning up papers. I'm not sure how much we'll be able to salvage, but I wanna try to save as much as we can.

I carry the wood around back, and start measuring to cover the door. It'll just be a patch job, but until we can get a professional over here, it'll have to do. By the time I get everything cut down and need Jacks to help me secure it, he's already collected all her papers in the office. He's also taken photos of things that are gonna need to be replaced, like the make and model of her office chair that's on the label attached to the frame.

He helps hold the wood in place, while I screw a brace on the back to secure it through the hole that used to be glass. Then we get to work on the inside. We get trash bags for the broken picture frames, and sweep up glass from the living room. Locate her vacuum in the broom closet, to clean up in there. The desk doesn't look damaged, but we load the busted monitor and drawing tablet and chair in the back of the truck to dump or recycle.

He looks furious cleaning up her nest, and I can't say I blame him, this is her special place, where she's supposed to feel safest. I leave him to it while I go start emptying the fridge and cabinets. The food is probably fine, but since we don't know if the guy tampered with any of it, I won't feel safe leaving it there. Jacks takes more pictures of things that need to be replaced, trying to make sure we keep anything special for repair, like a patchwork quilt that was torn open, or what looks like a handmade photo frame of young Candice and an older man, I am guessing is her grandpa. The glass is shattered, and some of the tchotchkes around the edges are broken off, but it looks special enough to try to repair it.

By the time we finish, it's almost one in the morning, and her house looks empty. The bed of the truck is loaded with bags to go to the dump. Jacks is still fuming, and I can't really blame him, but I pull my broken boy in for a kiss and rub my hands up and down his back.

"You ok, love? I know that's a stupid question, but how're you holding up?" I grab his hair, tilting his head so he has to meet my eyes.

He looks tired, but better than he did at dinner, and he tries to smile for me.

"Ok, let's get you home, cleaned up, and then omega snuggles, yeah?" That, at least, does earn me a smile.

We're both dragging by the time we make it home. I send Gabe a text letting him know we have an impending dump trip, and asking if we should just rent a dumpster so I can start renovations on the house. He can see it tomorrow, if I forget. Another speedy shower and I come out to find Jacks passed out in our bed, waiting for me. My heart lifts a little. I'm not jealous of the time Jacks spends with Candice, but I still need to feel needed for me. I crawl into bed behind him, kiss my bonding mark on his neck, and don't remember anything after that until Leo is knocking on my door, telling me it's time to get ready for work.

Chapter 30

I wake up sandwiched between Gabe and Leo, and it looks like it's still dark out. My bladder is full, and I need to squeeze out from under what feels like a two-ton arm pressing me into the mattress. No one is around my feet, so I shimmy down the bed and, ok, I stop to gape at the deliciousness in briefs and boxer briefs that I've been sleeping between...but fuck. Bathroom first.

When I finish washing my hands and come out, the room is pitch black, and I worry about stumbling around in the dark and hurting myself on unfamiliar furniture. It seems like as good a time as any to get a drink, so I meander downstairs to the kitchen, get a glass of water and now I'm awake...fuck.

I napped too much earlier.

To be fair, I've been kinda fucking stressed.

I hope Jacks and Xan made it back ok. I check out the front window and see the truck, so at least they made it home safe. It feels strange to be worried about two grown men, but I can't help it. They're important to me.

It's weird standing in the middle of the living room alone, so I head back up the stairs, noticing now that there is a big lump in Xan's bed, so I tiptoe as quietly as possible back to the nest, and crawl up the center. My vision has adjusted enough that I can see Gabe and Leo now. Gabe has his arms wrapped around Leo's waist, and Leo is rubbing his face on top of Gabe's hair. I kinda wish I had my phone on me so I could take a picture of this for posterity, or at least to show Jacks tomorrow to get a smile out of him. He seemed almost as broken as me today.

Not wanting to disturb them, I crawl into bed behind Gabe and settle against his back. This man is built like a grizzly bear, complete with fur, and while I always thought it would be a huge turnoff, it doesn't really bother me. He grumbles something in his sleep, then turns over and wraps me in his arms.

"Fuckin' hell, Baby, where'd you go? Woke up pressed up against this tall asshole." He pulls me against his chest and rolls back over, depositing me between them again, and only loosening his arms enough for me to get a decent breath.

I enjoy the dichotomy being snuggled between them. Leo is all smooth lean muscles on one side. So much golden skin covers well-toned abs that I want to trace with my tongue. Behind me, Gabe's chest hair covers most of a farmer's tan, all layered over thick slabs of muscle. They're both so big, but so different in form, appearance, and texture. I'm not sure if I want to draw them, or rub against them until they wake up and I can taste them.

I mean, I could wake them up by tasting them.

I should probably let them sleep.

One little lick won't hurt.

Fuck.

I need to check my calendar for how long until my next heat. Everything's been so fucked up lately, but I know it's coming up. Is that why I'm so horny lately? I crane my neck to look between the two alphas who have me pinned to the bed. There could be other reasons, I guess.

Snuggling down, I will sleep to come back, but it takes its sweet time.

By the time it finally does claim me, there's already light filtering around the blackout blinds.

Yeah, I slept in, but to be fair, I had a hard time falling back asleep. Jacks gets me up at ten with breakfast in bed. Everybody else has already left for work, and he wants to go over some computer stuff with me. He also wants to see about setting up my own room, not just the nest. The idea makes me squirm. Even if it wasn't for what happened yesterday, I'd still want to be around this pack, these guys—my guys.

I hope.

I'm also worried about being an inconvenience. I mean, I need to feel useful, so there's that, but we haven't known each other for long. They are so nice, and...well, ok, I'm not sure if nice is the right word. Still, I don't want to take advantage of them, and I feel like I am.

I talk to Jacks while I eat my waffles, and he asks about paint colors I might like for the nest and the new room. He says he might be able to pull parts off my old computer to build a new one, which is a relief to help me save some of my meager funds. I need to ask if we can go back to my house soon so that I can get more clothes and my own bathroom stuff. Then he sits with me while I finally turn on my phone. If it starts ringing again, I'm gonna ask him to answer it. I really need to access my calendar to find out when my heat's coming up. Then I have to answer messages and let my clients know what's going on.

He takes my hand while I wait for my phone to boot up, and leads me next door to what will be my room. We can discuss moving furniture around, paint colors, and moving Iggy in here once I get finished. Xan and Jacks share a room at one end of the hall. Next to it is Leo's room. Gabe's is directly across at the top of the stairs, then the other end of the hallway has what is now my room, and the nest is at the end.

But he must have already been working for hours, because when I walk in the room is already full of my stuff. The bed has several of my nest items on it from home. A lot of it is missing, but so much is still here. There are several stacks of sketchbooks and papers against the far wall. When I realize the paper has been taped together and stacked neatly, I can't hold back the sob that erupts from me, both from my life being torn apart, and these alphas trying to put it back together.

There's even a stack of photographs that I recognize from my living room, several are scratched or badly cut from the glass in the frames breaking, but they're here, and maybe I can get some of them restored. I drop my phone in my haste to hug Jacks, and he starts purring again, rubbing his hands up and down my back.

"I told you I'd fix it. This is just the start, so don't worry, ok? Xan and I went over and boarded up the back to keep anyone else out, and cleaned what we could. I need to ask you about a few things that I can't repair, if you wanna keep 'em for sentimental reasons, or if we can replace them."

Nothing will get replaced right now. I can't afford it, and just the thought of trying to sort out my computer and drawing tablet causes fat tears to roll down my face. I untangle myself from Jacks—much to his annoyance—and pick my phone back up. There are several online messages from people asking if I'm ok since I haven't been online. Then I log onto the forum to make a general announcement about the break-in and my computer getting trashed, but also to assure everyone that most of my work is backed up.

Jacks comes up behind me while I'm trying to type out information on my phone screen. He wraps his arms around me and nuzzles into my neck, and his hot breath across my skin sends an electric pulse skittering over my whole body.

Fuck, I need to check my calendar.

Switching over to my tracking app—*holy fucking shit*—next week. Next week I'm supposed to start my heat. Jacks draws in a sharp breath behind me, and I guess he saw it too, because his arms tighten and his purr gets louder.

"Mmmm...Xan better get those new hires done quick, and Leo will need to take some time off work." He pulls me tight against him, leaving a long trail of kisses from behind my ear to my shoulder, and I whine and shiver against him.

"I've...I've always taken care of them myself. I mean, Gabe is the first guy I was...." I stammer out, trying to pull away so I can meet his eyes.

"Do you want us to help you through it, or do you want to go it alone again, Little Lion?" His eyes are full of heat and he bites down on the corner of his lower lip, his purr thrumming loudly between us. "It's your choice, always, but we would be more than happy to help, however you need us to." He raises his hand, cupping his own neck before slowly tracing down his throat and resting against his collarbones, one finger tapping mindlessly, as he continues to suck and chew on his own lip...and fuck, but I wish he was doing that to me.

I try to shake myself out of the fog of lust he is giving off, but can't tear my eyes away from his mouth. I want to kiss him; I want him to devour me.

Fuck, it's too hot in here.

Jacks stalks me down the hallways as I back out of the room. We stop at the stairs. I'm not comfortable backing down stairs. I'll fall and break my ass or my neck, but I'm also not sure I want the game to be over. The only way out is over Jacks, unless I want to risk falling or invade their personal spaces. When I back down the hall towards the room he shares with Xan, his purr switches to a low growl that sends shivers racing down my spine.

"Omega, do you need us to help you with your heat next week?" His voice is a low rumble, my soft and snuggly alpha is nowhere to be seen. "All four of us...I can't wait to knot you with Xan." He tilts his head, thinking. "Or maybe knot you while he takes me."

The heat in his eyes is scorching, but I want to be burned. There is a surge of perfume and my thighs are covered in slick. Jacks groans, his growl thrumming louder.

"Not sure if I can make it to next week." He backs me into a corner, at the end of the hall, and I don't want to escape anymore, I want him.

His growl is driving me out of my mind, and his scent is spiking and mixing with my own. We smell like a fucking coffee shop at Christmas, and I want to lick the combined flavors off his skin.

"Please, Alpha. I need you," I whine, tipping my head back. His nose rubs up the column of my throat, breath heavy and hot on my skin.

"Fuck, Little Lion." He cages me in his arms, grinding his whole body against me. I can feel him vibrating with tension. "Not here, not without him." He bends low and scoops me over his shoulder, hand coming up to palm my ass as he stalks back toward the nest.

Holding me in place with one hand wrapped around my thigh, while the other pops the button on his jeans. My whole body is vibrating with the force of his growl and my panties and stretch pants are soaked through. I expect him to toss me in the middle of the nest, but instead, he lays me down gently on the mattress. He peels off my pants and panties in one swoop, holding them up to his face for a moment, breathing me in.

"Gonna need to save those for Xan later, so he can smell what he missed out on." His growl distorts his voice so much that I can barely recognize it.

His fly is open, but his pants are caught on his hips as he stares down at me, a manic smile on his face. He peels his T-shirt off and I'm struck again by the amount of colors adorning his skin. I just want to trace over them, study them all. I want to draw him, but this isn't the time or the place.

He leans over me in the nest, almost menacing in his beauty. He grabs the front of my flannel and yanks it open. Buttons fly every which way, "Don't worry, I can fix that," he grumbles, crawling onto the mattress between my thighs. "My omega, mine!" he growls, the reverberations from his chest sounding nearly inhuman. He slides his pants down over his hips, shaking them off the side of the nest.

Oh, a Jacob's Ladder...I've never seen one in real life before. I mean, I've drawn them a lot, they're super popular with certain clients but wow...

It really is a thing of beauty, long with a slight curve on the end, the row of barbells starting just below the head, six down to end just before at the top of his swelling knot.

This is totally not the time to go off on an art tangent.

My thoughts scatter as he settles his weight between my legs, his hard length pressing against my thigh. "My omega." He nuzzles against my neck, licking and biting over my pulse point. "Need to bite you, keep you forever."

Each word is punctuated by a nip, a tiny pinch against my throat, and I can't stop my whine at the feel of his teeth on me, or how my hips are tilting and rolling, trying to get friction.

"Wait, Jacks. Stop." And he does—he freezes. I don't even feel his breath on me anymore. It's like someone hit pause on my alpha. "I just...I wanna wait on bonding, please. At least....at least until the rest of the guys are here too...maybe...maybe during my heat. Please don't be mad."

His breath shudders out, and he wraps his arms tight around my shoulders. "Of course I'm not mad, Little Lion. I'm not even disappointed. I just got carried away." He rubs his chin against my forehead. "Always tell me if something is wrong or if I make you uncomfortable, ok? Always. Don't stress yourself out to make anyone else happy, yeah?" His big warm body is pressing me against the nest, and I want him to keep going, but now I'm worried I lost the moment.

He looks into my eyes and rubs the wrinkle that's forming between my brows. "Hey now, none of that. I didn't mean to get so intense. Your scent drives me crazy, sorry." He kisses me on the nose and tries to pull away, but I don't let go.

"Jacks...um." I bite my lip, trying to figure out how to ask. "I don't want to stop. Please, I just don't want to be bonded right now. Sorry."

Fuck, I'm saying sorry too much again.

He looks skeptical, searching my face for any hint that I'm uncomfortable, but he won't find it. I want this. I want this *so much* I feel like I might combust right here if he doesn't kiss me again. Satisfied with what he sees, he does, and oh, it feels so good. I feel like I should thank Xan later for how good of a kisser Jacks is, and of course that thought sends another spiral of heat twisting into my core.

Jacks is rolling his hips against me, stroking against my inner thigh. He's over a foot taller than I am, so things aren't exactly going to line up right for kissing during sex, but I need him. I shimmy down the mattress, kissing his chin, my tongue tracing down the pulse line of his neck, biting and sucking on his skin. He tastes so good. I nip sharp teeth against his collarbones, and bury my face against his chest and whine.

"Please, Jacks, I need you inside me. Please." He raises up on his arms, his hips finally pressed even with mine.

"I think we need to scoot back...otherwise I am gonna slide right off this mattress." He gives me a self-deprecating grin. And yeah, I was trying to position right, but I don't have his long body to worry about.

He loops one arm around my waist and drags me up to the pillows at the head of the nest. "Besides, I wanna taste you properly first, Little Lion, make sure you're ready for me."

I could tell him that I am, but I am not about to turn down oral, plus the piercings make me a bit nervous, but he's gentle. Oh, so gentle. Kissing me softly, his lips barely brushing against mine, down my jaw and the column of my throat.

Chapter 31

Jacks

She's so soft, and she smells so fucking good. I wish I could just lick her all over, but she's so tiny next to all of us, and I don't want to hurt her.

I don't buy into the hype that all omegas are fragile flowers. Hell Janey used to hold me down and noogie me on a regular basis, but size-wise, they're just tiny.

Fuck, I wish she were here, so I could ask her for advice on omegas. I bet she'd love Candice.

This is not the time to be thinking about that. That rabbit hole is more like a bottomless pit.

My dandelion's eyes are a clear icy blue with green and gold flecks, her hair is down and curls and frizz spill over her shoulders. She looks like some sort of primal fertility goddess, and I should worship her, give her anything. Everything. Everything that I am, broken as it is. But Xan put me back together, sort of. I think I might still be missing pieces, but maybe my goddess can fill them in. Maybe she knows where all my splintered bits went.

I kiss her lips softly, a barely-there breath across her own, and down her jaw and neck. She jerks and giggles, my dandelion goddess is ticklish, and I smile against her skin, nipping my teeth against her collarbone to take away the tickle. Down across the stiff bud of her nipple, my tongue comes out to lavish attention on one, while my hand comes up to pluck and tease the other. Soon she's whining, soft and sweet, and the sound makes my cock so hard that I could hammer nails with it. Switching sides, I move to torture her other peak with my tongue, trailing my hand down her rounded stomach. She giggles again and I use my teeth on her nipple, turning the laugh into a gasp.

Lower still, a thatch of curls, so much heat, so wet. I slide my fingers up her seam and it comes away soaked. I kiss down, following the trail my fingers made before. Biting lightly where it tickled earlier, until I've nestled fully between her legs, pushing them up higher so I can access the source of that torturous scent.

Deep pink and glistening, my mouth waters at the sight. My cock hurts, trapped between me and the mattress. I need to thrust, but any friction will set me off right now, so I lean down and blow cool air across her swollen folds, and she jack-knifes up off the pillows, her hand reaching out to cradle my head. With only the strip of my hair down the center, it's not easy to snag on a whim. But as she settles back on the pillow, her body is tense with need. I lean in again and run my tongue up the center from core to clit-the titanium ball on my tongue ring flicking hard over her swollen nub. She jerks and shivers under my lips. Her flavor bursts across my tongue, nearly making me come before I can even get inside her.

Fuck. I need more.

Burying my face against her, I lick and suck up any moisture I find, thrusting first my tongue inside to reach it, then bringing my hand up and using two fingers to gather it up to lick. She tastes so fucking good. Like those goddamned cookies, but better, richer. My fingers plunging into her hot depth, making her shudder, and I've almost forgotten what I was doing down here. I've never done this, and I lost my head for a moment from her tastes and the scent surrounding me. Pumping my fingers into her a few more times, I'm gauging her reaction, and she bucks and shudders against me, so I must be on the right track.

Needing more of her flavor, I go back to licking, and when I flick against her clit, she jerks hard against me, grinding down against my face...so that's a good spot. I find a good rhythm with my fingers and my tongue, licking, pumping, circling. She is strung so tight, she's practically vibrating. Xan likes when I suck him, so I try here, wrapping my lips around her clit and sucking and rolling my tongue piercing over it at the same time, and she nearly levitates off the nest.

She cries out and I'm soaked in even more of her slick as her body convulses off the mattress. I keep sucking and flicking and thrusting until she shudders and lies still. Her breathing is heavy, but her body lies languid and relaxed as I crawl back over her. Leaving small smacking kisses up to her face, a soft brush over her lips. Her eyes are huge, pupils so big that only the dark ring around the edge of her iris is still visible.

"How was that, Little Lion?" I smile down at her. She cups my face and pulls me down for a kiss.

"I don't think my legs are gonna work anytime soon. Sorry." Why would she apologize for that, I'm proud that I did that. She feels so good now and it was all me.

"We don't have to do anything else if you don't want to."

Please, please goddess, I want to. I beg silently in my head.

"I wanna feel you inside me, Jacks, please? I mean, unless you don't want to. You already made me feel so good." I kiss the apology from her lips.

"I want this. I want this so fucking much. I've only been with Xan, so..." I trail off, unsure how to finish that sentence.

Please be patient with me?

I want to make you feel good?

Tell me if I do something wrong?

I love you, and I want you to stay with me forever?

That last one reeks of desperation, and I don't want to guilt her into staying with us.

"It's ok, Jacks, I want this...just...go slow. I've never...with the piercings...please."

I settle above her, keeping my weight on one elbow. I kiss her forehead before lining us up with my other hand. Fuck she is so warm and wet, and it takes everything I have not to thrust hard and sheath myself inside her.

But yes, slow, need to go slow.

Watching her face, I slip just inside. And fucking hell, it is like nothing I've felt before. I lock my body down to keep from thrusting or coming early. I have to take some deep breaths, as much for her to adjust as me to hold on. I slide in slowly and she is still so wet. It's tight, but there is no real resistance, just a smooth glide and the shifting of my barbells as they enter her.

With each one, her eyes go wider, until she looks shocked when I'm finally seated completely inside.

"Are you ok? Nothing hurting?" I ask, kissing her fore-head again.

"Yeah, yeah, that's just...Wow," she pants out.

I feel smug, but now I need to move. I can already feel her muscles twitching around me and I need to make her come again before I lose myself. My knot's already starting to swell at the base of my shaft, and I know I won't last long.

I roll my hips experimentally, pulling out almost com-pletely before sliding back in, and it causes her to whimper.

I can do better than that.

I roll again, pulling out slowly before slamming back in so hard her body scoots up the mattress, and that earns me a gasp and a moan. Alrighty then.

I wrap her legs around my hips, lifting her butt up off the blankets just a bit, and stuff one of the pillows under her ass. Now, with a little leverage, I pull out and snap my hips forward again to another long loud moan, and her muscles tighten around me.

Fuck, I am not gonna last long this way, but hopefully neither will she.

I repeat the motion, supporting my weight like a push-up, rolling out and then snapping forward, her cries get louder, and she starts mumbling and cursing with each following thrust. I can feel the sweat between my shoulder-blades, but I can't stop. I am so fucking close.

She moans and writhes beneath me, my dandelion goddess, looking more disheveled by the moment, and I can't hold back anymore. I balance on one arm, and reach down to flick over her clit like I did before with my tongue and suddenly she is squeezing me so fucking tight, I can barely move. My hips stutter, not sure what to do, as her hands scramble across my shoulders and chest, seeking purchase, pulling me closer.

"Knot, Jacks, please...I want your knot. Please Jacks."

And my body takes over before my brain fully registers, pushing forward against the resistance. She is still so slick, and that's the only reason I can force my knot inside, where it locks us together, and I come so hard I feel like all my energy drains away with it. So, not just a goddess, but a succubus.

I can think of worse ways to go.

Chapter 32

Gabe

Jacks took Candice home this afternoon. She collected the rest of her clothes, since we're not sure how long she'll be staying with us. It just feels right having her here, like some piece was missing, but now everything's how it's supposed to be. Her scent is already all over the house, and I can't help but smile watching her and my pack together.

She likes helping Jacks out in the kitchen. She says she does better at baking dessert stuff than dinner, but the way they bounce off of each other, or I guess don't bounce off of each other while both working in that small area makes no sense. They seem to just move around each other without saying anything, almost like a dance, and I like it.

Jacks and Xan have set her up in the spare room, right next to the nest, and while it works for now, I think we're gonna need to rearrange a few things, maybe move the nest downstairs, and convert the den. Not like we use it anyway. I never did understand the need for a den and a living room, but the house had it, and right now it is mostly just storage. I'll talk to the pack later tonight and get their ideas. I think it might be better for her heat since the room's bigger, and downstairs, closer to the kitchen, but not as secure as upstairs.

Even now I'm wondering if it's too soon to ask if she wants to move in here permanently. I can safely say that all of us want her here, but I don't wanna push her to do something that makes her uncomfortable, especially so soon after this shit with her house. All I want is for her to feel safe, and make sure she's comfortable here, but I fuckin' hate waiting.

Xan and Leo are cleaning up the kitchen now. Xan's already had six people contact him about the mechanic positions, so at least we have some place to start. I should probably go over the applicants with him tonight, but we spent a lot of time the last couple days doing catch up with Trey still out sick. This is the first time he's asked for time off since we hired him, so I don't feel comfortable saying no, but his timing could've been better.

All I want right now is to cuddle up on the couch with a sweet little omega in my lap until she falls asleep again, then carry her into the nest, and sleep for a full eight hours. Another point in favor of moving it downstairs, no fear of her tripping going up or down the stairs.

Why the hell did we buy a two-story house anyway?

If we have kids, that's something we will need to worry about too.

I wonder if the guys will be ok turning the old nest room into a nursery, or if we should consider Xan's idea of adding on.

What the hell is wrong with me? When did I start thinking about kids? Shit!

I shake my head to dislodge the wild thoughts that are swirling around in there. Better just go grab a shower for now, I can sort all this out tomorrow. Heading up the stairs, I pull my shirt off as I go. The sooner I can get under the hot water the sooner I can get these damned muscles in my neck to relax. I know Candice is safe here, but whoever the fuck is after her has a lot of pain coming their way if I get a hold of them.

I hear talking coming from the end of the hall, what used to be the guest room, and I walk that way, just a quick check in to make sure everything's ok. But when I pass the nest the door is wide open and hot damn...it smells like Candice, Jacks, and a lot of sex.

Smells like they weren't just busy going back to her old place today.

Fuck, smells like a fucking holiday coffee shop...and now I'm hard. Well, fuck.

Turning around, I can take care of this in the shower. There's no reason for her to feel awkward just 'cause I can't control how my body reacts to her, but I draw up short when I hear the voice break with a loud sob. I rush back to her room, I don't wanna intrude, but I need to make sure she's ok.

Looks like Jacks and Xan cleaned up as much as they could. Hell, those two probably already have a twelve-step fuckin' plan to get her to move in, starting with getting all her pictures fixed or replaced and hanging them up here.

When we were kids, Xan insisted on trying to teach me how to play chess. Unfortunately, his attempts included thinking seven steps ahead, bullshit was just confusing as hell. Nope, he and Jacks like to play it together, and Xan most often wins—but not always—and I think that's cause Jacks is a crazy fucker who never plans for anything and so Xan can't predict his moves. But I tried a few times, and I just can't think that way. I can't plan ahead like that.

Also got tired of the two of them handing me my ass when I tried to play. No real point in it if you lose every damned time.

Candice sits on the floor, beside a stack of torn and beat up old photos. Some of them are in decent shape. She seems to have them scattered around her on the floor in various piles, depending on how badly damaged they are. She's holding one to her chest, her head bent over it, big tears rolling down her cheeks, and before I know what's what, I am sitting behind her, arms around her, and pulling her into my lap. I've never purred before Candice, but now I can't seem to stop the one that rumbles out of me. It's not as smooth as Leo or Jacks, but her body softens against me despite all that.

"Shhhh, it's ok little omega. What's wrong? I bet we can fix it." Fuck, I don't know if I can fix anything but a car, but I damned sure aim to try. Anything to help her be happy again. Her sniffles slowly die down as I rock us both back and forth, holding her and rumbling like I need my muffler replaced.

"It's just...It's my grandpa, or his picture...and my parents' pictures. They're all I have to remember them by. I kept meaning to scan 'em in, make digital copies, you know...but stuff kept happening, and I never had time, and now..." She lets out a loud sob, shaking in my arms again.

"It's ok, sweet girl. It's ok. Shhh." I continue to rock, and rub my jaw along her hair, catching the fine strands in my stubble. "I can guarantee you that if Jacks and Xan don't know how to fix these already, then they'll figure it out right quick. They're the two smartest bastards I know. This is nothin' for 'em. Don't you worry, we're here now, ok?"

I wish I still had my shirt on, as she rubs her face against my chest...it feels hot and sticky in my chest hair and now I really need that shower.

But, hey, bonus, no more boner.

My involuntary shudder startles her and she pulls back. "Oh my god, I am so, so sorry. That is really gross." She stands up, pulling me up and trying to wipe my chest off with her sleeve.

"That's not really workin', but I sure do appreciate the effort." She sniffs loudly before she starts giggling.

"Fuck, that is so nasty. Let's get you cleaned up." She runs into her bathroom and turns on the shower to warm up, then brings back a handful of toilet paper that she tries to wipe me off with again. It works marginally better than her shirt.

"It's ok, sweet girl. Get yourself cleaned up and get a change of clothes on. I was headed for my own shower before I heard you anyway, so it's all good. Wash off, get into some comfy PJs, and meet me in the living room for a movie, alright?"

She sniffs again, but nods, takes her handful of tissue back to the bathroom, and closes the door behind her. I wipe at my chest without much success, and head back to my own room. After I get cleaned off, I'll talk to Xan about the applicants we got today, and about fixing these pictures for her.

Things'll settle down soon...hopefully.

Chapter 33

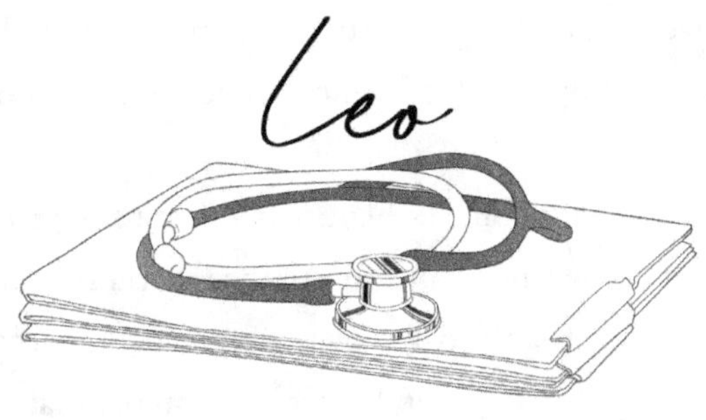

Jacks smells like my kitten, and while part of me wants to thrash him in jealousy, the other part just wants to stand in the kitchen and sniff him.

Yes, I realize I sound psychotic.

But my kitten makes me feel that way, out of control, lost from my normal sense of logic and structure. My own mind no longer makes sense when she's around. That's hardly a complaint. I'm enjoying every moment of the madness, however, I often feel out of sorts whereas before I felt...if not happy, at least content. Now I think about her constantly. I worried about her safety before she was staying with us. Now I know it was for a good reason.

Even before my kitten, I was a firm believer in the strength of the fairer sex. True, they had to work twice as hard to build muscles, but that is simple biology. Even I will readily admit that several of my female colleagues are more intelligent than myself, or at least they have more worldly experience and insight into our work. That may be partly due to my specializing in exotic animals as opposed to a general practice, but it holds true nevertheless.

Now, I just want to bundle her up in her nest and care for her, bringing her shiny things and sustenance. I still feel that most women are more than capable of taking care of anything that comes their way, but with her, I can't help this damnable primal urge to not let her do anything for herself, and it is beyond madness.

Logically, I know she's lived alone for the last three-plus years. I know she can feed and care for herself, but my fucking alpha isn't listening, and the feeling of being cleaved in two is disturbing, to say the least.

She arrives downstairs, looking simply delectable in a pink flannel nightgown, and I can't help but wonder what she has on under it. I was never a sex maniac before. I have enjoyed the company of women, mostly while I was in college, but I never felt like the raging pervert I feel I have become. Never felt the desire to be with anyone the way I want to be with her.

Getting off the couch, I walk over to her, wrapping her in my arms and just breathing her in. She is so tiny. Yes, she is an omega, and I understand that they are, as a rule, small. But I am also the tallest of our pack, and her head barely comes up to my nipples. Though I suppose even that would be useful for some things.

Dear God, what is wrong with me?

Bad alpha, stop being a pervert!

As I pull her close, my body relaxes, taking in that she is safe and among my pack, and no one will harm her within these walls. I would trust my packmates over anyone else in the world to protect our omega, but having her settled against me just lets me breathe easier. I lift her up, and she laughs as she reaches over my head to touch the ceiling fan when we pass it.

"Sorry, I need a ladder for everything. How does it feel to be so tall...this is so cool." She laughs in my arms, breast pressed against the side of my face as she flails her arms in the air. "Wow, if I could get a saddle made, I could just ride you around like a horse and look down on everybody." She slides down my chest, kissing my cheek in passing. I don't think she realizes the double meaning in her words, and I groan at the thought of her riding me anywhere.

I fold myself onto the couch, settling her into my lap so I can breathe in her heady scent. Jacks comes to sit on one side, rubbing his hand along her spine, while Xan sits on my other side and pulls her feet into his lap. We discuss movie options, I want something romantic, something I can enjoy with our omega cuddled in my lap, possibly Shakespeare in Love. Jacks and Xan groan at my suggestions, but agree wholeheartedly when the omega suggests a cartoon with a walking trash-heap,

Howl's Moving Castle. I haven't voluntarily watched a cartoon in years, but for her, I will try to pay attention. I may even enjoy it. I suppose there are romantic cartoons.

Twenty minutes into the film and I am pleasantly surprised that yes, they do make romantic cartoons. At least, I hope that's where this is going. Gabe finally makes it downstairs to join the rest of us, and sits in the chair beside Xan, talking quietly about applicants and work. I know he feels the need to rush everything along with Candice's heat coming up so soon, but I dislike when they talk about work at home, it means they don't relax, and if they don't relax, then Jacks won't relax, and if he won't relax, then I can't either because everyone around me will be keyed up and just...shit.

I'm working myself up over nothing. Take a deep breath of my kitten, yes, that's it.

My muscles relax and I turn my focus back to the television...where we have a talking fire. Strange, but ok. Candice is curled against my chest and my purr is a quiet rumble, lulling her to sleep. She blinks a few times, trying to stay awake, but after the stress of the last few days, I don't think it will be long before she is out for the evening.

I turn to Gabe. He shares my recent stress about her, my fear of what might happen when she is away from our protection. Now he's asking Xan something about photos. Ahh, it must be all the family photographs they retrieved from her house. I pet her hair, half-listening to their conversation. Gabe wants Xan and Jacks to look into photo restoration, since several of the damaged images were of her now deceased family. I pull her close to me, mentally dissecting the bastard that invaded her home and destroyed her sense of safety, and she lets out a weak grumble and thrashes lightly until I loosen my grip.

Of course Xan and Jacks will work on it, he says, but they should start calling in applicants tomorrow with her impending heat, or look at closing up the garage for the duration of it. I have rescheduled all of my appointments for the next two weeks, just in case. I have four coming in tomorrow, and then more on Friday. After that, I will work as needed and be on call to assist with providing time off for the doctors that have to cover my shifts while I am out.

My gaze wanders back to the television, and yes, as it turns out, this is a love story. I'll need to watch it again sometime then, with my kitten, but for now, I would rather get her to bed.

"Kitten, Kitten wake up. Do you want your nest or your bedroom?" I stroke her hair gently.

In truth, I would rather her go to her nest, so that I might snuggle with her there. Thus, I am not trying hard to wake her up. But I don't want to take away her choice if she would be more comfortable in the bedding that Jacks brought back from her home.

She burrows her face against my chest. "Leo," she murmurs, and my heart melts more at her gaining comfort from my scent. I guess that means we'll go to the nest again tonight.

Oh no, how awful.

I don't even try to hide my smile as I leave Xan and Gabe to their discussion. Jacks slides over to my now vacant spot, probably to discuss more about our omega's photos, as I slowly take the stairs, reveling in finally having time alone with her, even if it is just to sleep wrapped around her soft, warm body, and drift off to the sound of her breaths.

Chapter 34

Xan

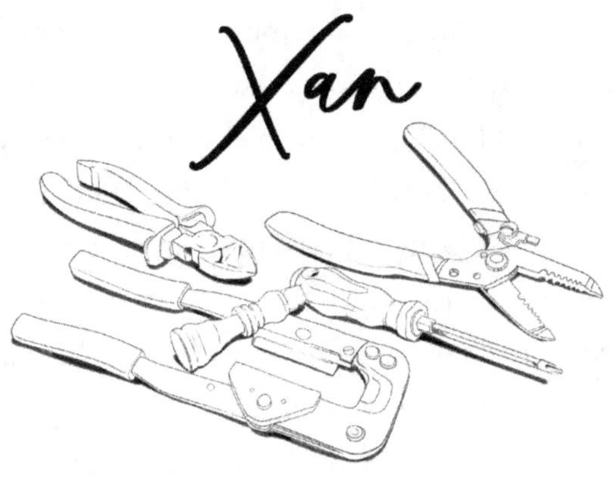

I've picked out the top three applications for the mechanic job to call in for interviews. Kelly has two more printed out that were sent in overnight. And I need to do some research on photo restoration during my break.

It's not that I mind dealing with the applicants. The garage is pack owned. That makes it is as much mine as Gabe's, but a lot of people tend to get bent out of shape if they talk to me, assuming I am just some sort of beta assistant. They insist on talking to the alpha in charge. Little do they understand, they're lucky to talk to me.

Gabe can be an asshole. I love him like a brother, but he doesn't deal with people well anymore. He feels protective of us and has a hard time letting anyone get close after what happened to Janey. It's like the man thinks he can seal us all in emotional bubble wrap if he doesn't let anyone get close. Now, give him an engine and the man is in heaven, make him have an actual discussion, and it's like pulling teeth from an angry alligator.

I don't bother looking at names on these applications, instead looking for education and experience. So it is a bit of a surprise when the first call I make, a woman answers. Normally, people give me their cell numbers, but this could be a landline. "Yes, this is Xan from Gabe's Garage. I need to speak to Sully Andrews." Rich deep laughter meets my request.

"Sally, Sally Andrews. How can I help you?" I stare at the phone for a moment, but what the hell.

"Yes, sorry, I got your application for the mechanic position and I was wondering if you had time to talk, or possibly time to come down to the shop for an interview?" I push on, looking at her resume again.

No, it shows she has the vocational certification for automotive work, as well as four years of experience in working in the tire and lube center of the big box store in Springfield. She is the most qualified, I'm just surprised.

"Yes sir, I can talk now, or if you want me to come in so we can meet in person, I can be there in about ten minutes." Her accent is fairly strong, but not so much that I have trouble understanding her. After working with Trey, this will be a delight.

"Thank you, yes, if you wouldn't mind coming into the shop so we can meet in person, and I can go over job duties, that would be great. We'll see you in about fifteen minutes. Thank you." At least this way I can get a better feel for how she'll work with our setup and how we operate.

Popping out to the garage to start on an oil change, I leave it to drain while I do this interview—then wander over to Gabe and tell him I am gonna need his help in the office for a few right at the thirteen-minute mark. If I tell him why, he'll just avoid it, so it's better to just surprise him and hope for the best. He won't agree, but that's a problem for future Xan. Current Xan has his hands full and will use underhanded tactics if he needs to.

The front door opens right as I'm leading Gabe back inside and a tall alpha woman walks in.

Oh, this is a surprise. Alpha females are nearly as rare as omega males. Not unheard of, just like winning the genetic lottery, it's rare for everything to line up just right for that. I wipe my hand off on my coveralls. "Hi, Sally Andrews?"

She takes my hand, she's close to my own six feet tall, and gives me a firm handshake.

"Yes sir, that's me." I give her my version of a professional smile, easygoing; no teeth, and try to relax my shoulders.

People tend to be more honest and straightforward if you give off the impression of being laid-back. I've been cultivating that outward appearance for most of my life to put other people at ease. Jacks often accuses me of being a people pleaser, but really, it's just a way to make my life easier.

"Good to meet'cha Sally. This here is Gabe, he's the boss, but I'll be doing your interview today. Sound good?" Gabe offers her his hand briefly, growls at me, and then stomps back out to the shop. "Yeah, he isn't really a people person," I say, watching him go. When I turn back to Sally, she's just looking at me.

"Can't really say I blame him there. I'm not exactly a people person myself. That's actually why I became a mechanic. I don't have to talk to many people, and if the thing I'm working on gives me too much trouble, I can smack it with a wrench." She smiles pleasantly, and I'm not sure if she's joking or not.

"Nah, I can relate." I chuckle. "Now moving on, this is Kelly. She works the front desk." Sally sticks her hand out and Kelly blushes when she shakes it.

Interesting, have to file that away for later.

"Kelly works here in the mornings, she helps us keep up with office stuff, 'cause Gabe also hates dealing with paperwork." Kelly blushes more, and suddenly finds something on her computer intensely interesting.

I show Sally the main office and explain various rules and policies, including the no phone at work rule, and the lockbox we all put them in, then out into the garage. Not everyone gets upset about the lack of a cell, but we've had a few people who refused, so better to get it out of the way now.

"As you can see, we have three regular bays. We do sometimes work around back behind the shop, but that's super rare so don't even worry about it. Normally it's Gabe and Trey here full time, and I work when they need me, but we've had some family stuff come up lately, and have been leaving poor Trey alone way too much. I'm hoping we can get a couple people in here full time so that neither of us *has* to be here if we have another emergency."

We walk around as I tell her about the layout. I point out the supplies, the bay features, and watch for any signs of discomfort or confusion. She seems perfectly at ease, and nothing she does rings any alarm bells. Her scent, a mild woody pine registers as relaxed with a few spikes of anticipation when I show her a couple of our tool stations. The biggest spikes are when I show her the pneumatic drills. They're Gabe's pride and joy that he splurged on when we opened the shop since they are *The Best*—so maybe they can bond over power tools.

I ask if she has any questions, and thank her for her time, before going to tell Gabe that we should hire her. He grumbles a bit, then I tell him she was super excited about his drills and he cedes that she'll probably be fine. I make a quick check with Kelly to ask the same—she's still blushing—but seems cool with it.

Marking off one new hire, I'll need to call her and let her know after I check into these other two applicants. The first doesn't answer his phone, and the next immediately starts trying to negotiate pay. His resume goes into the shredder. I collect the remaining ones I weeded out before, as well as the new ones from Kelly, to go over on my break so I can call Sally back to offer her the job.

Going into the garage to finish up the oil change I was working on, I'm relieved that at least one of our problems is halfway to being resolved. The morning keeps me busy, but I finish another three oil changes and two tire rotations, pick out another two applicants to call in, and leave a message for Sally asking when she can start. Then I tell Gabe I am taking off for lunch. If I stop by the house, I bet I can get a sandwich from Jacks. Maybe if I play my cards right, we can make a sandwich out of Candice.

Chapter 35

Candice

Xan is in a good mood. I can't take all the credit for that. Apparently, after he came home for lunch with Jacks and me, he went back to the garage and got two more interviews set up. He also called in a glass company to get my back door fixed, and I'll need to be there most of Monday for the install. He says he just enjoys getting shit done, and I can relate to that.

I'm a little worried though. He and Leo and Gabe have all alluded to needing to sit down and have a long talk about Jacks and his sister. I know they want to discuss it before we go too much farther in our relationship, and that makes sense. In truth, I want to know more about all of them, but they're worried this might be a deal-breaker for all of us. Which is ironic since Jacks is the only one I'm completely comfortable with. It's Friday, so hopefully this weekend we can get everything sorted out.

While part of me wants to reassure them that no matter what the problem is, it'll be fine. I know deep down that isn't true...sometimes things aren't fine. Sometimes, no matter how hard you try, things turn out bad. Sometimes happily ever after is just bullshit.

And now I'm just depressing myself.

Do I not want to offer reassurance because of anxiety?

I can think of at least three different scenarios where things aren't going to be fine.

Four...six if I dwell on it.

What if he is really sick, like, has some kind of horrible disease and is gonna die...oh fuck, I can't lose him now, I need him.

STOP.

Take some deep breaths. Count of four in...and out.

I need to go find Jacks now and get a hug.

I unfold my legs and stretch. I've been sitting on the floor in my temporary room, sorting through sketchbook pages. I can't express how much I appreciate Jacks and Xan doing all this for me. But like I told them, I know the stuff better than anyone, so I'll need to be the one to sort through it all for where to put it. I might be able to trim some torn edges and put things in sheet protectors and a binder, or clean up and tip the pages back into the book...but first things first with sorting, then after my heat I'll have plenty of time to take care of the rest of it.

Stretching my back and shoulders, I stand up and pad out into the hall and towards the stairs. I know I lose track of time when I'm working, but I'm still surprised to see how dark it is outside the window. My stomach lets out a loud rumble, and I realize I haven't eaten since after Xan went back from lunch.

Jacks jumps off the couch and wraps me in a hug as soon as I reach the bottom of the stairs.

"Are you ok? Did I do something wrong? Did one of them do something wrong? Are you pissed at us?" My mind spins with the rapid-fire questions, and I bury my face against his neck, breathing him in to ground myself.

"No, sorry, I just got hungry and figured I should come see if dinner was ready." Jacks and Xan exchange a look over my head, before Xan sandwiches me between them in another tight hug.

"Sorry love, I came by twice to tell you about dinner, and Jacks stopped in once...we just figure you were mad at us...sorry if we were too rough earlier." He kisses my forehead and then leans over me to kiss Jacks too.

"Oh, shit...sorry. I don't even remember you guys stopping in. I was just super focused." I reach both my hands up to pull their faces down. "And I really enjoyed what we did earlier, like, a lot, so please don't apologize. You apologize too much already."

Hello Kettle, this is the Pot calling, you're black.

My stomach takes this time to give out another loud grumble and Jacks squeezes me tighter for a moment before letting go and heading toward the kitchen.

"I made you a plate, and put it in the oven, so it's still warm. And it's not lasagna, so it should be fine," he says, looking pointedly at Gabe, who's still sitting on the couch. Jacks carries a plate out to the dining area for me and sets it down.

Not gonna lie, having a guy who can cook this well, and does so, for me, regularly—they are going to have to roll me out of this house if I don't start exercising again soon.

I dig into a big slice of shepherd's pie, and it's so good. Xan heads back to the living room and sits down beside Gabe again, resuming whatever discussion I interrupted. Jacks seems intent on hovering until Leo comes over and tells him to sit down. He watches me intently as I finish dinner, offering me seconds, a drink, or dessert. All of which I decline. I glance over at the clock, and notice that it is already 7:30. I must have been really focused to have zoned out through them trying to call me down for dinner three times.

I let Jacks lead me over to the second couch and pull me into his lap, where he starts purring for me, and all I really want to do is curl against him and sleep. With my heat getting closer I get hungrier and my body is tired more often. But if we need to have *The Talk* before it hits, then we should do it now.

"Hey, Gabe," I say, trying to pull out of Jacks's snuggles. "The shop's closed tomorrow, yeah?" It isn't really a question I need answered. I know they're closed tomorrow, but my mind is whirling with how to start this discussion, and I know I'm stalling.

"Xan and I were thinking of going in, just to do some cleanup, and get organized for having to be out part of next week for your heat. Why?"

Well, shit, there goes my knowing the answer.

"Oh, well, um, you said before we go through my heat we should talk to each other a little bit more about backgrounds...how you guys became a pack, how I started living with my grandpa, stuff like that. And I wondered if you wanted to do that tonight, or this weekend...or...sorry, I'm not great at talking about myself." I feel like my ears are on fire as I bury my face in Jacks's chest, but he's suddenly stiff underneath me.

I swallow thickly, pulling away, suddenly worried I've said something wrong, as I climb off his lap and settle in at the other end of the couch. He puts his hand towards me and my stomach sinks when he suddenly lets it drop and stares intently over at Leo and Gabe.

Fuck...and I ruined the mood! Good job!

"U-Unless you d-don't want to. I...I didn't mean to pry. It's just come up a few times, and with my heat next week, I just thought..." I trail off, nausea threatening to make the shepherd's pie a return performance.

Xan comes to sit between us, turning to pull Jacks into a hug, and rocking him back and forth.

I hear murmurs and then Jacks, a little louder. "No, no, she needs to know, right? It wouldn't be fair for her to get any deeper with my broken ass without knowing. But I...I can't. Okay? I'm just...I'm gonna go."

Xan is still wrapped around Jacks's bigger body, but Jacks is standing, up pulling him with him as he makes for the stairs. A fat tear rolling down his cheek. Xan finally lets him go, but watches him walk upstairs and turn towards their shared room. I don't hear the door close.

"I'm gonna go check on him, y'all can start without me," he says before plodding after his mate.

Leo comes to squat in front of me, and takes both my hands, looking into my eyes. Even crouched down, he's still taller than I am sitting on the couch. I'm eye level with his chin right now, so I think this is as close as we're going to get unless he sits flat on the floor, and I don't see the fastidious veterinarian doing that.

"It's not your fault, you know," he tells me, leaning down to kiss my forehead before sitting on the couch beside me, pulling me sideways into his lap, and wrapping his arms around me. Gabe watches us for a moment before he too comes over and sits beside Leo, behind me. He touches my shoulder, offering silent comfort before Leo continues.

"We moved to Shreveport when I was thirteen, and Gabe was in my class..."

Chapter 36

Candice

I didn't realize that big tears were running down my cheeks as Leo finished talking.

My poor broken boy.

What the actual fuck.

"What happened to that bastard, the one who..." I trail off, I can't finish.

Gabe speaks up behind me, hand still running up and down my spine. "He went to jail for a while. But he was young, and his parents argued that one *mistake* shouldn't ruin his life. He was an alpha with a lot of promise, an athletic scholarship for college."

His hand stops rubbing, and I can feel the tension in his arm where it rests against me.

"He got out after a couple of years. Though, I'm honestly surprised that they convicted him at all. Fucking bullshit that he got off with a slap on the wrist after..." His choked sob makes me jump, and Leo continues, "Janey was basically an older sister to all of us. Gabe grew up next to her, and Jacks and Xan were friends for years before I even moved to the area."

I'm aghast. "So that bastard is just running around free now, like nothing happened?" I stare up into Leo's pinched face.

"No, he died about six months after he got out of prison." I jump; I didn't realize Xan had come back. He's leaning on the banister at the foot of the stairs.

Gabe's head snaps up. "What? Why didn't I hear about that? What the fuck happened?"

"Car accident." Xan looks indifferent about the subject, staring up the stairs, towards their bedroom.

"Brakes..." he mutters, then clears his voice to speak a bit louder. "His brakes failed. He shouldn't have been driving at night, not after he'd been drinking, and certainly not with his depth perception issues." His dead stare swings back to Leo and his head tilts to the side as they lock eyes.

Gabe grunts behind me. "So, Little Omega, now you know. Jacks is kind of...broken. After everything went down, he turned inward. He eventually got his GED and did online school for computer programming. Not that he needed it, but it was a good springboard for him to learn more. He doesn't really leave the house." There was a long pause. I try to crane my neck to see him. "Well, until you. He gets in a mood every so often, twitchy and out of sorts, and Xan will take him in for a tattoo or a piercing."

I turn again to Xan, feeling like my head's on a swivel, but he's walking towards us, stopping behind the couch. He leans around Leo and rubs his jaw over the top of my head. "He says when he gets a tattoo or a piercing, the pain helps him feel."

I barely recognize my own voice. "Feel what?"

"Just...feel." Xan has finally lost that emptiness to his eyes, but the broken look that's replaced it isn't any better.

I take his hand and drag him around to the front of the couch to sit beside Leo. His legs unhinge and he collapses onto the cushion by my feet, his head falling into his hands. We all sit quietly, each of us deep in our own heads.

Finally, Xan scrubs his face a few times and raises his head, looking directly into my eyes. The intensity is unnerving.

"Bottom line, Pretty Lady, Jacks is broken, he wasn't exactly *normal* before this." He uses air quotes around normal. "But ever since Janey died, he's gotten worse. He takes care of us because he can't take care of himself. He's under some kind of fucked up belief that he owes us something because we were there for him after what happened, when his own family wasn't. He doesn't owe us shit. We all love him...Not like that, you perv." The corners of his mouth tip up in a smirk as he looks at me, but I know he's just trying to lighten the mood.

Leo strokes my hair. "As Janey was like an older sister to us, so Jacks is the baby brother that neither Gabe nor I had. His family fell apart when she died, and we were there to pick up the pieces." Gabe's hand starts its slow trek along my spine again. "That's why we needed to tell you love, we need you to understan' that Jacks is part of us. He may be broken, but I think it's pretty damned obvious to everyone how much he loves you already. And while we all want you here, he needs you. It's just gonna get worse the longer you're around. And if he helps you through your heat...well, it'd kill him if you found out about all this afterwards and left."

I'm struck dumb for a moment...too surprised to react appropriately.

"Ok, what the actual fuck?" I slide out of Leo's arms, brushing away Gabe's hand, and turn to stare hard at the three alphas sitting on the couch. "You actually fucking think I would do that? Fucking seriously?"

I start pacing, needing to move. "I know we haven't known each other that long...but fuck *me* guys."

I am breathing heavily and spots dance across my vision. I'm so livid my stupid accent has come out to play and it makes me even angrier.

Fuck, gotta calm down.

"Nice to know you have such a high opinion of me fellas. I care about Jacks. A lot...and while I will fully admit that *how* much I care about him already kind of scares the shit out of me...I just...Fuck...Really?!"

If looks could kill, I would be surrounded by dead alphas. "You seriously think I could do that? Leave Jacks just because someone fucked up his life?"

I turn to Xan. "You think I would leave him because he's not *normal*?" I mimic his earlier air quotes.

"'Cause let's be honest, y'all aren't exactly looking at the textbook normal omega. I'm squishy. I live alone—which is super illegal. I draw porn for a living. Let's not forget the depression, crippling social anxiety, and an aversion to physical contact." I check each statement off on my fingers, staring into the eyes of a different alpha with each one.

"I would list my dark and disturbing sense of humor as well as my penchant for severely outdated music and antique cars as other down sides, but considering who I'm talking to, I don't think those things are gonna be a problem." My eyes jump from Xan to Leo to Gabe, daring any of them to challenge me.

Gabe looks like I slapped him, Leo is staring at his hands in his lap, and Xan is just grinning at me. I take a deep breath, trying to stabilize my scattered thoughts and harsh breathing.

"If that's really all the confidence you have in me, then I'm out." I walk towards the stairs, trying not to cry.

I hate angry crying. I can camp here overnight, and then head back tomorrow. Hell, if Xan and Gabe are gonna be gone, maybe I can get Jacks to help me move my stuff over. I don't want him to choose between his pack and me...but fuck these guys.

I skip the nest and go straight to *my* bedroom, and like the calm fucking mature adult I am, I don't slam the door. I do, however, pull all of *my* nesting material over into the corner on the far side of the bed, as far from the door as I can get, before I curl up into it and cry myself to sleep.

I wake up sometime later, and the room is dark. Strong arms are wrapped around me and I recognize the coffee and cinnamon scent that is Jacks—the only alpha in this house I'm not pissed at. I drift back to sleep to the sound of his purr and the feel of its deep vibrations against my back.

Chapter 37

Gabe

Last night was a colossal fuck-up. I know words aren't my strong point, but fuck, there has to be a way I could have handled that better. I dragged Xan into the garage this morning at the ass-crack of dawn because neither of us were getting any sleep. We might as well do something constructive. Not that we need to worry about taking time off for Candice's heat now, unless we can convince her that we don't think badly of her...we just suck at explaining shit.

Xan is on his sixth cup of coffee as he sorts through the filing cabinet. He hates non-digital files and is updating our database with anyone not currently in it, backing up all the data onto a second hard drive, and a cloud...whatever that means. Scanning it, just to make sure we have a copy, and then shredding the original. The front desk is covered in little diamonds of shredded paper from his self-imposed punishment.

Meanwhile, I'm cleaning...I had to go get more degreaser, and cleaner with bleach, but the back office is now spotless, and the smell will burn out all your nose hairs. I'm about to head into the garage to start cleaning and organizing tools when the front door opens and Leo walks in, collapsing into one of the office chairs. Xan turns to look at me, eyebrows raised.

"Jacks refused to let me in the kitchen or make breakfast, and he called me an asshole. Then he hid the keys to the Jeep, so I had to walk to the diner for breakfast," Leo grumbles, causing Xan to snort laughter, sending tiny shreds of paper all over the floor—that I just cleaned.

"Fine, you can hang out here if you want to, but you're gonna have to clean too." I hand Leo the broom and dustpan, as well as the bleach spray and point him towards the waiting room.

"Lemme know if somethin' doesn't make sense," I call over my shoulder.

Leo sputters incoherently, finally wailing, "But I'm just terrible at talking about emotion." He turns quickly, pointing between Xan and me. "See. See. This is why I told the story. I can tell stories, even depressing ones. You want facts? I can do facts. You want hard data? I can do that too...I can even do an amusing anecdote about the incontinence issues of a fifteen-year-old Chihuahua. But I can't fucking talk about entangling emotional issues. So I told the story, and you two were supposed to do the explanation for our concern...but you didn't!" His shoulders are drooping and he looks panicked.

"Don't think I didn't notice how you conveniently left out your part in *that motherfuck's depth perception issues* when you told the story," Xan snarks back, returning Leo's glare.

Leo puffs up. "Oh, my part? My part, Mr. Brakelines? Really!" Leo is vibrating with anger at this point, stalking back towards the counter.

Xan just shrugs. "I didn't cut anybody's brake lines. What kind of idiot do you think I am? That would get noticed. You don't really need to anyway, just loosen the caliper a bit...just like draining the fluid on a break job. Every time the car stops...you lose a little more fluid...loosen it enough and you lose a lot. If he had been paying attention, and not drunk off his ass, he would have noticed they were feeling a bit...squishy." Xan goes back to shredding papers while Leo and I gape at him like idiots.

Finally, nothing more to say, Leo turns, and the good doctor shuffles towards the waiting room, cleaning supplies in hand.

We work until almost 5:30 without taking a break. I dread going home to an upset omega and her occasionally violent protector. Leo goes and collapses in the truck while Xan and I lock up and turn on the security system. I wonder if Jacks will still be pissed off enough not to cook...or if we should try to go by the diner to grab dinner.

"Hey, Jacks is probably least mad at you. Can you message him and ask if he wants us to grab dinner on the way home?" I ask Xan while we wait for the keypad to stop beeping, confirming that the system is armed.

"I don't know man, he has higher expectations from me, so I think he is gonna be even madder. Maybe you should do it. You *are* pack lead after all." I groan, knowing he's right. I rarely give orders or have to use dominance, since our house is so chill, but if Jacks will listen to anybody right now other than Candice, it's me.

I pull out my phone and see a text message received twenty minutes ago from Jacks, asking me to pick up an order he called in to the Chinese place on the other side of town. I often forget that he can feel Xan through their pack bond, and I should really stop being surprised when he makes plans around our schedule, despite not being with us.

Firing off a quick affirmative, I ask if he needs anything else. I consider asking how Candice is doing, but if he *is* talking to me, I don't want to rock the boat. Once I'm in the cab and behind the wheel, I let Xan know we need to stop and grab the dinner Jacks ordered, and he just smiles vaguely to himself. Leo is mumbling complaints in the backseat about fickle love-struck alphas and food. That man takes his eating seriously. Guess that much height requires regular feeding.

I pull into the parking lot at the strip mall and Xan goes in to get the pickup. He comes back carrying seven takeout boxes and I wonder briefly at the amount, but decide that is a problem for later. Soon he has everything passed off to Leo, who is sniffing at the boxes amongst continued grumbling.

Home is just a few minutes away, and when we get there, we each take a couple of boxes in, with Leo taking three, one of which he insists is his.

"Whatever man, your funeral if you don't give it over to Jacks." Leo grumbles all the way to the door, but sets all the cartons on the bar top when we get inside.

Candice is nowhere to be seen, but Jacks wraps his arms around Xan.

"I love you, but you suck at talking to people," he croons in Xan's ear, but loud enough for all of us. "Still, I appreciate it...I know you've been super frustrated all day...remember?" He rubs his face along the inside of Xan's neck, over their bonding bite.

"And I talked to Candice. She is...upset"—he turns a flat look at both Leo and me—"that the three of you would think she was shallow enough not to care about me just because I have...issues."

"Now wait just a minute!" Leo starts before Jacks's stare turns hard. "We just...we want her here, but you're family. We were just trying to make sure she had all the facts...fuck, I can't get my fucking words right." Jacks reaches up and slaps him lightly on the cheek.

"Yeah, big man, you suck at this." He turns towards the kitchen, leaving us all watching him from the other side of the bar.

"Luckily for you, I am *much* better at talking, and I know from how messed up Xan has been all day that you guys are just really terrible at saying what you mean. So, while you spent your Saturday cleaning..." He pauses long enough to eyeball each one of us, and then pinches his nose. "*I* was convincing our omega not to leave all your asses behind, and just keep me. You're welcome...now go take a shower, you stink. I'll finish dinner and wake up my Little Lion." As he talks, he starts shifting the takeout boxes around, taking down plates, and pulling out silverware. He gives one more parting glare before heading into the pantry to fill the rice maker pot, effectively dismissing the lot of us.

I turn to plod up the stairs, thankful that Xan talked us into doing a tankless water heater when we replaced the old one, but also dreading the lack of pressure from three of us showering at once. Ahh well...maybe we can add in a second one if Candice decides not to leave, and put in a bigger tub in the downstairs bathroom.

If we didn't fuck this up too much.
Girls like bubble baths, right?

Chapter 38

I wake up with Jacks's hand stroking my hair.

"Hey, Little Lion, you ready for some dinner?" he says, kissing me on the forehead.

Ugh, the pre-heat exhaustion is hitting harder than normal, and I wonder if it's because I'm around so many alphas—as opposed to my usual solitary existence. Whatever it is, it's kicking my ass, hard.

I lean into Jacks's warm hand, just enjoying how good it feels to touch him, before stretching my back and arms, trying to get my back to pop. I've been so used to sitting at a desk for most of the day and having scheduled times to make myself get up and move around that it's harder to acclimate to not being on a schedule. Add in the extra hours I'm sleeping this week, and I feel stiff and uncomfortable in my own skin.

"So, do you prefer steamed or fried rice?" Normally conversations with Jacks flow pretty easily from one topic to another, so this random question stops me short and I actually have to think about it.

"Um...probably steamed. It kind of depends on how it's cooked, I guess. I've had some really good fried rice, but it can be kind of heavy and greasy at times."

"Fair enough," he says, taking my hands and pulling me up from the bed. "I made steamed, but I ordered two cartons of fried, and I know that's the go-to for Gabe and Xan, but there should still be plenty...or they can just not have any if you want it all." He smiles at me, tugging me against his chest. He has been really clingy since we woke up this morning, and I don't hate it.

We had a long talk while the guys were all gone. He said Xan has been miserable since last night, and he finally left their bedroom when he wouldn't stop tossing and turning. But if he had known how upset I was, he would have been here sooner. I don't give a shit what the others say about him being normal. At least he can talk to me about feelings, and make sure I understand instead of just accusing me of things.

He told me they weren't *trying* to accuse me of anything, and that they pretty much all have the emotional intelligence of a rock. He asked that I give them another chance—at least to explain themselves better. But also, that he's mine, for as long as I'll have him, and they can all fuck off if they don't apologize properly.

The irony of his threatening to leave them—because of how they think I might react to him—isn't lost on me. In truth, I don't want to go anywhere. I like being with these alphas. Not just for sex, though that is so much more than I ever could have imagined, but just being around them.

When we're together, I don't feel as anxious—and while my depression can rear its ugly head at any time, I'm hoping it will also improve with soothing interaction. I love Iggy, but she's not great at holding a conversation. And I miss Sunny. Even his horrible cat breath yawns.

If I start down this path there will be a lot of tears, so it's better to stop now. I don't want to be weepy when I have to deal with the rest of the pack. I need to have my head on straight and my mind open. I want Jacks, and if he happens to come with some emotionally constipated packmates, well, we need to work on that.

Still in my pajamas, I go downstairs. Jacks is setting out food, some of it on serving platters, other items still in the takeout foam. I haven't had Chinese in a few years; it's always hard to order for just one person.

After he's done, he leads me over to the head of the table—Gabe's usual spot—and insists I sit there, sitting himself beside me. I hate being in the spotlight, and it feels even more awkward a few minutes later when Gabe comes downstairs in his pajama pants and tank top. He stares at me for a minute before moving one of the other chairs to the opposite end of the table. But of course, Jacks put all the food at our end, just out of reach of Gabe's new spot.

I don't want to be a part of whatever power play is going on here, so I try to leave, but Jacks just puts his hand on my shoulder, gently, but firmly keeping me in my chair, and glaring at Gabe. The two alphas are still locked in a battle of wills when Xan and then Leo come downstairs and join us at the table—Leo on my left side, and Xan beside Jacks.

No one reaches for food, no one moves, no one says anything other than Gabe's grumbling. He never even looks at me, just staring intently at Jacks. After a few minutes of uncomfortable silence, Jacks breaks eye contact, fills a plate for me, and sits it in front of me, prompting Xan and Leo to fill their own plates.

Leo looks longingly at all of the crab rangoons that Jacks has piled on my plate...I don't want the damned things...whoever thought cream cheese and crab was a great taste sensation clearly had defective taste buds, but Jacks loads me down and I have to wonder if this is supposed to be a punishment for me or the alphas.

I eat a few bites of the steamed rice and choke down a piece of sweet and sour chicken before Gabe gets up, glaring at Jacks, and moves to Leo's other side. Leo is stealing glances at my plate as he finishes off a giant pile of steamed rice, two servings of General Tso's Chicken, and three spring rolls. He continues staring at my plate while reaching for the container with the orange chicken. I sigh, not really feeling up to eating with all this tension, and push my plate towards him.

"I don't really like those. I mean, I can eat 'em, but you are more than welcome to them if you like."

He reaches over, taking all six off my plate. I am not sure how Jacks thought I could eat that many, anyway. Leo offers one to Xan, who shakes his head, and then puts two on Gabe's plate before crunching down on the rest himself.

"Sorry," he mumbles after he bolts down the first two. "When I was little, my mom used to make these each year for my birthday. They're one of my favorites, and the Jade Dragon has a recipe that's very similar to hers." He dips another one into the sweet and sour sauce before taking the whole thing in one bite.

I turn to glare at Jacks. "So, are you trying to make me uncomfortable, or is that just a bonus to whatever the fuck you're doing to them?" Jacks at least has the wherewithal to look sheepish.

"I just need them to understand that you are the most important. You come before Gabe, or Leo, or even Xan...sorry you know I love you." He adds the last part, leaning back in his chair and looking at this bonded mate.

"Nah, man, I get it," Xan says, rubbing his shoulder. "Just next time try not to give Leo an aneurysm, ok?" He kisses Jacks on the cheek and goes back to eating.

Gabe wipes his mouth and then lays his napkin beside his plate. "Ok. So I guess we're doin' this now then?"

He looks between me and Jacks a few times. "Listen, we suck, alright. None of us can talk about emotions for shit, ok? I admit, I should have handled that better, but I think there was some confusion on who was supposed to be the best one to actually express our feelings...and then we all did a fucking lousy job."

He pushes his chair back and starts to stand up before giving up and sitting down again, elbows on the table and head in hands.

"Ok, let's try this again. We care about you, a lot...all of us. We want to bond you and want you to be part of this pack if you want the same thing. But, we also want you to come into it fully informed that we all have problems. We're not perfect, and it's not just Jacks. Leo left a few parts out that don't paint him in the best light, and I'm sure you've probably guessed a few things from what Xan added that we are all sorts of fucked up. But we want you; we want you to stay with us. But only if you want to, and before you can make an informed decision, you needed all the information, or at least the important parts." He trails off, his head still in his hands, staring intently at the table.

I stand up and walk over to him, draping over his back and hugging him from behind.

"Ok then, fair's fair. You guys finish eating, and I am gonna go get cleaned up. When I get back, we can talk some more." I turn to Jacks. "Was this really necessary? Save me some of the sweet and sour chicken, and General Tso's, unless Leo already ate it all."

Leo looks abashed as he stares down at his plate. And I head upstairs to get a hot shower and think about how to explain the three weeks I lost when I was nine, and how I went to live with Grandpa.

Chapter 39

Candice

*U*p until I was nine, I lived with my mom and dads, two alphas and a beta. I don't know if I ever knew which one I was biologically related to, they were all just Dad. We were heading home from visiting Grandpa. He was Mom's dad. The last one. Grandma had passed away when I was four, so I don't remember much about her, but my Grandpas were dying out as well. It's hard to keep a pack together after they lose their omega.

I don't remember much. I had been playing with Mom and Grandpa and was super tired; I think I fell asleep in the car.

Arms tighten around me, Mom and gray-eyed Dad holding me tightly in the back seat, a loud scream and the arms squeeze so tight I can't breathe. A flash of light and everything slams forward, a jarring pain, then nothing.

Loud beeping wakes me up, and I squint through sore eyes. I don't know this room, with its scratchy white sheets. The air smells funny and itches my nose. My left arm burns like it is on fire, but when I reach over to touch it wires and tubes that are wrapped around my scrawny right wrist pull tight. Needles stuck in the back of my hands, taped in place. Where is everybody? I can't see or smell Mom or Dads.

I startle fully alert, panic constricting my lungs. The door opens and finally; I see a familiar face. Grandpa, the one we were just visiting. He crosses the room on shuffling steps. He looks older than he did a couple of hours ago.

Has it only been a couple of hours?

My head hurts.

I want to go home.

Where are my parents?

"Hey, little bit, looks like you're gonna be staying with me for a while. That ok?"

I don't want to stay with him. I want to go home.

I stare at him, my throat too dry to offer any more reply than a frog croak. He hands me a cup of water and a straw and I take several small pulls, the cold water stinging my mouth.

"What about Mom? I want to go home with them." Grandpa's shoulders start to shake and his head drops. A tear hits the white blanket, a startling spot on the otherwise blank white fabric.

"Yeah, little bit, they can't come home with us. Your mom and dads are gonna go stay with Grandma." He chokes on the last bit. "It's just us now, but we can do this, right, Girly?"

I remember vaguely that he calls Mom that sometimes. I nod limply, not sure what other response I can give. I feel like my mind is spiraling out of control and I want to shut it off, to go back to sleep.

I burst into tears, and Grandpa finally hugs me, crying quietly along beside my braying sobs.

After several minutes, he pulls away, unsure how to comfort me further. I love Grandpa, and we visit at least once a month, but this isn't the same. I'm still sniffling when the nurse returns. She talks quietly to him, but I don't care to listen to what they're saying. None of it matters, not really.

She finally makes her way over to me and tells me I'll feel better when I wake up. She puts a needle into one of the tubes plugged into the back of my hand, and my eyes are too heavy to keep open. Everything goes black.

S ix days later, I'm finally out of the hospital, cast on my arm, head fine other than a big bump. Grandpa says we have to go home, which finally pulls a smile from me. I miss home.

Maybe Mom and Dads are there, says a small dark voice in the back of my mind. I know it's lying. If they were there, if they were ok, they would be with me now. But still, a part of me hopes.

Grandpa gets me checked out of the hospital and we make our way out to his old station wagon in the parking lot so he can drive us home. I always thought his car was silly, with funny wooden panels down the sides, but it doesn't even draw out a smile now.

I'm not sure how long the trip lasts, I don't know how far away the hospital is, just that the tiny voice keeps whispering louder that everything will be ok when we get home, everything will be just like it was. Part of me wants to believe it so much that when we finally get to the house, my tiny hope dies at the moving van and large men moving our furniture out into it.

"Grampa? What are they doing?" I look over at the old man, my only family left.

"I am sorry, little bit, but without your parents here...well, we can't keep their house and ours. Mine is all paid off. So, this one is gonna get sold. But these nice men are making sure all your parent's stuff is kept safe. We're gonna get them to help us load up your important things, and...and..." He trails off, his eyes brimming with tears again. Does he miss Mom too?

Suddenly he slaps his thigh. "You know, after this, we're gonna go to the shelter. Every little girl needs a kitten, right?" The change in subject seems abrupt but has the desired effect of distracting me.

"I've never had a kitten. Do I get to pick her out?"

"Of course, she's gonna be your friend. It's only right you should pick her out. Now, stay sittin' right here for a few minutes while I go and talk to these nice men. Think about what kind of kitten you might want, and what you might want to name her. I'll be back in a bit, and then we can go."

I try to think of good names, but I'm still exhausted from what had happened. The next thing I know, I feel the car dip as the men Grandpa told me about start putting boxes in the back. When they finish, Grandpa is true to his word...we go to the shelter and I get a kitten, and then we take him to my new home.

After my shower, I come downstairs and snuggle up on the couch with the guys to tell them about my parents, but even after all these years, it still hurts to talk about it. So I curl into Gabe's chest. His arms around me chase away the cold feeling of being abandoned.

"Mom and two of my dads died in the crash. The third was in the ICU for four days, but he had passed before I woke up the first time." Gabe squeezes me tighter, Xan on one side rubbing his hands up my arm, Leo on the other braiding small sections of my hair. Jacks is sitting on the floor between my feet, purring and nuzzling against my shin.

"I know my parents didn't leave on purpose, I know it's not what they wanted. I know Grandpa loved me...but by then his own pack and mate were gone. He had been ready to go himself. But after Mom and Dads died, he had to stay to take care of me.

I don't think he resented me, per se, but sometimes it felt like he was just killing time."

"By the time Grandpa was diagnosed with cancer, I was about to graduate college. He told me he worried about me being alone, but I knew he was past ready. Less than six months after I had my degree, he was gone—just about three years now. He had done what he could to keep me from getting stuck in an omega sanctuary, even though he told me outright I should register on my own so I would be safe."

Gabe rocks back and forth, as best he can with a couch full of alphas, pulling my legs up and turning me sideways to tuck me under his chin. Jacks looks irritated at first, but then leans in closer to keep touching me, wedging himself between Gabe's knees. Gabe grumbles but doesn't try to move him away, just rubs his chin on the top of my head, his stubble catching strands of my still-damp hair. I am so going to need to use a heavy conditioner if this is going to be the norm here.

I want to stay here, safe and warm, but I can't stop my mind or my mouth, and I babble nervously. "So, yeah...just...the way you guys sounded last night, like you thought I would leave just because Jacks has some problems. It kind of felt like you were trying to get rid of me." I'm suddenly surrounded by low rumbly growls instead of purrs. "No, I mean...I hear you say that you don't want to...but sometimes it feels like everyone either leaves or can't wait for me to leave. And I know...deep down, I know...that isn't logical. But the logical part of my mind rarely syncs up with the part that gets anxious."

I give a small self-depreciating laugh. "Like, logically, I know the chances of someone finding out who I am online and then trying to bond me against my will are super low. I've taken every precaution I can." The growls surrounding me are louder and angrier now. "But, the anxiety part of my brain is always on high alert that somehow something slipped, I trusted somebody I shouldn't, or something...and now the person who slashed my tires and broke my car, and broke into my house is a creepy stalker or some shit and wants to kill me. But logically, I know that the chances of that are super slim." Another shaky laugh.

"So, yeah, I didn't mean to freak out. I'm just not used to people wanting me around...or at least not for a good reason. Sorry." I lean into Gabe, and his growl changes like a switch was flipped, back to his rumbly purr.

The man sounds like a fucking motorcycle—which I guess is appropriate considering he works with engines all day. I'm still so tired, and the vibrations are so relaxing. Before I know what is going on, my eyes are drifting closed. I wake up briefly with my face pressed against Gabe's bare chest and Xan cuddled against my back. Feeling safe and warm, I quickly fall back asleep.

Chapter 40

Leo

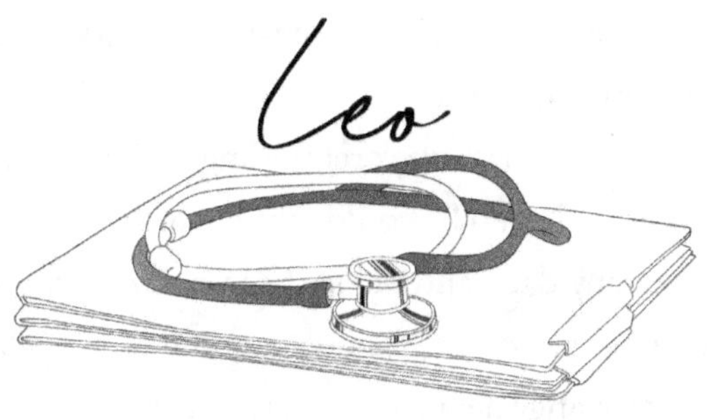

Sunday is fairly relaxing. The garage is ready and deep cleaned for at least one new hire to start on Monday, and I've rescheduled every appointment I could to have a week off. I'm still on call in case of emergencies, but otherwise, we're golden. We did call the firehouse and tell them that we would be shorthanded if they needed us. With our omega going into heat, we wouldn't be able to leave her alone completely, so Jacks, at least, would stay with her in case something happened.

Candice has tentatively agreed to move in with us, depending on how her heat goes. She says she needs to make sure we're all compatible, as none of us have really shared before. I can appreciate her caution when it comes to uprooting her life.

Xan, Gabe, and I still plan on going into work on Monday, Tuesday, and possibly Wednesday, depending on how she feels. Xan is worried that he hasn't been able to get in touch with Trey at the garage about their new hire. But figures he can introduce everyone on Monday, and hopefully get at least one more person hired next week, even if they have to wait and train after we all return to work.

Jacks has spent the last week rebuilding and upgrading Candice's computer. He said he could salvage the hard drive, so she shouldn't lose any data, and he has been ordering replacement parts to rebuild her system. Xan is spending today helping the two of them rearrange her room with the old furniture, the new desk, and Iggy's terrarium so she has a proper workspace. She says she doesn't want charity, but she seems to be taking Jacks's enthusiasm for gift giving in stride. I want to give her things too, but they seem to have all the bases covered. Feeling a bit useless in the whole courting process, I'm unsure of what I can do for her.

I guess I could ask if she knows any other romantic anime she wants to watch together. Though that is more for me than her.

Monday morning comes bright and early. I am ready to get through this week and I still need to figure out how to properly court my kitten. But one step at a time, first her heat, then I can help carry heavy things when she is ready to move in…then I can figure out how to make her need me as much as I need her.

This is a plan, or at least the start of one.

Work goes fine. I have three of my reschedules this morning, and everything is just standard checkup stuff. Then I have a bit of time before lunch, so I take one of Dr. Stephanie's clients since she is running behind, and I owe her for helping Candice. We have lunch, and I think Jacks is trying to build us up for the coming week. He included pasta salad and a protein shake. The post-it says it's for carb loading and endurance, and I can't help but chuckle a little.

I'm going to have to give him a quick lesson on nutrition if he insists on doing this. Still, I appreciate the effort. I gag my way through the pasta salad. Jacks is an excellent cook. I just hate pasta salad. It sticks to my teeth, and I can never get the flavor to go away until I can brush with toothpaste.

My cell rings as I'm cleaning up my spot in the breakroom. There are only a couple of emergency numbers that make it through the silence setting, so it has to be important. I look at the number on display and the bottom of my stomach drops out, my pasta salad threatening to make a reappearance.

My voice comes out as a croak. "Hello?"

The person on the other line is brisk and straight to the point. "Leo, we need you and your pack-mates now. Meet us at the station as fast as you can. There's a fire." They hang up before I can reply, and I'm dialing the garage as I sprint towards the front.

Gabe picks up on the second ring, and I don't even let him get through his standard greeting. "Fire. Can you and Xan pick me up on the way to the station?"

"Yeah, lemme jus'...Fuck, Trey's not back from lunch. Fuck it, we'll be there in two minutes." He pulls away from the phone, already yelling for Xan and giving instructions to someone else.

I stop at the front desk long enough to let them know I will be out for the rest of the day, then I bolt out of the building and start jogging towards the fire station. Gabe and Xan know that I won't just be sitting around waiting, and they can slow down enough for me to jump in the truck bed on their way.

I pull up Jacks's number on my cell. I know he and Candice were waiting for the window repair guy today, and he won't be coming with us, but I still need to keep him in the loop. He'll probably feel the stress from Xan anyway, but it's still important for him to know why. I stare down at my phone as it goes to voicemail, then hang up and try again.

Four rings later, I'm leaving a message as I haul myself over the tailgate and slap the back window. I let Jacks know that we are all on our way to the fire station. We love him, and to keep

Candice safe. Then I hang up, grab my gear, and hop on the fire truck as it's pulling out of the station, sirens blaring.

It isn't until the truck we're on turns towards the east side of town, Candice's side of town, and I see the column of smoke in the distance, that I start to get worried.

Jacks

Candice and I have been here all morning. We're waiting for the guy that Xan set up to repair the window. But while we wait, I'm helping Candice pack. The idea is that after her heat, she'll move in with us on a permanent basis. She can sell her house eventually, if she wants to. She says it'll help pay for renovations and her nest, but I'm not worried about that. It's after noon, and I'm just about to suggest a break for lunch. I packed us a picnic so we can share in her backyard, away from any stress she has from the last time she was here and the break-in.

"I'll get it!" I hear her yell from the kitchen, must be the glass repair guy, so a good time to get out of the house...but it does mean I won't be able to seduce her in the backyard while he's here.

Oh well, maybe after he leaves.

"Hi, no, thanks for coming...Do I know you?"

The voice that replies is vaguely familiar. "No, I don't believe we've met; I'm here to fix the door, Seth Thompson, with Thompson Glass." I can't see him from here. That weird twisty feeling in my mind is spinning like a tornado. Worrying that I'll embarrass Candice if I step out now, I stay in the nest where I can keep an eye on her, but not be seen from the front door.

"Oh, sorry, Mr. Thompson, yes, please come in and I'll show you the back door." She has a fake customer service voice right now, like she's trying to be overly polite, and that twisty feeling pulls tighter. I back away from the nest door, keeping Candice in my sight. She's not looking at the man walking behind her, but she's right, he is familiar. He has an ugly sneer pointed at her back, and a big bag of tools slung over one shoulder. Every alarm in my head is screaming at me to get my omega away from this fucker, and I don't seem to have any control over my legs moving me to do just that.

I grab Candice's tiny club from under the nest and step out of the door after he passes. I wait as he reaches into his tool bag. Candice is still turned away, talking about the back door and the glass, but as she turns back and sees me over his shoulder, the club raised high, her eyes widen. I don't want to bludgeon this dude without cause, but my hesitation and her sharp intake of breath lose me the upper hand. He spins around, bringing some kind of big ass wrench with him, and hits me under my raised arm with it.

The sudden shock of pain causes me to drop my own weapon and Candice to scream. I curl inward, my body automatically trying to protect itself from the stabbing pain around my ribs, but I need to stay upright.

I need to get Candice out of here, and I need to keep her safe until help gets here. But I know that face now, I know that angry sneer...and oh fuck...this isn't a glass repairman. He swivels his head between me and Candice, and I lower my arm on my injured side towards my pocket. If I can just press the panic button on her key, hopefully, they'll send someone out.

"You fucking bitch!" he screams at Candice, and I can't help the growl that erupts from my throat, dragging his attention away from her, even for a moment. "I finally get to meet you, in person, and what the fuck do I find? Some fucking piece of shit alpha in *my* omega's house."

He swings the wrench again, and I roll with the hit, getting clipped in the head and dropping to the floor but still conscious. My hand is in my pocket, slamming the panic button down over and over. The world spins, and Candice is screaming as he raises that fucking wrench over his head. I try to kick out with my legs, knock him down with me since his center of gravity should be fucked with that heavy ass wrench so high.

I manage to clip his ankle, but it just throws his aim off and he brings it down in front of my face instead of on my head, throwing up tiny wood chips out of her floor. Candice has her hands around his arm, trying to pull him away from me, and he turns and knocks her away with the back of his fist. My growl sounds bubbly in my throat, and I wonder if there might be something wrong with my chest from that first hit.

Candice is screaming at him and lunges for his throat, her hands hooked into claws. But though she is fierce, my omega is still tiny. She can't reach him before he swings again, and her head snaps back. She hits the floor, her skull smacking against the wood with a loud crack.

"Look what the fuck you made me do, stupid dim-witted son of a bitch. Fuck you, you fucking useless piece of shit." Trey kicks me hard in the face, and everything goes black.

Chapter 41

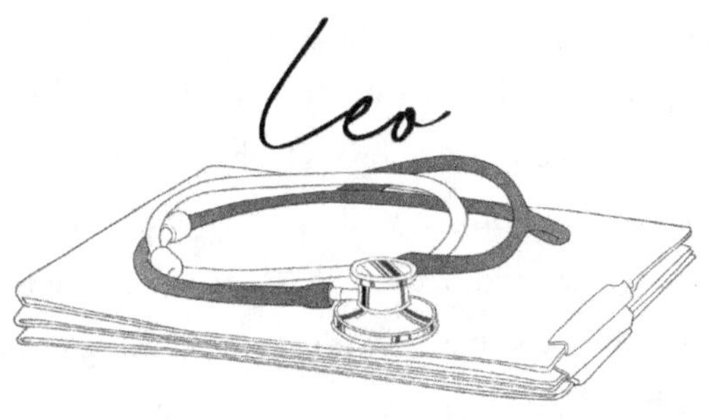

Gabe and Xan are both losing their ever-loving shit as we pull up in front of Candice's house. There are flames everywhere, and I still can't get her or Jacks to answer their damned phones. Joseph is trying to get both my pack -mates to settle down enough to put on their PPE so they can see if Jacks or Candice are in the house. Xan is screaming that he can't feel anything, and Gabe is raging back and forth across the lawn.

Joseph's brother, Samson, jumps off the back of the truck, already fully equipped, and heads towards the front door. Xan tries to rush past him, but Joseph hits him hard enough to at least get him to stop screaming, and hopefully hard enough to stop panicking. I finish getting my own gear on and run towards the door. Because of my height, I'm usually the last option to send in. However, my pack-mates are not coherent enough to be useful, so I am going to find our missing people.

I step into the burning house, smoke is everywhere, and I crouch down to try to see better. Something comes towards me through the smoke and I strain to make out Samson with a body draped over his shoulders. Judging by the size, I would guess male, so hopefully Jacks. I turn left, scanning the floor as I go, but no one is in the office. Through the living room, and it's boiling hot in here, trying to walk quickly in a crouch.

I yell through the radio asking Samson where he found the body. I can't think too hard right now of it being more than a body. Static fills the line and I can just make out, "li'ing…oom."

I head towards the nest, and there is nothing. Her nest is on fire, but I don't see anything resembling a person. It's too hot and my vision is getting fuzzy, but I need to find her. I check the bathroom, but the adjoining closet is nothing but fire, boxes and clothes still hanging up, all in flames. I need to check, but I don't think I can. I get down on my knees and crawl towards the closet, my hands blistering through the gloves as I kneel on the floor looking for anything that might be Candice. But the world is spinning and the black spots in my vision keep me from making any positive identification.

Yeah, I have totally fucked myself here. I try to stand and the world spins around me. Too much smoke, and I collapse against the wall, thankfully away from the closet. I try to use my radio to call for help, but my fingers feel like fat sausages and I can't press the button down.

Then another body is there—Gabe, pulling on me, dragging me through the nest and out the back door, into the yard, and away from the burning house. The world is spinning as we get into the clean air, but my skin burns on both hands and down my back where I hit the wall. He pulls off my helmet, checking my eyes while he calls into the radio to get help in the back. I hear a crack, and my brain pops up how pissed Candice is going to be that an alpha finally broke her fence.

"Shit!" says Gabe, loudly and with feeling, and I think he's reacting to my uncontrolled giggles at the image of my kitten ready to savage someone over her busted fence.

Joseph drops to the ground beside me, dragging a tank of oxygen, and swearing profusely. He pulls out three bottles of water, hands one to Gabe, and drops the other two on the ground by my head so he can put the oxygen mask over my face. My skin feels tight, and my face hurts, though I'm not sure if it's burned, or I am grinning like a delirious lunatic thinking about angry Candice.

"Sam got Jacks out. He said he didn't see anybody else. I'm gonna guess you didn't either?" He looks between Gabe and me. Gabe shakes his head and they both stare at me.

"No." My voice is almost gone, nothing but a raspy croak. "'S Jass?" I need to make sure Jacks is ok, but my voice won't work. Thankfully, they understand.

Gabe is still pacing angrily across the yard, but Joseph answers, "Jacks is…banged up. He needs to go to the hospital. He's starting to wake up, but not making a lot of sense. Xan is trying to talk to him now, but he seems pretty agitated. I better go get this fire out." He turns and runs back to the front to help the rest of the crew with the hoses and actually putting out the fire.

Agitated is a nice way of putting it, as Jacks comes stumbling through the busted gate, Xan following closely behind, arms out, trying to keep Jacks from falling. He is weaving like a drunk, dragging his own oxygen tank and taking periodic hits from it. Blood oozes from a gash in his forehead, and he is holding his chest under his arm, with the hand not dragging the tank.

He folds up on the ground beside me, his legs collapsing now that he has reached his goal.

"Didja find 'er?" He garbles out, blood leaking from the side of his mouth as he talks. What the hell? "That fuc'in fuc'...'e too' 'er...m'gonna 'ill 'im," he rambles, swaying back and forth. Gabe is staring at him intently. His own eyes are red and leaking from where he dragged me out of the house.

"Who? Jacks...Who took her? What the fuck are you talking about? What happened?"

While we are talking Xan finally catches up, dropping to Jacks's side, with the first aid kit and trying to clean the soot off his mate's face while he talks. He runs his hands over Jacks's chest, pressing in various places until Jacks hisses and flails at him.

"S'your fault...you hired that fuc'."

Xan takes a deep breath. "I love you, but you have at least three broken ribs, I am guessing a punctured lung by the way you dribble when you talk, and most likely a concussion. Your jaw is also swelling, but I can't hazard a guess on that. Now can you please explain what you mean so we can get you to the fucking hospital and go find our omega before I completely lose my fucking mind!" Xan's voice rises with each word until he is shouting in Jacks's face. I've never seen him this frantic before.

"Trey...that fuc'...he 'az here. Sa'd 'is name 'as Sef...Sef Thoms'on...he 'as here to fiss the winnow...Big wrench." Jacks holds his hands out like he is showing us the size of a fish he caught...looks like a big wrench, yeah.

"Hi' me inna fuckin' chess an face...hi' Can'ice wi' hi' fiss; knock'd out. Mo'erfuc'er kicked me inn'a face." He is dribbling drool and blood all down his chest, and Xan and Gabe are both staring at him intently.

Gabe marches over and squats down beside Jacks—reaching out. But his hand just hovers, not sure where to touch that won't hurt him. "Trey? The beta that works in my garage...that Trey?" Jacks nods like a bobble head, blood and spit flying.

"Son of a bitch!" Gabe yells, grabbing one of the water bottles and throwing it across the yard. He stands up, stalking back and forth again, scrubbing his hands through his hair.

He stops and turns to us. "Xan, get the paramedics. Take these two to the hospital. I need to talk to the cops, tell them Candice was taken and by who. I'll head back to the shop to pull up Trey's application information he gave us. The more info we have for the cops, the better, and he better hope like hell they find him before I do." He stomps off towards the front yard, yelling for the medic team to bring a couple of stretchers around back. Gone before any of us have a chance to reply.

Gabe

I hate that I need the cops. I don't mind working with them—we do it on the regular with stuff for the fire department—but I hate that I can't find Candice on my own, and I need their help.

Stopping in front of the house, the guys who were harassing Candice for her statement a few weeks ago are standing out in front of the burning husk that used to be her home. Watching the fire with their thumbs up their asses.

Boys in blue, take a bow, you're a credit to your station.

No, stop it. You need their help.

Shit.

I stalk over to them, looking every bit the raging alpha, and the first one that sees me coming reaches down to un-snap his baton.

Yeah, don't think I didn't notice that little action, piss-ant.

I try to seem less intimidating. I need them to listen. "Officers, I need your help. My pack brother's been beaten and our omega kidnapped. This was her house. The man who took her set it on fire."

They exchange a look before the tall one replies, "Sir, you must be mistaken, omegas can't own property. We have this residence listed under one Candice Manning, beta."

Well, fuck.

"Yes, sorry, sir, Candice is our mate, we haven't bonded yet, but we're courting her. She was taken by one Trey Benedict, he works at my garage...except my packmate said he gave another name earlier when he was here...so that might not be the right name."

The short one speaks now, the one who unclipped his baton. "So, sir, you're telling me that your un-bonded beta mate ran off with one of your employees, and now you want us to go after them?" He looks smug, like he caught me in some sort of lie.

"No, you smarmy little bastard, he's telling you that his omega mate—who was hiding out as a beta—was fucking kidnapped by the same bastard who set this fucking fire, and he is trying to get your help to get her back if you will pull your heads out of your asses long enough to do your goddamned jobs!" Joseph comes marching across the yard, away from the still sputtering shell that is all that's left of Candice's house.

"I've known her since she was a child. She's been passing as a beta since her last family member died a few years ago, and yes, this is her house. I was here replacing a lock a few weeks ago. You need to call your captain and send them over to Gabe's Garage to get the rest of the information he has on the suspect." Joseph nods towards me and the first cop turns white. Yeah, we're the only garage in town—guess who services all the police vehicles, and usually gives them a discount?

The taller officer is nodding numbly. "So, is that a yes? You'll meet me at the garage?" The nodding continues, so I quickly turn to Joseph.

"Thanks man. Listen up, I left Xan, Jacks, and Leo in the back. They need a couple of paramedics as soon as possible. They'll be going to the hospital. Xan needs to stay with Jacks. Do you understand?" I wait for him to nod. "I'm headed over to the garage to pull all the files we have on this bastard. Jacks said he introduced himself to Candice as Seth Thompson from Thompson Glass, but that might just be a made-up name. Can you take care of my pack? Please?"

Joseph grabs my shoulder and squeezes it. I'm surprised by the gesture, but Jacks told me that Candice's known him since she was a kid. Apparently, she grew up next door to his pack, so maybe that's why. "Go on man, I'll finish this up and get the guys to the hospital. You go find your omega. Yeah?"

He shoves me lightly towards the road and I realize I don't have the truck or the Jeep with us. I turn back to the officers, not wanting to have to ask them for anything, but I'll gladly swallow my pride if it'll get our omega back sooner, and in one piece.

"So...I was on the fire truck on the way over and seem to have left my truck at the station, can you guys give me a lift?"

They grumble at me, and I'm not super happy right now either. But the town is small enough that the fire station is right next to the police station, so they don't have to go out of their way at all.

When we get to the station, they let me out of the back of the patrol car. "I appreciate it guys. Is somebody gonna come on by the garage to get Trey's information?"

They both hem-haw around before finally agreeing, and I bolt next door to grab my truck and take it back to the shop as fast as I can. I look at the dash clock and realize it's not even three in the afternoon yet. Today has been nuts, but the sooner I get this shit together the better.

I walk in the door and Kelly jumps up from behind the front desk.

"Hey, sorry Gabe, Trey never came back from lunch, and with you and Xan gone to the fire department...I didn't want Sally to have to run the place alone on her first day."

I pat her on the shoulder. "Thanks for takin' the initiative here. I appreciate it. And I need all Trey's paperwork."

She starts pulling out work orders. "No, sorry, stop. I need all his hirin' paperwork. He has Candice, set her house on fire, and beat the shit outta Jacks...and Leo is in the hospital with him for smoke inhalation 'cause he was tryin' to find her. So things are kinda fucked right now, and I need to figure out how to find Trey."

Sally's head pops around the corner right as I finish speaking. "Well, if he's not coming back, I'm going to finish this brake job he started, ok" This is not the time to laugh, but I manage a quick chuckle.

"Thanks Sally, sorry you kinda got slammed with this shit on your first day." Her eyebrows draw down, and I worry for a second that I've offended her by saying 'shit'...if that's the case, I don't think she's gonna last long around here.

"Boss, I've told you five times already this morning to call me Sal, aright? Sally's the name of a doll in a musical with a singing skeleton. Cute, but not really me." She grins at me and ducks back out to the garage. Ok, yeah she should get along fine.

I turn my attention back to Kelly right as the bell jingles over the door and Thing One and Thing Two, AKA the officers from earlier, step through. I ask Kelly to make copies of the papers and she just gives me side-eye.

"Did you forget you and Xan went on a cleaning spree recently?" I'm puzzled by the question, but watch as she prints three pages off to give to the officers. "Did you gentlemen need these electronically, or will print be ok?" Thank fuck *she* knows what the hell's going on.

Xan scanned everything in. This office is now a paper-free zone, and I would have spent the next two hours searching filing cabinets for papers that no longer exist.

"Hey, can you print me up one of those too, so I can look it over." She rolls her eyes, but does as I ask.

I turn to the officers, paperwork in hand. "I know he calls from this number, and answers it when we have to call him in. Is there any way to trace that? Or find out who it belongs to."

Thing One, the tall one, nods again and pulls the transmitter off his shoulder to call it in. I really hope we're getting somewhere with this.

"Kelly, can you please call the hospital and see if Jacks and Leo arrived yet? Xan's with 'em, but he needs to stay with Jacks to keep him stable."

Chapter 42

Candice

*F*uck, *my head hurts.*

My face hurts.

My eyes feel crusted shut, and I am so fucking tired. I try to reach up to wipe the gunk out of my eyes, but my hands won't move more than a fraction, and pulling on them just hurts.

Alarm bells ring in my mind.

What the fuck was I doing?

I was waiting...with Jacks, we needed to get the back door fixed. He was packing up my clothes and my nest stuff so I could move in with them after my heat this week. I was almost done in the office, taking drawings and stuff off the wall and wrapping them for protection.

The doorbell and a familiar face, but he said he was with the glass company, Seth Thompson. Jacks was going to attack him, but I don't want him to go to jail for attacking some random guy. I need Jacks—the whole pack—to be there for my heat, and afterward, I just need them.

The guy lashed out...he hurt Jacks and I tried to help him, but...

That motherfucker.

I remember him knocking Jacks down. Then me when I tried to help. Everything was black until he was dragging me out. Hitting the pavement woke me up, at least a little. There was fire, and I could hear sirens.

That fucking fuck knocked out my alpha and set my goddamned house on fire.

I am gonna fuckin' kill him.

I pull harder on my hands while forcing my lids open. I need to see where I am. I need to see if Jacks is—where is Jacks? He was with me in the house...fuck...the fire. Did he set the fire while Jacks was still in there?

Panic robs me of my breath, and I flop around, trying to dislodge whatever the hell has my hands. It does no good. They're stuck tight and not moving. I look around the room. Maybe if I can get loose I can call Gabe. He's part of the fire department, he can go get Jacks. I twist and flail, trying to get loose, but it's dark outside now...no...it was only just afternoon. I can't...Jacks.

A broken sob scrapes my throat, and I lay there wallowing. All the fight draining out of me as the train of anxiety plows me under, filling my mind with thoughts of what might have happened. How the others will blame me for him getting hurt or killed. How even if he is somehow alive, he won't want me because I got him hurt. Before long I am curled in on myself, shaking uncontrollably.

I'm all alone, no one will want me, and no one is going to help me. I take a deep breath, then another, trying to center myself.

I can't very well check up on Jacks, or apologize for getting him hurt if I'm locked up. Ok, think logically. My eyes are sore as I try to keep them open enough to look around the room. I am on a bed; my hands are behind me, hard plastic cutting into my wrists. So, probably zip ties. I know grandpa had me take self-defense classes in high school, but my mind is blank on getting out of something like this. There isn't enough slack to twist them. And all those movies that show someone tucking their bound arms under their feet with their legs curled against their chest. Total bullshit, boobs do not allow you to bring your knees up to your chest...and I don't think I could be that flexible anyway.

The bed I'm on really is plush. A small omega part of my mind keeps telling me that this is a nice soft blanket, and I should stay here and burrow under it. Clearly, my omega has shit for self-preservation skills.

Well, we're not going anywhere until the room stops spinning, so just lie back, close your eyes, and try to save your energy. With your heat coming up, we want to be well-rested.

Fuck...So, I'm on even more of a time crunch. Shit.

But the snarky little voice is right, I won't be able to do anything in my present state, so I better rest up. I close my eyes, focusing on anything other than my already spotty vision. Mostly I smell smoke.

Probably from where this asshole burned down my fucking house.

Also dust...and something else. Something subtle, and rancid, like old grease that's been left to curdle. The smell makes bile rise in my throat, and I open my eyes again, trying to get some other sensory input to drive out that putrid smell.

Once I can stop focusing on that, I close my eyes again and listen. I hear boards creaking, someone is moving close by, and muffled voices, but I can't make out what they're saying. The creaking gets louder and then fades away again. I don't know how long this lasts, before I nod off, my body trying to preserve energy for a heat that I really don't want to go through now.

Not without my guys.

I wake up again to someone running a damp cloth down my face. My jaw and head are still throbbing, and I wince when the cool cloth drags over an open scrape on my chin. More details are coming back to me. That guy who works in Gabe's garage. I only met him a couple of times.

What was his name?

That asshole knocked out Jacks, and me.

I am so cutting off his fucking dick.

My eyes pop open in shock as my head is tilted and an ice pack is pressed underneath it.

"Now, now, Candy, don't jerk around. You're going to hurt yourself." The condescending tone would make me grind my jaw if it didn't hurt so badly already.

"I'm already very upset at how events transpired. What were you doing with that alpha in your house?" His hand that was adjusting the ice pack tangles in my hair and the pull on my sore scalp draws an involuntary yelp from my throat.

"Nobody but you and I should be in that house. Nobody! But not only did you let an alpha in to fix your locks a few weeks ago, but all of pack fucking Asher? Did you think I wouldn't find out? That you could just slut around and it would be fine with me?"

Clearly somebody's been eating their Crazy-O's this morning.

What the fuck?

The hand in my hair pulls tighter, tilting my head back and straining my neck. The face suddenly staring back at me is crazy. He looks nothing like the laid-back guy I've seen in passing at the garage. His eyes are wide and bloodshot; his hair looks less greasy, but it's a tangled nest where it looks like he's run his fingers through it repeatedly. Gone is the easy smile, replaced with a snarl and spit flies as he screams in my face.

"Did they fuck you? Slutty little omega had to go and fuck an alpha! Did you let them knot you, mark you?!" He shakes the hand holding my hair and my head snaps to the side. I can't stop the whimper that comes out, and suddenly his features shift to contrite.

"Oh, Oh, no, Candy, I'm sorry" He doesn't look sorry...not his eyes. "You just make me so mad, being a little slut. All omegas are, but I was hoping you were different."

"It's ok, though."

"Shhhh shhh, now. It's ok. We'll work past this."

He finally lets go of my hair, and hooks his hands under my arms, pulling me up the bed until my head rests against the pillows. He reaches up, smoothing his own hair back, and then pulls the bottom of his shirt down to straighten it.

"Trey..." All I can manage is a raspy croak; my throat wants to close up at the sheer insanity staring down at me.

"Seth. Seth Thompson with Thompson glass. Trey *is* my middle name. Though, *you* probably know me best as Wishbone."

The world tips, spins, and I have to bite my tongue hard enough to taste blood. I really don't want to pass out around this crazy asshole. This creepy fuck who's been following me online for at least a few years now, buying commissions and offering to send me money to help when unexpected expenses happen.

"You didn't answer my question, Candy. Did you take all their knots?" And I'm relieved that I can shake my head no.

Technically, I was only knotted by Gabe and Jacks. I'm seriously worried about what he'll do to me if he gets any angrier. He raises an eyebrow, skeptical of my answer.

"Did you let them mark you?" Again, I shake my head no.

"You know I'm going to have to check, right?" He yanks hard on the collar of my shirt and the top buttons fly off, exposing my throat and the straps of my bra.

"Hmm...nothing here, but alphas can be sneaky bastards." He yanks again and the rest of the buttons disappear. My shirt gapes open, revealing my breasts and stomach.

He pushes it off my shoulders, grabbing me by the nape of my neck and tilting me up so he can try to push it the rest of the way down, until it's bunched around my wrists. His hands run over my shoulders, down my arms.

"Sneaky, sneaky alphas." He mumbles under his breath as his hands continue to stroke my skin. He pushes me over, hands on my back, fiddling with my bra clasp, and I cringe and twist. I already feel like my skin is crawling, and so far all my bits have stayed covered. If he goes any further I won't be able to stay chill.

"You won't be able to get it off...it'll just get stuck on my arms too. If you unhook my arms, I can take the bra off for you."

Please don't agree to that—I'm trying to sound reasonable, but my gorge rises just offering to help.

His hands pull away, rolling me over onto my back again, and he looks at my face, trying to determine if this is a trick.

"No, no I can check later...they didn't leave any obvious bond marks." His gaze tracks down my torso, hungry eyes lingering on my breasts, and I am glad I am wearing a full coverage white old lady bra. I don't need to give this sick fuck any more ideas.

"We'll need to get you on a diet though; I want to make sure *my* omega stays fit and attractive." He lightly pokes at my belly squish, and it takes all my willpower not to glare. But, you lure more flies with honey than vinegar, so I clench my teeth and try not to react.

"Of course, Seth, I want to look good for you." I watch him from under my lashes, trying to hide how much I really want to just kick the shit out of him. He's momentarily shocked, but quickly recovers.

"That's a good little omega." And he pats me on top of the head. I cringe at both his touch and his repeating the same nickname that Gabe uses. But when Gabe uses it, it sounds like praise. This fucker just sounds patronizing.

"I'll get my chef to fix up some brown rice with chicken and broccoli. Doesn't that sound yummy?" He strokes my hair this time, like I'm some kind of pet.

"Thank you, Seth," I grind out, trying not to gag over how much he preens at my docile act.

"There we go. Now, would you like a hot shower? Get you all cleaned up so you can snuggle into your nest like a good omega. We need to make sure you're comfortable before your heat hits."

Two thoughts wash over me, one right after the other, and I'm thankful he is already turning towards the door, because I can't maintain this mask.

First of all, I am not getting naked and taking a shower around this creep...second, how the fuck does he know when my heat is supposed to hit?

Chapter 43

Xan

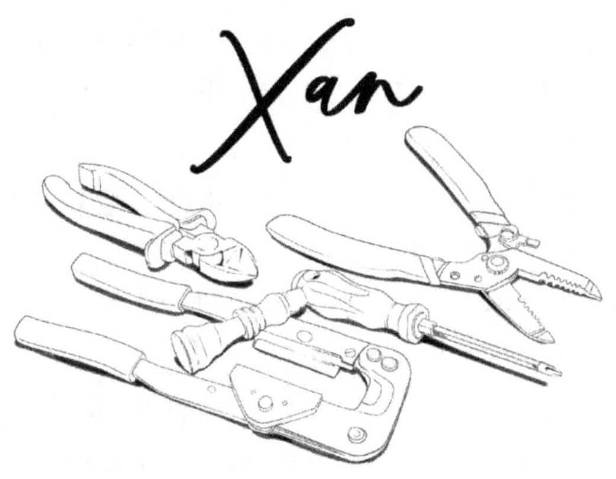

That motherfuck...I'm going to kill him.

I pace the hall outside of the X-ray suite that Jacks is in. Leo was fine being admitted for observation due to smoke inhalation, and second-degree burns on his hands and back. Jacks does have a mild concussion, and five broken ribs, not three, two of which did puncture his lung, thankfully not deep. He's also dealing with breathing in smoke, a variety of cuts and bruises, and a fractured jaw. I have to remind myself that it could be so much worse.

He's wheeled out on a gurney, and it looks like they gave him some really good painkillers 'cause he is grinning like an idiot. Maybe a low dose of Alsomna—that new sedation medication I was reading about for alphas. I was wondering if it would help him with his sleeping or nightmares. They gave him something anyway, not enough to knock him out, but definitely enough to make him loopy.

"Mr. Asher? Xander Asher?" A nurse follows Jacks out of the room, carrying a clipboard. Jacks reaches for me as they walk past, but I stay to talk to the woman calling my name.

"Yes, can I help you?"

"Mr. Asher?" she confirms again, wasting my time while my mate is getting farther away.

"Still yes. How can I, Mr. Xander Asher, help you today?" I grind out through clenched teeth.

"Oh, ok, well, I need next of kin information for Mr. Jackson Asher. We don't have anything listed on his paperwork, and he wasn't the most helpful...he just kept asking for you." Her eyes keep bouncing around the room, not wanting to hold my own, which are furious.

"*I'm* his next of kin. I'm his mate." I pull my shirt collar to the side, exposing his claiming mark.

"Oh, yes, but you're both...and...we saw the mark on his neck...and...isn't there a pack lead or an alpha we can talk to?"

I don't even know what the fuck this bitch is babbling about now, only that my mate has been rolled into an elevator and is now gone, and I give it less than five minutes before he goes ballistic on everyone around him without a familiar face to calm him down.

Putting on the best version of my easygoing persona that I can, I hold my hand out towards the elevators.

"Walk with me, will you? I don't want Jackson to be left without family nearby." I march purposefully towards the elevator, and she can either follow me, or fuck off, because I'm being serious when I tell her I don't like him to be without his family. She trots to catch up with me, calling loudly.

"If I could just speak to your pack lead; I just need to get his paperwork filed, and I need to know his next of kin, and who will be responsible for any medical expenses. We don't have any insurance on file for him."

Ahh...there we have it, the vulgar topic of payment. "Just mark me down as responsible. I'll take care of whatever bills he can't cover."

I'm spamming the up button on the elevator. I saw the display stop on floors three and five after he got on, so I can check the nursing stations at both of those if I need to.

"But, Mr. Asher, we really need a card on file, or some sort of insurance." And poof...there go the last of my fucks, right up in goddamned smoke.

Breathe, Xan...you won't be here for Jacks if security kicks you out.

Fuck

I spin on my heel, still pumping the elevator button.

"Ms..." I look down at her nametag.

"Ms. McGinnis." I try for a charming smile, but I can't guess at what it really looks like when she backs up a step.

"Ms. McGinnis. If you have something for me to sign, some document agreeing to pay whatever fees your hospital has...I will gladly do so. One of my pack members is being treated for smoke inhalation, my mate—who you refuse to address as such—is being admitted for several injuries, not the least of which is a concussion, my omega is missing, which, coincidentally is how my two pack-mates were injured, trying to protect her. My lead alpha is missing after going to the police to file a report and I am slowly losing my ever-loving-fucking mind…so if you have something for me to sign, please give it to me now, before I lose all sense of decorum, and have to be forcibly removed from your facilities. Do I make myself clear?"

The elevator finally arrives, and I am about to turn towards it when Ms. Mcginnis takes another step backwards. I hear Jacks giggling, and turn towards the sound. He's standing in the elevator, in nothing but his hospital gown. "Xan!" he slurs, staggering towards me. He's holding up an IV bag in one hand, but it's not doing much good since it is connected to the tubes coming out of the hand holding it.

"Excuse us, Ms. McGinnis!" I say loudly, taking Jacks's elbow and leading him back into the elevator.

"I do hope you're not causing problems, my love. Now, what floor did they have you on?" Jacks holds up five fingers.

"Right, up we go, hold on then." The door slides closed as I hold the button down for the fifth floor, my arm wrapping snugly around his hips.

"By the way, your ass looks really good in that gown." I smile up at Jacks, and he leans heavily against me, as we head back up to his room—hoping like hell there is no path of destruction to follow and he just slipped out after they got him situated.

Luck seems to be on my side as we get up to the fifth floor. The nurses all look our way as we stumble off the elevator, but no one stops us. Jacks hobbles down the hallway with a purpose, so at least they got him settled into a room before he escaped. He checks door numbers and finally pushes into 553, half-falling inside. The sooner I get him back in bed, the better.

I barely have time to take in the slightly burnt smell and the sheet that hangs as a room separator before Jacks yanks it back, stumbling into the side of the bed. Leo is there, his face pink and shiny, bandages on both hands, and tubes running up one arm.

"C'mon...Leo...ge' up!" Jacks looks at the bandaged hands and then grabs Leo's arm instead, carefully avoiding all the wires and tubes attached to our big alpha. He yanks a few times, but Leo only lets out a pained groan.

"C'mon, go'a go!" Jacks gives up on pulling and tries to push Leo out of the bed, but he barely starts to roll before Jacks drops to the ground, grabbing at his busted side.

The pain seems to have snapped him out of it, at least temporarily, and he looks up at me with tears in his eyes. "Xan?"

I help him stand up and limp over to the unoccupied bed. I get him stretched out across the covers and press the nurse call button. Nobody bothers replying, but a few minutes later a severe-looking older nurse appears in the doorway.

"Oh, I'm sorry, we only had one patient scheduled for this room." She stammers out a quick excuse as she takes in the situation. Leo groaning on his bed, Jacks curled up around my arm in the other bed. She hurries over and looks down at the hospital bracelet wrapped around Jacks's arm.

"Mr. Asher? Oh...Ohhh? Leo Asher is your packmate, yes?" I nod a quick affirmative.

"Yeah, Leo's over there, this is Jacks, and I'm his mate, Xander. Jacks doesn't like to be alone, so he came and found me down by X-ray, and then dragged me up here and made himself at home. Can you help him, please?" I don't like how my voice cracks at the end, or how her eyes get wider with each word.

Thankfully, she seems more professional than the woman downstairs and immediately gets started trying to help. She asks me what happened, and I try to explain while she checks Jacks's vitals. He's whimpering now, the cut on his forehead breaking open and oozing blood down his jaw. She calls down to the nurse's station and asks for Jacks's records, and it's only a couple more minutes before a younger man pops through the door carrying a stack of papers.

"Oh, now, technically this is the burn recovery center, but..." She looks at the paper. "That's fine, since he is also recovering from an inhalation injury. However, we are going to need to get a doctor in here to evaluate his concussion and get his chest taken care of before he can rest. If he can rest...the doctor will need to look at everything before we make a decision." She looks back and forth between Jacks and the paperwork. He has a death grip on my hand, his eyes screwed down tight.

"We're going to get you taken care of, young man," she says sincerely and then pats him on the ankle and smiles at me before leaving the room.

Hooking a chair with my foot, I drag it over so I can collapse next to Jacks. I'll need to check in with Gabe, but just need to rest my eyes first. Leaning my head against Jacks's bed I don't remember anything until the severe nurse shakes me awake.

Jacks

*F*uck *me, everything hurts. When I get ahold of that little shit-monkey I'm going to peel him like a fucking banana.*

Everything smells antiseptic, and they must have insane filters in this place. Warmth envelops one side of my body and I look over, catching a hint of Xan's bourbon and rain scent, *cozy*. He's asleep wrapped around my side that isn't bandaged, his fingers are intertwined with mine and his face rubs into my shoulder. I catch sight of a big lump over his shoulder, and it's Leo, hooked up to lots of machines, and heavily bandaged.

Poor bastard, I remember seeing him lying out in my little lion's yard after I woke up. They didn't want me to be in here, but I couldn't leave him in a room all alone. What if he has a nightmare with none of his pack around, and there would be no one to sneak him snacks. Nope, he's stuck with me, and Xan, by proxy.

I push the nurse call button and an angry-looking woman in a tight bun is at our door a moment later. "Oh, I wasn't expecting you to be up so soon. I thought he was the one buzzing." She looks down at Xan, and part of me wants to pull the blanket over him so she can't see him, but Janey would've kicked my ass so hard for being rude, so I remember my manners.

"No ma'am. I'm sorry to call you in. I was just wondering how long it's been since we arrived, and when we can leave." Her eyes widen with shock...shit, did I do something awkward that I can't remember?

"I'm sorry, Mr. Asher, but you have five broken ribs, and you had to have a procedure to re-inflate your lung...Mr. Leo Asher over there is suffering from singed lungs and burns. I'm sorry to say it, but it will be at least a few more days, if not a week, before we can discharge you. And that depends a lot on how long it takes you to heal. So, please, lie back down and get more rest." I look at her, dumbstruck.

"You've been unconscious for about thirty-six hours, Mr. Asher."

Shit...Fuck...Shit-fuck!

It's ok, I can work with this.

"Thank you ma'am, I sure do appreciate your help. Can you please be a darlin' and tell me how to get an outside line on here? I just wanna call up our pack leader and check up on our omega."

I point at the phone, smiling my most disarming smile. And yes, I am laying it on super thick, but I can't do Xan's effortless relaxed charm. So, let's try fake southern gentleman charm instead, and hope it doesn't get me in any more trouble. I clearly have no idea what I'm doing, but it works in movies.

Chapter 44

Candice

Shortly after Seth leaves, a woman comes in, starts a shower, cuts my ties, and offers to help me strip.

No, I'm good, thanks.

I ask for privacy, and while her pinched brows say she isn't any happier about this than I am, she refuses. However, she does stand outside the shower door looking towards the bedroom the entire time, so at least I'm able to get clean. I wash my hair a few times; it takes a while to get all the blood out, and there's a really tender spot on the back of my head. Not going to lie though, the conditioner in there is amazing, and my hair is now super soft.

I scrub hard in the hot water, feeling like my skin is going to melt off, but I have to get the sensation of Seth's touch off my body. By the time I'm done, I look like a big red lobster.

The woman hands me a huge fluffy towel, and I just want to bury my face in it…I didn't know something that soft could be absorbent, but it feels so good against my abused skin.

She leads me back to the bedroom and hands me a stack of fresh clothes to put on. My old ones are gone, which is no great loss on my destroyed shirt, but I want my underwear and bra back. The ones she has are about two sizes too small, but hey, stretch pants are known for stretching. Still, the T-shirt looks almost obscene stretched over all my jiggly bits.

Seriously, if this douche canoe is that rich, you'd think he could afford prisoner clothes that fit.

I hate tight clothes, partially because I'm heavy. They're pinchy, and expensive clothes that are tight are no exception. She leads me down the hallway to another room, there's a mid-sized table laid out with food, a steak, baked potato, and wine on one side, chicken breast and rice with a side of broccoli and a glass of water on the other, also a salad, but I don't eat salad because I am not a fucking rabbit. I mean, I usually eat the croutons and sliced carrots out of it, but I have a feeling Seth would get pissed if I try that here.

Not surprisingly, he's standing behind the chair with the steak, and his eyes bug out when he sees the spectacle that is my outfit. If he doesn't like it, it's his own fault for getting rid of my stuff and not having the right size. I feel like a sausage stuffed into a too tight casing. His eyes roam over me and he swallows a few times before he opens his mouth.

"You look lovely, my dear."

Oh, fuck...it's not disgust. He likes the jiggly bits.

Shit.

I lower my eyes demurely, but it's really just so I don't have to see him staring at my nipples poking against this fucking shirt. To be completely honest, I know a *LOT* of guys like plus-sized women, in theory—or at least in art. I get that request a lot, and you know, part of me really enjoys that there's an appreciation for a variety of body sizes and shapes. But the most common request, hands down, no contest...is big breasts. Anywhere starting with a C cup and just going up to impossible sizes, and ok yeah, drawings. But most straight or bi-guys who buy art from me like boobs.

I have been blessed, or cursed, depending on the day, with an ample supply. Most omegas are petite and slim, we are said to be the ideal female form, curvy in all the right places, but not too much. But, if we are discussing body types, my figure leans more towards ancient fertility goddess and less Tinkerbell. I made my peace with that a long time ago, but it doesn't mean I like to have some creep staring at me.

I hunch my shoulders and scurry towards the table...maybe I can put that fucking big bowl of salad right in his sightline between him and my boobs. As soon as I sit, I curl my shoulders in, trying to hide as much of myself as possible with the table. Undeterred, Seth circles the table and pushes me closer to my plate, running his hands across my shoulders and taking a moment to complete the perv trifecta and stare down the gaping collar of my shirt.

Open eye contact with nipples – check.

Pervy comments – check.

Looking down cleavage – check-erooni!

His hands linger longer than they should, fingers dipping towards my collarbones, before slipping away. He walks back to his own chair.

He takes a sip of wine, holding it in his mouth for a moment, and staring at me before he finally swallows.

"Now, Candy, I can understand your confusion here, but I would rather start over fresh. Let's put that whole messy business behind us, and get to know each other, shall we?" He smiles, and it makes me feel slimy, like I need to run back to the bathroom and scrub again. I sip the water to hide my grimace.

"I don't use the name Trey here. My name really is Seth Thompson, my fathers created Thompson glass, but I now own the company. What else would you like to know?" My mind whirls with questions.

Why am I here?

How did you know I'm an omega?

Why were you working for Gabe...no, wait, better not mention any alphas.

How long have you known I was an omega?

What did I do to slip up, and how can I fix it in the future?

Seth smiles at my confusion. "Let's start at the beginning, shall we? My fathers were alphas, my mother was a beta, and yet they were surprised when I never revealed as an alpha myself."

He chuckles like there's a joke behind that, but I don't see the humor.

"Of course I was groomed to be one, you know. You don't build and run a multi-million dollar company without trying for an appropriate heir, they were so certain I would be an alpha that they ignored all the doctors tests and common sense, and insisted that my designation would come in any day, I would start a pack, and get my own omega, the coveted prize that they themselves never managed to acquire." He swirls his wine around his glass like some fucking cartoon villain.

This asshole loves to talk about himself...but the food smells so fucking good.

I'm so hungry right now...but he isn't eating. He's fucking monologuing. I sit here and stare at my chicken and rice and wonder if he'll look away so I can pop a piece of it into my mouth.

"They, sadly, passed away just after I graduated high school, still determined that I would grow to be an alpha, and carry on their legacy. I figured I should start with finding an omega, and that would help me build a pack, even if my proper designation never came in. But omega sanctuaries don't want to talk to betas. You have to be an alpha to court an omega with them. Or at least be part of a pack of alphas." He tips his glass back, finishing the wine in one swallow, and a smartly dressed man steps forward to refill it for him.

"I was not about to lower myself to looking for a pack. Once I had the omega, they would come to me. But you know how hard it is to find one...free range...so to speak?" He laughs at his joke, and I just want to punch through his teeth.

"So I started looking into packs in the area, packs that had children who weren't registered, packs that might be hiding away a sweet little omega for me. But there weren't any." His smile is more of a grimace, as he takes another large drink of wine.

"So I dug deeper. We aren't a large area, so it's easier to keep under the radar here. Then I found a pack...a deceased pack, two alphas, one omega, and a beta. They had a daughter, now living with her grandfather." I can feel the blood drain from my face as he stares at me.

"Of course, there was no guarantee she would be an omega, not with one beta father, so I watched. I hired someone to follow you in high school, and you were always so small. Personally, I had hoped by some fluke that your friend Stephanie would be a surprise reveal. She's short too, but svelte. Alas, her parents are both betas, and it seems that there were no surprises by the time she left for college."

"But you, you didn't go away to college, did you? You took online classes only and lived with your grandpa. You didn't leave the house unless absolutely necessary, and even then, the man I hired could never get confirmation." I don't want this fucking chicken anymore. My stomach is rolling and if there was anything in it, I am sure it would come back up.

"Then, of course, dear old grandpa died. Cancer, such an awful way to go. And you became even more of a shut in. I began to look for a way to put myself in your path. The few times a year you would interact with other people were at the veterinary clinic, bank, or garage. I enjoy taking things apart, so I had Bernard here help me fabricate all the items I would need." He gestures vaguely towards the well-dressed man with the bottle of wine.

"There was a bit of a learning curve, and of course the wait for you to come out. But then, one day it happened, you called and set up an oil change for your car, and then I had your contact information. Some of which we already had from research, but every little bit helps. So, we searched more online."

"Candice Manning...you couldn't have thought up a better online name? CandyMan? Really? And look, you draw art for money. Well, artists are always looking for customers, so it was easy enough to become one of those. Bernard broke into your house—he's actually quite good at picking locks you know—and confirmed your designation. He said your whole house smelled like a thin mint cookie...I had to have his tongue cut out for going on about it, as if he had any right." My eyes flick to Bernard. But if he's upset by what happened, he doesn't react.

"Some things you were careful of, but you freely let it be known you lived alone with your pets. My condolences on your cat, by the way." He sneers and I wrap my hand tightly around my fork, ready to fling it at his head.

"And there's also the fact that you take off a week, like clockwork, every six months." He slams his wine down on the table, shattering the fragile stemware in the process.

"Of course, I could never get you to just take money. It always had to be an exchange with you, buy art, get an auction stream. Something! Like I want digital fucking art when I can just go buy actual art to hang in my home." He scoffs, and tears fill my eyes. I thought I was doing good taking care of myself. Fuck him.

"Then you stopped. You started missing streams, you weren't available as much, and I worried a pack had found you, and had turned your pretty omega head. I had to get closer, make it so you needed the money I offered, so the next time you came out, I slashed your tires. You would *have* to come into the shop, you would *have* to take the money I offered to repair your car...but you didn't." He stalks towards me.

"Then that fucking alpha, Gabe came back from lunch the next day, he and Xan both...and they smelled like an omega. They smelled like *my* fucking omega! Tell me, did they fuck you that day, or did you play this stupid coy act with them as well?" He grabs my shoulders, yanking me out of my chair and slinging me across the room.

I hit the ground and slide into a wall. But he isn't an alpha, he doesn't have their inherent strength, so while it hurts, I can still stand up, and the fork I gripped earlier is still in my hand.

He drags me up by my hair, wrenching a scream from me when it pulls against the still sore lump on the back of my head.

I don't have any pockets, so I tuck the fork along the inside of my wrist, the curve against my hand, holding it in place with my thumb as he drags me from the dining room and back down the hall the way we came.

I hear a bell ring in the distance and he bellows for someone to get the door, but never slows his stride. I could try to scream, but if the people here won't help me, I don't have any guarantee that the person at the door will either. I'm dragged back into the bedroom and he finally releases my hair, only to grip the back of my neck in one hand and tear the shirt down the back.

"Fucking omega whore...trying to lure me in, pretending you want me, and not just any fucking alpha knot that comes along." He's screaming at me, pushing me towards the bed.

"Which one was it, huh? That mentally challenged moron who owns the garage, or his equally deficient stoner underling? The tall freak of nature or the tattooed lunatic who they all just keep around to make the rest of them look better? Which one!"

He's shaking me by my neck, and I barely catch myself as I fall against the mattress, trying to make sure I don't drop the one small weapon I have. He grabs the stretch pants, which are already strained, and tears them down the middle. I curl in on myself, trying to hide my exposed flesh, but he doesn't stop.

"We have to check for claiming bites; make sure they didn't mark you. You can't tell with alphas. They can be sneaky bastards." He tries to roll me over and I kick out at him, but he just grabs my leg in his big hand and pulls it taut. His other hand trails up my thigh, and his breath grows rougher.

"Are you getting wet for me, Omega? Are you making all that lovely slick for Seth?"

Well, nope, my vagina is officially doing its best impression of the Sahara Desert.

His hand stops groping me and he tries to pry my thighs apart...my skin crawls as he gets closer to my center, and I don't think I'm going to get a better chance than this. Dropping the fork down the palm of my hand so the tines are sticking out against my thumb, I thrust it forward, jabbing at his eye. He never sees it coming.

He doesn't see it afterwards either as there is now a fork embedded in his eye socket.

Seth falls back, screaming and pawing at his face. I want to take time to cover up, but I don't know what my options are, so I grab the oversized towel I used after my shower and tie it around my chest as best I can. He is still screaming on the floor and a thick goop is sliding down the side of his face. Probably a good thing I didn't eat that chicken. Nausea rolls through my core.

I bolt from the room, holding my towel together with one hand, and jiggling my way down the staircase...I never thought I would miss a bra, but here we are. The woman who helped me with my shower earlier has the door open a crack, but I can't see who's on the other side, she seems to be trying to keep them from coming in, and right now that's good enough for me.

She's so focused on turning these unwelcome guests away, she doesn't see me barreling down the stairs and straight for her until it's too late. She starts to turn and I slam full speed into her, knocking her over and tearing the door out of her hand.

I sprawl in a totally unladylike position, sliding a few feet before I come to a stop at the foot of an entryway table with a big vase on it...*oooh fancy!*

Dammit, I think I hit my head again. Fuck.

My impact shakes the table enough that the vase wobbles and falls off. The loud crash makes me cringe.

I really need to pull this towel down...I wonder if I am loopy from a concussion, hormones, or low blood sugar.

Is that last one even a thing...I don't remember when I ate last.

Someone yanks me up, strong arms wrap around me, and I bring my knee up hard into their groin before I register the sweet scent of cherry tobacco.

Oh, shit.

Gabe lets out a loud "oof" of air, but doesn't let go. He has his whole body wrapped around me, curled over my sprawled form, holding the towel in place and trying to preserve what little modesty I might have. When an officer comes over to check on us, Gabe lets out a loud growl, and I have to lean around him to talk to the woman in blue.

My voice is overly chipper and a little hysterical sounding to my own ears. "We're fine...but you might want to check upstairs. There's a guy with a fork in his eye who just ripped off all my clothes, and he might need help." Gabe's head snaps up, his hands checking me over for injuries even as his growl gets louder and rougher.

Chapter 45

Gabe

My omega shakes in my arms, wrapped in nothing but a towel, and I want to go upstairs and stomp Trey—*Seth...what-the-fuck-ever*—into a sticky paste that the cops can then scrape off my boot and into a jail cell.

My body can't decide if it wants to growl or purr and all that comes out is a loud garbled mess, but I don't even care right now—she's here. Running my hands over her skin, she is so very naked other than a towel. I unbutton my over shirt and try to take it off so that I can wrap her up in it, but she whimpers when my arms start to loosen.

"It's ok, Baby Girl, I got'chu. I'm just gonna wrap you up better, ok?" Folding my legs, I tuck her into my lap as I talk, and then she lets me pull away long enough to remove my top layer and pull it over her head. She swims in it, but my alpha immediately relaxes now that she's wearing more, and covered in my scent. I wrap my arms back around her and pull her against me, tucking her head under my chin. She's going to need a medic to look over her, but for now I just *need* to have her in my arms.

She wiggles, and her ass rubs against me. The situation fires off my instinct to mark her, to make sure no one else comes near her again. But this is neither the time nor the place to do that. So I hold her hips still.

"Stop trying to tempt me, Little Omega."

She lets out a tiny whimper and freezes and I wonder if I hurt her, or if I said something wrong. But she turns her face into my chest, takes a deep inhale of my scent, and settles quietly against me again. I settle my alpha by running my hands up and down her back and arms, just feeling her, reaffirming for myself that she's ok, and she replies with a tiny omega purr of her own. I can't help the grin that spreads across my face, omegas rarely purr, and only if they feel safe.

She jerks back and stares up at me, tears in her eyes, and I'm ready to tear something apart.

"Jacks? Is Jacks ok?" Fat tear drops roll down her cheeks, and I wipe them away.

"Jacks is fine, Baby Girl...just fine. He's at the hospital with Leo and Xan."

Shock widens her eyes.

"Oh, no, they're fine too. Leo got a few burns and breathed in some smoke at your house, and Xan is just there to keep Jacks relaxed." Her eyebrows go up.

"Smoke?"

Ahh...Fuck!

"So I wasn't wrong...that little shit stain really did set my house on fire." I'm so surprised by her calling him a shit stain that a laugh bursts out of me.

"Yeah, I'm sorry honey, he did, but we got Jacks out, and he's gonna be ok. A few busted ribs, banged up jaw, and some smoke, but he'll be right as rain before you know it." I don't tell her just how bad Jacks was injured, just skim over the ones that will be obvious when he comes home, and she curls against me again, her tiny purr starting back up.

As fucked up as everything is right now, it still feels like everything's right. Both our boys should be coming home in a few days, but I'll see if she wants to get some heat suppressants to hold off until they're better. I know we were all looking forward to that and bonding, but right now I think they all need time to heal...and I'm pretty sure Jacks will try to fight me if I tell him that.

But for now, the commotion has died down. I stand up and carry my omega out to the waiting ambulance. They have Trey strapped to a gurney, with gauze over his eye, and I wonder again at the tiny woman in my arms, how I got lucky enough to find her. We talk to the paramedics, and they have about a hundred things they need to ask about what happened. The more she answers, the angrier the EMT gets until he's glaring at Trey, even as the questions continue. I don't envy that little fuck on the way to the hospital, but thankfully the EMT says Candice can go home. He offers her a blanket, and I try not to growl. He's just doing his job. And technically, yeah, his job is checking out my omega right now. I still want to growl.

I get Candice back in the truck, all buckled up in the front seat, she's wrapped in my shirt and the paramedic blanket, and looks like a fluffy burrito, leaning against the passenger window. I start down the road and hit speed-dial for Xan, and I'm relieved to hear him awake and Jacks jabbering away at Leo in the background.

"Did you find her? Is she ok?"

"We got her, she's ok, we're in the truck headed home. A little bumped and bruised, I'm gonna try to talk her into letting me take her to the hospital, but I think she just wants her nest right now. How's it going on your end?" Jacks has stopped talking, and even the occasional grunt from Leo is silent.

"Well, Jacks managed to track down the nurse while I was asleep earlier and is trying to get discharged early. But I told him no way. Leo is awake on and off. He has a bit of a cough, but other than his hands and back hurting like hell, he says he feels fine."

"Glad to hear it, man. Take me off speakerphone, I need to give you a heads up." I wait until he comes back on.

"Trey is headed to the hospital. Seems our girl here was going down fighting. She stabbed him in the eye with a fork when he tried to...well I wanted to let you know so Jacks didn't get hurt or kicked out trying to get revenge." My growl is back to full throttle right now, and my fingers tighten on the wheel till it feels like the bones are about to break through the skin.

Unbroken silence, I almost think the call was disconnected.

"*This* hospital, you say?" His voice is cold as ice.

"Yeah, it's the closest one, so it's just a guess. Oh, and you can tell Jacks thanks for the tip. Seth Thompson is the name. It matched up with his phone bills. But I need to let you go. I wanna focus on the road since it's startin' to get dark again." We say our goodbyes and hang up.

I recognize that flat sound in Xan's voice.

Jacks would go off and stab the motherfucker, Leo would probably just snap him in half like a twig...but Xan waits, he plans. Now that he knows who to look for, and where, I'm sure he can come up with something, even if it is just making absolutely sure that he goes to a prison where they like squishy beta men. I look forward to seeing what he comes up with.

The drive home is quiet. Candice is snoring beside me, soft, cute little snores. As she tucks her head down into the blanket and nestles her nose against my shirt, I'm not sure what else I can do. So I pull over and do a quick online order for grocery pickup. It should be ready in a couple of hours, mostly instant stuff that I can't fuck up, but still make sure she's fed. Frozen lasagna—if Jacks were here, he'd kill me—frozen veggies, different flavors of canned soup, and bread for grilled cheese sandwiches. I'll readily admit that Jacks is a much better cook than me, but I make a mean grilled cheese.

Order placed, I start to pull back out on the road to go to the house, but then I hear her whimpering in her sleep, and I am struck with indecision. I think her nest would help her sleep; it smells like pack and Jacks went all out. At the same time, I would rather her go to the hospital to get looked over, and if we happen to run into the guys while we're there, wouldn't that also be good? Decision made, I take the next ramp out to the interstate and drive North 4 exits. She's still whimpering in her sleep, but I have my hand on her now, and she curls away from the window and as close to me as she can get with the seatbelt on.

I pull into the hospital visitor parking lot and lift her out of the truck, still asleep, and still wrapped in blankets. She doesn't have any shoes on, and I don't want her to feel awkward. As I walk in the main entrance, they offer me a wheelchair and I wave them off. I am glad to carry her. I do tell them what the EMT said, but that we mostly came to see the pack. Maybe Xan or Jacks can talk some sense into her. I don't feel comfortable pushing after everything else she's been through today.

The front desk directs me to the fifth floor, and an angry-looking nurse meets me when I get off the elevator. She's a beta, but she looks like she could give Jacks a run for his money on being stubborn. Her arms are crossed and I can see straight away I am not getting by this woman without a good reason.

"Asher pack, I'm here to see Jacks and Leo...and Xan." Her face lights up at that.

"Oh, is this Candice? I'm so glad to see she's ok. Can I get her anything? The poor dear looks like she's been through the ringer." I smile at her kindness, and say thank you, but I think seeing her pack would do her good right now. She just nods and smiles and points me to a room.

I don't bother knocking, which is probably for the best. Leo is sprawled out across his bed, head back, snoring loud enough to wake the dead. Xan is sitting beside Jacks's bed, a rolling tray between them, playing strip poker. Xan is down his shoes and socks, and I know he is letting Jacks win, because he only has on a hospital gown. They both turn their heads when I come in and Jacks tries to scramble out of the bed, stopping and wincing, holding his side as he hobbles over, IV pole in hand. I lower Candice enough that they can both see her in my arms, and Jacks sobs loudly, startling her awake.

Then they're both crying. She scrambles out of my arms, losing her blanket in the process and limping on bare feet towards him as he crawls back into bed. She cries harder when she sees Leo bandaged up in the bed beside him. Xan pulls her into his arms, and plants his ass on the side of Jacks's bed, so she is stuffed between them, all three of us purring loudly for our omega. Even Leo's snores taper off into more of a rumble, and I think he's trying to purr in his sleep.

Xan looks at me. "The doctor says that there's a lot of inflammation and scorched tissue from the smoke, so he'll probably be snoring for at least a few weeks. He suggested a cool mist humidifier to help keep the area moist. Jacks's lung is healing well, but his ribs are never going to mend if he doesn't get more rest, and his jaw has a small fracture, but none of the teeth are damaged." I smile, glad to hear the news, until Candice turns and glares at me.

"A little banged up, huh? Just a few busted ribs?" Her arms are crossed as she stares at me.

"Ok, but to be fair, I didn't want you to worry or blame yourself for them getting hurt. I know you worry…about everything. You don't need to worry about this, they're ok. I even brought you to see that they're ok." Before she can say anything else, the angry nurse comes in.

"Here you go dear. I brought you some fuzzy socks and a spare pair of sweatpants we had at the nurse's station. I know it can get chilly up here." Candice beams at her and thanks her, before returning her angry glower to me.

The nurse just smiles indulgently, but Xan pulls Candice towards the bathroom to get dressed, and whispers in her ear something that's probably going to come back and bite me in the ass later.

Chapter 46

Leo

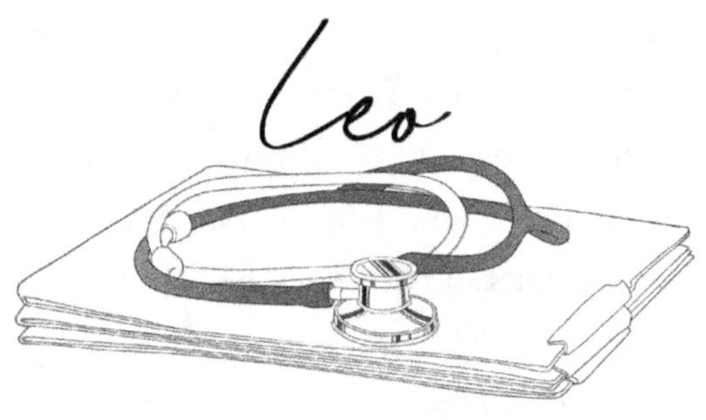

I missed my kitten's first visit to the hospital, but I was awake for the rest of them. She talked to the doctor and got some medication to hold her heat off for a few weeks, since half her alphas were incapacitated. I still haven't thought of a good courting gift, and we're headed home today. Xan comes alone to drive us home, so that Jacks doesn't try to get frisky with the omega in the back of the truck. He's *mostly* healed, but broken bones take more than just a couple of weeks.

I make Xan stop before we leave so I can hit the gift shop and get her some flowers. It's not a courting gift, more just an I-missed-you gift. Jacks is mad that he didn't think of it first. When we get home, Xan helps Jacks into the house. My skin still feels a bit tight in places, but I can easily make it around on my own, and they sent me some oxygen just in case my breathing gets difficult with my singed lungs.

Candice is in the kitchen—in a cute little apron covered in pink hearts—and Jacks makes a beeline there as soon as he sees her. She gives an exasperated look to Xan, who manages to peel him off and lead him over to the couch, where he pouts while staring at her. She blows him a kiss to settle him down, and goes back to the oven, pulling out a roasting pan. I'm not sure what's in that thing, but it smells really good...so does she, and I want to stalk her up the stairs and make her melt with my mouth and hands.

She came to our room almost every day we were there, but I couldn't really touch her, not the way I want to...the way I've wanted to ever since I first saw her at the clinic. I should have known something was up then, even without being able to smell her. My body knew, it just took my brain a while to catch up, and soon she should start her heat. I know she's been on blockers for the last couple of weeks, to make sure we were healed enough. Even now, Jacks is supposed to be taking it easy, but he told Xan he would escape the hospital and walk home if they didn't release him now, so we were all cut loose.

I want to eat, I also want to eat her, and I am a bit torn at the moment between which one my body needs more. Conversely, she did go through all the trouble of making dinner, and I don't want her to think I'm ungrateful. Maybe we can pawn kitchen cleanup off on Gabe and Xan since we've been at the hospital, and I can take her upstairs after we eat.

This sounds like a good plan. I like this plan.

Idea in place, I hum to myself as I head towards the kitchen to see if she needs help. I didn't notice it before, but she has the radio on and turned down, her hips swaying along to an old Def Leppard song about sugar, so I grab her hips and slide behind her...my rhythm sucks, and the height difference makes this almost impossible, but she turns in my arms and cuddles against my stomach anyway.

"I missed you." It's a soft whisper against my chest, and my hands slide from her waist to wrap about her back, pulling her against me.

"I missed you too, Kitten. When we started driving towards your house on the fire truck, I couldn't breathe. I just kept telling myself it couldn't be you, you were safe with Jacks, and then we got there, and I couldn't think—none of us could. I don't want to do that again. I love you. I was already pretty sure, but this has just kind of solidified that thought."

I pull back enough that I'm able to get down on my knees, still not quite eye level, but at least I can see her face now, and her eyes are red. "I love you too, Leo. All of you...though Gabe is still a grumpy ass. I'm sorry I worried you all...I really didn't mean to." A tear escapes her eye and rolls down her cheek. I brush it off, cupping her face with both hands, and leaning my forehead against hers.

"Of course you didn't, Kitten, none of us think that. I'm just...I'm sorry we weren't there when you needed us. I'm sorry you got taken in the first place, and that we let that asshole get so close to you. We love you, and we want to bond you, if you'll let us. Make you officially part of Pack Asher."

"I mean, you already are, but...shit, I'm messing this all up." I'm stuttering over my words, but I don't want to give her any reason to think we don't want her, don't already know she is ours in every way.

"I want that too. I want to be able to feel you all." Her arms come around my neck, and she stretches up to kiss me on the tip of my nose. Not romantic, but definitely cute, like kitten kisses.

"Is it ok if we wait till my heat? I wanna make sure I do this right, and I don't know what I'm doing. Um, I took my last suppressant yesterday, so it'll probably be soon...maybe two or three days. Sorry." She blushes, her ears turning bright red. I chuckle against her hair.

"Whatever you want, Kitten, however you want to do it, it's all up to you, ok?" She nods, and pulls back, wiping her hands under her eyes and sniffing.

"You wanna help me with this roast? It is not real light...and flaming hot right now, so I don't want to hurt myself, or drop it on the floor trying to get it to the table."

Gabe must be listening because he comes bustling in and grabs the potholders off the counter to take the pan before I can get it.

"We want to make sure this makes it to the table." He winks at me and leaves. Candice looks startled, but bounces back quickly.

"Ok, then, um, can you get the cake?"

Xan comes in and grabs a large platter with a cake off the counter, but we all freeze when we hear a screech from the dining area, and all of our heads swing towards the table.

"You are not fucking telling me you put that hot goddamned pan on my fucking table without a fucking trivet, are you? What the fuck, man!" Jacks storms around the bar and grabs several dish towels out of a drawer, while yelling over his shoulder. "That is no way to treat natural wood you fucking savage!"

Candice busts out laughing so hard she doubles over, hands on knees...and I wonder if I can get her to laugh that hard later...in the nest...while not wearing pants.

Xan shakes his head, takes the cake and leaves, setting it on the server before going to console Jacks, and look up videos on how to repair scorched wood. I get back to my feet and offer her my arm to lead her to dinner.

Candice is a good cook. She says she got used to cooking when she lived with her grandpa, and it was always harder to just do it for herself when she could nuke a frozen burrito. She also jokes that this is the reason she's squishy, and I growl at her self-depreciation. She's beautiful just the way she is.

Gabe is on dish duty, though it's more in penance to Jacks and the table than anything else. Soon after dinner and welcome-home cake, we retire to the couch. There is another anime on—this one has a talking cat in a top-hat, and I seriously have no idea how my kitten finds all these strange movies, but maybe I need to broaden my horizons.

After food has time to settle, I lead Candice upstairs to wash all the hospital smells off of my skin, and make sure she knows just how attractive I find her.

I pull her towards the nest bathroom. It doesn't have the biggest shower—that's downstairs—but it should still fit us, and it has all her favorite soaps. I want her relaxed and boneless in my hands, so I'm going to do whatever it takes to make her comfortable.

She likes her water hot, but not turned all the way up, so I toss a couple of towels in the warmer and then get the shower started. Once the room starts to fog up, I hit the fan and turn the water temperature down, barely one eighth of a turn, just how she likes it. I strip out of my own clothes and throw them at the hamper. I want to undress her too, but it looks like she beat me to it, this time, and when I turn around, the rest of the room melts away. All I can see is her.

My feet move on their own, crossing the room in two long strides. I wrap my arms around her, picking her up so I can taste her. My lips crash into hers, and her tongue thrusts into my mouth. Fuck, I've waited so long for this. Small chaste kisses, little pecks on the cheek or lips as I was leaving for work or getting home. But this, I need this. I curl my hand under her ass and stabilize her against my chest. She is making little whimpering moans into my mouth as she nips and sucks against my lips. My cock is already so fucking hard, and I try to keep her lifted above it, because any friction right now is going to make me come.

Her hands wrap in my hair, pulling and tugging, twisting my head to the angle she wants so she can devour me. Her core is hot against my stomach, and the scent of her slick is heavy in the room, as she slides her hips back and forth over my abs, seeking her own friction. I move my fingers forward, circling her thigh, and giving her something hard to grind on. I groan into her mouth and she swallows it down, shaking in my arms.

Did she...did she just come on my abs?

Her body relaxes against mine, rocking against me, but no longer frantic. Her head tilts back and her expression is sheepish.

"Sorry Alpha, I've been stressed I couldn't, um, finish lately. Sorry."

I laugh and kiss her hair. Releasing my grip, I let her slide down my body, hissing at the slick friction as she slides over my erection. "Soon," I assure it.

Grinding against her before I release her to get clean. I do a quick scrub on my hair, then pull her under the spray with me so I can wash her hair, it curls around my fingers, and I really want to wrap my hand around it, pull her head back, and ravage her mouth some more, but clean first. I get her rinsed and conditioned, then grab her soap and get all my important bits. I'm going to smell like a peach orchard after this, but if she doesn't mind, then I don't care either.

Once I'm clean, I kneel in front of her...and tilt her head back to remove the conditioner. Then I put her hands on my shoulders so I can reach down and wash her feet, making sure I get her tiny little toes, up the calves, tracing my hands up the inside of her thighs slowly. By the time I get to the top and pull my hands away, her breathing has gotten heavy and rough...and she tips her head out of the water to give me a dirty look when I set her foot down and move to the other leg. Same procedure. Wash her foot, rubbing my thumbs into the arch, gentle pressure to relax her while I get her clean. My big soapy hands up over the calf, swirling behind the knee...she jerks and giggles...I guess her knees are ticklish. I file that away for later. I stop just at the top of her thigh again, earning me another annoyed glare.

Still on my knees, we're close to the same height. I tilt her head back, making sure the conditioner is out, and then start soaping her neck and shoulders. I want to avoid the sensitive spots, tease her by not touching them, shoulders, stomach, around the out-side edge of each breast, avoiding her nipples. Being this close to them is torture. All I want to do is lean down and draw them into my mouth, circling my tongue over the stiff tips. Pulling and rolling with my tongue...fuck I'm leaking pre-come, thank fuck we're in the shower.

If I were here alone, I would take care of this now, just touch-ing her is the sweetest torture, but I'm already so close, and

I need to draw this out to make sure she gets at least a few more, because I know I won't be able to last once I'm inside her. Orgasm denial has never been a kink for me, but I can sometimes see the appeal. Today is not one of those days...I'm so hard, I feel like I could fuck my way through a concrete block right now.

Once we're both cleaned, I pull the towels out of the warmer and bundle her up, wrapping another one around her hair. Originally I planned to go for the full pampering experience, and smooth lotion all over her, but I don't have the patience for that right now, and with how she is leaking slick, neither does she...plus, it would taste terrible, and I need to lick her.

Towel around my own hips, I scoop her into my arms and make my way back to the nest. She's rubbing her thighs together and whimpering. I finish blotting all the water off of her skin, drawing this out, and I want to whimper right along with her as my hands trace over her skin. I don't want to leave the damp towels on her; I don't want her to catch a chill, but her skin is so warm...too warm, actually.

Is she getting sick? She was at the hospital a lot with us. Maybe she picked up a bug.

"Kitten, do you feel ok?" I put my hand on her forehead, and yeah, she is definitely running a fever.

Fuck my life. I can't seem to seduce her. My timing is just shit every fucking time.

Suddenly it registers that she hasn't replied. I cup her face and look closely in the dim light of the nest. Her face and chest are flushed, her eyes glassy, and her whimpers have become a steady whine in her chest.

"Kitten, Kitten, look at me." I tilt her face, trying to get her attention. "Kitten, how long did the doctor say it would take your heat to start after you stopped taking the suppressants?" I'm swinging madly between terrified and overjoyed. I want her to be in heat, but not until she's ready, and she thought she had a few more days.

Her thighs rub together, and the scent of her perfume is making me lightheaded. It's stronger now, and so sweet.

"Hurts." It's a whisper, barely a breath, but I hear it.

"What hurts, what can I do Candice?" I know I sound angry, I'm not angry, I'm just worried, and I want to help, but I don't want to do anything she's not comfortable with.

"Please, Leo...Alpha, please. Make it stop." She paws at my towel, loosening the knot until I look like a fucking coatrack with that damned thing hanging off my erection. If she wasn't so needy right now, I would be embarrassed. But she does need me, and I lean her back against the nest.

"Shh, Shhh. It's ok. I'll help, just relax." I stare down at her, laying at the edge of the mattress, her legs draped over the side.

I slide between them, stretching them gently, and draping them over my shoulders so I can finally see her. Her thighs are covered in slick, and her pussy lips are all pink and swollen. I should at least let Gabe know that she's going into heat early...but after...after I help her. I lean forward and lick the slick off of her thighs. A loud groan erupts from my chest. Fuck, she tastes so good.

I lick deeper this time, flicking my tongue across her clit, and then tracing it down to thrust inside of her, there's so much slick it's dripping down the blankets, and I kind of want to call Jacks in here to help, so we don't waste it. I don't normally even think of sex and my packmates at the same time, but all the time we've spent together in the nest lately, it seems like the next logical thing. I don't find them attractive, but I know omegas usually like being shared.

Fuck, I hope she likes being shared.

She's moaning and writhing on the bed, and I have to wrap one hand around her hip and hold her down with my palm splayed across her pelvis. I cover as much of her core as I can with my mouth, using my tongue like I want to use my cock, thrusting it into her over and over, collecting all her slick. She tastes like heaven, but I can't seem to get her to orgasm this way. I use two fingers, sliding inside her. She's so fucking tight, and I'm about to come before I can even get any friction for myself. My other hand is still spread across her hips, keeping her pinned.

She's bucking and rolling her hips along with the thrust of my fingers, and her hands come down, scratching along my hand and arm, flailing for purchase. I cover her clit with my mouth and flick my tongue a few times before sucking hard on her little nub. Her channel clamps down tight on my fingers, trying to suck them back in—her nails score my skin. I think I might be bleeding, but I don't care at this point. She lets out a long, keening cry before collapsing limp on the bed.

I pull my fingers out, sucking and licking to make sure I get all her slick. And slide onto the bed beside her. Her eyes are closed and her muscles languid as she smiles up at me.

"Pretty Kitten, do you feel better?" She rolls against me, rubbing her face on my chest.

"Thank you Alpha." She kisses and licks between my pecs and I am about to come all over her stomach if this keeps up. My balls ache from being denied, but I need to make sure.

"Candice. I think your heat started. Is it ok if I go get Gabe and the others?" Gabe, specifically, since he is the head of our pack, but I know Xan and Jacks will want to be here too.

Her eyes shine up at me. "Leo, please...I want you." I pray to any god that will listen to give me patience and resistance right now.

"You can have me Omega, I'm yours. But do you want the others as well? Can we knot you and bond you? Please, this is important." She tries to rub her palms down my chest and stomach, but I pull her hands away, and she starts to pout.

I stand up and she whimpers again, reaching for me. I hate being the responsible one.

But temptation is a difficult burden to bear, and I only manage to make it to the door of the nest, yelling out for Gabe or Xan to come upstairs now, before she gets a chance to drag me back to the bed, because I know I can't resist anymore.

Chapter 47

Candice

Knowing someone is big is not quite the same thing as *knowing someone is big*! Case in point, Leo is a tall guy. I think Jacks told me he was six-foot-seven, and there are times I want to climb him like a tree and feel what it's like being that tall. By the law of averages, this would mean that Leo is also well-endowed, and holy fucking shit, I'm not sure if that's going to fit.

I know omegas are made to be stretchy, and yeah, logic dictates that if a baby can come out of that, then a giant penis should be able to go in. But the tree analogy was not far off, and that thing is like a fucking log. My inner omega gives a little happy wiggle.

That bitch is crazy.

My mind is clearer than it was. Leo has long, thick fingers, and he knows how to use them. But now I'm burning up again. I feel like my skin's on fire, and I need him to come back here and knot me properly, but he keeps trying to pull away. It's enough to make a confident and empowered omega cry...and I'm neither of those things. I sniff loudly, feeling even worse about myself. Who starts crying in the middle of their heat? I know it's not attractive, and I doubt it's doing me any favors with my already squishy body.

I curl in on myself, trying to cry quietly. It hurts, and I need a knot, but I can understand why Leo doesn't want me...the man is gorgeous, the whole pack is, and I'm kind of a frumpy nerd. I wish I'd paid more attention to how to be attractive when all the girls talked in high school about makeup and exercise and giggled about how to seduce somebody. I just didn't care. It was never important to me, but now I feel like I'm missing some pretty crucial knowledge.

A big warm body curls against my back, and the scent of oranges is stronger than the chai right now, zesty. It's not fair. This man smells like a hot cup of tea and an orange roll. Fuck. I curl farther into myself, trying to get as small as I can, but his big arms wrap around me, keeping me from hiding. "I know it hurts, Kitten. I'm here to help. Just tell me what you need."

But how can I tell him like this...I need a knot. *Oh, could you lower your standards just for a few days?* Once again, the logical part of my brain tells me that he wouldn't touch me if he didn't find me attractive. He wouldn't be curled up against my back with a lead pipe pressed against my ass if he didn't want me...but anxiety, ain't she a bitch? She says it's all pheromones and nobody could really want me, I can't stop my body's shaking from the need and the tears, and I don't have the courage to tell him what's wrong.

He squeezes me tighter. "Ok, Kitten, let's try this...do you want to wait for Jacks or Gabe? We can do that, but is there any way I might be an acceptable substitute? If not, I'm going to need to go take a really cold shower and have a lie down, alone, with a lot of lube." He pauses, kissing the back of my shoulder.

"It's ok if you don't want me, I know I'm not dominant like Gabe, or fun like Jacks or super smart like Xan...I'm just kind of a big freak of nature." He sighs and kisses my hair.

"Do I need to beg here? Because I need you, I'm so hard it hurts, and if you don't want me, I would really rather not be here when they come in." He hugs me tight, but my brain is still trying to process what he's talking about when his arms loosen and he pulls away.

It takes me longer than it should for all that to filter through. Hormones or pain, I don't know, but I roll over and grab his hand before he can leave the bed. I pull, and he lets me bring him close. He looks so sad, and it's such a far cry from his usual easygoing smile that I start crying for both of us. "It's ok, Kitten, I know what I am." He kisses my hair, but I don't let him pull away again.

Grabbing his face, I pull his mouth to mine. While I'm probably salty and unappealing...I don't think Miss Omega Manners ever covered how to deal with anxiety crying during a heat. I never read her column anyway, so that's just a guess.

He doesn't leave me guessing for long, after the first few tentative kisses Leo is kissing me back, sucking on my lips, and I gasp in surprise—he uses that opening to thrust his tongue into my mouth. I writhe against him as his big hands hold me down, caging me in as he plunders my mouth. He's all I can feel, everywhere and everything I need, devouring my moans and whimpers, his possessive growl rumbling across my skin, making my nipples harden and more slick gush from my core.

He leans over me, his knee going between my thighs, spreading me wide for him, one of his big hands slides down to my hip, holding me in place as he drops and rolls his body against mine, the other fists tightly into my hair as he ravages my mouth. I feel like I'm going to combust if he doesn't fuck me soon, but when I try to pull away to ask, I can't. I'm trapped by his hands and tongue and teeth, and I do the only thing I can I bite him.

He pulls back, looking down at me, his pupils are blown wide, and he's breathing heavily. His hand on my hip moves up to touch his lip and the tiny drop of blood there. His eyes flick to the blood on his fingers and back to me. Regret mars his face.

"Please, Leo...my alpha. I need you inside me. Please, it hurts, I need you." A flash of relief crosses his features before he kisses me again, fast and sweet, but with copper tints to his orange flavor. He hooks his arm around my waist and pulls me higher on the bed.

"How do you want me, Omega? Do you want to present for me?" I immediately roll over, scrambling up onto my hands and knees before dropping my arms and looking back over my shoulder at him. He runs his hands over my hips, then up my spine, raising goosebumps.

"I think we need pillows," he murmurs and thank fuck for Jacks, because I have a shit ton of pillows in here. I start grabbing them and tossing them over my shoulder. I think I smack him with a few in my fervor, but then his arm circles my hips and lifts me again, stuffing the pillows under me until I feel like my legs are hanging in the air by the time he stops.

"That is a delicious view, Kitten." Then he bites my ass cheek, not hard, but I'm sure I'm gonna have a mark there tomorrow. I glare over my shoulder at him this time.

"Sorry Love, you just look good enough to eat." But I'm distracted again as his fingers wrap around my hips and he holds me in place to rock against me. Just the feel of his hard shaft pressing against me leaves me whimpering and leaking slick all over him.

He groans loudly, grinding against me harder. One hand pulls away to rub his cock head up and down, getting him slippery with my juice.

"Is this ok?" I barely manage a nod, before he's lined up and pushing into me, and the stretch is both pleasure and pain.

The friction makes me moan, but if I wasn't an omega, there's no way this could work. I feel like I'm being split in two, as he slowly inches his way in, stopping to breathe and pulling back to rock forward with more force. The burn is almost too much, and when he bottoms out inside me, his knot pressed tight against my entrance, I don't know if that's going to be possible.

My inner omega gives another excited little squeal and dance.

She is gonna fucking get us killed, I swear.

A big hand strokes down my spine, and his low purr kicks up, loosening my muscles and helping me relax around him.

"You ok there?" I reach back and pat his hand, because words are not something I can do right now. A low chuckle is my only warning before he pulls out and slams back in hard. My teeth click with the impact and a small part of my brain wonders if we're going to survive this.

But what a way to go!

Leo is huge, and strong, and he lifts and maneuvers my hips, dragging my body back against him every time he thrusts forward. I feel like a ragdoll, a very overstuffed ragdoll, as I'm pushed and pulled by this giant alpha. Used for his pleasure. It's a heady experience, and I can't do more than twitch as my release slams into me, making white lights explode behind my eyes. My whole body seizes before it relaxes, my muscles become jelly when it happens. All I can do is hang limply in his arms as he thrusts into me, grunting as he works me over, stretching me for his knot.

"Alpha...knot. Bite...please..." I'm not sure if I'm making sense, but he gets the gist of it.

He pulls out completely, and I feel empty and devastated, until he rolls me over, and slides one hand under my ass and the other against my back. He lifts me up to his chest, and my legs go around his lean hips. He holds me tightly against him as he slams back into me, filling me with one thrust. I give a strangled cry as my whole body lights up.

He moves me over and over, thrusting me up and down on his shaft—his loud groan shaking my whole body.

"Fuck, Candice. I-I can't hold on. I want you, please...can I...?" He raises me once more and pulls me down hard against his knot and it hurts, it hurts so bad. I wiggle against it, trying to escape the pain, but my movement and my weight provide the last nudge it needs to slide inside, locking me against him.

He's sitting back on his calves, neck bent at a harsh angle, kissing and licking my neck, and I tilt my head to give him better access. I feel so fucking full right now, I'm lightheaded, and worry filters through that I might pass out. I reach up and pet his hair, the only permission I can give right now, but it's enough, and with one last lick he opens wide and sinks his teeth into my neck where it joins my shoulder.

Another internal explosion rocks me, my eyes rolling back, and my body twisting and convulsing around him as all my muscles seize. He straightens and his head tilts back as he lets out a roar loud enough to shake the windows in their frames. He's still holding my body against his, locked in place by his knot. And I can feel my body milking his release. He's filling me up. I flail against him, my hips trying to buck. His hand slides from my ass to snake between us, long fingers dipping down to rub my clit—keeping my orgasm going as he twitches and jerks inside me.

My mind feels stuffed with cotton, the edges of everything all soft and fuzzy. His arm wraps across my back, and he lowers us to the side, his big body still wrapped around me. I can feel warmth radiating in my chest, a cozy feeling like being wrapped in a fuzzy blanket, and I know it's Leo.

"So, did you just fuckin' call us up here to watch you knot and bond our omega without the rest of the pack?" Gabe's growl startles me out of my snuggly repose, and Leo tenses against me, pulling me tighter to his chest.

"I actually called you because her heat started, and I wanted everyone to get ready and join us." I can hear the smile in Leo's voice. "The audience for knotting and bonding is just a happy bonus."

Xan's loud guffaw breaks some of the tension and Leo kisses the top of my head.

I'm still locked against him, and I bask in his warm satisfaction that I can feel through our bond.

"Well, Old Man, you're more flexible than I realized. I admit I was curious how you were gonna pull that off with her being so short—it was quite a sight to see." Xan chuckles darkly. "Let me lock up, feed Iggy, and get Jacks in here. Gabe, can you grab some water bottles and stock the mini-fridge? I don't think any of us are going anywhere for a few more days."

Chapter 48

Gabe

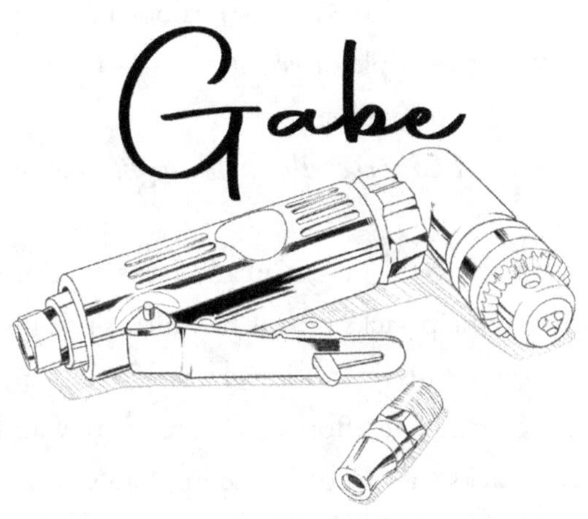

The growly lead alpha part of me is mad. Leo gave her a bonding mark first, but realistically I know she was in pain, and Leo was nearby. He's also the only one who hasn't been with her yet. I know Xan has yet to knot her, but we'll all be offering her our services over the course of the next week.

I grab a case of bottled water out of the garage, a couple of boxes of different kinds of protein bars—*and what the hell*—the fruit bowl along with the bananas sitting in the middle of the table, just in case. I stack everything on top of the water and carry it up the steps to the nest, putting a couple of waters in the mini fridge. I don't know if our omega likes her water room temperature or chilled, but I want to be ready either way.

She's still curled up against Leo. Her eyes are closed, but her hands rub up and down his forearms in a soothing motion. I grumble again, because my inner alpha wants to be in his place. Once their towels are collected from the floor and in the washer downstairs, I snag a couple of yogurts out of the fridge and a box of chocolate chip cookies.

Gotta to be sure I have everything she might need or want on hand.

When I get back to the nest, Xan and Jacks are already back. Xan is having to help Jacks out of his shirt, since his ribs are still healing. I can see his frustration at trying to be gentle, while Jacks is pulling against his efforts, trying to get to Candice. I go stand between Jacks and the bed, meeting Xan's eyes.

"You need any help?" But Jacks stops yanking when he loses sight of her and Xan smiles at me.

"Thanks, man, I appreciate it. It's like having a fucking two-hundred-pound puppy that wants to jump up on every-one." I wait until he gets Jacks's shirt off and leave him to try to wrestle him out of his pants alone.

I've got an omega that'll be needing me soon. The room is already filled with her perfume, and I think it's part of what's making Jacks so feral. I've been hard as fucking stone since I walked in earlier, and I don't think it's going away anytime soon.

Leo's groan speeds up my hands. It sounds like his knot is finally going down, and she is going to need help sooner rather than later. Omega heats can be difficult, and with everything else that's happened since we met, we haven't really gone into specifics with Candice on how she wants to handle it. Other than her giving consent in advance for knotting and mating bites, and her birth control situation—which involves a shot from her OBGYN. I am glad at least one of us had foresight for that. Peeling my undershirt off, my eyes latch onto her throat, mentally mapping out *my* spot. Right on the opposite side of Leo's, I can see the pulse jump in her neck.

That spot is mine.

As I unbutton and lower my jeans, Leo tightens his arms around her and slides her up his chest, dislodging his still hard cock, and tending to his mating mark on her neck, kissing and licking the fragile skin there. She is so tiny against him, and I'll admit that Xan was right, it was an impressive sight to see them together.

I was a bit worried at the end about the knot. It's like the man has a fucking softball at the base of his dick, and I don't know if she'll be able to take it any time other than during her heat, but that's a worry for another day. I step out of my jeans and leave them there. Jacks huffs at me, but he's hardly in a position to complain since he's busy fighting Xan to get his shoes off and get on the bed. As soon as he frees himself from his sock, he scrambles across the mattress to Candice, sandwiching her between his chest and Leo and starts kissing her, nipping across her jaw and down the far side, across from where Leo is taking care of his own mark.

Right in my fucking spot. And the little asshole knows it, judging by the shit-eating grin he just threw my way.

Candice is rubbing her thighs together, whimpering and writhing between the two of them. I growl my dominance at Jacks, who clearly has no sense of self preservation, since he just ignores me. Other than giving a satisfied little smirk as he continues to taste her skin.

"Xan, get up here and get your boy before I lock him out of this room for his own good," I snarl, and Jacks just giggles like a brat, snuggling closer to our omega as her arms wrap around him. This time *she* gives me an angry look, and I'm flustered.

"He's gonna hurt himself again if he gets too active. He needs to calm down," I tell her, pointing at Jacks as Xan tries to peel his arms off her without hurting his ribs. Her eyes are sad when she turns her face back to him, but she pulls him close for a soft kiss, and then presses lightly on his shoulder, so he lets Xan pull him away a bit on the bed.

"I'm not sayin' you can't have him, my Little Omega, just that we need to be careful, and he's not bein' careful right now." Her eyes widen and I can see how much she relishes the pet name. But she *is* mine, she's ours, and it's time to make sure no one else fails to understand that fact.

With Jacks no longer pressed against her front, she reaches for me, a small whine escaping her throat. "Gabe." It's a breathy little sigh, but just having her call my name causes my cock to start weeping pre-come. I flick my eyes to Leo to confirm and he meets my gaze and pulls back, effectively passing the wiggling omega off to me. Her hands are frantic on my skin, caressing and scratching, fingers tracing lightly over my muscles one moment, only to squeeze and pull against me the next. Her body is shaking with need, and I groan as she attacks my mouth with fervor—kissing and biting. I roll her under me, trapping her body with mine and keeping her from wriggling away. Thrusting my tongue into her mouth in the way I want my cock to already be inside her.

She moans into my mouth, and I swallow down all her whimpering cries. "Do you want me, Little Omega? Do you want your alpha to knot and claim you?" Her movements grow more agitated, her body rolling against mine, her thighs tightening under me—trying to trap my cock between them, and I taste her pleading moans against my lips. "If you want my knot, you need to be a good girl and calm down. Can you do that?" The thrashing slows, but her whimpers ratchet higher.

"Fuck, you are so fucking good for me." I raise myself up on my arms and slide my pelvis forward. "Now, open your legs, yes, just like that...such a pretty girl." Her head tilts until she's looking down between our bodies.

Holding myself up on one arm, I wrap her leg around my hip and take my shaft in hand—giving it a couple of long, hard strokes, teasing us both. Her eyes are huge and glassy, staring down at me, and she chews on her bottom lip. I lean forward to lick her mouth and stop her before she breaks the skin. Her eyes ping-pong between my face and my weeping member, but close entirely when I push forward into her, just the head.

I stop and her eyes fly open, glaring and angry. "No, pretty girl, look at me. I want you to watch me." Her eyes slide down my body, settling on where we're joined, as I slide the rest of the way into her hot core. Even after Leo, she's still tight. I don't have to fight as much as I did the first time, but she feels like fucking heaven.

I wrap her other leg around me, and she locks her ankles behind my back, pulling me tight against her. "Oh no, Little Omega, no topping from the bottom...that's not how this works." I chide gently, rolling my hips against her and drawing out a long, low moan. "I thought you wanted to be a good girl for me. Good girls don't demand, they ask nicely." I roll my hips again, grinding against her clit. "Can you ask nicely?" Another hip roll, and then a pause, waiting for her reaction. I know that once her heat hits hard, I won't be able to play as much, but for now my alpha wants to dominate her.

"Please, Gabe." It's barely a murmur, but I reward her with a tiny teasing thrust.

"I'm sorry, Pretty Girl, what was that?"

A little louder this time. "Please, Alpha, please, I need you." And I groan at her breathless little plea, more than ready to take care of us both. I pull back far enough to kiss her on the forehead, and then thrust forward, allowing my mind to get lost in the pleasure of our bodies together. Her legs are tight around my waist, her arms come up to circle my back, and her nails dig into my skin as I pound into her harder. Sweat rolls down my back, stinging as it slides through the long tracks she's made on my skin.

Fuck, I am already so fucking close. My arms wrap under her back, pulling her hard against me as I rut into her tight little body. She's crying out, pleading over and over for me, and I need her to come. I need to knot her, but fuck. "That's it, that's my good girl. You ready for my knot, Baby? You ready to be ours forever?" She screams out her plea against my chest, and I can feel her muscles tighten around my aching shaft.

Thank-fucking-god, I thought I was going to die if I had to hold back any longer. She goes limp in my arms, and I roll over, her body flopping loosely on top of me. I grab her hips in a bruising grip, my fingers digging into her flesh and pull her hard against me as I thrust up into her, my knot stretches her, causing her to cry out again and spasm around me, and then it's in, locking us together. I groan loudly, my release finally washing through me as my cock kicks inside her, filling her up, and a deep aching part of me wishes she wasn't on birth control. It wishes that after this heat she would be pregnant, but that can come later, if she wants.

Pulling her taut against me, and tilting my head down so I can mouth her neck and shoulder. Fuck, she tastes so fucking good, and she keeps murmuring, "Please, please, please," over and over under her breath. I strike, biting that special spot I picked out, lead alpha's prerogative, right over her heartbeat. I feel it fluttering against my tongue as I bite down, breaking skin, and her coppery taste coats my tongue. A warm light blooms in my chest, a soft golden glow where I can feel her warm and content, beating right next to my heart...and through that, Leo, still smug that he bonded her first, and so fucking happy that she's ours.

I pull back enough to tend to the mark I left on her, laving her skin with my tongue, leaving soft kisses, before settling back purring to ease any lingering pain. I stroke her hair gently until she looks up at me, chin resting on my chest. "So, was I a good girl?" She smirks at me, and I snort laughter.

"Yes. You were a very good girl, but if you snark at me like that, I am going to redden that pretty little ass of yours." Her cheeks burn a deep pink, and her eyes flip back to stare at my chest. I think my little omega might enjoy being spanked sometime soon.

We're still stuck together when Xan slides across the nest towards us, two water bottles in hand, and I hold her against me as I sit up, wrapping her thighs around my hips and settling her into my crossed legs. I have to lean her back to get her to drink, since she doesn't want to move from where she's plastered to my front. But hydration is important, and better to start now than have to play catch-up later.

"Thanks Xan, can you grab me a warm washrag, please?" He just grins at me, but goes to the bathroom to get it anyway.

He knows it's important for me to take care of my pack. While the care I need to provide for my little omega is different than for the rest, it's still important, especially right after intimacy. When he returns with a warm wet cloth and a towel, I trade him for the now empty bottle.

"Hey, don't wash the bonding marks yet. They need time to heal properly before you get 'em wet," he tells me, like I don't already know.

Xan is a certifiable genius, but sometimes he says some dumb shit. Not on purpose, he just doesn't seem to realize that some things are common knowledge. Other things that he takes for granted, nobody else knows, because it is random and obscure shit. Unfortunately while he's helping me, no one is corralling Jacks. Who comes over to fawn over Candice, stroking her hair and kissing her shoulders. At least he realizes that she does need a break at this point, and snuggles down against my leg so he can pet her thigh.

I settle her against me again, and run the washcloth over her face and neck, carefully avoiding the bonding marks on each side, then down her back and arms. It's not very warm by then, so I send Xan back for another as I lean her back on the bed on top of the towel. Jacks promptly moves above her on the nest, reaching out to touch her arms and shoulders. My knot softens, and I am loath to pull away from her heat, but she needs to be taken care of, at least until the next wave hits. I run the warm cloth over her hips, taking note of the bruises there, and cursing myself internally. It takes another two washrags before I get to her core, and clean up the mess that Leo and I left. She flinches a little, and I'm not surprised that she's a bit tender.

Chapter 49

Jacks

Finally. Finally, my little lion is in heat, and I can't seem to stop touching her. Any time my skin isn't in contact with hers, I feel like whimpering.

Alphas aren't supposed to fucking whimper, dammit.

Xan strokes my back, helping keep me grounded. I know I need to heal, but I also need her. I've touched her and tasted her more than any of the pack, but I don't think I'll ever be able to get enough of my sweet girl. Her scent is richer now, more decadent, and while I know it's from her heat, I think I prefer her normal scent. The normal one means she isn't in pain. It means she is calm and happy, and feels relaxed. This scent means she's in pain, or at least might be in pain if she can't get the knots she needs.

She told me before that her heats were never that bad, but this seems much more intense than she led me to believe. Is it because she has alphas right now? I don't want to be the cause of her pain. I slide closer to her, touching her anywhere they'll let me. I'll feel better once the bond is complete, then I can know how she feels, what she needs. She's resting now after Leo and Gabe, and I feel lost without her, even though she's right here. I need her.

Xan kneels behind me. He's amazing and strong, and I love being with him, but she feels like the other half of me, and I want to love him together with her. Make sure she knows that no matter what, we'll always be together.

He puts on a good front, but really, he worries about putting himself out there, worried that people will think he's faking being smart. He doesn't try to look like it. Most people don't realize the laid-back grungy mechanic is the real mask. He likes working on cars, figuring out the puzzle behind them so they work again, but the carefree attitude is all an act to put other people at ease. It's only us, and now Candice, who gets to see my brilliant mate in all his splendor, his real face, as it were.

Candice murmurs sleepily. She fell asleep after Gabe cleaned her up, and I think it's been at least a few hours. I wonder if I should go get her something to eat for when she wakes up. Will she be hungry? Her heat's just started, and she's still mostly coherent. So we aren't into the full throes of it yet. Once we are, I know it'll be harder to get her to eat or drink anything, so maybe I should make sure she does now.

Watching her sleeping face, I enjoy the shy smile she gifts me when her eyes open and she catches sight of me looking over her. She's the sweetest little omega, and I want to give her everything good in life.

"Can I get you anything, My Little Lion?" I return her smile, stroking my fingers down her neck, circling the bite that Leo left there.

"Why do you call me that? I don't think of myself as especially fierce." I grin at her misunderstanding.

"Well, I started calling you a little lion because you looked like a dandelion sticking out of the omega burrito I wrapped you in. But I think the fellow you stabbed with a fork would find a point of contention with you saying that you're not fierce." She swallows thickly and gags.

Shit...too soon?

"Sorry, that was just really gross. And I don't look like a dandelion." I chuckle, pulling her into my arms, and she moans softly. Her skin is burning up again.

"Do you need another knot, my fierce Little Lion?" I can't help but smile at the scowl she graces me with. She is fucking adorable. But her hips twist and her face pinches, and now is not the time to tease her.

"Do you want me alone, or do you want Xan and I together?" Her eyes grow wide, and she bites her lip.

"Together, this time" She ducks her head when she answers, and I grin at how shy she is.

But my smile doesn't last as Xan wraps a hand in my hair, and pulls me up, my back pressed against the front of his body, taut as a bowstring, my hips pushed out so that my head is level with his. He gently bites against my bonding mark before smirking down at Candice.

"Were you talking about me, loves?" Her eyes grow big, looking up the line of my body, and she licks her lips, rising on shaking arms. She twists and settles in front of me—my eyes drop to watch her take in my straining cock.

Her eyes flip up to Xan, and I can see him smiling down at her like the Cheshire cat from where his chin rests on my shoulder.

"You wanna make him beg, Pretty Lady?" Her head bobs rapidly, her eyes never leaving my hard shaft. Her tongue comes out to lick her lips again.

"Teamwork then? You can have the front, and I'll take the back?" Her eyes finally flip up to Xan, and she nods again.

His hand tightens in my hair, and the other hand cups my hip, holding me in place as her tongue comes out and flicks across my weeping tip. He lets out a low moan of appreciation, and I nearly come then, caught between my two lovers. Xan releases my hair and steadies my hip, pouring lube down my ass-crack, and massaging it in. His hand strokes from my hip up my back, tilting me forward as he circles my anus with one finger, pushing gently against the tight ring of muscle after every circuit, he thrusts in and out of me, loosening me up, and applying more lube as needed until he can add a second finger. I'm already panting with need for him—my eyes closed—when a warm wet mouth envelops my tip, and her soft little tongue rolls over my piercings every time Xan pumps into me.

Fucking hell, I don't know if I'm going to last long enough for him to even fuck me at this rate.

I groan loudly as he removes his fingers, adds more lube, and pushes three in at once. She takes that moment to suck me down deeper, her lips almost touching my knot as I bump against the back of her throat. I pet her hair, wanting to tangle my hands in it and fuck her mouth, but that's not what she needs. She lets out a little whimper as I thrust against her. Xan stops and pulls away.

"Well, we can't have you abusing the omega, now can we?" He laughs darkly before biting the back of my neck and moving away. Candice is still on my cock, but my hands aren't on her. Without the extra stimulation I have more control, but I'm already getting close when Xan yanks my hands behind my back, and I feel the cord loop around my wrists.

"There now, pretty as a picture. All tied up, and no place to go." He slaps me on the ass, causing me to thrust forward into Candice's hot mouth again. Her needy groan matches mine.

Xan's hand comes back up and wraps around the back of my neck. We both know I could escape if I wanted to, but that's part of the game, it's just there to remind me. His other hand returns to my ass, freshly lubed and thrusting three fingers in harder than before. I want to lean back into it, but that would take me away from Candice's heat. His fingers slow, and then stop, still lodged inside me.

"Do you want me to fuck you, Jacks?" he whispers in my ear, nipping at my lobe.

"Do you need me to take you hard and fast while she sucks you off?" His fingers thrust again, scissoring wider, opening me up for him.

"Or do you want her to present, so you can fuck her and knot her? Bond her while I pound your tight little ass?"

I barely croak out, "Yes!" Then the fingers are gone, and the blunt head of his cock is lined up with my tight ring of muscle.

He pushes in, more gently than I expected, until just the head pops inside, and we both groan at how fucking good it feels to have him inside me.

His hips flex and retreat, gaining a little ground inside of me. Candice bobs her head, swirling her tongue around my tip each time she comes close to the end, and it's making my muscles twitch and tighten around Xan as he pants in my ear.

"Fuck...Omega, Omega stop." It is not a full bark, just enough to get her attention.

She pulls back with a loud pop and I dribble seed onto the bed at the sudden cold air against my heated skin.

"Such a good little omega, My Pretty Lady. But he's going to come too quickly if you keep doing that. You make him feel too good." His hips snap against me, and he is finally fully seated to the knot.

He bites my shoulder, moaning around my skin.

"You feel so fucking good Jacks, but I was about to lose it watching her suck you off....I just need a minute," he whispers into my ear.

His voice rises for her, "Can you present for your alphas, turn around so he can knot you properly and bond you like he wants to so badly."

His hand reaches around, stroking me once and squeezing my knot hard. My hips buck against him, and my breathing stutters.

Candice scrambles around, thrusting her ass in the air and wiggling it at me. Fuck me, she's so wet, slick dripping down the inside of her thighs, and I want a taste. I want to bury my face in her core and drink her down. But it's not the time for that. For now, I need to feel her. Feel her wrapped around my aching cock, feel her flesh between my teeth, feel her warmth in my chest, snuggled close to Xan's. He touches her hip, guiding her closer. Her legs are between mine now, brushing the inside of Xan's thighs. He reaches forward, gathering her slick and smearing it all over my shaft, stroking me hard and fast until I let out a strangled moan, and then he lines me up with her dripping pussy.

"Now, fuck our omega!" he hisses into my ear before slamming into me hard, causing me to fill her with one thrust.

My fingers spasm as my hands pull against the bonds. I need to touch her, to stroke her, to wrap my fist in her hair, pull her head to the side and sink my teeth in behind Gabe's mark. I can see the perfect spot, Xan and I can overlap right over her spine.

But Xan's fingers are back in my hair, holding my head in place, or I would already be sinking my teeth into that perfect spot. Claiming her as mine, as ours. My teeth ache with the need to mark her, and my jaw throbs where it was recently fractured, but I can't seem to loosen the muscles to relieve the pressure.

She moans and writhes against me, pushing back even as Xan is fucking me into her savagely. Little whimpers reach my ears as she braces her hands against the mattress, pushing back, trying to get closer, trying to knot herself on my dick. I completely lose it, pulling against Xan's hand in my hair, snarling and snapping in frustration. His hand drops, releasing my scalp, and pulling the ties loose from my hands, freeing me to touch her, like I need to do so badly. But then he growls against my back and grips my hips tight, nails digging into my skin and I faintly register the tickling sensation of blood running down my skin as he slams in me, forcing me deep inside her. She looses a keening cry, her muscles clamping down on me as my knot forces its way inside, and I pump her full of my come, her body milking me for all I'm worth.

"Now, bite her, bond her...make her ours!" Xan shoves my head down towards her, as he growls and empties himself inside me. He seems to be riding the razor's edge of a rut, and I have no doubt he would knot me right now if he could. Being an alpha, my body isn't built to take a knot, though sometimes I wish I could. My teeth are on her, that perfect spot, and I bite, causing her to cry out again, as she continues to come wrapped around my knot, draining me dry.

I feel like collapsing between the two of them, dark behind me, light in front. But I need to take care of my new mark, as I feel her warm and bright growing inside my chest. The contrast is a bit startling between her and Xan. Her little spark is like a tiny sun bringing light and warmth into my chest. Xan is warm, but dark, like a hot breath on the back of your neck when you knew you were alone. I love him, but sometimes I forget how black he can be. I feel quiet echoes of Leo and Gabe as well, and they reflect Candice's tiny sun right back to her. Xan pulls me back against him.

"You truly are the most amazing thing to ever happen to me." He kisses my neck just below my ear, then pulls out, causing a shudder to run down my spine.

He guides me to help Candice lie down on her side, since I'm behind her, and still buried inside her, not leaving anytime soon. Maybe I should apply for a change of address, and just take up residence. I smile at my own ridiculous joke, and run my fingers through her hair, gently loosening tangles and fluffing it out so the sweat can dry from her skin.

Chapter 50

Xan

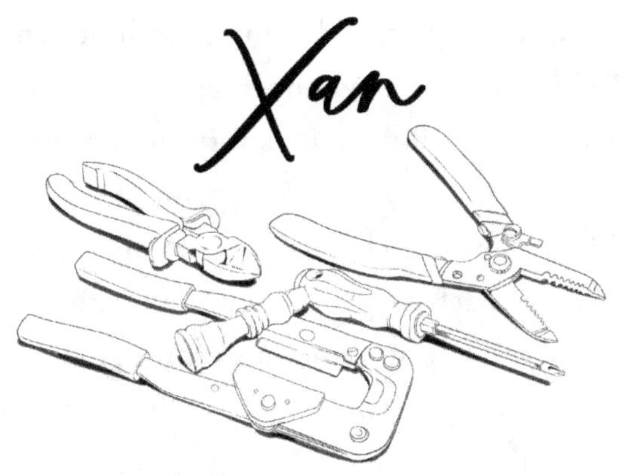

I make my way to the shower. My legs are still shaking, but I need to clean up in case Candice needs another knot soon. It would be a lie to say I didn't also want to leave my mark on her perfect neck. Finally tied together with the rest of them. It's more than I could have hoped for. Gabe and Leo are more like brothers to me than anything else, but I'll still rest easier knowing I can feel them, and knowing they're safe at any given time.

I want to feel Candice like I do Jacks. That man's bond is like a sparkly fucking unicorn dancing around my dark chest. I can feel the echo of her through the bond Jacks and I share, but I want it for myself, too. Maybe that's greedy, but I don't care. I'll allow myself to be greedy for this.

Once the water's hot enough, I step under the spray. My back twitches and the muscles loosen under the heat. I rarely let myself go that far with Jacks. He's too soft and sweet, especially when it comes to Candice. But sometimes you just need to let it out to play, and I think they both enjoyed it. I know Jacks likes being tied up sometimes, and Candice *might*, so that's something to look forward to trying. Ugh, I should probably pace myself. We're gonna be at it for a few days, and I don't want to burn out too soon.

I scrub my hair, debating if I should cut it or not. I haven't bothered in years, and it just keeps growing. Jacks likes to play with it now, so I'll probably just have him trim the ends up. My mind wanders, relaxing under the steam and clearing my head. I know once I get back into that room and Candice's perfume hits again; I am gonna be fucked. I damned near tipped into rut earlier with Jacks, and I don't want to risk hurting him, ever. Fuck, her scent, the sounds she makes, the feel of her skin...I'm getting hard again just from the memory, and I don't think it'll be long before I do go into a rut if I'm not careful.

I mean, ruts and omegas go together like...well...chocolate and peanut butter, we were made to satisfy them, and I'll gladly do everything in my power to keep her healthy, happy, safe, *and* satisfied.

Fuck, I need her. I love Jacks, but I don't think I've ever felt this way about anyone. I just don't want to do anything to make it awkward.

Like fucking him hard into her with no warning...yeah, no chance of awkward there.

Fuck.

I wrap my hair in a towel and put another one around my hips before stepping back into the nest. Jacks is still wrapped around her, and they look sort of perfect together. My bright colorful alpha with all his sharp edges, and our pale sweet omega, soft and cozy. The balance between them really is stunning.

But, I'm getting distracted. I grab up the towels and washcloths from earlier, and head downstairs to put them in the washer along with ones I'm currently wearing. I walk into the dining room to grab an apple out of the fruit bowl and it's gone...dammit. Gabe must have grabbed it to take upstairs when he was picking out snacks last night, so I cross the kitchen and reach into the pantry to grab some jerky before heading back to the nest. My cell is plugged in and laying on the counter, and the screen flashes with a voicemail when I walk by. A tiny alarm bell rings in my mind, and I look back towards the stairs. It should be fine. Everyone else is up there with her.

I pull open my voicemail and enter the code, and wait for it to click over. It's Kelly at the garage, and she sounds really upset. What the hell.

"Xander, sorry, I know you guys are busy with your omega, but Trey...er...Seth. He came by the shop. He was so mad, he threatened me if I didn't tell him where you live. Sally's here though, and she told him she'd put out his other eye if he ever comes near me again. Oh god, Xan, I was so scared. He looks crazy. I don't…I didn't tell him your address, but it's not like it's a huge secret. Just…be safe, ok. Please be safe."

The message ends with a click and I save it instead of deleting. Fuck, I am gonna need to tell Gabe about this. I stomp across the room towards the garage, calling the police station as I go, wondering why the fuck no one told us that the crazy fucker who attacked our omega was loose again. Once the line rings through I open the door and step out onto the cold concrete floor. I don't want Candice to overhear this conversation, so it's better to do it downstairs, and as far away as possible. She has enough going on without this shit.

"Oak Flats Police Department, how can I help you today?" I sigh, trying to hold my temper in check.

"Yes, this is Xander Asher. I just received a call from one of my employees that Seth Thompson came to our place of work and threatened her. The last I heard, Seth was in jail after kidnapping and trying to rape my omega, so I want to know why I wasn't informed of his release and what you can do about him harassing my people."

There, totally civilized. I can fucking do civilized.

"Oh, yes, Mr. Asher, I'm sorry. But Mr. Thompson was released on bail last night. We tried to call a Mr…." I hear papers shuffling in the background. "Mr. Gabe Asher, as a courtesy, but were unable to reach him to let him know. I wouldn't worry too much about it, but if you'd like, we can send a patrol car over to your place of business to drive around and keep an eye on things."

I grind my teeth, and by sheer fucking force of will manage not to scream or throw my phone.

"Thank you, that would be greatly appreciated. Thank you for your time." I manage to maintain a calm tone and hang up, which I think deserves a fucking award.

I gotta figure out how to talk to Gabe about this. But when I open the door to head back into the kitchen, Leo's standing in the living room, tearing at his hair. "Oh, thank fuck."

Panic fills my veins as I march towards him. "What, what's wrong, what happened?" He looks a bit shocked at my tone, and I try to calm down.

"Candice, she...she wants you. She's crying. She said she needs you. I came downstairs, but you were gone, and...what's wrong, man? You look like you've seen a ghost." I scrub my hand that's not holding my phone down my face, and give him a whispered rundown of what happened since I came downstairs looking for a snack.

"What the actual fuck? Why would they let that bastard out?" Leo is growling now. It's a rhetorical question, so I don't bother answering.

"Can you get Gabe out of the nest, fill him in while I take care of Candice?"

"Of course, just...don't fuck her until I get him out of the room. It seems to galvanize him, and then I'll never get him moving." He chuckles and pats my arm.

"Good luck, brother."

He trots back up the stairs while I try to get my mind off all the shit going on and back onto our omega. I take some deep breaths, frustrated that our omega's first heat with our pack was interrupted by this. This ought to be a time for more than just the physical bonding. Clearly, she trusts us to some degree, or we wouldn't be doing this, but this is supposed to be a time where we can focus on each other in all ways, physical and emotional.

That little ass-wipe is fucking it up.

I've waited long enough for Leo to get Gabe's attention and head back to the nest. When I arrive, they're standing near the door, Leo talking quietly to him. Gabe's head snaps towards me as soon as I walk in. His features are hard and set, angry, considering how much perfume our little mate is pumping out into the air. I go hard instantly, my gaze drawn back to the bed where Candice is curled around herself. Jacks is petting her hair and stroking her skin. She shakes harder as sobs wrack her body when Gabe and Leo leave the room. This is all sorts of fucked up.

I slide into the nest beside Jacks, letting my hands join his to stroke and pet our sweet girl, pulling her hair away from her wet cheeks. Big eyes blink up at me from wet lashes. Her nose is red and I want to growl again at how messed up this is. How everything feels off kilter. Even before the phone call, something felt wrong, not with her, never with her...but something not quite right tickled the back of my mind. She reaches for me and all other thoughts disappear. I nod once to Jacks, who sneaks away and follows Gabe and Leo out of the room, then I fill my arms with the soft sweet omega before me. Pulling her against my chest.

She looks around for a minute and whines when she realizes we're alone.

"It's ok love, of course they want you." A big tear rolls down her cheek. "They just need to clean up a little bit, get a snack, then they'll be right back. None of us wants to be away from you longer than we have to."

Some of the tension leaks from her body. I know she's anxious, she worries, even now, that we might not want her. Which is ridiculous. I'm fairly certain any one of us would gladly dismember someone to keep her safe and protected.

The more my hands rub over her skin, the more relaxed she becomes, melting against me, a tiny rumbling omega purr issuing from her chest. My own chest swells with pride that I caused that. I hold her face and kiss her forehead, her cheeks, her lips. She wraps her smaller body around mine, and it feels so good to have someone smaller than me to take care of. Everyone thought I was going to be a beta, and even when my designation came in, I never got taller. I just barely hit six feet high and stayed there, but it makes me feel ten feet tall as I tuck her head under my chin. My purr rumbles through me, soothing her stress and helping her relax.

Sadly, it doesn't last long, and soon she's whimpering and wiggling against me, twisting her tiny body against mine. A low whine builds in the back of her throat, the need from her heat overwhelming the calm. I lift her face and look into her eyes. She nods slightly, and I know we're on the same page, even before her quiet plea reaches my ears.

"Xan...Please...Alpha. It hurts."

I pull her face to me and kiss her quickly, pulling back and then laying her down on the bed.

"Don't worry, Pretty Lady, I'll take care of it. Just relax, and let me make you feel good." I kiss her lips again, lightly, then make my way down her body, leaving small soft kisses in my wake.

Tracing my tongue down the column of her throat, kissing and sucking on the delicate skin, careful to avoid the fresh marks my pack left. I tease her collarbones with my teeth, scraping along the sensitive flesh. Pulling back to look at her face, I take her breasts in my hands, flicking the hard nipples with my thumbs, rolling them gently, taking in her reaction to each sensation. She wriggles against me, her hands coming up to touch and stroke my shoulders and hair.

That's not good enough.

I lower my face and flick my tongue over her hard peak, and I'm rewarded with a tiny gasp...I suck hard on the nipple and she moans and twitches against me.

There's the reaction I was looking for.

My other hand gently pulls on the nipple I'm not worshiping with my mouth. Tugging and rolling the stiff tip as her fingers dig into my scalp, pulling me against her as I bite down, just a little sting before my tongue laves over the abraded flesh, soothing it.

I don't want to stop, but she needs me to keep moving. Pulling away, her taut peak leaves my mouth with a popping sound. I trail kisses down her stomach, my hands reaching down to spread her legs wide so my body settles between them, my shoulders pushing them apart as I get closer to her heated core. She smells like peppermint mocha with cinnamon...Jacks didn't clean her up yet.

Fucking hell, I can't stop the groan that escapes me as I breathe in their combined scents. My cock is trapped under me, and leaking into the bed, and it rubs against the blankets as I stretch forward to taste her. Even though I finished once with Jacks already, I'm getting close again. I need to wait until I'm inside her, knot her, bond her...but fuck me. It's hard to resist any longer and I push forward, thrusting my tongue inside, tasting their joining and it is fucking amazing.

Eagerly lapping and sucking against her core, I drink down their combined flavor and my resulting growl vibrates both of our bodies. Fuck, I need to mark her like he did...but she needs to come first. Once I've gotten all that I can with my tongue, I use my hands, spreading her open and thrusting inside with two fingers.

She is so fucking hot and wet, and I suck on her clit, silently begging her to come so I can fuck her properly. I vary the speed of my fingers, scissoring them back and forth, finding a rhythm that makes her moan as I flick my tongue over her hard nub, and she's so close...I can feel how close she is...but she doesn't seem to be able to push through it. Pulling my slippery fingers out of her, I switch to my thumb, still pumping in and out. I use my slick coated finger to probe her back entrance and she twitches hard.

There we go.

Gently circling her back hole, I test for resistance, waiting for her to protest, but when nothing comes, I push one finger inside, my thumb still buried in her core. I nip at her clit with my teeth, and I'm rewarded with a fresh wave of slick covering my hand. She lets loose a high keening wail and convulses, her legs twitching. I keep my hand and tongue moving until she stills, her hand goes back to stroking my hair instead of pulling on it. Slowly retracting my hand, I kiss the top of her mound as I crawl up her body.

"Was that ok, Precious?" She looks up at me with glazed eyes and pulls me down to kiss her.

"Mmm, that was wonderful...thank you...You taste good," she mumbles, rubbing her face over mine. "I'm so sorry I got all weepy on you. These hormones are horrible and...I...I'm sorry."

"Shh...it's ok. I just want to make sure you're ok...Are you ok?" I stroke her hair, trying to meet her eyes, needing that confirmation before we continue.

"Yes, thank you...but...can I feel you inside me? Please, I want you, and I want you here beside Jacks and Gabe and Leo." She touches her chest, right below her sternum, and I smile.

The tender moment is broken when I hear her mumble, "Gotta catch 'em all, I guess."

I snort laughter, not sure how I lucked into such a sweet nerdy omega, but she amazes me at every turn.

"God, you're such a geek, I love you." My confession startles me as much as it does her, I didn't mean to say it. But she just smiles up at me.

"Oh, like you're one to talk." And she tugs at my attempt to grow a beard. "Didn't chin pubes go out of style in the 90s?"

Laughing again, I descend, covering her with my body, devouring her lips. Her giggles turn into sighs of pleasure and sweet moans as I plunder her mouth with my tongue. Feasting upon her sweet cries as I grind against her, and when I look down into her glazed eyes, she gives the faintest nod. I line myself up against her and push inside. She's so wet for me that I slide in with no resistance, fully seated up to my knot on the first stroke. It's like being wrapped in warm wet velvet, squeezing me, and I gasp and almost come immediately. Holy fuck...This is going to be difficult.

I pull back almost all the way out and help her roll onto her side. Lifting her leg up in a half split over my shoulder, I tease myself, thrusting lightly into her entrance...I *have* to hold on, and this way I can also stroke her clit and her back door if she needs that. Once I'm re-positioned, straddling her thigh, I push all the way in again. She moans out my name as I snap my hips forward, and my cock jerks inside of her, almost losing the battle.

I lean forward, folding her leg towards her chest, and pound into her, her little mewls and gasps pushing me closer and closer to the edge, and when I feel her start to pulse and tighten around me, I'm lost. I lean my weight forward, straining and pulling against her, needing to have my knot inside her before I finish, and she cries out as it finally slides into place and seals us together. Her muscles clench around me, dragging my release from me, I couldn't stop even if I wanted to. Her body won't let me as I empty myself inside her tight, hot channel.

"Now, please." It's barely a whisper, a soft breath.

I push her shoulders forward and lean down to strike...burying my teeth in her skin. My mark intersects Jacks just above her spine. The final bite finishing the collar of marks around her neck, the pack fully linked together. She cries out again, the bond locking in place, and I feel her tiny light blossom in my chest right next to Jacks. The two together make me feel bright. I can find them both now if they get lost—but I won't let them get lost. They're mine in every way now.

I run my tongue over the new mark, cleaning off the tiny trickle of blood and kissing it reverently before pulling back and straightening her body.

"Sorry, I wasn't trying to turn you into an Escher girl." I smile down at her, and her laughter is high and clear as she returns it.

She reaches up to cup my cheek, her brows furrowing. She wipes away moisture I didn't know was there, then tilts her head, and I can feel her wondering if I'm ok.

"I'm fine now love, just fine...rest."

It takes a bit of wiggling in this position, and still locked together, but I finally settle behind her. The big spoon, holding her tightly and letting my mind wander to explore these new sensations in my chest. She and Jacks are both bright lights. His tiny unicorn now has a spinning disco ball and is practically vibrating with excitement at the bond being completed. It's amazing, but also a bit unnerving to feel so light and empty. Like everything is right and nothing could ever go wrong.

I have to guard my thoughts and my feelings, as I pull the tiny omega closer to me, I know how wrong things *can* go, and now that I have this feeling, I'm never letting it go.

I will destroy anyone who tries to take it.

<h1 style="text-align:center">Chapter 51</h1>

Candice

My heat continues for three more days. Three of my pack are around me at all times, but one is always missing. My inner omega is both anxious that someone might not want her and pissed at them for not being there. I've been knotted so many times, I feel like I'm going to walk bow-legged for the rest of my life, but my head is finally starting to clear.

I remember the first day clearly, being knotted by each of my guys, the bond sliding into place as each one marked me. I look around at the three alphas sleeping under and near me. Xan is wrapped around Jacks, and I passed out the last time with Leo still knotted inside me. While cock-warming isn't a kink of mine, waking up this stuffed doesn't feel bad at all, and I can see where I might enjoy it in the future if I wasn't so sore already.

The clouds in my mind clear and now I feel sticky and disgusting. I flail out of the nest, landing in a heap on the floor and letting out a loud groan. Jacks whimpers in his sleep, and Xan grumbles, pulling him closer. I smile watching them. Xan looks like some kind of laid-back surfer dude, and Jacks could have fallen out of a British punk band, but the need to be clean calls, so I turn and stumble to the shower.

I get the water started and wait for the steam. Getting a cup and chugging three glasses of water while it heats, my stomach growls in protest for my not including food. But I'm afraid if I try to make it to the kitchen right now, I'll have so much alpha leaking out of me that it will create a slip and slide on the stairs. So for the safety of all and the comfort of me…shower!

I adjust the temperature from volcano-hot down to boiling-alive hot and step under the spray. I miss my waterfall shower head from my house—probably need to get one for here now. A sharp pang fills my chest as I remember that I don't have a house anymore and I try to put it from my mind. Allowing the hot cascade to rinse away the dried come and slick that covers my body, I reflect on the last few days. This was the strongest heat I've ever had, and I don't remember all of it. There was a deep aching need, but all of my alphas were there at some point to help me through it. I trace my fingers lightly over the necklace of marks wondering why I didn't mark my alphas in return…or really arrange the nest myself, and it feels like a cold finger of dread slides down my spine at why my omega didn't do those things. I mean, I feel safe here. I have my alphas.

Is something wrong that my omega brain senses that I don't?

My body aches, still feeling the need to be knotted again, but it isn't as strong now, and as I dry off and pull a long shirt over my head, I resolve to talk to the guys about it once they wake up. Looking down at myself, the shirt I put on comes almost to my knees, and when I bring the sleeve to my nose, I realize it's Gabe's—who is not here. Now, on top of finding snackage, I need to locate my pack leader, so I concentrate on feeling him through the bond. I think he's asleep—but why isn't he here with us?

I leave the room as quietly as I can, closing the door behind me so I don't wake the guys up. I walk gingerly down the stairs, a death grip on the railing, since my legs still feel a little like Jello. And since I live here now, I have to agree with the guys about moving the nest downstairs before my next heat. It'll be a good chance for us to paint the room beforehand, like Jacks wanted.

When I get to the bottom, I see Gabe in the living room, lying on the couch. He doesn't look particularly comfortable. However, the bond is peaceful, so I'll wake him up and drag him upstairs with me after I find food. A clear plan in place: I march towards the kitchen...tripping over my own feet a little and stumbling forward. I have to lean heavily on the bar to steady my wobbly legs. Standing there contemplating my own clumsiness and trying to get my legs to solidify, I notice the garage door wasn't pushed closed all the way. It's not open, it's just not latched.

I walk towards it, intent on pushing it closed. I feel a tingle at the base of my skull, a low warning buzz telling me something isn't right. Fuck the snack. As soon as I get this door shut and locked, I am gonna go wake up Gabe and get his help. My fingers brush the door, pushing against it, but instead of sliding closed it pops open, and a hand grabs my wrist, pulling me forward and unbalancing my already wobbling legs.

My mind spins as I take in the figure in front of me. A scream bursts forth as I yank my arm as hard as I can, trying to fall backwards instead of towards the snarling asshole who burned down my fucking house. He looks the same. Same fancy clothes. Same messy hair. Same enraged snarl. Same angry eyes...eye...there's a patch of gauze over the other side, and a small part of me is glad that I stabbed him since he hurt my alpha and burned down my fucking house. Hell, he pretended to be my friend, and stalked me.

I scream again, as loudly as I can...knowing that at any moment my alphas will come, and I'll be safe. Time freezes as I don't hear any movement in the house, and I think of all of them sleeping upstairs and Gabe sleeping on the couch. My eyes track down his body, seeing the gun in his hand. A tranquilizer gun? I don't know, but they're not dead. I would feel if they were dead, wouldn't I?

This little motherfucker!

He sneers at me again. "Oh, are the big bad alphas all asleep?"

He drags me through the house, his big hand like a manacle around my wrist. I kick and scream, but Gabe doesn't stir from where he lies on the couch.

"What...what'd you do?" I say, yanking on my wrist, trying to get to Gabe. I need to make sure he's ok.

"It's so hard to get medication to knock out alphas. There are all these hoops to jump through. I had considered just using horse tranquilizers, but those aren't guaranteed to knock one of those big bastards out fast enough. *You* have put me through a lot of trouble, little omega." His face twists into a maniacal grin.

"Let's go check it out." He holsters the gun and pulls me towards him—reaching up to rip down the collar of my shirt.

"Fucking omega slut!" He takes a deep breath. "That's ok...the bond looks new, so if I kill them now it should fade fast enough. It's going to hurt like hell, but we can just consider that part of your punishment.

"Let's get rid of the three upstairs first. If the bond breaking wakes them up, I would rather only have to deal with the one down here." He pulls me towards the stairs and I go limp, making him drag my body behind him.

"Do I need to knock you out too, omega?" He fingers the gun at his belt...I don't know what effect alpha tranquilizers would have on an omega, but I seriously doubt I would live through it.

"I wanted you to be awake when they died so you could feel it, but if you're going to fight me this much, it might not be worth it." I let him pull me up, I can't do anyone any good if I'm unconscious, or worse.

He pulls me up the stairs and I follow, stumbling on numb legs.

At the top, there sits Iggy, staring up at me from the railing at the head of the stairs. She looks desperate for attention after being separated for most of the week. I yell at her, trying to get her to leave because I would so not put it past this asshole to hurt my iguana. Her head tilts to one side, then the other, and I see what she is planning too late. I grab at her as she leaps, demanding attention. She hits Seth in the chest, scrambling towards his head, her tiny claws sinking into his shirt and skin.

Turns out, Seth is not a lizard guy *and* he screams like a little bitch. He flails backward, teetering on the edge. I grab again for Iggy, but she is dead set on getting on his head now and skitters across his shoulders. Seth screeches again, letting go of my wrist, his hands beating at his own chest and head. Thank fuck, that's enough for her. Iggy reaches the pinnacle of Seth, decides he isn't worth her time or affection and leaps again, landing on my bare thigh, her tiny claws sinking in. I don't even notice as I watch gravity take hold of Seth and down he goes, screaming.

I turn away, pulling Iggy up to rest on my shoulder in her preferred place. There are a couple of loud snapping noises as he hits stairs on the way down, and his scream cuts off. But I don't look back, I just run straight into the nest to find my phone. After locking the door, I call 911 while I shake my alphas, trying to rouse them.

The emergency dispatcher answers before the second ring. I'm glad she has experience understanding incoherent babbling, because I don't think I'm making sense at this point. I keep shaking Leo, but he just mumbles. I try Jacks and Xan, and nothing. I'm trying to explain everything as best I can to the operator, but thankfully she finally stops me and asks me for my address. I almost give her my old address before I remember it's changed. She asks me to stay on the phone while she sends the police over, and I tell her we need a medic too because my guys aren't waking up.

As a lastditch effort, I pull open the mini fridge and bring a couple of bottles back over to the nest...cracking the seal and pouring the cold water over Leo. He jack-knifes off the bed, sputtering and blinking at me. It's only a second for him to take in my tear-streaked face and panicked expression and then he's pulling me into his arms, holding me and purring a soft, soothing rumble. Then he hears the dispatcher on the phone and gently takes it from my hand. He confirms the address, admits he just woke up, and asks how soon they will be here. Hanging up, he looks back down at me.

"You know, there are less...wet ways of waking someone up. For instance, I keep smelling salts in the first aid kit." He smiles at me gently, but I just cry harder, my hormones are still high, and I really want him to hold me, tell me it's going to be ok, knot me again, and go back to sleep...but that option is off the table, at least for now.

So I go with him to get the smelling salts, but when we get to the top of the stairs he looks surprised, and a little green. I follow his gaze down. Seth is lying at the bottom, his neck at an awkward angle and his eye staring open and empty at the ceiling.

Leo asks me to go wait in the nest for him. Still wearing Iggy, I go back and spend my time poking at my two sleeping alphas while I wait for Leo to get back. It takes longer than I thought it would, and I need to ask him where the hell they keep the first aid kit. If it's this hard to find, I don't think it is going to be super useful. But when he finally returns, Gabe is with him, looking a bit groggy and very pissed off. Leo wakes up Xan and Jacks and then we all scramble to get dressed when the doorbell rings. The police have finally arrived.

Once we're dressed and downstairs, I tell everyone what happened, from waking up on top of Leo to pouring cold water on him to wake him up. Xan looks at the stairs and my iguana and mumbles some stuff about safety. The police look around the house, and find that the lock on the garage door was forced open, and that's probably how he got into the house. Xan mumbles something else about enclosing the garage and putting in a carport.

The next few hours are uncomfortable, not just because there's a dead body at the foot of the stairs, but also because my heat hormones are still running through me. I really want to shove the cops, and the EMTs, and the dead body out the door and drag my alphas back to the nest, but they won't let me...I asked. Jacks agreed, but Gabe vetoed it.

Spoilsport.

Chapter 52

Candice

By mid-afternoon, I'm about to combust. Jacks brings me upstairs to help long before the house is empty, but it can be hard to relax when the house is full of strangers. Jacks offers to change the sheets out, and while I let him remove the wet one, I don't want to get rid of the others just yet. I need to fix them though...so I pull everything off and re-fit the sheets...then the blanket.

No, not that blanket. I need the other blanket.

I place pillows and smooth creases...and then do it again. Trading out fabrics and textures to different spots until it finally feels perfect. By the time I finish, the last officer has left, and Jacks is grinning at me like he just won the lottery. When the rest of the pack wanders in, he is bouncing up and down on his toes like a little kid.

He leans into Xan and whisper-shouts, "She likes the nest I got her!"

It takes Xan a minute of looking to see what Jacks is talking about, but then he just smiles and pulls him in for a quick kiss, before turning to me. "Well, Omega, are you going to invite us into your nest?"

"Well, no. Not dressed like that." I smile at him, and he and Jacks race to see who can get their clothes off first. Jacks wins because he was only wearing sweatpants since his ribs are still injured. He scrambles into the nest, bowling me over and flattening me into the mattress, kissing and nipping at my lips and chin. Grinding his length against me and whimpering.

I'm a little relieved when Xan appears behind him and offers to tie him up for me if he doesn't behave. Jacks lets out a low, shuddering groan, but allows Xan to pull him away.

Gabe is next, and he kisses me slow and deep, pulling me into his lap, his hands cupping my ass as he holds me against him, his shaft already hard and rubbing over my clit makes me gasp into his mouth. Then there are more hands. As Leo reaches between us, his fingers trailing over my breasts, teasing my nipples, his mouth coming down to kiss and lick at the bonding marks on my neck. My body melts between these two huge alphas, my skin tingling and sparking everywhere they touch.

Soon Gabe tilts me back into Leo's lap, stretching me between the two, and I almost come off the bed when his big hands settle against my core. Three fingers push inside, and I'm already so wet that while there is a little stretch, he glides in easily. He groans loudly, and bites his lip, staring down at where his fingers are buried inside me. He pumps them a couple times before his thumb comes down on my clit and starts a slow, heavy rhythm in time with the thrust of his fingers. His other hand strokes his own shaft, occasionally bringing the head down to thump against my hard nub.

Leo has my hair wrapped around one hand. He turns my head to the side and there's his monstrous shaft, already leaking copiously from the tip, and I want to taste him. He loosens his hand enough that I can tilt my head and lick up the side, but it's not enough. Between being teased with Leo and by Gabe, I am soon writhing, tangled in their legs. Leo's fingers reach out and stroke up my breasts from my stomach. His big hands almost cover them completely, but they still spill out between his thumbs. He smiles down at me as he plucks at my nipples, rolling them between his fingers, before squeezing the entire globe in his hand. When he finally releases me, his thick fingers wrap around his shaft and pump it again. I need to come; I need them inside of me, but no one is. They just tease me.

I look to the side, searching for Jacks. He and Xan will let me come, they feel so good...but they're otherwise occupied. Xan on top, holding Jacks down and kissing him deeply, thrusting against his stomach and grinding him into the mattress. No help there.

"Please, Alphas...Please let me come. I need it," I whimper and Gabe stops, pulling his fingers out of me with a wet squelching sound.

"You don't like how we play with you, Little Omega?" he asks, thumping his cockhead against my clit again, and sending little shivers through my body.

"I, I need more...please."

He just smiles at me. "You hear that Leo? She doesn't like how we're playing with her. She needs more."

Leo grins back. "Well then, let's give the pretty omega what she wants."

Gabe's hands are on my hips, Leo's on my shoulders and they flip me over. Still facing each other, Gabe brings my hips up and licks me from clit to ass, then thrusts his tongue inside of me, repeatedly spearing me with it.

"Do you still want more, Kitten?" Leo asks, one hand wrapped around his shaft, the other tangled in my hair.

"Y–Yes, Alpha," I manage before he raises my head and brings his giant fucking cock to my lips. He taps twice against them, smearing them with pre-come.

"Open up Kitten, time for some milk." There is a loud moan behind me as I gush more slick all over Gabe, but I open my mouth, licking my lips clean before taking his swollen head inside.

I have to stretch wide and the angle is difficult until I can get my hands underneath me to hold myself up. Leo's hand is still in my hair, guiding me up and down his shaft until it bumps the back of my throat. My eyes water from the strain of stretching my mouth that wide.

"Oh, fuck, you look so good like that. You are being such a good girl for your alphas," comes a voice behind me, but I can't turn my head with a giant dick stuffing my mouth, so I silently preen at his praise.

"Can you take another?" I nod, trying to answer, but nothing comes out other than a muffled moan.

I feel Gabe slip out from under me, holding my hips in place as he lines himself up with the entrance to my pussy.

"Such a good little omega." He slams into me hard, pushing me down on Leo, and I gag slightly, but I can't swallow with this thing lodged in my throat. Leo groans and shifts too, so he is kneeling in front of me, my head tilted back, opening up the column of my throat and easing some of the pressure.

Gabe pulls back and thrusts hard into me again, and I have a moment to breathe before Leo's cock is back in my throat. Leo groans again, and the next several minutes are a blur of Gabe's murmurs of praise and the sounds of Leo's pleading. Soon Leo is gasping for breath. "We need to switch, I'm about to blow and I need my knot inside her again."

Gabe slows down, his hips still thrusting, but not as fast or hard. "I think I have a better idea. Lie down for our omega to ride you."

Leo scrambles to comply, his big body surprisingly graceful for his size, as Gabe lifts me up, still impaled on his hard cock, and walks across the mattress towards Leo.

"We're going to make a little switch out here, Little Omega. Leo can have your hot little cunt to knot, and I'm gonna take your ass, ok?" I whimper with apprehension. While Xan has played back there one time, no one has ever done *that* before. Gabe lifts me up, settling me on top of Leo's shaft and pushing me down. The stretch isn't as painful as it once was, but it is still a tight fit as he slides me all the way down so I'm resting against Leo's knot.

"Now, I know you're probably a little scared. Have you never had anyone back here?" he asks me, his hand rubbing lazy circles across my ass-cheek. I can't meet his eyes.

"No, I mean...Xan's fingers, but nothing else." He smiles and a low purr rumbles through his chest.

"That's because you're a good girl. Don't worry, I'll make sure it feels good. It might sting a little, but just at first, ok?" He ruffles my hair and I feel like I should remind him that I am a fully grown adult and don't appreciate being patronized, but it's hard to do that when someone is busy shoving a finger up your ass.

Gabe gathers more slick, smearing it from my core to my anus and slides his finger in and out...Leo is shuddering under me, and I lean forward to get a little friction, and give Gabe better access.

"That's my good girl," he says again, thrusting deeper, gathering more slick and adding a second finger.

This is as far as Xan got, and my body tingles with anticipation as Gabe scissors his fingers back and forth, stretching me and opening me up. I rock slightly against Leo, forcing strings of incoherent words from his lips. It's kind of satisfying to see my eloquent doctor so tongue-tied, but I grunt and my rhythm falters as Gabe adds a third finger. There's a burning pinch and I try to pull away.

"Shhh, shh...it's ok Baby...you're ready now." He pushes his hand against my back, flattening me against Leo. Then I feel the blunt head of his cock pushing against my back hole. If I wasn't so stretched out, impaled on Leo, I think I would clench up. But none of the muscles in my lower half seem to be working as Gabe pushes slowly inside, using my own slick for lube. Gabe growls long and low.

"Fuck, Little Omega...Holy fuck...You're so tight." He pulls back and thrusts forward again, gaining another inch, and Leo lets out his own strangled growl.

"Oh fuck, do that again." There is a dark chuckle behind me and Gabe slides back and thrusts in, harder this time, gaining more ground.

Leo's hands clamp around my hips. His eyes are wide and wild. "Fuck, Kitten...I." He looks over my shoulder. "Hurry the fuck up, Gabe, I am about to lose it."

Gabe grunts in response and pulls back again. Snapping his hips forward, bringing his knot all the way to my tight ring of muscle. Leo snarls, holding my hips in place and thrusting up into me. Gabe growls louder behind me, and then he is rutting against me. Slamming his knot against me with every thrust, trying to push past that tight ring. The dual sensations are too much and I cry out as an orgasm rolls over me, drowning me in sensations where all I am is feeling. One big raw nerve exposed to pleasure, throbbing with it.

I slump between them, boneless, until something prods against my face. It feels sticky. I look up, expecting to see Leo's hand, but Jacks is smiling down at me. "Hey Little Lion, you want a treat."

Xan is on the other side and they are both standing beside Leo's chest, cocks out and ready...Jacks was poking me in the cheek with his. Gabe has slowed behind me, and Leo is vibrating beneath me.

I open my mouth, needing them to do the work, since I am boneless right now. And work they do. Holding my head, they take turns fucking my face. First Jacks, being careful of the metal on his piercings, then Xan, trading me back and forth between the two. Leo's hands clamp down on me, bouncing me up and down against his knot while Gabe continues to thrust from behind. It takes less than a minute before Leo lets loose a growling roar, pulling me hard onto his knot. It's not as difficult as the first time, but I am so full already with Gabe in my ass that I worry for a moment before he pops inside and locks in place. His cock kicking inside my overstuffed pussy as he fills me with jets of come, setting off another tiny orgasm for me.

Gabe is next as he grinds out, "Shit...fuck...'s too much." Slamming into me again, and I can't move.

Locked to Leo. It burns when he forces his knot inside me. It pushes me over the edge again, and I can feel myself tightening around both of them, to their mutual moans of pleasure. Xan's hands are tangled in my hair, holding me in place as he fucks into my mouth. Jacks tries to push him out of the way to take his turn, but Xan doesn't stop. He groans, holding me tighter.

"That's it, take it all." His chest is heaving, his eyes squeezed shut as he pumps down my throat, erupting, and I swallow as fast as I can, but I can't get it all before some dribbles down my chin. Xan collapses to the side, sitting down heavily.

Then Jacks is kissing me. "Don't want to waste it, love." He licks up my chin, shoving his tongue in my mouth and then is back on his feet, taking his turn with my mouth. He's more gentle than Xan, caressing my cheeks and stroking my hair.

"You are so beautiful, Little Lion. So beautiful, and you feel so good." His hip movements grow frantic, and soon he comes down my throat as well. He doesn't move away, instead he holds me as he sits down, laying both our heads on Leo's chest, and staring into my eyes.

"Thank you." He kisses me on my nose, and it seems so strange considering what he just did.

"For what?" I manage to mumble out.

"For being with us, for being amazing...for being you." He kisses my forehead and closes his eyes. Soon I'm sandwiched between and surrounded by snoring alphas. And yeah, it has been a hell of a couple of months, so I pull Jacks's hand up to hold, and fall asleep against them all.

Chapter 53

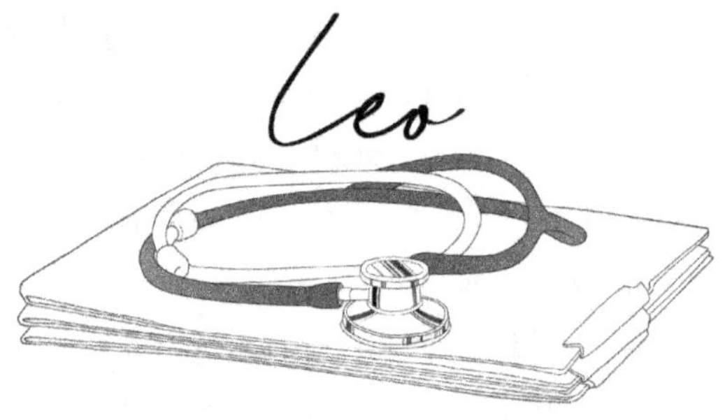

Leo

Three Months Later

I lead our omega down the hall. She knows we're at the clinic, because I didn't blindfold her for the trip over, but I did once we were in the building. Everyone is playing along, and I appreciate it. Laura was not happy that I am bringing Candice in for this. She thinks if I am in the office, I need to be working, but this is important. Also, I hate to say it about anyone, but Laura is kind of a bitch.

Maggie is standing by the kennels with Dr. Stephanie, bouncing up and down on her toes, and they both have huge smiles on their faces. I have both of Candice's hands in one of mine as I lead her to the cat cages. We've had a lot of strays recently, and one momma cat whose kittens are almost ready to be adopted out. I wanted to make sure Candice got first pick of the litter...not that she knows.

I stop and put my hands on her shoulders, before untying the blindfold and stepping out of the way. She blinks up at me before focusing on the pen full of kittens in front of her.

"Oh my God, they're so stinking cute!" She does a full body wiggle.

"I know that you loved Sunny, and nothing can ever replace him, but...if you want to, I thought maybe you could pick out another friend or two, but only if you want to, no pressure at all." I rush through what I wanted to say, suddenly worried this was a stupid idea and she'll think I am trying to replace her deceased cat.

She looks up at me, tears in her eyes. "Shit, sorry, this was a bad idea. We...shit. Never mind. How about ice cream? I can take you out for ice cream?" I stammer, trying to salvage the situation.

She sniffs and wipes her eyes. "Well, while I would love some ice cream, thank you...let's pick out a couple of new family members first. How much longer do they need to stay with their mom?" She looks back down at the litter of seven kittens, all different patterns, but we'll get the mom altered once everyone is weaned and send her back to the colony. With luck, we'll find loving homes for all the kittens, and adoption fees include shots and alterations on them as well.

Candice reaches down and rubs a tiny black ball of fluff behind the ears, and it hisses and tries to scratch her with its little needle claws. She holds the back of her hand down into the pen until one of the other kittens comes over and rubs against it, purring loudly. She picks up the tiny ginger, tears in her eyes.

"So, do you wanna be Sunny two?" The kitten paws at her nose and closes its eyes, leaning into her.

She rubs her face against it. The little black kitten she originally tried to pet is now meowing loudly, looking up at her, so she scoops it up and holds them together against her chest, their dual purrs loud enough for the entire room.

"And you can be Moon. How's that?"

I fill out the paperwork for the two kittens while Candice plays with them and a feather, then she kisses them each on the nose and promises to come back soon. The mom and kittens will go back into solitary to keep everyone healthy, and Candice makes me promise to bring her back in a few days so they won't forget her.

We stop by the house and get Jacks before heading out for ice cream, because he'll pout if he finds out later. He hands Candice a tiny box with a shy smile, and she opens it looking perplexed. Even I'm a bit mystified because laying inside on a pile of tissue paper is a fucking cassette tape. Who even owns a cassette player anymore? But Candice has more tact than I do, and just smiles and thanks him.

Jacks laughs; he's laughed more in the last three months than he has in years, and it feels good to hear it.

"It's a mix tape, Xan and I made it for you, it has all those weird old songs you listen to when you dance around the house and don't think anyone's watching." Her responding laugh is loud and bright, like her.

"Thank you, both of you, but I'll need to find a tape deck, I don't think I have one." He just keeps smiling at her and brushes her hair off her forehead.

"No worries Little Lion, we have one at home, obviously, since we made it...but there's also one in your car." She shakes her head, still smiling.

"No, no, I think I would know if there was a tape player in my car. Still, I appreciate it, and I can't wait to listen to it later." She leans over the seat to give him a kiss and a hug. "Though, I'm kind of curious why, I mean, what did I do to get gifts?"

But before he can answer and ruin the surprise, we are pulling into Gabe's Garage. Sally waves from the first bay, and calls into the back—soon Gabe wanders out from the front office. Candice undoes her belt and hops out.

"Hey, we're going for ice cream, you wanna come? You can have the front seat." She sing-songs that last bit, waggling her eyebrows, but our pack leader just chuckles, pulling her into a hug.

"Maybe later, love. I need to get some work done. But I think Xan wanted to talk to you." Just then, Xan appears around the side of the building, driving an old Ford Mustang.

I know nothing about cars, but I recognize the hood ornament. Candice, on the other hand, gets super excited and runs over to him.

"Wow, this is beautiful. I haven't seen it around town before." She reaches out like she wants to touch the faded paint, but pulls her hand back, looking guilty.

"Oh, yeah, well, it's been sitting under some tarps in the back for the last few years. Gabe and I pulled it out of a guy's field so I could rebuild it. The motor runs great now, and I might even be convinced to redo the paint...for the right price." He grins lasciviously and waggles his eyebrows, but Candice is looking down at the car, rubbing her hand across the hood.

"Well, you did an amazing job, both of you." She looks over at Gabe and smiles. He just smiles back and shakes his head at her.

"Aww, don't be like that Baby, I'll even let you play with the gearshift if you ask nicely." Xan tries again with no response other than her looking longingly at the car.

With all of us standing around staring at Candice as she stares at the car, Jacks finally has enough, and goes over and slaps Xan in the back of the head, earning himself a glare.

"Oh my god...you! You are the owner...fuck. Candice, I've had this fucking car under a tarp for two years...you think I suddenly got off my ass and fixed it for anyone else?" Xan sounds frustrated, but he's laughing by the time he finishes.

Candice turns towards him with tears in her eyes, and he trips over his words trying to explain. "Shit, I'm...I'm sorry, Baby. I been busting my ass trying to get it ready in the last few months, and with the new hires and everything going crazy, I haven't had time to paint it, and…I'm sorry." She is crying fully now and Gabe lets out a loud growl as Xan wraps her in his arms rocking from side to side and making shushing sounds.

"I'm sorry…I just…no one's ever done anything so nice for me before." She sobs against his chest. Clearly she doesn't count the kittens I just gave her, but we haven't brought them home yet, so fine, I'll allow it.

"But…why, why the kittens, and the tape, and the car…what's the occasion? Did I miss something?"

Jacks bounces over. "It's our anniversary!"

Candice eyes him skeptically. "No, we met just less than five months ago."

He hugs her, sandwiching her between himself and Xan. "Three months ago, you told us you love us, and let us bond you…though I'm still waiting for you to mark me back." He kisses the top of her head, and she cries harder against Xan. Her words are muffled against his chest.

"Thank you, all of you, for loving me back."

But we can't stay like that, the guys really do need to get back to work. So Xan pulls the car back behind the shop to finish getting it ready. Gabe goes back inside after claiming several kisses with promises for more later. Candice, Jacks, and I go out for ice cream, then home for Jacks to make dinner, and Candice to finish repainting the den so we can move the nest downstairs before her next heat. She already promised to give us each our own bonding marks during that one.

Chapter 54

Candice

Two Years Later

I finish the last stroke of paint and put down my brush. Iggy looks fabulous, in a long red cape, and armor, riding a horse...ok, so it is a large anthropomorphic iguana, but she did save me, and I felt the need to immortalize her in paint. It came out so much better than I expected.

I have the rest of my recent work hung up around the room, but they're all under painters' cloths right now, waiting for the big reveal. Xan, Jacks, and Gabe renovated the old nest and put in more windows for natural lighting, and it is an amazing studio and office. Shortly after it was done, I started working on paintings for each of them.

I go downstairs and collect my guys. It's the weekend, so everybody is home. I grab Xan and Gabe out of the garage; I can't get them to leave cars alone even on their days off. Leo is in the office downstairs that he shares with Jacks and now Xan, and Jacks is pulling a cake pan out of the oven.

Double chocolate fudge cake. Smells so good!

I lead them all upstairs and into the studio, standing them each in front of their gift. I had to wait until they were all done, so I didn't ruin the surprise. Jacks gapes on his way through at the painting I just did of Iggy.

"Wow, Iggy's lookin' good!" He laughs, I don't do as many commissions anymore, mostly just for fun, but I still take some on to feel like I'm contributing. Though the money I got from selling my house after it was rebuilt means I wouldn't have to worry about money anyway, it's still nice to stay busy. Plus, a lot of the clients I had at the time are friends now, so I don't want to just leave them hanging.

"Yes, she's lovely, but look what I did for you." I turn Jacks back to the covered canvas hanging on the wall, and once he is in position, I pull off the cover.

"Holy fuck, Little Lion...It's amazing...what is it?"

I bump him with my shoulder. "It's you."

"Oh, well, yeah, I recognize me, but..." All the others are looking at the canvas in front of Jacks right now.

"It's how I feel about you, how you feel in here." I tap my chest. I look at the canvas again, and it *is* Jacks, it took a long time to get the face just right, photorealistic has never been my strong suit. He's lying on his back in a field of flowers. It's very *Sound of Music,* but with more rainbows, and butterflies, and a unicorn with a disco ball after a comment that Xan made once.

"I did one for each of you. You're not the only ones who have trouble with words sometimes, and I figured if I couldn't tell you how I feel properly, then at least I could show you how you make me feel."

One by one they each removed the cloth covering, staring at each one before moving on to the next. Xan is second, standing beside Jacks and he pulls down the cloth. His painting is heavy on the shadows, and he tilts his head looking at it from different angles, before chuckling a bit.

"Jekyll and Hyde, eh?" He smirks at me, and yes, his image is two-faced.

"Xan, I love you dearly, and you are the most amazing and brilliant man I have ever met in my life, but sometimes you are also a right bastard." He looks at me and blinks several times before shrugging.

"Eh, that's fair." He kisses me on the cheek and we move on to Leo.

He pulls down the cloth and even I blush a little bit, and I painted it. There stands Leo in nothing but a tiger loincloth and a taiko drum. He looks at it for just a second.

"You painted me as Raijin?" Gabe and Jacks both look at me and Xan cackles.

"Yes, I did, you are huge and powerful, and amazing, you make me feel safe and protected, and I thought a god of thunder would suit you...totally did not just want to paint you in a tiny loincloth...not at all." I grin up at him, but his only response is to lift me up and kiss me until I feel like I am melting into a tiny puddle of omega goo.

"*You're* amazing," he says against my lips before putting me down on my wobbly legs.

"Now I'm a little afraid of what I'm gonna see here," mumbles Gabe, as he pulls off the last cloth. His mouth drops open as he takes in the image of himself, wearing a bearskin hood and barbarian style armor, a long battle-ax in one hand, the other reaching towards the viewer.

"Ok, yeah, I'm a badass." Gabe smiles, puffing out his chest.

Xan snorts again. "Check the foreground." Gabe looks at him and blinks. "Look at the hand, Mr. Badass."

Gabe's head swings back to the painting, squinting to take in the details. The kind eyes and soft smile...and the teddy-bear hamster cupped in his painted palm. He grumbles a little, but I can still see the smile in his eyes when he looks between me and the paintings.

"These are amazing, Little Omega. Thank you." He pulls me close, and whispers in my ear. "But I kind of feel like you deserve a spanking for that last one." And I can't stop the shiver of anticipation that runs down my spine.

Jacks' Journal

Pack information   to make gift buying easier

♡ Candice ♡   Likes
Age - 27   Height - 5'2   Pack   old cars
Scent - Chocolate peppermint (so good!!)   Cats   anime
Favorite Color - Purple   Iggy   old music
                                               Favorite food - paninis?

Gabe   Action movies
Age - 32   Height - 6'5   briefs
Scent - Cherry tobacco   Cars
Favorite Color - Red   Tools

Leo   food
Age - 32   Height - 6'7   Romantic comedies
Scent - Oranges and Chai   boxer briefs
Favorite Color - Teal   animals

Xan   Mystery Movies
Age - 28   Height - 6'0 (my love is short! ha ha!!)   Chess
Scent - Burbon and petrichor   boxers (ugly!!)
Favorite Color - Green   building and fixing stuff
                                                        Books

Jacks (ME!)   Candice
Age - 29   Height - 6'4   Xan
Scent - Coffee and Cinnamon   Cooking
Favorite Color - Orange   Tattoos
                                               Science Fiction movies
                                               Candice (yes, again!)

<u>*Acknowledgements:*</u>

To my husband Eric who goes above and beyond to do all my art, because he is as kind as Leo, as fuzzy and huggable as Gabe, prone to bouts of useless Jeopardy trivia like Xan, and not quite as neurotic as Jacks, but just as much of a caretaker. Love you my tallest.

Huge thanks to my alpha reader: Alice, she is wonderful and supportive and I can't say enough how much I appreciate her!

Another thanks to my beta readers who are awesome: Angelique, Heather, Debora, Renee, Morgan, Catherine, Blaire, and Kimberly.

An enormous thanks to Marie Mackay who is an awesome person who has been super helpful in answering lots of question about publishing and strange random writing stuff. She is also a great writer so if you don't read her stuff yet, go check it out.

Lastly, this book is dedicated to Hathor, the original Sunny. I miss you, you grumpy old bastard. You were my best friend and made me realize I had an allergy to cat dander.

<u>*Afterword:*</u>

Thanks again for reading my first book...this was a wild ride for me. First off, I appreciate any and all feedback, if there was something you loved, or hated, feel free to send me a message or an email. I have a facebook, discord, or you can email me at galadreal.simmons.author@hotmail.com and I am currently reading each review on Goodreads. Reviews there and Amazon are always appreciated. Please follow me on either one for updates.

What comes next?

Well, I already wrote a 10k bonus scene that takes place during Candice's second heat. It will be posted for free on the Facebook group—Galadreal's Book Case—and discord group and I'm working on setting up a newsletter and website so that it can be downloaded there www.Galadrealsimmons.com

"Building a Pack is Ruff" is story 2 in the Pack Pets Omegaverse and will feature Rufus and Jake as our animal companions, two big friendly doggos that want all the cuddles. Mostly Jake. Rufus is Kelly's family's dog, and he stays living with them. Jake becomes as obsessed with our resident beta as the rest of her pack. So hang on tight for that.

Next up is Sarah's story "Hopping for a better Pack" She's rattling around in my brain, demanding to be written, so hopefully that will go smoothly.

Thanks again for hanging out, and I hope to end up on your watch-list soon (unless you are the FBI or something, then I don't wanna end up on your watch-list, but thanks for reading the book.)

About the Author:

Galadreal Simmons was born at a very early age. She doesn't remember much of it, as she was tiny and squishy. Regardless, after 45 years...she's still short and squishy.

She was named after an elf proving that nerd genes run in her family. It is spelled differently, because try teaching a five year old how to spell something that long. When she was of an adult age, she had it legally changed to include the misspelling.

She lives in a not overly remote location in the southern United States with her husband, two small creatures that share her genetic material, and a cat named Nyx.

She enjoys reading, avoiding human interaction, and feeding crows in the hopes that they will form a crow army and do her bidding. So far, that hasn't worked out, but she continues to do it anyway—because they might be hungry.

www.ingramcontent.com/pod-product-compliance
Lightning Source LLC
Chambersburg PA
CBHW071730110726
47908CB00006B/1557